Next time

YOU LEAVE

ANDREA GONZALEZ

next time you leave

Flat Caps & Wheels

Book One

andrea gonzalez

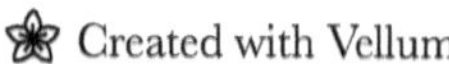 Created with Vellum

author's note

Hello, beautiful reader.

Thank you so much for choosing Next Time You Leave as your next read. Even if you end up not liking it, I'm grateful that you gave it a chance. It's been quite a ride. I wrote the first draft in a month after a huge loss in my family and spent the next three years editing it.

Please be aware of the trigger warning list so you can protect your mind and heart before reading.

That being said, this story and the characters are dear to my heart; they all have a little bit of myself in them. Especially Carmen.

A few details about her before you get into her story:

When she started talking to me, I didn't know the depth of her wounds and insecurities and how similar they were to mine. The more I got to know her, I realized that although we both have completely different backgrounds and traumas, the resulting fears and doubts we have are exactly the same. She's a badass, an optimistic soul and a woman who gets what she wants when she wants. Still, she might have some self-deprecating thoughts here and there during her journey that might annoy some of you. Her self-love is a work in progress, just like mine. Sometimes it's all the way up, sometimes it's all the way down.

Healing doesn't have a deadline and it's never linear. So please be patient with her, just as you would be with any friend of yours. I know we all want a secure and confident heroine, but the truth is… some of us are not there just yet, but that doesn't mean we're not worthy of love, romance and a happy ending.

And if like Carmen or myself, you're still struggling with seeing yourself as the ultimate prize you are: please don't give up on yourself and never stop believing you deserve good things. Always. No matter what. Your insecurities are just that… insecurities. Lying thoughts. They're not you. They don't define you, your future or the life you're destined to have.

Again, thank you for reading. I hope you enjoy this story as much as I enjoyed writing it.

Love,

Andrea.

playlist

Candlelight by Relient K
Flare by Relient K
Things I'll never say by Avril Lavigne
Dear Maria, Count me in by All Time Low
Honey and the bee by Owl City
The great escape by Boys Like Girls
Tongue Tied by Grouplove
1, 2, 3, 4 by Plain White T's
Patience by Tame Impala
Can't Complain by Relient K
Houdini by Foster the People
When we first kissed by Hellogoodbye
Cameo Lover by Kimbra
Every single time by The Jonas Brothers
There is a light that never goes out by Anberlin
Uncanny by Anberlin
You belong here by Anberlin
Love Song by Anberlin
Down by Anberlin
Take me (as you found me) by Anberlin

Orpheum by Anberlin
Mi persona favorita by Alejandro Sanz ft. Camila Cabello
Love you like I used to by Russell Dickerson
Not Over you by Gavin DeGraw
After all by Elton John ft. Charlie Puth
Innocent by Anberlin
When I'm alone by Lissie
Over it by Relient K
Walking on a dream by Empire of the sun
Don't go yet by Camila Cabello
Safe and Sound by Capital Cities
Must have done something right by Relient K
Midnight Swim by Brock Berrigan

contents

*To my eleven year-old self: We did it, baby girl. We wrote a book.
I hope you're proud of me, because I'm proud of you.
I love you. Always have. Always will.
P.S. That teacher ain't shit.
You my love, are THE shit.*

1

carmen

"Fuck, I'm late… like, really late. The guys are gonna kill me."

I'm never late.

"Shut up, you're always late," my sister, Rocío, says from the other side of the phone. "Besides, it's just Jacob, Ethan and Antonio."

Yeah, my two best friends, Jacob and Ethan Rodriguez, and my cousin, Antonio Lopez, let me get away with anything, but today is not just another day. This isn't just a family gathering. This isn't just another 'let's get tacos and beers' kinda day.

"Do I need to remind you what type of event we've been planning, Evelyn Rocío? It's the event of the year."

Scratch that, this is an event of a *lifetime*. The first BMX competition this neighborhood has seen after ten years of being retired from the sport. Not that we ever rode professionally, but it was our daily bread for years since Jacob and Ethan's dad taught us all how to ride a bike. It was the sport that practically made us family, and what determined the rest of our lives.

We only have about two days to solidify plans and we're

already behind schedule. Antonio asked me to come a little earlier.

"I know, I hate that I'll miss it." Rocío says.

"What are you talking about? You hate BMX."

"I don't hate it; I just prefer books to sports. Still do, but this is different."

I almost fall as I open the door of Hope Center, the community center my friends and I manage.

I say hi to a couple of people and find the classroom where I know the guys will be. Ethan's chuckle roars in the hallway as I approach the door.

"Do you want to say hi to the guys?" I ask my sister.

"Uh… maybe, but not now."

"Come on, they'll love to say hi. When was the last time you talked to them?"

She says something I don't really pay attention to since I'm approaching the classroom. That's when I hear the guys talking to someone. The topic of conversation piques my interest, so I stay next to the open door, careful not to make them aware of my presence.

"Chip, you still there?" my sister says.

Chip, the nickname my late brother Angel gave me when I was just five years old. He said I was so tiny I looked like a chipmunk and the nickname never really went away. My sister was one of the last people jumping on that bandwagon but eventually couldn't resist the temptation of reminding me of my size with one single word.

"María del Carmen Morales, answer me."

"Esperate un ratito." *Wait just a second.* "I want to know what they're saying."

"Ay ay ay… What have we talked about eavesdropping, Carmen?" she says with an exasperated tone.

"Don't act like you don't want to know, too."

"It's official, then?" A voice asks. It's my friend, Fred Lynch. He used to be my boss in my previous job and has been volunteering here at Hope Center for a long time now.

"It is," Jacob laughs. "Carlos Martinez, Sean Williams and Mickey Acevedo are officially competing in the X Games."

I smile at the comment. These three kids are mentees at Hope. The three of them are some of the first students we welcomed when Hope Center its doors. They're the whole reason why we're opening the memory vault to host this event. They got into the Sports Program when they were freshmen in high school and surprised us all when they chose to chase professional BMX riding. Just last year, they signed their first contract with Elite Bikes Co. One of the biggest BMX brands in the country. I don't like to dig too much into that company because the owner of said company is someone very close to us. Someone I used to know and would rather forget.

Still, I'm glad he still remembers where he comes from and that he saw the potential in these kids, giving them the chance we never had. The dream my brother Angel died with.

"I still don't really understand what the X Games are, is it like the Superbowl of extreme sports?"

"Something like that," Ethan says. "It's one of the most important Extreme Sports events in the world for sure. It's organized by ESPN and sponsored by major brands, and it's *extremely* exclusive."

"Yeah, you have to be invited to be able to compete," my cousin Antonio interferes.

The X Games were our ultimate dream growing up. Once upon a time, when life was really perfect. The guys always wanted to compete, but to me, that dream looked a little different. Of course I wanted to be part of the event, but not on my bike. I wanted to be behind the camera.

I fell in love with BMX at the same time I did with photography. Just two years ago, I was hired as a Layout Designer and Photographer by Ride Xtreme, one of the most important extreme sports magazines in the country. Not that my life has been rainbows and sunshine working for them, I haven't even touched a camera at all for the magazine. But I can't complain. They're making one of my biggest dreams come true this summer: I am going to be part of the team of photographers covering the X Games.

That's worth every pain in the ass I've had in that office.

Things are not exactly what we were hoping for when we started talking about this all those years ago, but very close. Seeing Carlos, Sean and Mickey making it a reality is almost as good. Those kids remind me so much about the guys back in the day, it's like we're getting those dreams come true through them.

"We knew these kids were going to eventually make it after Elite Bikes sponsored them, but we didn't know it was going to be this fast," Jacob keeps going. "By the way, have you told Chip?"

"What?" Antonio replies. "I thought Ethan was going to tell her; he's cold blood for these kinds of things."

Stop. Rewind. Repeat.

Tell me what? Is someone sick? Did someone die? My heart rate spikes, and I get my ear closer.

"Oh my God, what is it now?" Rocío says from the other side. "Why are you breathing like that? What are they saying?"

"They're talking about me, shut up."

Ethan scoffs, "Pot, this is kettle… Besides, I told you I didn't want to do it. I thought that's why you were going to pick her up from work tomorrow."

"She's like a little sister to all of us, not just me… *You* two are Oliver's *brothers. You* got the news first. *You* get to deliver them."

And there it is.

I get shivers down my spine as I hear his name after all this time. The name that used to feel like honey on my lips every time I said it. Now it feels like it was only a dream. Many people would say a nightmare, but if there's one thing I know, it's that I could never label him as such. As much as it hurts me to remember him.

I feel my legs turn to rubber and before I lose my nerve, I snap the door open. The four men jolt as they turn to look at me standing tall… or as tall as a 5'1 woman can be.

A wave of anxiety makes my stomach turn but still I look at them with an eyebrow raised.

A second passes.

Two, three…

"Look at you all looking so guilty." I give them the fakest smile. "Did I hear you need to tell me something, or was it my imagination?"

"I, ummm…" Fred hums, standing up uncomfortably from a desk. "I think I'm needed in the kitchen."

I want to laugh at Fred's awkwardness as he walks by me, but I glare at the three individuals in front of me as they look at each other with annoyance. I don't like the dread running up and down my spine, but the worry in their eyes as they look at me doesn't make it any easier. I'm used to these guys telling me everything, so the fact that they're finding it difficult to say whatever it is makes me anxious.

"Well?" I ask, "What the fuck is it with you?"

"And this is why I asked you to do it," Antonio mutters to Ethan.

"What?" I demand. After a couple of seconds, I talk again, "Don't make me twist your arm."

I see them all tense up at the remark. We do not talk about twisted or broken arms in this family.

I feel a pinch of guilt and groan, "Okay, bad joke. Sorry." I run my hand through my hair. "I just… Could you please just point and shoot? You know I hate it when you keep secrets from me."

"Okay, come here," Jacob says, extending his hand to take mine. I carefully put my phone inside my pocket upside down so Rocío can still listen as Jacob keeps going. "You see… Oliver called us the other day… He, ummm… He, uhhh…"

"Oliver is getting married in three months," Ethan blurts out, welcoming a pause that feels like forever.

He could've just sucker punched me. Same effect anyways, which is surprising. It shouldn't have that effect, it's been ten years, but it does. It feels like all the air just left my lungs and my chest is starting to hurt.

You knew this would happen sooner or later. It isn't supposed to hurt. Why? Why is it hurting after all these years?

Is it the fact that they haven't mentioned his name more than necessary through the years, giving me just the basics of his life? Or is it because deep down inside of me, I was still hoping for something to change on his part?

It doesn't matter.

It fucking stings.

Oliver is getting married.

To a woman who isn't me.

"It's going to be super small," Ethan goes on. "Just family, courthouse style. No party."

The three of them look at me with worry in their eyes when I don't say anything for a moment. I don't even know how to react.

I'm sure I need words. Words? What are words again?

"Oh… good," I let out a long breath, "good for him. I'm sure he'll be very happy." I fake a laugh. "I thought someone was dying or something."

"That's… not all," Antonio says, running a hand through his face. "He's coming back two weeks before the X Games and will be around for a while. He's staying at Alberto and Marta's."

"That's in two months," I mutter, pulling away and making the biggest effort to sound as uncaring as possible. "I still don't understand why you are acting so creepy."

They all exchange a knowing look. I'm full of shit and they know it.

Antonio keeps going, putting his arm around my shoulder. "Look, I know we haven't touched the subject in a long time… but we know it's still a very tender spot. We just wanted you to know and make sure you're okay."

I scoff nervously and shake him off. "Ya'll act like I'm still sixteen and delusional. Of course I'm okay!," I put a strand of my hair behind my ear. "Why wouldn't I be?" *Because I'm not.* "It's not like the dude has been talking to me every day for the last ten years." *I need another hug. Can I please get another fucking hug?*

"Ummm… exactly why is he going to be around for so long? That's weird; he hasn't been here in a while."

"He wants to be here for Mickey, Sean and Carlos personally." He shrugs. "He was so excited when he sponsored them last year. They remind him of himself and Angel. Same neighborhood, same backgrounds. He wants to see them in action."

I hate how that makes me swoon a little. Fuck those butterflies.

But how can it not? Oliver and my brother Angel were best friends since they were in kindergarten. Jacob, Ethan, Antonio and I were only one year below them and had the same connection they had when they met. I was six years old when Alberto invited Antonio, Rocío and I to Jacob's birthday party. Their cousin Vince was visiting from up North and our friend Alex had just moved across the street. It was a different type of love at first sight, but just as life changing.

Alberto saw that bond from the very first second and from that day on, he took us in as part of their family and gave us all what we desperately needed and didn't even know it yet: a real sense of home.

We've been inseparable since then. Almost like having a pack of big brothers looking out for us.

And me? I had the biggest crush on the oldest of the Rodriguez siblings from the moment I saw him for the first time at that party. He was always so cool and had the biggest, most contagious smile I'd ever seen. As loyal as someone could get. Always backing up my brother whenever he had to defend Rocío and I at school. Supportive as any other of the guys and always finding a little time to make me feel special. More than anyone else.

Everything gave a one-eighty turn the moment Alberto gave his sons their first BMX bikes. The day I saw Oliver flying on his BMX over a ramp, his arms extended to the sides and landing perfectly with his hands back on the handlebar…

It was like seeing Prince Charming riding on a white horse, except that I didn't only want to get that prince for myself—I wanted to get on that horse and jump exactly as he was doing.

Meanwhile, the gang went bike crazy and *never* looked back. Except for Rocío, who was never interested in sports and always had her nose inside a book instead. Still, she tagged along wherever we went, cheering and rooting for everyone from the stands.

Needless to say, extreme sports became life.

We all became very good at it, but nothing compared to Oliver and Angel. They took the hobby and made it a passion, then rewrote the meaning of that word.

They were the BMX kings of the city. The most talented and accomplished riders, defeating only each other in each Midwest competitions, organizing city and statewide events, opening skateparks in surrounding neighborhoods, including ours.

Their dream was always to go Pro and get sponsored by important brands, and they worked hard every single day to achieve it.

We were a team, and they were our leaders.

Wherever they went, we followed.

Angel wasn't only my brother anymore. He was my hero, my best friend, and my mentor.

And Oliver?

He was my shooting star. A bright, unreachable and too-good-to-be-true star who I found impossible not to fall for.

Oliver was the one who put a camera in my hands for the first time.

Oliver gave me my first kiss *and* my first heartbreak.

When Angel died in that terrible car crash, we all knew things were going to change forever, no matter how hard we tried to put the pieces back together. I just didn't know how much harder it was going to be.

Oliver *disappeared*.

He vanished out of my life without an explanation.

I know he never made any promises. He never asked me to be his girlfriend, never said he loved me. Still, the abandonment felt as if he had.

He didn't show up at the funeral or call to see how I was coping.

Next thing I knew, he was already living in the UCLA campus, on his way to become a Mechanical Engineer. We all thought he was still pursuing a sponsorship as he originally planned, but instead, he and his friend Damian Williams, who was also a rider, designed this amazing bike for a class during their Senior year. It caught the eye of a retired Pro Rider and in less than a year, they all partnered up to found Elite Bikes.

I thought he had cut ties with everyone and had abandoned us all without notice. But slowly, I figured out it was only me. He was still calling Antonio and sending texts to Rocío.

He never once called *me*.

I tried to figure out what I had done to push him away. I repeated the last moments we had together over and over in my head, trying to remember what I'd done wrong, but I gave up when I couldn't come up with an answer.

My brother was right when he warned me to stay away from him. Angel somehow found out about my kiss with Oliver and told me not to get my hopes up. Like an idiot, I didn't listen.

Ten years later, he still has his looks, plus the money and influence of his position. He has everything he's ever wanted. I must be the last person in his thoughts right now, whereas he's been a constant in mine.

Jacob's voice pulls me back to reality.

"He also wants a bachelor party," he keeps going. "Well... *his* style of a bachelor party, which will probably be pretty boring anyways. Now that Vince moved back to Minneapolis, Alex is flying from Florida that week too. He's getting everyone tickets to the X Games and—"

"You're reuniting without me? Without Rocío?" I interrupt, the tears I've been trying to hold making their way out now.

Well, at least now I have a good excuse for them.

"Chip," Jacob says as he tries to reach out for me. "I swear we don't want you or Ross to feel left out. We love you to death, but Ross can't stand him anymore and with you guys not talking and all—"

"Rosy doesn't hate him, she's just still mad at him for ditching us and ghosting *me* but I know they talk." I look down my lap. "And I… well, I just haven't figured out what I did for him to just disappear on me forever. What I did that was so wrong for him to cut me off to the point of all of you having to pick sides."

Translate it to: Why did he never love me but made me think he did?

I've always loved the respect everyone has had when it comes to this topic. They always stop when they've shared too much, but try to make me feel like it had nothing to do with me, when I know well it did.

"Nothing," Ethan blurts, his jaw ticking. "Hear me? You did nothing. This was all on *him* and his stupidity."

Yeah, right.

I know they've always hidden something about this whole thing. That there's so much I don't know but they do, and I probably won't ever find out because I don't want to ask. This is all water under the bridge. Chapter closed. Page already flipped.

"Well, whatever it is. Thank you for telling me," I say, wiping my tears. "I just need to get mentally ready, that's all. I'll be at the X Games anyways, so I need to adjust to the idea that he'll be around and taking all your attention. He does too."

"You know it's not like that," Antonio says.

"Would you excuse me for a second?" I say before he starts talking again. "I just need a moment. I'll be right back."

"Wait, but—" Ethan tries to hold onto my hand, but I turn around to leave the room.

I can still hear them calling my name but I ignore them. I know enough and don't want to dig into it more than I have to. Once I'm safe inside a bathroom stall, I take my phone out to see if Rocío is still on the phone.

"Are you still there?"

"Ese hijo de la gran puta," *that son of a bitch*, she cusses. "He's an asshole and that's a low blow. He's leaving me out because he knows I'm gonna beat the shit out of him. God… I'm so sorry, babe."

"I'm fine."

"It's **OK** if you're not." She whispers, "Just remember you're a badass bitch who kicks ass. You've survived worse in your life, and you will get through this."

Rocío was Angel's twin, but always acted like the oldest. He always protected us and wanted to keep us safe, especially from our mother. When he died, it was almost as if his spirit had stayed inside Rocío's heart, and we both became even more defensive about each other than we were before. When one is down, the other one picks her up. Always.

"Rosy, it's really not that bad."

"You and I know that's bullshit. We both know this is gonna fuck you up."

Rocío has always had the crazy idea that Oliver was in love with me. That he and I were meant to be together, but he blew it all up. There was a time when I wanted to believe her, but it only broke my heart even more and I refuse to go down that road again.

"You mean my silly crush?" I laugh without amusement. "You know I got over it a long time ago, Ross. It's not like I've been wallowing about him. I've dated."

"Yeah, dating others doesn't mean getting over your first love."

"He wasn't," I say with a little annoyance. She laughs a little, but I keep going, "But you're right. I can get over a few weeks with Oliver around. I just need to get ready for it."

"That's my girl."

We say goodbye to each other, and I make my way to one of the sinks to splash my face with some water.

I can do this. I can do anything. I repeat as my mantra for a couple of seconds before going back to the guys. We have a plan we need to wrap up today and can't waste any time on nonsense. I walk back to the classroom but don't find any of the guys there. For some reason, I get a pinch of anxiety poking in my chest as I walk around the building without seeing any of them. Something tells me to go to the parking lot and before I even get out of the building, I bump into Antonio.

"Hey, where were you guys?" I ask. "I'm sorry, I—"

"Alberto," he says.

The broken tone he uses sends a wave of panic down my throat. The same tone his mom —my aunt Carmela—used when she told Rocío and I about Angel's accident. The same tone that feels like death.

"What happened?" I say, swallowing my panic.

"He… uh…" He takes a couple of breaths, putting his hand on his chest. "He just had a heart attack."

Another punch to my chest.

"What? When?"

"Just now… Jacob got the call just five minutes after you ran out of the classroom. He was supposed to be here too." He takes off his cap and scratches his beard. "The guys are already on their way to the hospital. I just came back to let you know. You can come with me if you want to, but—"

I don't let him finish. I just grab his hand and pull him out to the parking lot. My heart is trying to get out of my throat. The tears I'm trying to hold start falling as Antonio breaks the silence, voicing the fears I'm trying to kick out of my mind.

"He's not going to die, is he?" he says as we buckle up. "He didn't die last year when he fell off that ladder; he can't die now, can he? He can't leave us too."

"Tony, stop," I say, cupping his face and pulling him for a kiss on his cheek. "He's not going to die. Alberto is a fucking fighter. He's going to pull through. He'll be fine."

He has to be.

His only reply is a nod before he wipes a tear with his sleeve and starts the car.

As we make our way out of the parking lot, the only thing going through my mind are prayers.

I can't lose focus right now for something that's well buried in the past.

I can't waste my energy.

Not even for *Oliver Santiago Rodriguez*.

2

oliver

Can the world please stop for one second?

One second. That's all I need.

One second to hold time and space so everything can stay the same for just a moment. One second to get ready for the next one when everything will blow up in my face.

This is my prayer.

My recurring thought.

I've been drowning in it since Sunday night when I got the second most devastating phone call of my entire life.

One no son could ever be prepared for.

My dad had a heart attack.

My life was going as usual while I was sitting in my living room with my fiancée, miles away and oblivious to the fact that he could've *died*. I was losing him without even knowing. Without a warning. Without a goodbye.

Life really doesn't give a shit, does it? It has changed unexpectedly ever since I can remember. One day you're the happiest you've ever been, about to go to college with your best friend, ready to take your BMX career to the next level. You just kissed the girl of your dreams and are about to make every single one of your dreams come true. Then, all of a sudden…

Your best friend dies in a car crash you should've prevented. You see your girl being kissed by another guy and you're unable to hop on a bike again for the rest of your life because you know you don't deserve it and everything you've known is crumbling to the ground in the blink of an eye.

People say time heals all wounds but that's not true. You just get used to the pain, to the new normal, and then in the moment you least expect it, everything changes *again*.

It's Tuesday night. I came home early from the office because I couldn't stand my hands being tied between papers, financial statements and whatever crap the accountants were talking about. I usually spend most of my time at the factory, supervising and working side by side with the engineers and welders that have all the action. I'm a guy who works with his hands, always have been since Papá taught me and my brothers to work with wood and metal. I'm not the type of person who belongs behind a desk. Still, Damian, my friend and business partner, needs me sometimes to do the boring part of our job at the office with paperwork, signatures, and meetings, and I have no other choice.

The downside of being the boss, he says.

But I couldn't concentrate at all. I couldn't think of anything else but my father being in the hospital and me being all the way here. He's supposed to be discharged today. His heart is weak but should be fine according to my brother Jacob, although he says they wanted to check on something else that caught the doctor's attention. He didn't give me specifics, but I'm really hoping it's nothing serious. We've already had enough adrenaline rushes with him. Last year, he suffered a mild concussion after falling off a ladder doing a kitchen installation. Now *this*.

I put on my work clothes and walk to the carpentry and welding shop I set up in my backyard. It's not big, but it's equipped enough to build whatever I need or want. Everyone keeps telling me I should profit from it, but what else do I need when I co-own one of the largest BMX brands in the country?

I never thought these skills were going to make me rich in the first place.

When Damian and I made our first bike for a developmental class our Senior year in college, we never thought people would actually want to use it. It was lighter than most bikes at the time and easier to jump flip in the air than the most sold bike that year. At least, that's what Damian and everyone else said since I couldn't bring myself to even think about riding a bike. Not too long after, people started asking for parts.

We joked around about having our own factory someday and it was the source of a couple of laughs. Even when we were building good parts at low cost, no one really trusted that the skinny Mexican kid from South Minneapolis and the geeky Black kid from the Bronx had it in them to build an empire—until Aaron Johnson, a retired Pro-rider, heard about us. He believed in us from the moment he met us and surprised everyone when he decided to make an offer to found Elite Bikes Co.

It's been a whirlwind of events since then. Haven't had much time to do anything creative just for myself in the last five or six years. This shop gives me exactly the distraction I need to tame a little bit of my anxiety.

Today I need it more than ever.

I open the sliding doors towards my backyard and Juanito, my black and white Pitbull, jumps from his bed and follows me. Everyone who knows me knows Juanito is always right next to me.

I start the MIG and try to concentrate on the frame of a drawing desk I'm making for the lady who cleans my house. My mind gets distracted about Papá for a while and I can't get it to shut up. If it's not about him, it's the same thought that's been parading my mind for ten years.

What happened to you, Oliver? When was the last time you felt like yourself?

I have a rock-solid business, a house, a family and friends who love me, and I'm getting married to a wonderful woman. I'm supposed to be living the dream.

Then why do I feel like nothing makes sense?

What's a bike business if I can't ride a bike anymore? What's a big house if it's completely empty and the people who are supposed to make it feel alive are a thousand miles away from you? Who runs away from home because he refuses to accept the fact that the dream life he wanted in that place will never happen? What kind of crazy, selfish person convinces his good friend into marriage just because neither of them wanted to be alone?

My train of thought is interrupted by my phone. I almost drop it as I take it out in a rush, my mom's number popping up in the caller's ID.

"Mijo lindo," Marta, my mother, sighs. "Your Papá is doing better; we just came back home from the hospital and he's about to take a nap. He'll be on bed rest for the rest of the month, and we'll need to be checking his blood pressure constantly before the next doctor's appointment."

"Good, that's good," I breathe a sigh of relief. "What else did they want to check?"

She doesn't say anything for a couple of seconds and my heart rate goes up.

"They, ummm…" She clears her throat. "They are concerned about–about how things happened, and they ran some MRIs of his brain."

"His brain?" I frown at the phone. "Why would they run an MRI of his brain after a heart attack?"

"Mijo, I'm scared," she says, almost in a whisper. "I told you kids this before and you didn't want to listen. He's been acting strange for a while. Repeating the same story over and over, asking *me* to repeat myself over and over. His sudden change of subjects, can't find his keys or wearing mismatched shoes—"

"That's just aging, Mama. It happens to everyone," I interrupt. "I still don't understand what you are getting at with this."

"He *got lost*, Santiago," she finally says.

"What? What do you mean he got lost?"

"He got lost on the way home from the grocery store," she says, her voice breaking with tears. "He says he got into some brain fog and couldn't recognize where he was. He had a panic attack that triggered a heart attack. The doctor found it so strange and ran all these MRI's and memory tests… They wanted to look for brain damage and rule out a couple of things. They said he needs special scans to look for—"

"Don't say it," I say like an idiot. As if not saying it will change anything.

"They think he might be in the first stages of Alzheimer's disease. He needs special testing to see if there's protein accumulation affecting his brain function."

I feel my legs giving out and I fall back against the wall, breathing hard.

No. It can't be. It's not possible. It can't be.

Alberto Rodriguez is young, strong and has the sharpest mind I've ever witnessed in my life. These lapses of forgetfulness don't mean a thing. Doctors misdiagnose Alzheimer's all the time. *This* doesn't mean anything.

"No puede ser." I*t's not possible.* I start talking fast and stand up to walk towards my living room. "They must've gotten it wrong. He's too young; he's not even sixty, Mamá." I breathe hard. "I'm flying you here. I'll make an appointment in the best hospital and we'll get a second opinion. I'm not—"

"He's too weak to fly," she interrupts.

"He's too young to have Alzheimer's."

"I know," she sniffs, "and it's not a definite answer either. He still needs to be tested for it."

"Then why wasn't he?"

"Because Alzheimer's symptoms mimic other diseases, so they have to rule them all out before running the tests he needs to see if there's plaques in his brain. He needs a specialist for that, and they don't have the equipment in this hospital."

"Find the best one."

"What?"

"If you won't fly here, then find the best specialist in

Minnesota and make an appointment," I say, throwing myself on the couch. "I don't care how much it costs or if his insurance will cover it or not—just find the best one."

"Santiago."

"They're wrong." I feel my heart coming out of my throat. "That doctor is wrong. You said it's not a definite answer, so let's find one. I'll pay whatever is necessary… We're probably freaking out for nothing and the sooner we figure it out, the better."

My head is spiraling in a never-ending loop. My hero, my teacher, my protector, my guide. I refuse to believe he has to go through something like this so young. Alzheimer's doesn't even run in our family. Don't get me wrong, I trust medicine. I believe in science, but just like everything else on earth, it's not flawless. Doctors are human beings who make mistakes and I'm sure they made one now.

"OK," she finally replies.

"How's he taking it?" I ask, not really wanting to know the answer.

"He's… processing it. A little quiet since they mentioned it."

"Hey," I say, attempting a smile with my voice, "it's alright, Jefita. He's going to be OK. I know it looks bad but there's gotta be an explanation. We're not going to give up and we'll find it. You sure you don't want to come here? Let me take care of you."

"You *are* taking care of us," she whispers. "You've done so much for us already. We wouldn't be able to afford this life without you. You'll have the time to be with him. You también tengo mis dudas, sabes?" *I'm also a little doubtful, you know?* "But let's not act without thinking first."

"Alright," I say, feeling defeated.

"I love you, mi amor lindo. We'll talk soon, okay?"

"I love you too. Todo va a estar bien." *Everything will be alright.*

I hang up and throw my head back to the couch, my breath intensifying as I cover my face with my hands.

A wave of memories floods my brain as I feel tears rolling down my cheeks.

I am who I am because of that man. He's my number one fan.

He gave me my first bike and taught us all how to ride it. He taught us by example how to work for what we wanted.

I've gone to him for *everything*.

He was the first one to encourage us when Angel and I wanted to ride professionally. He believed in me when I didn't think I could get into UCLA. He was my rock when Angel died and wiped my tears away the day I saw Carmen in the arms of another guy. How dare there be an illness that could potentially take away his brightness and wisdom forever?

My thoughts are interrupted by the sound of Juanito barking at the front door, where Susan, my fiancée, walks in just seconds later.

"Ollie, what's wrong?" she asks as she sits down next to me.

I take refuge in her arms and let out the sobs I've been holding. She doesn't say anything for a while and lets me be. When I finally calm down, I tell her about the call.

"Oh, Ol, I'm so sorry," she says, wiping my tears with her thumb, "but if they're telling you to go to a specialist, it means there's no diagnosis."

"And there won't be," I assure her. "They got it all wrong. They won't fly here, so we'll have to make an appointment in Minnesota."

"He just had a heart attack, it's only natural, but…" She hesitates. "I think your mom is right, getting lost on the way home sounds a little bit off."

"Sue, he's a workaholic who hasn't taken a break in thirty years." I sit up straight, "He's a business owner who doesn't sit back to watch others do the heavy job. He's an action guy who never stops and stresses too much. I'm sure that had something to do with it. He's just getting older."

The words leave my mouth but even as I try to make sense of them and everything that's happened, I know there's something weird about it. They've lived in the same house since I was born; he has walked the same road thousands of times. Thinking about him getting lost is scary as fuck but I refuse to say it out loud.

"Well, the only solution I see here is if you fly home and see it for yourself," Susan says, giving my shoulder a little squeeze. "It would take a load off your mind, and it would make him happy after everything that's happened."

The tone and suggestion send a shiver down my spine. Not because I don't want to go see my parents, but because of what it would entail. Susan knows exactly what that is.

"I, uhhh… I'm going anyway," I mutter. "I'll be there for two weeks for the X Games."

"Oh yeah, I almost forgot about your plan to avoid reality."

I ignore her sarcasm and walk to my mini bar. "What are you suggesting then? Are two weeks not enough?"

"For your dad, right now? No, I don't." She scoffs. "Ol, it's been ten years already."

I've been to Minneapolis a total of three times in ten years and Susan knows exactly why. We confide in each other like best friends. She's been the closest I've ever been to a woman in years, sans the romantic feelings everyone believes we have. Not that we don't find each other attractive. We hook up whenever we want to let off some steam, but we've never been more than that.

Susan swore off men when her ex-fiancé eloped with her best friend a few years ago. I'd given up on relationships by then, but found in her a person I was able to be fully honest with, the company I needed without the emotional bond that only ends up in tears. She's been through the same pain I have and understands why I need to guard my heart. But she's also a big believer of *'fight your demons and let go of grudges'* and that often means facing your past.

Something I don't think I'll ever be ready for.

"Please. *Please* don't," I warn, taking my glass to the couch.

"Don't you think it's time?"

"For what?" I motion with my hands. "Admit that I'm a chickenshit who can't visit his hometown because I can't handle how much I messed everything up?" I scoff. "I've already admitted that, and you know the deal, it'd be too much. Knowing what Papá went through hurts enough."

Seeing her will hurt even more. The reminder of what could've been different.

"Time to finally accept that your life changed and move on." She takes my hand and rubs it gently. "I've always respected your decision of living in this delusion of yours where nothing ever happened to Angel and Carmen never existed, but I think it's time for you to open your eyes."

"I could wait until Papa gets better. I'll book a flight for all of th—"

"Ol," she interrupts, "I'm sorry if I'm being harsh, but this is *bullshit*. Every time you want to see your family or friends, you fly them here. *Always*. But this time is different. This time it's *them* who need you *there*."

"Sue," I plead.

"You always say you'll do anything for them; well, here's your chance."

I lean forward to leave my glass on the table and wipe my face with both hands. "She'll be there. All the time." I turn to face her. "You know that, right? She's like a daughter to him… In fact, I bet she's there as we speak." I shake my head. "It's taken me years to get over her… and she… she terrifies the hell out of me. If I see her again, I don't know if I'll be able to stay away from her for too long, and will get my heart broken all over again. I can't repeat the story, Sue. I can't go through that again."

"Look, I know it hurts." She cups my face. "I understand. It also took me a long time to get over what Caleb and Helen did. I don't know what I would do if I had to face them again… but I also know nothing they ever did could ever keep me away from my dad in that situation. I know deep down inside of you, you're dying to go but you're letting your fear win again."

"I'm not—"

"And you do it all the time. Just look at this bubble you've built where you pick and choose who you let in… and you can't even enjoy it because you can't make peace with what's outside. With your past. You won't be able to until you slay that dragon. By the looks of it, life is forcing you to do it now. But you're strong… you can do it."

"I'm very happy with my life." I take a sip of whiskey.

"Are you, really?" She smiles knowingly. "Why did we agree to get married in the first place, then?"

Because we were craving company without expecting feelings in return, just to fill a void.

"That's what I thought," she says when I stay silent. "But that's not the point. You've let your past dominate your life for far too long." She punches me gently on the shoulder. "Grow a pair. Book a flight for tomorrow. Go home, Oliver. Be with your family. Face Carmen once and for all and let her go."

I wince and scratch my head, considering it for a moment. Damian has been pushing me to take a vacation for years—I know he'll even open the door and kick me out of the office if I ask for a couple of months. I don't say it out loud, but Susan is right. I want to go. I want to stay at my parents' house, take care of Papá. I want to hang out with the guys like the old times. Feel a little bit like the old Oliver for just a moment.

Except that it wouldn't be like it used to be.

"Come with me," I blurt out.

"Oh, no," Susan laughs, "this is your fight, bud. Not mine." She kisses my hand. "Just imagine your dad's face having all of his kids under the same roof for a while."

I smile at the thought. Sue's right; we may not know if he's sick or not, but that, plus that heart attack, may be a sign that I need to make some changes in my life. Starting with going to my family instead of making them come here like I always do. I've missed my gang, my home. I take my phone out to text the group chat with my siblings.

Oliver: What if I tell you I'm coming home tomorrow?

Jacob: And going back when?

Oliver: Same day I originally planned.

Ethan: Two months? You're staying for two whole months? Are you serious?

Oliver: Dead serious.

Jacob: I'll kick your ass if you leave earlier.

I let out a chuckle and look at Susan. "Alright, you convinced me."

Susan is right about one thing; this is what my familia and I need.

But she's wrong about something else. When it comes to *María del Carmen Morales*, I've never been that strong.

3

carmen

Finally, a good day after a couple from hell. I'm still trying to get past the adrenaline rush of having Alberto almost dying so I can begin to process the fact that he might have Alzheimer's. Ethan and Jacob aren't feeling alright about it, but I'm feeling hopeful. The fact that they said it was a possibility is giving me peace, and I choose to hold onto it with my whole heart. They're going to the Mayo Clinic next month to run the rest of the tests he needs and will have the best doctors looking through them.

No matter what happens, we'll be right there with him.

I only wish he would be here at Hope Center for today's event. The Jam is already here, the BMX competition we've been planning for months for Mickey, Sean and Carlos. They're not competing today, but they'll be the jury like the bosses they are. It should've been an exciting day for all of us, but it feels more emotional and heavier than I expected. Not only because of Alberto, but also because I can't help to remember the good old days.

I let the sadness sink in for a moment before shaking it away. I won't let anything ruin this day for me. This is the sport we love. What made us familia. What made us who we are today.

Today will be unforgettable.

I've been teaching photography every Wednesday for the last six months here at Hope Center, and today my students and I will be photographing the event, just as I used to do back in the day for Oliver and Angel. Maybe even better. These kids are crazy talented. That's one of the many things I loved when Jacob started Hope Center with his friend, Juliana. He turned it into a place where our community can have the best opportunities to explore their abilities and grow to be what they want.

Even Fred wanted to contribute to my class today. He's been learning all about Extreme Sports and was excited when I invited him to supervise the kids with me.

Everyone's been here since early to set everything up and the environment is already lit up. The guys were here last night to stage the track in the parking lot with ramps, tabletops and bars, so contestants and visitors are riding around already. The food trucks are starting to open, and the speakers are blasting our favorite music.

I take a deep breath and let my heart enjoy the sight.

"I wish I would've gotten into BMX when I was younger," Fred says, while admiring the track. "What prizes are you giving away to the winners, anyways?"

"Everything is sponsored by Elite Bikes," I say, taking my camera lens' cap off. "The first prize for each category is a new Elite Pandora bike 2019, and the second and third places are getting gift cards."

"Well, that's quite a prize." He lets out a surprised chuckle. "What are the rules of the contest then?"

"There aren't as many as you'd think." I put my camera belt around my neck. "Each contestant has forty-five seconds to use the track and get as many tricks as possible, but they must be clean tricks. Meaning that the contestant can't fall off the bike or put either of their feet down to gain balance while riding if the trick doesn't require it."

"Only forty-five?" He raises his eyebrows.

I smile. "You have no idea the number of things you can do."

Memories start falling again the second I finish the sentence.

When, in those forty-five seconds, everything disappeared and nothing else mattered more than BMX. When Oliver and Angel would steal the show every single time and would shock everyone watching.

When following with my camera, riding on my bike next to the rest of our friends was life.

The same bike and camera that made me find my purpose.

The same bike and camera Oliver gave me.

I shake the thought out of my head as my students start to arrive with their cameras ready. We have a lot to do, and I don't have time for all the sadness nostalgia brings. We're not only having our first competition in years, but also almost all of the gang will be here. Vince Rodriguez—Jacob and Ethan's cousin— just moved back to Minneapolis to be close to his boyfriend after living in the North Shore for a couple of years. He grew up with a bike in his hands with the rest of us and had to be here today.

We start doing some rounds with the bikers currently on the track. I explain the dynamics of the sport, the kind of tricks and movements they should expect from each category, and the angles they need to pay attention to. We do a few shots and start playing with the camera settings as the crowd gets bigger in a matter of minutes.

I'm helping Ruth to focus her lens when I hear a bark behind one of the ramps. Because my curiosity is bigger than my head, I look around trying to get a glimpse of the dog. I spot the black and white American Pitbull right in front of the main building's back door, pulling on his leash, and I freeze when I realize who the owner is.

Oliver?

He's here? How? Why? He's not supposed to be here. He's supposed to be in L.A., living his best life with his fiancée. I'm supposed to have two months to get ready to face him. *I'm not ready.*

His dad just had a heart attack and they found out he might have a terrible illness. Of course he's going to show up for his family without a warning.

Fuck!

Oliver. Is. Here.

He's here, showing the world those dimples I used to tease him about when he'd give me one of his killer smiles. He's talking to Mickey, who's stoked to be in front of him. How can he not? Oliver's a local hero, a legend to this neighborhood, just like my brother Angel. He's done so much for the community over the years, even though he hasn't set a foot here in a long time. Everyone worships the ground he walks on.

My heart races and I find myself surprisingly out of words. Stopping this nostalgia is impossible now. All the feelings I thought I'd successfully pushed away for the last ten years are all on the surface again.

Oliver is *here*.

In all of his sexy, six-foot-two, gorgeous brown-skinned, raven-haired, and charismatic glory.

Seems like I'm still the little girl who can't get the hint and get over a stupid crush for the same stupid boy who discarded her when he left.

Boy?

I mean, Mr. Drop-dead hottie.

He should know what he does to a decent lady wearing that flat cap backwards. I always loved that look on him…

When did he get all of those muscles? And why did he have to make them look even sexier with all of those tattoos all over them? He's grown so much. So beautiful.

Sweet mother Mary. I think my left ovary just melted.

"How about a panoramic from the top of the big ramp?" Fred asks, but my eyes are focused on Oliver, who is still oblivious to my existence.

It won't be long before he notices me, and I can't keep staring at him like an idiot.

What will he think? Is he going to ignore me like he's been doing for ten years? Is his fiancée with him?

"Hey," Fred says again, "you okay?"

"Fantastic," I say, before letting out a pathetic sigh. I turn to him in a trance. "Yeah, sure."

Right when I'm about to turn around, I hear the dog barking and I swear I can feel Oliver's eyes on me. I haven't seen him, but I know. I've always known. I've always been able to feel those dark eyes on me.

Guess that hasn't changed either.

The gooey sixteen-year-old in me drains the last drop of common sense out of my mind and I turn around, regretting it instantly. He's looking directly at me, completely dumbfounded, his brows all the way up as if he's seen a ghost.

We make eye contact for two seconds and my brain begs my body to run away, but as always, my body decides to ignore what's best for me. I swallow hard and force myself to the other side, but it's too late.

"Chip?" I hear Oliver calling.

Dear Lord, why did he have to call me by my nickname as if nothing ever changed? Why? And how is his voice even deeper now?

"What's going on with you?" Fred asks at the same time I hear Oliver calling me for a second time.

"Oh, God," I say, breathing hard. "Ummm… nothing. Just… yeah, let's go to the other side."

I start walking behind Fred but end up losing track and walking with no clear direction. My legs feel like a ton of bricks at this point, and I can feel my heart trying to come out of my chest. I wasn't ready to see him, let alone talk to him. I make the mistake of turning around again and see him walking. *Right. Towards. Me.* He looks as shocked as I am, but is walking with determination, his cute dog jogging next to him.

My logic must be on vacation today because I even see a hint of a smile forming on his lips. Must be my imagination.

Run! My brain commands and this time, my body obeys… in the wrong direction.

"Chip, wait!" Oliver screams, right at the moment I notice I'm running backwards.

The next thing happens in a matter of seconds. Taylor Wallace, a volunteer here at Hope, is currently skateboarding on the track and has the wonderful idea of falling behind me. I can hear the *ooohh* from the crowd around us, but when I turn around, it's too late. I step on his board and fly backwards, falling on my back in front of everyone. My camera takes this opportune time to land on my face.

Kill. Me. Now.

I try to save my dignity by not moving and keeping my eyes shut. But just when I thought my humiliation couldn't get any worse, his deep voice calls to me with worry. Before I can even move, I feel the raspy tongue of his dog licking my face.

"Chip, are you OK?" Oliver asks, kneeling down and grabbing my head with his strong hands. His cedary smell and warmth of his body invades my atmosphere, making my heart rate go nuts.

"Ouch," I murmur as I open my eyes and look up to him, smiling at me as if time never went by.

"There you are," he whispers with a soft smile in his tone. "Hey."

"Hey, Ol," I say, suppressing a sigh and ignoring the butterflies still in my belly. "How's it going?"

Why, God? What did I do to deserve this?

4

oliver

Just when I thought I couldn't be more stupid.

Why did I have to do the opposite of what I said I was going to? Why did I get myself into this? Get *her* into this? Literally running away from me should've been a hint that she didn't want to talk to me.

I'm an asshole. A worthless nickel that can't resist her magnet, but an asshole anyways. Even when just looking at her for the first time in years hurts like hell, I can't help the urge to get close to her. Never could, never will. You can't fight the natural laws of this universe. I knew it from the moment I bought that ticket home, and this just proves my point.

I wasn't expecting to see her so soon though. I arrived yesterday. My parents were thrilled with the surprise. Papá is a little weak but still shed a couple of tears when he saw me coming out of Ethan's truck. As much as my brothers and I promised not to stress out about his memory issues until we have a final diagnosis, I couldn't help but to pay attention to him. Besides his tiredness and the side effects of his heart medication, he seems fine. So, I decided to take this entire situation as a wakeup call and make up for the lost time.

I told my siblings I wasn't coming to the contest from the moment I arrived. I didn't think I'd be able to handle the memories and nostalgia. But just as Papá told me, this place is ingrained in my bones. This neighborhood, these streets, the people. They were all my sanctuary for many years when Angel and I were getting started and I didn't even know how much I missed it until I made the decision to show up unannounced.

Without thinking about the consequences.

I hadn't been here for too long when some of the riders and neighbors stopped me to say hi. I logically knew she was going to be around but for some reason, I thought I'd be able to avoid her.

Wrong again.

I felt her before I saw her.

Then I turned around and instead of panicking as I thought I was going to, it felt as though I hadn't been breathing for ten years and I was finally catching my breath. As if time had never really passed. Camera in her hands, her ravishing light brown skin was lit up by the sun. Her long, brown hair tied in her two signature long braids. Not a girl anymore. A woman, with beautiful curves I'd never seen before, but the same glow in the same perfect smile.

The same beautiful caramel eyes I've always been obsessed with.

One look and I was completely disarmed, almost making me fall to my knees.

People say things shine brighter against the sun, but Carmen Morales makes the sun shine even brighter. Staring at her can make me go blind, but if I don't, it gets fucking dark and scary. The same way I've felt since I had to accept she never wanted me as much as I wanted her.

Still, I had to talk to her. Be around her for one second.

Worst idea I've ever had.

"How's it going?" I chuckle nervously as I help her sit up. "You just flew three feet and probably got a concussion, and you're asking me *how's it going?*"

She keeps her hand where her camera hit her without saying a word. I'm trying not to distract myself by noticing the little things that are making my mouth water and my heart beat faster. Like how her soft skin feels on my calloused hands, the goosebumps all over her arms while I hold her, the citric scent of her perfume, or the fullness of those pouty lips.

Get a fucking grip, Oliver!

"Jesus, Carmen, are you okay?" Juliana asks as she rushes towards her, interrupting my thoughts.

Jacob is right behind Juliana. "What the fuck, Chip? Are you hurt?"

"Hey," I snap out of instinct, "can you give her a little space?"

That's when Jacob sees me kneeling down next to her, and Juanito sniffing and whining all over Carmen as if he wants to make sure she's okay. Jacob didn't know I was here and the way he's glaring at me tells me he'll give me shit later.

"Can you stand?" I ask Carmen, giving her a hand.

"I'm fine," she says but falls to her right side.

"Whoa, okay." I quickly catch her in my arms, lifting her up. "Let's find some place where you can rest."

"There's no need to carry me, Ol," she says.

"I don't mind." I hold her even tighter. I turn to my brother and hand him Juanito's leash. "Can you take Juan with you?"

Jacob raises an eyebrow without saying a word and takes the leash. *God, I'm gonna get so much shit about this later!*

"Okay, there's nothing to see here," Jacob says to the crowd, while bouncing his eyes between me and the beautiful woman in my arms. "Riders! Time to warm up. Amateurs, to the track."

Juliana walks next to us as we head towards the main building. Carmen and I keep exchanging awkward looks as we walk. She's avoiding my gaze at all costs and although it stings, I understand. It's been ten years of silence. Ten years of being nothing to each other. How hypocritical is that of me?

When I left for college, I explicitly asked my family and friends never to mention Carmen again. Not that I didn't want to know about her.

I wanted to know *everything*.

What she was doing, who she was dating. Everything about the amazing life I was never going to be part of. They fought me on that for a while, especially her sister, Rocío, who didn't talk to me for a long time after I left. Carmen was suffering. Because of Angel, because of me. My absence and my inability to be what everyone else deserved of me. With time, Rocío and everyone else understood, although they never really forgave me.

"You can rest here for a while," Juliana says, opening the door of her office. "Do you want to go to the ER? Should we call Dr. García?"

"That's a good idea," I say, lowering her to the couch. "You should get checked."

"I'm fine," she says, looking at Juliana. "I definitely saw stars for a moment, but I'll probably just get a bruise. That's all."

"Alright," Juliana smiles, "but don't feel like you need to stay."

She nods and Juliana walks away, leaving us alone. The air is uncomfortably thick around us; I can see Carmen swallowing hard and looking everywhere but at me. My self-preservation is telling me to leave her alone and go back outside, but I can't find the courage to do it.

I'm just helping her, I just want to make sure she's okay, right?

"Are you sure?" I ask, kneeling down in front of her. "Are you nauseous? Any pain? Dizzy? How many fingers do you see?" I hold two fingers in front of her.

She laughs, taking a little bit of the awkwardness away, along with a piece of my sanity.

That laugh. When was the last time I heard it?

"I'm fine."

I get a bit closer. "You sure you don't want to go to the ER? I can take you."

"Oliver," she whispers.

I clear my throat and stand up. "I, uh… I just want to make sure you're okay."

Her smile fades a bit and she finally looks me in the eye.

"Since when?"

Boom!

I've always known I hurt her by just disappearing. We were friends, after all. She became my confidant, my biggest fan and supporter, the person who made me laugh the most. I felt guilty for a long time for banning her completely from my life because I knew she never wanted to hurt me. It wasn't her fault that she wasn't as into me as I thought, and I couldn't just stay here while she was with someone else who wasn't me.

I know I deserve her bitterness. Still, I can see it in her eyes that she regrets what she just said, even if I deserved it. This woman is allergic to grudges and would never treat me the way I should be treated, which makes me even more of an asshole.

She opens her mouth to say something else when we're interrupted by the door opening. A tall, blond guy who looks like a damn magazine model comes in, looking all concerned.

"There you are," he says, throwing himself at her feet. "What happened to you?"

"Where the hell were you?" she asks, sitting up straight. "I was looking all over for you when I tripped and fell. It was embarrassing."

"I took the kids to the top of the ramp as I told you. I thought you were behind me. Oh, I'm sorry." He looks my way and stands up, offering me a handshake. "I didn't see you there."

"Oliver," I say dryly.

"Oliver?" he echoes. "Oliver Rodriguez? Jacob and Ethan's older brother?"

That makes me smile. "The same."

"I'm so glad to meet you. Wow. You and Ethan look exactly alike." He grins. "Everyone's told me so much about you. I'm Fred, by the way. I didn't know you were going to be here today."

I look at Carmen, who's been glancing nervously between Fred and me.

"Yeah, well… I didn't plan to come this fast but," I put my hands in my pockets, "I'm sure you've heard about my dad."

"Of course, I'm so sorry. How's he doing?"

"Much better, thank you."

"I'm glad," he says, taking a card from his wallet and handing it to me. "If you ever need anything, and I mean *anything*, please let me know." I take it and put it in my pocket as he turns to Carmen. "Are you sure you don't want to rest? We've taken great shots so far. We've got this."

"Be there in a minute." She gives him a tight lip smile.

"See you in a little bit then." He shakes my hand again. "It was a pleasure meeting you."

"Likewise," I say.

Acid burns my stomach as I see him go and fight my need to ask Carmen all the questions I have about Fred. It's pathetic. I should stop the guy, ask him to come back and let him take care of her. But the green-eyed monster cut my words short.

You have no right, asshole.

"Feeling better?" I manage to say once we're alone again.

"Yeah, thanks," she says, taking her camera. She fakes a smile at me and starts walking away and I can't stop myself from following her.

"So," I say as I reach her and walk next to her, "qué onda con el güerito?" *What's up with the blondie?* "Is he your boyfriend?"

She stops and lifts an eyebrow, "El güerito?" She clenches her jaw. "His name is Fred."

"Yeah, right. Fred." I breathe hard. "So, is he?"

"What? What the hell, Ol?"

Yeah, what the fuck, Oliver?

"I… I'm sorry," I wipe my face with a hand, feeling embarrassed as hell. "Fuck… I'm an asshole, I'm sorry."

"Yes, you are." She shakes her head. "What about you? When's the big day?"

"What?" I ask, genuinely oblivious to what she's asking.

"Your wedding…when's your wedding?"

"Oh, yeah, well—"

"I mean, not that I was expecting an invitation," she interrupts, "since we haven't been close in a while but…"

I raise an eyebrow and she keeps going on and on. It's amazing how after ten years, I still know this woman better than I know myself. She's always sucked at disguising when she's nervous, making the cutest poker face I've ever seen, and talking faster than anyone I've ever met.

She's still the same person she was back then around the edges, but there's definitely a different light and maturity deep inside.

Which is exactly why you need to back the fuck off.

I mentally slap my dumbass head back to reality as she keeps talking.

"…Do you have a photographer lined up already?" She tilts her head. "I assume you do, but still, I've done weddings, pregnancies, and engagements too. You know, you just need to ask. I mean, if you want me there, of course. I'll understand if you don't. I don't want to impose, you know? I'm just saying."

I've been nodding in agreement, fighting a grin as I listen to the almost imperceptible shake in her voice and the way she's drumming the top of her camera.

She's still so adorable.

"So, what do you say?" she insists. "I can give you a friend's discount. I mean, if you still consider me your friend."

I jolt at those words, feeling them as a well-deserved slap to my face.

"I'm sorry," she says, shaking her head. "I'm talking too much, aren't I?" I start interrupting her but she keeps going. "It's just that I haven't seen you in forever and I wasn't expecting you here and then bam!" She mocks an explosion. "You're here… in front of me… as if nothing ever happened. And you're getting married." She whispers the last words and runs towards the door. "I'm sorry, I've gotta go."

"Chip, wait," I rush forward and grab her arm.

Let her go.

But damn, I missed her…

She turns around and looks up at me.

"I know you might not believe it," I say quietly as I let go of her hand, "but it's really good to see you."

"Well, if that's true," she smiles, "next time you leave, don't be a stranger. I won't bite, I promise."

I attempt to laugh at the joke to disguise how broken it makes me feel to realize it's true: we became strangers. And after just an hour of interaction, I don't want to keep it that way.

Is it worth it, though? It's obvious that I'm still a complete idiot when it comes to her and my heart is still too damaged to take another hit. Especially from her.

"And Ol?" she says before opening the door. "You know you can always count on me, right? No matter what happens, all of you are still family."

I know she's talking about Papa's appointment next month. For a moment, I imagine myself pulling her into my arms, asking her to please talk some sense into my heart. Telling her all my doubts and insecurities. How scared I am of losing him, because I know she will always know what to say to make me feel better, even if she can't solve anything for me.

But I shove the thoughts out of my mind and just nod. She smiles in return and walks away from me.

Once she's out of my sight, I take my phone out and send Susan an emergency text.

Oliver: Coming to the contest was a bad idea.

Susan: OMG, you messed up ALREADY? *facepalm emoji*

Oliver: Don't judge me.

Susan: Details *eye roll emoji*

Oliver: Saw her. Followed her. She fell and hurt herself running away from me. I tried to help but it was awkward as hell. Met her boyfriend and acted like a jealous prick. She was a sweetheart anyways.

Susan: Dude! *six eye roll emojis*

Susan: You're an idiot.

Oliver: I knoooow. I just couldn't help it.

Oliver: I don't know if I can do this, Sue. I'm already feeling too much. I'm fucked.

Susan: Oliver, get yourself together. You'll be fine. She moved on a long time ago and you deserve to finally move on too.

Make amends, be her friend, get closure. If she's still the same sweetie you've told me so much about, then I'm sure she's missed you as a friend and will want to reconnect.

Susan: Is the event still going?

Oliver: Hasn't even started yet.

Susan: How do you feel about that?

Oliver: Weird. It feels like Angel is going to show up at any moment.

Susan: Focus on today, Ol. Your family, your best friends. They're all there as always. Enjoy them.

Susan: I'm about to drive. TTL.

Be present. Today. Enjoy today.

I repeat the words and make it my mantra with a couple of deep breaths before opening the door to walk outside.

I can't help but scan through the crowd to look for Carmen and her boyfriend.

Carmen Morales has always been my kryptonite and my dynamite at the same time. She can push me to the limit of every emotion there is and at the same time, drain my heart till the very last drop. My crush for her was strong from the very first day but I couldn't help falling in love with her from the moment I saw her picking up Angel's bike and jumping inside a bowl like she was born to do it, and I've never stopped loving her.

Probably never will.

5

oliver

"Care to explain what the hell was that?" Jacob asks as I approach the jury's table. He smashes Juanito's leash against my chest and I take it, leaning down to scratch my dog's neck.

"What the hell was what?"

"Don't play fucking dumb with me," he sighs. "Dammit, Oliver. I don't understand you. You said you weren't coming; then you show up unannounced. And *then* you have the *audacity* to act so shocked to see her."

I stand up to face him, my cheeks burn with anger. At myself for putting everyone in this position, but still taking it on him like an idiot.

"You could've warned me she was going to be here," I say, not finding a better excuse.

He scoffs, "*No mames, cabrón.* You're the one showing up out of nowhere." He shakes his head. "She's always been here. It was *you* who turned his back on her and ran away. *You* wanted this, now suck it up and *leave her alone.*"

I shake my head and shut my mouth because he's right.

"Look," I scratch the back of my neck, "I was just trying to help her, alright? It went a little bit out of hand."

"Bullshit," Ethan's voice comes from behind me. I turn around to see his brows furrowed, cornering me between Jacob and him. "You better not start with this shit again, carnal. For her good, and especially your own."

"I…" I stutter, exchanging looks between both of them. "I… okay, you're right. It's just… It was just the shock of the moment. I wasn't thinking, happy? It won't happen again."

"Better not," Ethan works his jaw. "Pendejo," he mutters, before bumping my arm as he walks by.

Jacob and Ethan are Irish twins. Ethan's older by ten months, but everyone says in a previous life, both of them—along with Antonio and Carmen—were born quadruplets. They became best friends almost at the same time Angel and I did. The four of them were the ones who stuck together after the accident, and they've defended each other tooth and nail. Especially when it comes to Carmen.

Jacob is still glaring at me. "Please, Ol. You're getting married, and she's happy where she's at."

"Yeah," I sigh, "I just met her *boyfriend*."

I want to hit a wall as I say it. I expect a little bit of sympathy from my brother but instead, he lets out a loud chuckle.

"Her *what?*"

I lift an eyebrow. "Her boyfriend?"

He laughs again and shakes his head, walking away and leaving me in limbo.

What the hell was that?

I want to ask but it's not healthy for me to keep digging for more information I don't need. There's a reason why I haven't asked about her during all the years. Still, Susan made a good point, I need to make amends. I'm not sure if that will be possible with how tense and awkward I made everything today, but I at least need to try.

I walk around with my dog, trying to clear my thoughts and admiring the great setup the guys put together. The atmosphere is already up, the riders are still warming up, and I feel a wave of pride as I see Elite Bikes Co. all over the air every time one of them flies on a perfect Barspin or 360.

Getting emotional is inevitable but I can also feel a wave of excitement in my lungs, even though nothing is as it used to be.

The track is clear again after the Amateur category makes the first round. Mickey, Carlos and Sean take advantage of the space to give a short performance as the Intermediate contestants line up. People I don't know come and introduce themselves, and some others I haven't seen in a long time come to say hi and ask about Papa's health.

It's so weird being here without him.

He used to be the first one to show up whenever we had an event going on back in the day, or whenever any of us was about to compete. He said he was going to watch the Facebook Live, but I know he's missing us as much as we're missing him.

I'm letting Juanito be petted by a little girl when I feel a tap on my shoulder. I chuckle and feel my chest tightening when I turn around. Antonio and my cousin Vince pull me into a hug and right when I'm about to say something, I feel a heavy punch on the back of my shoulder.

Alex Polanco, my compadre. He was born in the Dominican Republic and came to live here with his mom and older sisters when he was just five years old. He was an amazing BMX rider like any of us and I let him borrow my bike for a year until his mom bought him one for Christmas. We talk through Facetime all the time, but I haven't seen him in person in at least three years.

"What the hell are you doing here?" I ask, putting an arm around his neck and pulling tight. "When did you get here?"

"Landed an hour ago, Vince picked me up," he says with a grin, which fades a little with his next words. "I couldn't not come after what happened. Alberto is the only father I've ever known, I needed to be here." He smiles again. "And then these guys throwing a BMX party like the old times? You bet your ass I'd be here."

My heart breaks a little but I smile anyways. "I've missed your dumb ass."

I see Carmen from afar, who snaps her mouth open when she realizes Alex is standing in front of me.

"Alejandro?" she screams and Alex turns around.

"What's up, Chipmunk?" He opens his arms. "Missed me?"

He hasn't even finished the question when Carmen lets out a squeal that makes everyone turn around as she jumps to Alex's arms.

I try to ignore the pinch of jealousy in my chest, and I turn to Vince and Antonio who are already looking at the first Intermediate contestant. I join in as Ethan and Jacob approach us. I do my best not to look at her, but it gets harder with each passing second. She's always been the heart and soul of the gang.

Juanito is also having a good time. He hasn't stopped moving his tail in excitement and rolling over so people can pat his belly.

The entire setting fills my heart with a mix of emotions. Sadness, longing, happiness. All the things I've tried to repress since Angel died but now are stronger than ever. The memory vault is wide open and that's when I realize the entire gang is all together for the first time in years. We're just missing Rocío.

Damian and I sponsor major competitions worldwide through Elite and have organized events all across the country. But *nothing* beats being back in my neighborhood, seeing Papa and Angel's dream come to fruition.

During my teenage years, Papa encouraged us not only to be the best riders but also to give BMX a good reputation. And we did. We spent years trying to make people see the value, complexity and high quality of this sport and how underrated it was back in the day.

Not that my job ended there. I'm still honoring that mission. Our purpose as sponsors has always been to find ways to make young riders confident enough to pursue BMX as a career and not just a hobby. Give them the opportunities so they don't feel the need to give up on the sport they love in order to have a future like many riders of my generation.

Seeing so many local riders competing at this level and being supported by a crowd this big is nothing but rewarding.

We keep our places right by the jury table as the competition goes on and flashbacks start invading my mind. I close my eyes for a moment and hear the music mingling with the crowd, calling my name. I can feel my hands gripping the handles and my feet pushing the pedals as I come alive on my bike.

Where the only person I was competing against was *myself*.

I didn't care if I won every single contest.

I just wanted to ride, make a living out of my bike, and be happy.

"*Winning contests gets you sponsored,*" Angel used to say whenever we had that conversation. He always competed to be the best, no matter what. But what was the point if I was never going to be satisfied? I wanted to enjoy every second of the ride and I did with a smile on my face every single time. I have pictures to prove it. That's how I got the nickname 'The Quokka', as the little smiley rodent.

But when Angel died, the smile disappeared. I couldn't go on.

I clearly didn't give up on BMX. I still got involved in the culture and followed the sport in California. Damian and I would go to every contest and event during college. My hands were still itching to jump on a bike, but it wasn't my place anymore.

I didn't feel competitive or motivated to do it, even just for fun.

I didn't have my people around me. Nothing was the same.

Carmen wasn't next to me.

My thoughts are interrupted by the crowd giving a standing ovation to one of the riders on the track. My friends and I cheer and shout, seeing them fall and perform. We tease each other, joke, laugh, and remember the old days. We take pictures together, discuss the best tricks and styles of the new generation. I end up giving the prizes to the winners at the end.

And in the midst of this joy, a pair of beautiful caramel eyes keep following my every step. Filling me with the same longing I've tried to avoid for ten years.

As much as I want to resist them, I can't take my eyes off her either.

6

carmen

Embarrassed? Confused? Angry? Surprised?

All of the above.

After almost getting a concussion in front of every single person I know, including the one and only guy who would make my entire will power drain and my knees weak, how could I not?

Hence the fall.

Handsomeness and hotness aside, who the fuck does he think he is to demand explanations about who I'm with?

Ten years of silence and he thinks he can take over Angel's duty to get all 'big bro' on me? I wanted to believe for a second that he was jealous, but I know better. He's engaged to a *Vogue Model.*

How can he be jealous of *me?*

Don't get me wrong, I know I have my something. But a *Vogue Model?*

I'm not that delusional to even think I can compete against that.

Yes, I googled her.

Yes, I regret it.

I wish I'd called my sister before doing that. She could've told me googling the fiancée of the guy I've loved since I was six years old was going to do nothing to help my self-esteem.

A little girl with a crush. Seems like I'm still behaving like it. But how can I not? He still looks at me the same way he did back then. I know I was a naïve teenager, but he kept giving me reasons to believe I had a chance with him. He never treated me as some delicate flower like Angel did. I was his equal. Still, he made me feel special with his attention, support and comfort.

To everyone else, I was *'the princess with a bro spirit'* of the group, who didn't mind the farting, burping and the dick jokes. But never to Oliver. Even with the attention of every girl in a ten-block radius, who flirted shamelessly and threw themselves at him everywhere he went, he made me feel like I was the only girl in the world.

We all thought Oliver was going to become the next Dave Mirra. BMX was his DNA. There was no way he would've done anything else. Everyone wanted to be like him, be around him. But he never let it go to his head. He had the attention of the entire world and still he made me feel like I was *his* world.

But I misread all the signals.

"You doing okay?" Jacob asks, putting his arm around my shoulder while I finish taking the last picture of the day.

"The time of my life." I give him an exaggerated smile.

Jacob snorts. "I love it when you try to fool me."

I look up at him and shrug.

"What do you want me to say, Jakey?" I sigh. "You're all going through some shit and I'm glad he put aside whatever it is that I did to him and finally came home."

"You didn't do anything," he says, giving my arm a squeeze. "He's an idiot who has his head stuck in his ass and can't communicate shit."

I let out a chuckle. "Whatever it is, I'm fine. I already made peace with it."

"I'm sorry I didn't tell you he changed his plans. It was very short notice. I wanted to tell you sometime today, but it was super busy. Besides, he said he wasn't coming here today."

"It's okay, don't worry about it. I'm glad he's doing well."

"I know you don't want to talk about it," he takes my hand, "but you know I will always worry about you and the last thing I want is for you to hurt more than you already have."

"I know. I love you for it."

"Love you too, Chip." He presses a kiss to my hand.

The conversation changes and right when I'm about to start putting my camera gear inside my bag, my phone buzzes inside my pocket.

Mamá: Primero me voy a morir antes que me vengas a ver. *(I'll die before you come to see me.)*

Araceli Morales, the drama Queen of drama queens. She's a very melancholic and bitter person and likes to guilt trip me to do what she wants when she knows I'm busy. We have a… complicated relationship full of painful baggage I don't like to talk about. The guys don't like her very much, even Antonio being her nephew. Not to mention Rocío, who can't stand her for longer than an hour. They say I let her manipulate me and lie to me, but I just hate seeing her being alone, even when she lives with her sister. She needs me and I need to know she's alright.

She understands English but can't speak it. I have no idea how it happened, but ever since we were kids, we got used to talking to her in English, even if all of her responses are in Spanish.

Carmen: I was there on Friday. It hasn't been that long, mami.

Mamá: I used to change your diapers full of shit every day. Never heard me saying "it hasn't been that long" for that, right?

I let out a frustrated sigh.

Carmen: Is everything alright?

Mamá: I ran out of medicine last week and I'm filling out an insurance form I don't understand.

Carmen: When do you have to file it?

Mamá: Tomorrow.

Carmen: Why didn't you tell me you ran out of medicine and why didn't you tell me about that form until now?

Mamá: You know what? Go back to your friends and your bikes. I don't know why I bothered. I'm sorry, I won't bother you again. God bless you, mija.

"Oh, Jesus," I sigh, scratching my head.

"What is it?" Jacob asks, closing the clasp of my camera bag. I show him my phone and he rolls his eyes. "Clever as always." He shakes his head. "You leaving then?"

I nod. "Have to."

"*Have* to?"

"Yes, I have to," I groan and wipe my face with a hand. "Please don't start. Not today. I've had enough headaches today and I really couldn't take a lecture."

He opens his mouth to say something but closes it again, shaking his head.

"Okay," he rolls his eyes, "not saying anything…*for now.*"

Okay, maybe she does manipulate me a little bit. But I love her. I hate what anxiety and depression have done to her. The extremes she's gone to because she refuses to go to therapy.

It's never been a secret that Angel was her favorite child. When he died, her already tough demeanor and aggressive personality turned her into the most bitter, vengeful person I've ever met. I don't justify her actions, but I understand her. My aunt Carmela says she suffered a lot of trauma growing up as the oldest daughter. They came from a very dangerous area in Guatemala when the military was massacring entire villages in the eighties. Their dad used to beat the hell out of them and my youngest aunt, Sucely. After my grandmother abandoned them to join the guerrillas, they didn't have any other choice than to run away. My aunt Sucely to Guatemala City, and my mom and aunt Carmela to America.

She was still too inexperienced and naïve when she came to the country and fell in love with the asshole of all assholes who cheated on her and abandoned her right before I was born.

When Carmela divorced her husband and brought Antonio to

live with us, both her and my mom started a Central American restaurant called *Las tres morenas* which became very popular with time. I just wish that would've given my mom a little motivation to be a different type of mom to us.

I lost count of the times she hurt me and Rocío with words and slaps when we were kids for the smallest and most insignificant things. Even Angel got in the middle several times because he knew she would listen to him. I thought Angel's death would soften her a bit towards us, but it was the opposite.

Rocío couldn't handle it for too long and left for Chicago to pursue a career as a journalist. I don't blame her for leaving, but for a while it put a strain on our relationship. I wanted us to be a happy family like the Rodriguez's and tried to push Rocío to come back and talk to our mother many times; it ended up pushing her away for a while until we had a long talk to make her boundaries clear. I go see her all the time, but she only comes back for her birthday, when we all go to Angel's grave and have a picnic with his favorite food and snacks, celebrating his and Rocio's lives.

I've always thought there was something else that happened between them, because even though Rocio still contributes when Mamá needs help, she wishes she could ban her from her life. She might be right; she's done the worst to me too. But I don't think I'll ever have the heart to hit the delete button on her.

I walk to the jury's table to say my goodbyes, trying my best not to stare at Oliver. I hug Ethan first.

"Don't go yet," Ethan says over my shoulder, hugging tighter. "Let's go for drinks."

"I wish I could." I kiss his cheek. "Araceli needs some help with some insurance paperwork."

"Uh huh," he says, and I punch him on the shoulder, making him laugh. "Let us know if you need anything… like an excuse to escape."

I lift an eyebrow and turn around to hug everyone else. When I get to Alex, I squeeze tight. I still can't get over the excitement of his visit, but I'm not surprised he's here.

"Dinner tomorrow night?" he asks.

"Bet." I turn to the rest, "Vince? Tony? Dinner tomorrow night?"

"Sure," Antonio says. "Yo! Jake, Ethan, dinner tomorrow night? What do you say, Ol?"

"I… uhh," he stutters, "I made plans tomorrow night."

I ignore the pinch of disappointment and turn to Alex. "Cool, I'll text you tonight."

After saying goodbye to everyone for the fifth time, I finally get to my car where I let out a long breath and mentally prepare to be emotionally and mentally drained. My mother still lives in the same house I grew up in, just ten minutes away from Hope Center, so I take advantage of the short drive and give myself a pep talk before arriving.

There's always a reason to smile and make people smile, María del Carmen. You have the power to make someone's life better in some way. This time is your own mother. You can do this.

I find her at the kitchen island cutting some vegetables like she doesn't have any care in the world, but the moment I approach, she starts crying.

"Hi, mami," I say, leaning down to kiss her cheek. "What's wrong?"

"Nada." *Nothing.* "Just here thinking I might need a lawyer but can't afford it."

My heart starts racing and I refuse to pay attention to all the worst-case scenarios playing in my head.

"Um, okay" I swallow hard. "And why would you need a lawyer?"

"I was talking to Cristina just this morning," she says, "and she told me about her mom. She had the same pain in her stomach before she died." She presses against the upper side of her stomach. "I told her about the nausea and palpitations, and she said her nephew is a good lawyer and can help me to figure out what to do with the house once I'm gone. She says she can talk to him to give me a good rate."

I take a deep breath and press the bridge of my nose.

Did I mention she's also a hypochondriac? Ever since Rocío

went to college, she convinced herself that she's about to die from some disease. We've been to the doctor many times and the answer has always been the same: she needs to go to *therapy*. But instead of following the doctor's recommendations, she always finds a way to complain to other people who tell her she "isn't crazy" and ends up taking advantage of her.

Many of her symptoms *are* real. Her high blood pressure, the shortness of breath when she's having a panic attack and, in this case, the gastritis she's gotten due to all the over-the-counter medicines and vitamins she self-prescribes or her friends recommend.

"Mami," I say softly, tucking a strand of her hair behind her ear, "We went to the doctor for this, remember? He said it was gastritis. He gave you medicine for that; have you been taking it?"

"But Cristina—"

"Cristina's mom must've had something else, Mami."

"That's what I'm saying!" She smashes the knife against the counter. "I must have *something else*."

I grab her hand. "You have gastritis and you're not going to die from it, Okay? I don't think spending money on a lawyer is a good idea. At least for now."

"But spending money on God knows how many cameras is more important than your mother's last wishes?" She shoves my hand off. "You know I don't make as much as I used to in the restaurant. Why can't you just give me the money? Or tell that ungrateful sister of yours. She makes more money than you do. It's Cristina's nephew."

That's exactly why, mother. Cristina's nephew is a scammer.

"My cameras are what puts food on my table, Mami," I breathe hard. "A lawyer is not important right now. Let's focus on your insurance paperwork, okay?"

"What insurance paperwork?"

Please, not again.

"The paperwork you asked me to help you with?" I bite inside my cheek. "Mom, did you lie to me again?" She huffs, and I keep going on. "Why, Mom? Why do you always do that? Why do you always make up a lie so I drop everything and come running?"

"No me digas mentirosa, patoja malcriada." *Don't call me a liar, you brat.* She yells at me, her nostrils flaring hard and her eyes getting redder by the second. When I try to take her hand again, she shoves it. "Fuera de mi casa. Estoy harta de estas dos hijas tan malagradecidas que no pueden atender a su madre como se debe." *Get out of my house. I'm sick of these two ungrateful daughters who can't take care of their mother as they should.*

"Mami," I insist, "you said—"

"GET OUT!" she yells, muttering more cuss words in Spanish.

It's always like this with her. She calls, I run to her. She makes up a problem I can't fix because it doesn't exist. She gaslights me and gets pissed because I couldn't please her, and then she kicks me out.

Story of my damn life.

I nod, biting my lower lip. "If you still need help, text me. I'll be home."

I drive with tears in my eyes and get to my house more exhausted than ever. A cup of tea is all I need.

I used to avoid tears at all costs; I thought they were a waste of energy. But when Angel died, Alberto gave me the sweetest take on tears: *"Tears cleanse your soul, mi niña. If you don't cry, you'll poison yourself to death. Feel it and let it go."*

Although I haven't cried again as much as I did when we buried my brother, I always take my time to feel my feelings, cry a little bit, and move on. Which is exactly what I do before sitting down at my desk to edit today's pictures.

As if my mommy issues weren't enough, I get caught up in an avalanche of emotion.

Oliver is there. *In every. Single. Picture.*

Reminding me of how blind and naïve I was to believe the silent promises I thought he made.

He never said he loved you.

He never said he wanted to be with you.

He never said that kiss was real.

Still, I waited like an idiot.

Then I became a bigger idiot when I forgave him without an apology.

For going away without a goodbye.

For abandoning the gang when we all needed him the most.

Because it wasn't just an accident that scarred us all. It was the fact that Angel wasn't by himself when it happened. Jacob was right next to him and the rest of the guys were driving in a car behind him. They witnessed it all. Antonio tried to pull Angel out of the car. Ethan made the 911 call. Vince and Alex found Jacob unconscious and bleeding just a few feet away from the scene.

It wasn't. Just. An accident.

It was a traumatizing tragedy.

We were beyond broken and couldn't even try to piece ourselves back together.

I blamed Oliver for making it worse for a long time. Maybe if he would've been here Alex wouldn't have enlisted in the Army as a way to cope. Probably Vince wouldn't have moved with his mom up North for good, and Antonio wouldn't have hidden in the room he shared with Angel without talking to anyone. He wouldn't have shut down and stopped being the joyful, playful guy he used to be. Ethan wouldn't have started with all the secrecy and disappearing to God knows where every now and then.

I would've had someone to cry with, instead of drowning in the darkness of an empty room and enduring Araceli blaming everything on me.

Alberto put us back together.

He helped us all heal. He would make up any excuse to invite us over to do stuff together and just talk about things. About Angel. About memories. Even when it was the hardest thing to do. He was the one who started the picnic tradition for Angel and Rocio's birthday. He paid for my sister's tickets the first few times. He even got matching tattoos with all of us to remember Angel: *a bike handlebar with angel wings.*

We slowly came back tighter than ever. Even when we started leaving Oliver and BMX on the sidelines of our lives.

Eventually, Jacob, Ethan and Antonio got into car mechanics, and I went to school to become a graphic designer. The emails we wrote to Vince, Alex and Rocio became texts, then Skype and Facetime calls. And finally, little reunions from time to time.

The new normal was painful, but it was still full of a true love that never faded. Even if the one person I wanted to love me was the missing piece.

The people who chose me have always been enough for me.

They still are.

7

oliver

We wrap up the event, clean up the place and decide to check on Papá. This reunion was perfect for him, despite being a bit weak and tired. He's been the same jokester and teasing guy he's always been. After about an hour, he goes back to his room to rest, and we take advantage of the time and go get drinks.

Despite the unexpected events and uncomfortable encounters, we had a great day.

I'm in awe with the hard work the guys have done at Hope Center. Jacob started it as a place to offer education and resources to Latinx families and to help immigrant parents to adjust to their new life, introducing them to others and building relationships. They had so little expectations and never imagined the impact it was going to have on the community. They currently have all kinds of classes and workshops, mentoring programs for future athletes, tutoring for immigrant kids who are still struggling with English, and many other programs for adults. I couldn't be prouder to be a sponsor through Elite Bikes.

"Ol, you need to keep an eye on him," Ethan says as we make

our way inside the bar, talking about the kid who won the Advance category prize. "Did you see that final Barspin? I'm impressed."

"Yeah, I already talked to Damian about him," I say as we sit in a booth, "but we still don't know what we'll do next. There's talent everywhere and we want to go to Mexico, Guatemala and Costa Rica next year to catch talent."

"Do you have someone in mind already?" Antonio asks.

I nod. "We've seen a couple of videos of some kids in Mexico, D. F. and Oaxaca. There's also a bike shop in Guatemala City that sponsors events frequently and we want to check it out." I pause for a moment as the waitress serves a bowl of nuts, chips and salsa and gets our first round of drinks. "They built their own park in front of the store and have been selling Elite merch for a while. We want to get in touch with them. I want to take some riders down there to give their bikes away, just like I got mine, remember?"

The comment opens a can of worms and we all start remembering the day Craig Reynolds suddenly handed me his bike during a contest. We talk for a while about memories and the good old days but I'm eager to catch up with my cousin.

"So, what's new, Mr. Richie Rich?" I say to Vince. "Haven't seen you since you flew to L.A. last new year's. Ya ni me llamas, carnal." *You don't even call me anymore, dude.*

Vince is the son of my dad's younger brother Vicente and a very wealthy woman named Marissa. His parents separated after he was born and spent all his summers with us in the neighborhood. He's the CFO of his grandpa's company and we like to tease him about being a rich mommy's boy.

"I feel like I live inside conference rooms; that sums it up," he laughs. "Now that Daniel and I are thinking about living together, I might sell some of my shares and start a nonprofit."

"That's amazing, loco," Alex says. "What kind of nonprofit?"

"Our goal is to help reduce the homelessness in the state." Vince rests his back on the chair. "I'm still in the research process, but I might partner with someone else to do that."

"Let me know if you need some of the contacts from Hope," Jacob interjects. "Juliana knows pretty much every organization and shelter in the cities."

"Thanks, Jake, I will." Vince smiles and turns to Alex. "What about our very own Dominican Tank of Muscles? How's the new season with Judge Roberta?"

"Bro, believe me when I tell you, somedays I feel like I'm going crazy," Alex laughs, wiping his face with his palm. "You have no idea how difficult it's been to keep my shit together with all the weird things I have to see every day in that show."

Alex is an Iraq and Afghanistan war veteran. He came back to the country directly to Miami from his last tour, where he became a security guard of the Cuban celebrity judge, Roberta Marin in her family courtroom show '*Tell it to Judge Roberta*.' I've seen the show thousands of times and always laugh watching Alex keeping order, passing evidence, breaking up fights and carrying screaming ladies out of the set.

The entire table explodes in laughter and I have to wipe my tears, hearing him talking about the most ridiculous lawsuits people take to that court. Even Antonio lets out a snort.

"I'm telling you," Alex keeps going, "esa vaina es the locos."

"Alright, I see you Muscle Tank." Antonio punches him on the shoulder. "My mom never misses an episode. She's always bragging about her boy on T.V."

"Bro, I seriously need to see Tía Carmela before I leave," Alex replies. "How about you? How's everything going at the shop? How's Luis treating you?"

Antonio, Jacob and Ethan work at Synergy Garage, a well-known car shop in Minneapolis. Jacob is a front-end alignment technician, Ethan does body shop and detailing, and Antonio is an expert in engine restoration and classic car modifications. They've been working together for several years and always have hilarious stories to tell.

"Same ol' same," Antonio answers too quickly.

We all look at him quizzically and Ethan starts laughing.

"Don't mind our buddy Tony here—he's just pissed because the new girl is getting on his nerves."

"Shut up, asshole," Antonio warns, pointing a nacho chip at him.

"What do you mean, the new girl?" Alex asks, taking more nuts. "Did Luis hire a new secretary?"

"Look at you assuming some sexist shit, damn," Jacob shakes his head. "Ramona isn't a secretary; she's the new *restoring techni-cian*, bro. That girl is a *beast*. Tony's had a lot of workloads for the last few months and Luis tried to hire someone to help him out and from the five people he's made cry in the past few months, Ramona is the only one who hasn't left," he chuckles. "*But…* not a day goes by that we don't hear both arguing with each other."

That makes me chuckle. Antonio has always been the tidiest, most perfectionist sucker of all of us and he hates it with passion whenever things aren't done his way. I want to ask more about this, but Antonio clears his throat and speaks before I can say anything.

"Hey, too bad Chip couldn't come," he says as he shifts uncomfortably. "What did Tía Araceli want with her?"

"Help filling out some insurance form or something like that," Jacob says. I can see him shooting me a look.

"That's a shame," Vince says, resting his arms on the table. "I've missed that loca."

Carmen is the only topic I never bring up with them as a rule. *Never.* I should listen to Jacob and let it go. I should listen to my better judgment and stay away. But my curiosity is *killing me* and now that they brought it up, I can't keep myself from asking.

I clear my throat.

"What's up with that Fred guy?" I ask, failing miserably to sound casual.

I can feel the silent judgment in everyone's looks. Jacob shakes his head, Ethan raises an eyebrow and clenches his jaw, Vince purses his lips and looks away, while Alex straightens his back, joining his hands to play with his fingers. Antonio strokes his beard and smirks before talking.

"What's up with him?" he asks.

I sigh in frustration. "Who is he?"

After a couple of seconds, Ethan lets out a long chuckle and everyone follows in laughter. Antonio shaking his head. I just sigh with annoyance as everyone else keeps making fun of me.

"You're *pathetic*, Oliver," Ethan shakes his head as the laughter dries down. "Really, what's with the sudden interest? You haven't even wanted to *mention* her name since you left and now you're worried about who's she with?"

"I'm just… curious," I shrug, taking a long swig of my beer. "You guys know him well?"

"He was her boss in the agency she used to work at," Jacob says, while Vince asks for another round. "He's a good guy and has been volunteering at Hope a lot."

My tongue speaks before my brain is able to catch up. "How long have they been dating?"

"I thought this was exactly the information you were trying to avoid," Ethan says, lifting both eyebrows.

Our drinks arrive and we take our first sips. Ethan has always been the most straightforward of us, so his direct question doesn't surprise me.

"Well," I say, "I bumped into them without even trying and anyone telling me—don't blame me for wanting to know."

"You said you weren't coming," Antonio argues, "but that's still not the point. You could've just ignored her like you've done for the last ten years. Besides, you're engaged, why would you care?"

A sting of guilt pokes my chest. The only thing I've ever hidden from them is the nature of my engagement to Sue. They don't know about our arrangement and why we decided to get married. I shake my head and glare at him.

"I know and I would've," I say, "but I couldn't exactly ignore her when she was laying on the floor. *Again*, I'm just curious."

"If I remember correctly," Jacob intervenes, narrowing his eyes, "she was laying on the floor because she fell running away from *you*."

I open my mouth to retort, but Ethan beats me to it. "And then you were all over her like a creep," he scoffs. "Güey, admitting you're jealous would give you back a little bit of dignity. But again… *you're fucking engaged.*"

"Can you just answer the damn question?" I adjust my cap nervously. "Are they dating openly, yes or no? I just want to know."

I'm pissed to see how much they're enjoying this little round of torture. I feel my stomach turning with anger. Jacob wipes his face and finally answers.

"I told you to leave it alone, Santiago," he says with an annoyed tone, "but just because you're probably dying inside, I'll take that weight off your shoulders. No, they're not together. Not even close, mano. They're just good friends, that's all."

I don't know how but it does take a huge load off my mind. I know she will eventually find someone to be with, but at least I don't have to witness it.

"Out of mere curiosity," Alex says, crossing his huge, tattooed arms, "what was the last thing you heard about her? Like, real news."

"Last time I heard, she was dating that guy from college?" I shrug with my head down. "Andrew? Armand?"

The news had broken me at the time. According to my mom, it was pretty serious, and there were even speculations that he was going to propose. I almost had a panic attack when she told me.

"*Alan,*" Ethan growls. "Fuck that *puto.*"

"Hijo de la chingada," Vince says before I can comment. "I still can't believe she didn't let me end him when we could."

My entire body tenses up. My back and neck are hard as a rock, and I'm scared to ask the next question.

"What are you talking about?" I ask Vince.

"Didn't you hear that son of a bitch broke her arm?" he says casually.

"*He what?*" I roar, scaring everyone at our table and making a few patrons look over.

I don't think I heard it right. I *better not* have heard it right. I can feel the flames from the living hell inside of me; there's no possible way someone would do such a thing to the sweetest person that has ever walked on this earth.

"Wait a second," Vince looks at me with confusion in his eyes. "You really didn't know? The entire neighborhood was talking about it."

"No, he didn't," Jacob scoffs, "*surprising.*"

"Well, wait a goddamn minute," I glare at Jacob. "One thing is I didn't want to know about Chip's happy life, but this is completely different shit. *Why the fuck* didn't you tell me about this?"

"A ban is a ban, Oliver," Ethan replies with a shrug. "You said you didn't want to know about her, and you didn't. We thought you'd hear about it eventually, but you never asked, so we never mentioned it. We didn't find out until it was too late, if you ask me."

"What the hell happened? I thought they dated for years?" No one opens their mouth, and my anger intensifies. "Are you going to tell me or not?"

Antonio clears his throat and rolls his eyes.

"They did," he says. "Everything looked great for the first few months. She seemed happy. But then… she started hanging out with us less and less. I asked her what was up, and she confessed Alan didn't like us around her and she didn't want to upset him." He sighs. "I told her that was the first sign of a fucking abuser, but you know how she is. She trusts easily and wants to believe everyone is good and kind… So, she told me I was crazy, but she still shut us out."

"She didn't even invite us to her graduation," Ethan says.

That hits me like a bucket of water over my head. The fact that she loved someone so much to even push the guys away is beyond me. It only makes me want to find the guy and kill him with my bare hands for hurting her.

"Anyways," Antonio continues, "she got an internship at the agency with Fred and had to work till very late this one night. It was a motocross event she was photographing, and Fred offered her a full time job, so of course she was ecstatic and accepted. But the motherfucker kept calling her like crazy. When she called him back, he was pissed about the new job. Said she was a whore and was probably fucking some executive because she wasn't that good to get a job like that without sleeping with someone."

My jaw clenches even more with each passing word, my hands balled in fists, and it takes all my willpower to stop myself from breaking the table as Antonio continues.

"She broke up with him. We all picked her up, brought her home… but the guy didn't leave it alone. He insisted on apologizing, and she agreed… because she's a fucking saint." He shakes his head. "So, they met at a mall. When he started barking why they shouldn't have broken up and how he was doing her a favor by taking her back, she got up to leave… but the motherfucker tried to kiss her… When she pulled away, he grabbed her by her arm and twisted till it broke."

"Are you alright, Ol?" Alex asks hesitantly.

I have never been this fucking angry in my entire life.

"No, I'm not fucking alright," I mutter, fighting the lump in my throat, my fingers pressing the bridge of my nose. "I'm not fucking alright. Please tell me you hunted this motherfucker and chopped off his balls."

"We didn't but it wasn't because we didn't want to," Jacob says to his beer. "Chip managed to call 911 and pressed charges. Son of a bitch did one year and got out on parole." He takes a swig of his beer. "It was the longest night of my fucking life. We didn't know where she was, and she wouldn't answer her phone. We were about to go look for her when she showed up in a cab with a fucking cast. I feel like we messed up somehow, you know? We didn't see how bad it was until this happened. He was always treating her like shit, manipulating her with his crazy jealousy. We didn't see it until it was late."

"I told her she didn't have to settle for a lousy restraining order," Vince crosses his arms. "I wanted to pay for lawyers, appeal the parole and end him. But she refused. She said Karma was a bigger bitch and God would do justice."

"Yeah, that was surprising," Ethan agrees. "Araceli defending him definitely wasn't."

"What?" I scream-whisper.

My heart rate accelerates as Jacob looks at Antonio, as if he's not certain about telling me this part of the story I'm desperate to know. When Antonio nods, Jacob talks.

"Araceli said Chip must've done something to provoke him." Jacob fixes the collar of his shirt. "She said she screwed up because he was never going to take her back now and he was the best offer she was ever going to get."

I smash my hands on the table, not measuring my next words.

"And why are you talking about this like it's the most natural thing? Fuck! They hurt our girl!"

"Tranquilo, bro." *Calm down.* Ethan pats my back. "It's not like we didn't react the same way. But that was almost *three years ago*. Yes, it's Carmen. She's our girl, and it sucks you didn't know. But *that* is *your* own fault, cabrón."

I suddenly feel sick; my head is spinning, and the overwhelming realization of my failures crashes my nervous system. The pain and anger of this reality I wasn't aware of is unbearable.

I failed her more than I thought.

I should've been braver and stronger. I should've taken her rejection like a man, moved on, and come back like I was supposed to. Be the friend she needed and protect her from this and God knows how many other things. I suddenly *need* to know it all. Every single detail I purposely avoided for ten years. The names of every single person who have hurt her in any way.

I stand up and start walking without looking back. I hear the guys calling my name, but I can't stay. I need air. I can't believe someone would do this to my girl. To *any* girl.

I walk with no direction, the warm air hits my face, drying the tears I wanted to hold but now I can't.

"Ol, wait!" I hear Antonio coming after me.

I turn around and wait for him to reach me as I try to pull myself together.

"Hey," he says, grabbing my shoulder, "it's okay, bro."

"No, it's not," I say, finally breaking down in tears. "I can't believe I did this to her."

"You didn't do anything." He tries to catch my gaze. "It was *him* that hurt her. No one else. Ethan was just trying to make a point; you know how he is. Dude needs to learn how to filter himself."

"You know what I'm talking about," I whisper, "and he's right. I left. *I* decided to leave her and never come back."

"Yeah, I know. Still, what happened to her wasn't anyone's fault but that motherfucker's." He drops his hand off my shoulder. "Look, I know it's too much information all at once and there's still a lot you don't know. But don't let your guilt lie to you. Try to focus on today and the chance you're getting to show her you never stopped caring. Because I know you never did."

"What do you mean, there's a lot I don't know?" I tense my shoulders.

"You've been out of her life for ten years, Oliver." He lets out an unamused chuckle. "There's a lot that happened."

I wait for a couple of seconds. Cars are passing by, and the streetlights are starting to turn on. The world is spinning as usual, but it feels like mine just stopped.

"Tell me she's dated good guys, Tony," I finally ask, tiredly. "Tell me she's been treated like the queen she is after that fucker."

"I wish I could." He gives me a sad smile. "Life hasn't been easy for her, especially in the dating department. Jake and Ethan might disagree with me, but if you really want to make amends, man the hell up and talk to her." He pokes my chest twice. "You need to talk about what happened back then and the reason why you left like you did. She deserves it. And you know there's no way she'd reject you, you know she's that good." He sighs, "She's missed you, Ol."

"I don't know if I can do that without getting involved, Tony." I clear my throat. "I'd never admitted it out loud… but you all know already I *never* got over her. Not even a little… I don't know if I ever will, and that's fucked up."

"It is, but you have to face it and learn to live with it. It's not fair to her and not fair to Sue." He shakes his head. "You need to let it go, once and for all. You're getting married and she… Well, she's made peace with the past and is truly happy. Now it's your turn."

"This is too much to process in one day." I throw my head back and lean on the nearest wall. "I wish I could go back in time and try to be her friend, even if she didn't want me like I did."

"Dude, you've really got too much to clarify with her. I'm sorry you can't go back in time, but you can try to move forward."

I nod and he pulls me into a hug.

"Now, let's go back to the bar." He signals with his head. "We've been apart for too long, loco. Let's make the best of this time."

We walk in silence and take our seats again. No one mentions her or our previous conversation again, but I can feel myself dissociating. My thoughts go back to Carmen and the enigma of the last ten years. Antonio and Susan are right, I need to show her I never stopped caring.

I was terrified that I was never going to be able to stay away from her, but maybe it's not as bad as I thought. It doesn't have to end in tears.

I'm an engineer; I'm sure I can find a mechanism to get closer without stirring up old feelings…

It shouldn't be so hard.

8

oliver

Nothing like waking up from a power nap and not knowing what year it is or how you got there. I'm awake before I open my eyes and for a second, I think I might've been dreaming. The sound of a familiar song by Vicente Fernandez, the king of Rancheras, coming from downstairs makes me open my eyes. The memories of the last two days start falling as I look at the posters of the BMX legends Dave Mirra, Bob Haro, Van Homan and Ruben Alcantara on the wall in front of me.

It wasn't a dream. I really am home.

I stretch a little bit and look at the time on my phone. It's late in the afternoon and I've spent the day sleeping like a baby. I follow the sound of the music and find my dad sitting on the living room floor with Juanito curled up on his lap. He's looking at his record collection.

Papá said that BMX and music saved his life, carpentry gave it purpose, and Mamá gave it meaning. He came to the U.S. from Oaxaca when he was very young and grew up in the barrios of L.A., getting in lots of trouble with gangs. He met Mamá when he was a teenager during a BMX dirt bike competition. He fell in love with her at the same time as he fell in love with the sport.

Yeah, sounds familiar.

He wasn't exactly poor but still couldn't afford the luxury of a good bike. So, he and Tío Vicente, who was only a few years younger than him, started working in a carpentry shop of a furniture company after school and during weekends to be able to buy their own bikes. The company they were working for moved to Minnesota in the early nineties and brought them both with them. He couldn't be away from Mamá, so he proposed right after her high school graduation and started their life together in the coldest of the states.

Not too long after, he and Vicente decided to go their own way and started their own business building kitchen furniture.

When we were kids, Papá used to have his hair a little longer in a tiny ponytail and had a thick chevron mustache that he used to wiggle to make us laugh. He always had a cholo vibe that used to intimidate some people, without knowing he was the softest, most compassionate guy in the world. He shaves his head now and is a little chubbier, but he's still the same guy with the same heart.

And I could've lost him.

He looks up and smiles at me, interrupting my thoughts, and turns down the volume. I can't help but smile back.

"Watcha' doing, viejito?" I ask, making my way towards him, Juanito wagging his tail and throwing himself at me as I sit on the floor.

"Just looking through these old things," he says, motioning to the records. "Thinking about my Papá."

"When was the last time you took these out?" I say as I point at the albums of the music my abuelito used to play on his guitar. Papá used to play them during road trips or to go to work. We used to hate it, but I've been secretly playing a track or two from time to time as I've gotten older.

"A while. But I've been wanting to listen to them." He smiles. "You know, having a heart attack makes you think. I've been so caught up in work, Hope Center and... well, so many other things, that I forgot how important it is to enjoy the little things like music."

A lump forms in my throat and I fight it. We haven't really talked about what happened to him and what's going on with his health. Mainly because I don't want to stress him more than he is. It's already traumatic to have gone through something like that to add more by making him relive it.

"You want to enjoy the good life?" I say after a couple of seconds. "Just say the word and whatever you want is yours." I attempt a smile. "Do you want to go somewhere? Buy something? Just say it and I'll get it for you. Lo sabes bien." *You know it well.*

"Ah, I almost forgot I have a rich son." He waggles his brows and narrows his eyes for a second. "You know, there's actually one thing." He sighs. "If I end up having something like Alzheimer's—"

"Don't say that," I interrupt, but he keeps going.

"If I do," he puts a hand on my arm, "and I lose my mind… get all my favorite books and read them to me. Get all my music and play it all. Show me my old BMX tapes. I want to experience the excitement of the first time all over again."

"You *do not* have Alzheimer's." I take his face in my hands and breathe hard. "You hear me? You don't. Stop thinking about that. Stop putting more worry in your heart. You're still weak and you don't need more stress."

"Ay, mijo," he says and pats my cheek twice. "I know you hate this, but reality is, I might. I've been thinking about it. Researching and, well… it'd make sense if I do."

"What do you mean?"

"I haven't been feeling like myself for a while, Santiago. There are some things going on that make me feel like I'm changing in a weird way. The confusion… the uncertainty… it really scared me." He turns to pet Juanito. "I want us to have answers. I want you all to be ready if this happens again."

I can't resist it anymore and throw myself into his arms, swallowing hard. I want to ask him everything and know every single detail of what happened to make sense of it. Find that crack in the wall of that story that will make him see that his fears are not a reality. That *my* fears are not a reality. That it isn't true, that it's not possible. That life can't possibly hit us this hard again.

"Listen to me," I whisper to his ear, "we already scheduled an appointment with the best neurologist in the state. You'll have the best evaluations, the best people looking into them, and the results will come out clear. It won't happen again, you hear me?"

"Mijo—"

"I don't want to hear you saying anything like that again. You can't have Alzheimer's."

"Why not?" He raises an eyebrow, almost sounding amused.

"Because it wouldn't be fair." I snap my arms open. "Why does it have to be you?"

"You qué se?" *I don't know.* He smiles. "Why not me? Mijo, I'm not saying I want to be sick. I don't. I'm saying you need to accept it's a strong possibility." He kisses my cheek. "You think you can get an explanation for everything, to stop things from happening just because it's terrifying, but you can't. That's life. It doesn't give you warning or a remote control. It just happens. You don't get to decide what it will bring. The only thing you have control over is whether you live it to the fullest no matter what."

He shakes his head. "I've lived a wonderful life thanks to your mom and all of you kids. You've made my life unforgettable, even if my fate is that someday I will forget. Life is not *fair*, Santiago. But it's *beautiful*."

"I feel like it hasn't been for a long time."

I sniff and hold back a sob. He notices and cups my cheek. "Hey. What have I told you about crying?" He frowns. "Los hombres también lloran mijo." *Men also cry.* "Let the tears out if you need it. I didn't teach you that macho bullshit."

I bury my face in his chest and the tears I've been holding back since I arrived start falling. I cry like a little kid. Juanito approaches to sniff and whine at our feet while Papá hugs me tight, scratching my hair and whispering sweet words in Spanish.

"I just wish things could stay as they are for one fucking second," I whisper.

"What's the fun in that?" He chuckles, pulling away. "Can I ask you a question?"

I nod, feeling a pinch of fear. He has the ability to question everything I know as true in a life-altering way with just a couple of sentences.

"What the hell are you doing with your life?" he asks with a teary smile. "And I'm not talking about the money you have in the bank or any materialistic bullshit. I know you're successful on paper; I'm talking about here," He pokes my chest. "What are you doing to make your life unforgettable?"

"I don't know." I swallow hard, letting out what I've been trying to deny for so long. "I'm in auto-mode. Going through the motions, doing what we're all *supposed* to do. The house, the job… The marriage. But I don't know if I'm happy, or just settled."

"Ay, mijo." He shakes his head. "Worse than forgetting your life is not having *any life* to even forget. Stop wasting time on things that are not bringing joy to your life, things that are void. And I'm not just talking about the things you want, what makes you happy. I'm talking about the hard things. The real joy that comes from overcoming pain and fear, when you look at that one thing you waited so much for and realize it was all worth the difficulties."

He smiles. "You need to stop running away from reality when you think it's getting tough and start appreciating the beauty of hard things… stop giving up on life when it doesn't fit your expectations. That's when life surprises you the most… don't deprive yourself from it and be grateful for everything it will bring to you. *Today* is a good day to start."

Today. Why does everyone keep mentioning it? Maybe because there's something there I need to listen to. Maybe *it is* all about today. Because today, Papa's still here. I let that sink in for a moment. I forget about what happened, forget about the possible outcomes of that appointment, the fear of losing him and focus on his words.

"I love you, Papá," I say, cupping the back of his neck. "Eres mi héroe y siempre lo serás." *You're my hero and you always will be.*

"I love you too, mijo."

We hug for a little while and I help him to put the rest of his records back in the box. Suddenly, Juanito stands frantically and runs towards the front door, scratching the bottom and barking before the doorbell rings.

"I'll get it," I say as I stand up. When I open the door, the air leaves the room, and my heart starts beating faster.

Carmen.

I freeze for a couple of seconds. I see the shock in her eyes.

I wasn't expecting to see you here, either.

Why do you always have to look so beautiful?

"Hey," I say, clearing my throat.

"Hey," she smiles. "Oh, whoa," she jolts as Juanito keeps jumping in front of her, waving his tail so hard half of him moves from side to side.

She laughs and kneels down to pet him.

"Oh, look at you!" She lets him lick her face. "*Whosh'* a good boy? *Whosh'* a good boy?" She chuckles and stands up. "I guess he loves me."

Who in his five senses wouldn't?

I shake that thought out of my head and attempt a smile, moving away so she can come in, and force myself not to check out her ass as she walks by me.

"Well, look who finally decided to visit!" Papá says behind me. "La niña más linda de todas." *The most beautiful girl of all.*

"Albertito lindo," she gives him a hug.

"Juan, knock it off," I mutter to my dog, who's trying to knock them over. I grab him by the collar and take him to the backyard. I take advantage of the moment and level my breathing. When I get back inside, they're both in the living room. Papá in his favorite chair and Carmen at his feet. I'm about to offer something to drink but I get distracted by their conversation.

"I thought you forgot about me," Papá says.

"Ay tan exagerado!" *Such a drama King!* "I'm here almost every day. You can just say you missed me."

"I did. I always do. You know you and your sister are the daughters I never had, right?"

"Can you imagine?" She pats his knee. "You would've spent all these years praying for patience."

Papá lets out a silent chuckle that sends a shiver down my spine. Even though it sounds like a genuine laugh, it's not his loud, joyful laughter. It feels as if he's trying to cheer himself up and my heart breaks at the thought.

"Ay, mija," he sighs, "I would've been grateful to have you as a daughter… I'm still hopeful that one of you will marry one of my boys, you know?"

Dammit, Papa! I look away.

Dude, just step out.

Carmen starts laughing, trying to disguise the blush I can see all the way from here, and pats my dad's hand.

"Are you sure they would be able to handle any of us?"

"With a beautiful soul like yours?" He shakes her chin. "Who wouldn't?"

She shakes her head and laughs again. "You'll make me blush!"

"Do that favor to the world."

Sly old man!

I shake my head with a huge grin on my face. I turn around and close the kitchen door, but I keep listening right behind it.

"I want to ask you a favor," Papá says. "I've been thinking a lot these days and waiting to talk to you alone… Well, you have always been the glue that holds the group together. Promise me you'll keep doing it forever. That I won't have to worry about anyone."

"Alberto," she argues quietly.

"Take care of my boys."

"Alberto. You're still young and strong. That heart attack didn't take you down, it was just a sign you needed a little rest. That's all. We're not losing you anytime soon."

"But I won't be here forever," his voice breaks, "and whenever that happens, everyone's going to need you. Especially Santiago."

I understand the heart attack scared him, but I didn't understand how much until now. I don't want to keep listening but I'm frozen. Carmen stays silent for a moment and replies quietly after a couple of seconds.

"I'm sure his wife will take care of him," she says after a couple of beats, and the pieces of my heart that were already broken turn to dust.

I press the bridge of my nose with my fingers, trying not to sob loudly, and take a couple of deep breaths.

"But he misses *you*," Papá continues. "Don't look at me like that, he hasn't said anything. But I know him. My boys are my entire heart. When they're hurting, I do too. I know he does. I know you kids don't talk about this, but now that he's here, it's important for you to understand… He hasn't been the same without you." He pauses. "Promise me you'll take care of them if something ever happens to me… I can't help getting old, you know."

"Maybe old, but still very handsome."

He laughs. "Promételo."

"I promise."

"Eso mero." *There you go.* "Now, my next request. Would you take pictures of my familia?" I can hear his chair rocking. "It's the first time we're all together under the same roof in a long time."

"Of course!" she says excitedly. "I'll talk to him, and we'll set a date."

"Si, si… alright." He mutters something I can't understand and laughs a little. "I, ummm… yes…. You—you know what sounds like a great idea? Pan dulce. Don't you think?"

"Ummmm, sure," Carmen says. "Do you want me to get some now?"

"Yeah, why not? Bring it all," he laughs, his voice shaking a little bit. "Take Santiago with you."

"I, uhhh…"

"Santiago!" he shouts. "Santi, ven acá."

I suppress a smile and walk towards the living room. She's ready with her purse over her shoulder and my dad is sitting on the floor again.

This matchmaking old man has never had any shame when it

comes to Carmen and I, and I love him for it. He might fail with his meddling this time, but I can take advantage of it and use this opportunity to talk to her and patch up our relationship. I want to have her in my life in any way she wants to be, even if it's just a friend.

"Yes, Papá?" I try to sound casual.

"Go with Carmencita to La Oaxaqueña and bring some pan dulce, si?" He looks around. "And where the hell is your Mamá?"

"She didn't tell you?" I raise an eyebrow. "She was supposed to be at Hope for a meeting, but she should be back soon." I turn to Carmen. "Sure, I'll go with you."

Carmen walks towards me and I get goosebumps when she approaches to touch my arm.

"You don't have to," she whispers.

I'm about to say something when Papá beats me to it. "Yes, he does. Go."

We both laugh. I look at Papá then at Carmen.

"I could use a walk," I shrug. "Let's go."

I grab my cap from the coffee table and put it on backwards before leashing Juanito. I open the door for her and try to push all my feelings to the back of my heart and focus on what I need to do.

I could use a walk and a friend. If that's all I can get, I'll take it.

Even if it isn't enough.

9

carmen

We walk towards the Mercado Central in silence. The only sounds I hear are our steps on the concrete and Juanito's raspy breaths as he walks between us. The air is filled with familiarity. Old feelings that remind me of a distant home. An old me. The old *us*.

"Thank you for stopping to see him," Oliver breaks the silence, "you're definitely good at making him smile and I… I really appreciate it."

"It's really not a problem, Ol." I smile shyly. "I feel bad for not calling before though."

He turns to me and frowns, "since when do you need to call to come over?"

Since you decided to come home without anyone telling me.

"I don't know," I laugh nervously, "we're grabbing dinner with the guys later and I thought… well…"

"I'm sorry if I made you feel like you have to do that," he says. "My parents love you and I'm more of a stranger to this house than you are."

"I didn't mean to imply it was your fault," I say, looking at the concrete. "It just… it feels weird to have you here, to be honest, and I don't want you to feel uncomfortable with me stopping by whenever I want."

That makes him stop and look at me, wiping his face with a hand before talking.

"God, I really fucked it all up with you, didn't I?" He keeps going before I can reply, "You know, I'm really happy you stopped by today. I've been meaning to talk to you and this is the perfect opportunity."

A single, unwanted butterfly starts flopping around my belly. It confuses me. I don't know if I should be excited or terrified. Do we need to talk? Most definitely. There's so much that needs to be cleared up and explained but I do want to know? Part of me wants to know everything, but do I want to relive the humiliation of his rejection?

"Wh— what do you want to talk about?" I ask, wrapping my arms around my chest.

"Look, I know I made it awkward yesterday and I'm sorry," he takes my hand, "I've been the worst person in the world and so unfair to you and me," he sighs and lets go, "I know I don't deserve your forgiveness, but I really am sorry. I'm an asshole for just going away and ghosting you for all these years. Then acting like an idiot yesterday."

"Well," I swallow hard, "you did give me an extreme case of silent treatment and I just… I just want to know what I did for you to do that."

He shakes his head and I brace myself for impact. I regret asking now.

"Nothing," he looks around, then at me. "You did nothing. It was all me and my bullshit. You have no idea how much I hate myself for it." He takes his cap off and runs his hand through his thick black hair. I try not to stare at his biceps as he puts it back on and continues. "After everything happened… It took me so long to put my feet back on earth. I admit I didn't process my pain the right way and what was supposed to be a bad phase became a never-ending cycle. I didn't know how to cope," he frowns and shakes his head, "I'm sorry. This is still very heavy for me to talk about and—"

"It's alright," I say, putting my hand on his arm, "it's hard for me to talk about it too. Not as hard as it used to be but still. Losing Angel fucked everyone up in different ways. I get it. We don't have to talk about it if you don't want to."

"Just know that I'm sorry," he takes my hand again and squeezes, "I know it doesn't cut it, but please… forgive me."

That's a vague apology for ten years of absence, I want to say, but I can't find the courage to do it. Maybe because I understand where he's coming from. Talking about our past means we need to relive that horrible day and that's always painful.

But how can you close an old wound if you're not willing to touch it?

Nothing ever wipes away the pain of losing someone so close. I still cry sometimes when I remember that night. However, going to therapy, talking about it with Alberto and the guys, has helped us to navigate the pain and live with it and keep pushing forward. By the looks of it, it seems like Oliver never did, and that worries me.

Maybe if we really recover our friendship, we can have a conversation about it in the future? I don't want to force him to open up if he's still not ready, but at least he's owning his fault. I know he's being sincere and my stubborn heart wants to take whatever he's willing to give.

I lift an eyebrow and give him a hip bump.

"I will if you buy me chocolate ice cream."

He chuckles, his shoulders relaxing.

"Still thinking you can solve all your problems with chocolate, huh?"

"No one is immune to chocolate, Santiago," I say playfully, taking the leash from his hands, "no one in their right mind."

"You know I never really liked chocolate," he laughs as Juanito pulls the leash, making me stumble.

"That's because you hit your head hard that one time when we went to Wisconsin Dells when we were like eight."

"God, I can't believe you still remember that." He chuckles, taking the leash back.

I try to ignore how his dimples pop by shifting my attention to the sound of his laughter, but it makes it all worse. Opening this memory vault is bad enough for my already bruised heart, but I can't help but crave this old feeling of comfort and familiarity.

So, I give my heart permission just this once to open up and receive Oliver's attention as we keep talking.

We enter the Mercado Central and walk to La Oaxaqueña, Alberto's favorite bakery. Oliver buys almost every pastry and piece of pan dulce they have, and I take a little box for my mom. I send her a quick text telling her I will drop it off at the restaurant later, before walking to an ice cream kiosk, where I get my chocolate fix and Juanito gets a little icy snack before walking out.

"Tell me about your fiancée," I say, finding a bench near a park. "How did you meet her?"

Yeah, nice self-torturing question, you idiot.

He hesitates before answering and rubs his hands.

"Her name is Susan Riley." He takes a lick of his ice cream. "She was Damian's wife's roommate. She introduced us during their rehearsal dinner two years ago, and well," he shrugs, "we hit it off."

"Let me guess," I waggle my brows, "you couldn't wait to ask her out, and asked for her number?"

He laughs. "It was actually the other way around… *She* asked *me* out. We hung out a lot but didn't become a couple until much later."

"Well, look at you," I wipe my mouth with a napkin to disguise my discomfort. "How long have you been dating?"

"Promise not to judge?" He lifts up an eyebrow.

"I would *never*." I bring a hand to my chest.

He laughs. "About six months."

When he sees me snapping my mouth open and shut, he laughs again and keeps going. "Yeah, I know, it's kinda fast for a marriage but… we've been good friends for a long time. We know each other well and get along amazingly. She just… gets me, you know? It felt like the right thing to do."

A wave of mixed feelings pokes my chest. I used to be that friend; the one who got him. The one who supported him and knew everything about him. He's got to be really in love with Susan then. It took an eternity for him to kiss me just once and he proposed to her in a heartbeat.

Susan is very lucky.

Every time I've asked a guy out, they've turned out to be assholes later.

Maybe someday I'll meet one of the good ones. One that would be so desperately in love with me that he will want to stay. Someone who won't want to change me and will love me with everything I am, scars and ugly parts included. He won't be Oliver, but I believe there are still more great guys out there.

"Did you do a big proposal?" I ask, trying to sound interested.

Why do I put myself through this?

"If a *'hey, I think we should get married'* on a Friday night after eating our entire weight in tacos counts as a big proposal… then, yes." He shrugs.

"Listen, never underestimate the power of tacos," I fake a laugh, "but if you're crazy about each other and you can't live without her," I tug his arm, forcing my next words, "I'm happy for you, Ol."

I look up at him and he doesn't say anything. His penetrating gaze makes me feel self-conscious and intimidated. For a split second, I imagine him leaning down to kiss me, but he swallows hard and looks away.

"What about Fred?" he says after clearing his throat.

My face feels hot. "Yeah… about that."

He lifts up an eyebrow and smirks. "What about it?"

"You're such a damn liar," I punch his shoulder. "You already know he's not my boyfriend, don't you?"

He starts laughing and I shake my head.

"I'm sorry I let you think he was," I say. "I wanted to clarify but it was… I don't know. Weird, to say the least."

I didn't want you to think I was such a loser.

"It's alright, I had no right," he adjusts his cap. "Damn, I still have no right."

The silence turns uncomfortable for about five seconds, but Juanito—who's been laying on the floor at our feet—suddenly starts barking at a squirrel climbing on a tree. Oliver pulls his leash to get his attention.

"Que te pasa, cabrón?" *What's wrong with you, dude?* He mutters to him while rubbing his chin. After calming down, Juanito rolls over so Oliver can scratch his belly.

My little heart.

"So," he smiles, sitting back on the bench, "Graphic designer and photographer. I want to say I didn't see it coming... but I think everyone did."

Thankful for the change of subject, I tell him about my journey through college, how I got my internship in the agency, and how it led me to work with Fred before transitioning to RideXtreme.

"I freaked out when Fred hooked me up with the former editor in chief," I continue. "He said he was impressed with my portfolio, which wasn't that big then," I shake my head at the memory. "He offered me the same salary I had at the agency if I accepted the job as a Layout Designer too. I couldn't say no."

"That's amazing," he says, "but... I don't think I've seen any of your pictures."

I shake my head and purse my lips. "You haven't, but if you find all the pages well balanced and easy to follow with your eyes, you can thank me."

"No, seriously. Why haven't you been taking pictures if you were hired as a photographer?"

I debate talking about this as I do with everyone else since it's the fakest part of my life at the moment. Everyone keeps asking me the same question and I always say it's because my graphic design skills are more needed than my photography ones. But reality is that Simon Miller, my pain in the ass boss, and I had a very ugly meet-hate when the former editor retired and Simon started working for the magazine. He mentioned the newspaper he used to work at, and I commented on a piece I hated about one of my favorite skaters without knowing Simon was the one who wrote it.

It was one of the most awkward moments of my entire life.

Since then, to say that Simon hates my guts is an understatement. I haven't touched a camera since then, but he had to eat his words when he had no other choice than to send me as an official photographer for the X Games. Deep down, he knows I have what it takes; he just doesn't like me because I insulted his ego.

I decide to give Oliver half of the story.

"Well, my boss thinks I still need experience." I stand up.

"Bullshit." He follows me. "You've been taking pictures of riders for years. Why does he think you need experience?"

"He says photographing street riders isn't the same as doing it professionally, but you know it's pretty much the same." I shrug. "But he had to suck it up. The two main photographers resigned last month and had no other choice than to send me as an official photographer at the X Games."

"For real?" He lets out a surprised chuckle. "That's awesome, Chip. I know you've always wanted to do that."

"I know, right?" I bite my lip, "well… I'll see how it goes. You know how clumsy I get when I get super nervous."

"Hey," he stops and takes my hand, "you're one of the most determined, stubborn, and talented people I've ever met. I've always admired how much of a badass you are—this won't be any different."

We smile at each other as he releases my hand, "is that what you want to do long term? Work at a magazine?"

"Not really," I sigh, "my dream is to be a BMX photographer full time. Follow the Pros all day, maybe get a ride or two on a good bike."

"Like the old times, but with a paycheck? I love the sound of that." I see him smiling in the corner of my eye, "well, we're planning more sponsorships next year, we'll need photographers for sure."

My heart skips a beat at the suggestion. Photographing Elite Bikes riders? It would be a dream come true, but I don't want him to feel obligated to have me.

"You don't have to do that," I say.

"I know," he turns and smiles sideways, "but you deserve it. I'm proud of you, Chip."

I need to look everywhere else but him. I can't let him see the longing in my eyes. The veil just dropped, and it might reveal what I've been trying to deny all of these years. The fact I've been trying to protect myself from: *I never stopped loving him.*

I swallow my feelings and a text from my mom brings me back to reality. I reply quickly saying I'm on my way and turn to Oliver.

"Do you mind if we stop by the restaurant and leave the bread?"

"Nope," he motions with his head, "let's go."

Next time he leaves, he'll leave as my friend. He won't be a stranger anymore.

I walk next to him in silence, trying to convince myself that's all I need.

10

oliver

Restraint, thy name is Oliver Santiago Rodriguez.

If abstaining myself from kissing her more than once today hasn't tested my self-control, I don't know what would.

I'm done lying to myself and pretending I'm not as crazy about her as I've always been. I'm still in love with her goofiness, her positivity, and the selflessness she treats people with. I want to keep the mask on but it's impossible. Even Juanito seems infatuated with her already. I can see it in the way he waggles his tail when she pets him, rubs his belly or gives him little kisses.

Lucky dog.

We keep walking in a comfortable silence. For a moment I allow myself to daydream about being hers, but stop it as soon as I remember the main purpose of this conversation. I need a full reset and to train my heart to resist her now that we've re-established our friendship. Because having her close again won't be easy. It'll feel like walking through a desert without being allowed to drink water.

Putting my heart on the line would be setting myself up for another break.

A deadlier break this time.

Then

BMX, school and friends.

That was our entire life since Middle School, when Papá started planting the idea of getting sponsored. School would always come first, but the rest of our time was dedicated to either practice or watching BMX videotapes. Angel and I let everyone take turns on our bikes until the entire gang got their own. It didn't matter how hot or cold it was outside.

It was a constant. Just like Carmen's company.

She and Rocío never left Angel's side. Wherever he went, they were there too. We all thought Carmen was the cutest thing in the world. She was the most enthusiastic when it came to BMX. Always clapping frantically whenever one of us achieved a new trick or perfected one we were struggling with. Little by little, she became one of us and I even started to miss her when she wasn't there.

Angel had no problem with having his sisters around everyone else, but he made it clear they were forbidden. He wasn't very open about what was going on in their house, but we all knew Araceli wasn't too nice to the girls, so it made sense to all of us that Angel felt overprotective about them.

But Carmen became the gravity of our entire team. Everyone wanted to be around her. Especially *me*. Her laughter, her energy, her smile, and the way she wanted everyone to be okay just because she genuinely wanted happiness for everybody... It was my undoing.

I tried to avoid it. Really. I tried to ignore my feelings, but the day came when I couldn't resist it anymore and had to admit what was really going on inside my heart. I was fifteen years old. We were trying different things to take pictures and videos. Papá had been given a professional camera and told me to use it. My first instinct was to hand it to Carmen so she could play with the settings and try different shots of us. We were so impressed with the first photos she took that we decided to make her our official photographer for the rest of the summer.

It was Saturday night, after we'd been riding all day around the city. We were waiting for her and Rocío at the skatepark as always. There was nothing peculiar or different about that night, but the moment I saw her coming from two blocks away, I had to stop my bike and stare. The closer she got, the more my breathing slowed down and I couldn't look away.

What the hell was happening?

She was riding on the sidewalk that led to the park on a skateboard Ethan got for her. Rocío was walking next to her with her usual book under her arm. Carmen was wearing jean shorts, a black t-shirt knotted at the bottom in a little bow, showing a small portion of her skin and accentuating a figure I'd never noticed before. Her long hair knotted in two braids.

I stopped dead. She was the most beautiful girl I'd ever seen.

I had to fight my urge to pedal in her direction and meet her halfway to kiss her breathless. The desire that flew all over my body was freaking me out, as a million different scenarios played in my mind.

The guys approached to say hi and talk to her, but I couldn't move from where I was. She took turns to hug everyone and I had to fight the need to push my way to get to her. In my denial, I turned around to get my bike and pedal away, but the sweetness of her voice made me pull back.

"Hey, Big Guy," she said from behind me.

I turned to face her and froze.

She was wearing makeup.

She'd never worn makeup before. For some selfish reason, I imagined she'd worn it for me.

"Hey, Chip." I swallowed hard.

She smiled at me, but before she could say anything else, Jacob called her from behind me.

"See ya in a bit," she said and walked away.

The next thing was the most simple, trivial thing in the world.

If you'd seen it, you'd probably thought it wasn't a big deal. Yet, it made me lose sleep that night and every other night after that:

She smiled, took the skateboard under her left arm and slightly brushed mine as she walked by me. It was a millisecond of contact, but the air was instantly charged with her scent and flew in my direction as she passed. It filled my nose and went straight to my chest, making my heart race a thousand beats per minute.

I closed my eyes shut for a moment before turning my head a little to see her while she walked away, but when I did…

She was already looking at me over her shoulder.

She bit her lip and fucking *winked*.

My knees turned to rubber, and I couldn't erase the stupid grin off my face.

Jesus, I like her. A lot.

And I think she might like me too.

Everything changed that day.

I couldn't stop thinking about her and couldn't fight my feelings anymore or keep my mouth shut, but it was one of those secrets everyone really knew. The pull I felt towards her was impossible to keep ignoring. I was an idiot for her, always wanting to get her attention or talk to her whenever she was near.

I despised when other boys would try to talk to her. She never understood the effect she had on guys. Every guy in school had a crush on her but she never knew. She never paid attention to any of them, and that fact shouldn't have been as satisfying as it was. She deserved a better guy than I was. But I wanted her for myself and needed to make it happen.

I knew I was playing with fire and risking my relationship with my best friend, but I had to take my shot. I had to know if the look in her eyes and her secret smiles meant what I wanted them to mean.

The perfect chance came when she said she wanted to learn how to ride like us. She'd jumped a few times on Angel's bike before, leaving us all in awe, but never really practiced any tricks until later. Angel was a little scared of letting her. She was so tiny, but never as fragile as Angel thought. She was a badass, a fighter, and so determined I just couldn't say no. She loved BMX just as much as any of us and deserved a chance.

That's what made me give her my bike the day I was given a brand new one out of the blue. A Pro-BMX rider surprised us with a visit to one of the contests we organized and out of nowhere, he handed me his bike, saying he wanted a new talent to have a bike that matched their level.

Everyone started congratulating me, asking me to sell the parts of my old bike, but I knew what I wanted to do the second I got the new one.

"Are you serious, Ol?" Carmen said when I handed her the bike.

"I am," I said, taking her hand and placing it on the handlebar. "It's yours, if you want it. But I have one condition." She lifted an eyebrow, and I kept going. "You'll only let *me* teach you."

"Are you kidding? Of course, yes!" she said, before throwing herself in my arms. I held her tight. Before I realized what was happening, she placed a kiss on my cheek, and I felt it everywhere. I wanted to say so much more, but her giggles interrupted my thoughts.

She jumped on the bike and started pedaling around with the most beautiful grin I've ever seen.

That was the moment I knew I would do anything to keep that smile right where it was.

Angel wasn't exactly happy. But when he saw her picking it up so fast and becoming as good as everyone else, he couldn't have been happier and more proud. She didn't need my help for too long, but I kept going with our BMX classes after training with the guys for years.

Everything I felt for BMX, I felt it twice as much when she was there.

Enjoying my passion right next to her was the most amazing experience I've ever had.

I fell in love with it even more while falling in love with her. Without even knowing.

I crushed on her in silence for three years.

It was about time everyone noticed.

The guys said Angel had started talking about it and I needed to be careful.

It was nerve wracking. But the more I spent time with her, the more I realized I didn't care anymore about what anyone said. If I could only prove to everyone this was real, maybe I could have it all.

Angel and I got full rides in the Mechanical Engineering program at UCLA.

We were already in contact with some brands for potential sponsorship and were going to make the most epic road trip to L.A. and be roommates. It was my last summer in Minneapolis, and I wanted it all.

I needed to know if there was a chance for me and the girl of my dreams, once and for all.

It was a Friday night—we were sitting down at the edge of a bowl in the skatepark after a rough training session, our bikes on the floor. We were talking about everything and anything. About how things were changing. About the future.

When the laughter and conversation died down, we stared at each other in silence.

"Whatcha thinking about?" she asked.

My face was hot as hell, not just because of all the exercise, but because I didn't know how to initiate the conversation I needed to have. I wanted to tell her I thought she was beautiful. How proud I was of her. How much I was going to miss her.

God, I want to kiss you so much, I wanted to say.

But I was scared of her reaction.

What if I'd misread everything and she didn't want me?

Make a move, asshole.

"I…" I stuttered. "I'm honestly scared to tell you. I don't know how you're going to take it."

"You know you can tell me anything," she took my hand, "good or bad, you can talk to me."

I finally looked up and saw the worry in her eyes and realized I couldn't wait anymore.

Still unsure of what I needed to do, but the thought of going away without even trying was like a punch in my chest.

"Would you get mad if I kissed you?"

She raised both eyebrows and waited a few seconds. I was about to apologize when she spoke.

"You… you want to kiss me?"

"I haven't been able to think about anything else for a long time."

"I…" she breathed hard, "I'd like that very much, Oliver."

That was everything she needed to say.

I cupped her warm face in my hands and pulled her gently to close the gap between us, bringing her trembling lips to mine. I wanted the kiss to be sweet and smooth, but the moment she opened up a little, I couldn't resist. I devoured her mouth. She wasn't my first kiss. She wasn't the first girl I had laid eyes on. But she was the very first I wanted a future with. Kissing her felt a thousand times better than anyone else I'd ever kissed before. I felt like I'd found the gold I'd been digging for the last three years and made me forget whoever I'd kissed before her.

We kissed for the longest time and yet it felt like it wasn't enough. When we finally pulled away, I couldn't bear to stare at her for a moment. I was so happy I was going to burst. When I looked at her again, she giggled.

"Well," she said, "I'm not mad at all."

I laughed and hugged her. We didn't say anything else for the night. We stood up and walked back. Kissed her again when I left her on her doorstep and promised to call her later. I didn't want to say or do anything else that might screw everything up, so I smiled and walked away once she was safe inside.

I wasn't too far ahead when I heard someone pedaling behind me. When I turned, Angel jumped down from his bike, grabbed me by the collar of my shirt, and slammed me back against the wall.

"What the hell, Angel?" I pushed back.

"What the hell are *you* doing?" he demanded. "I didn't disfigure your face the moment you kissed my little sister just because I didn't want to make a scene in front of her." He breathed heavily. "But this fucking game ends right *now.*"

"What? What game? Who the fuck is playing any games?"

"You know exactly what I'm talking about." He pulled back, "if you keep going with this, you and I are over, Oliver. I mean it."

I scoffed and stepped forward. "You really trust me this little? Unbelievable."

"I don't trust anyone when it comes to keeping my sisters safe and you've always known it," he snapped back. "I'm not gonna let you break her heart and just leave. You're gonna fucking kill her and ruin everything we've worked for." He pushed me, "why, Ol? Why her? From all the girls you could've picked, why did it have to be my sister?"

My anger toned down for just a second.

Carmen and Rocío were the apple of his eye.

And he was worried about her and what playing with her would mean not just for her but for everyone else. But he didn't know how I really felt. No one really did.

That was the moment that changed everything. It was right in that second when I realized this wasn't just a simple crush anymore.

I was in love for the first time in my life. In love with a girl that shouldn't have been forbidden but was.

I cleared my throat and smiled.

"Dude, you act like you don't know me."

"Seems like I really don't." He scoffed.

"Angel I…" I swallowed hard and smiled, "I'm not just going to play with her and leave. I'm serious about her. And I think she might feel the same way."

"You're kidding me, right?" he shook his head, "first, we're going away, bro. There's no way you're going to feel the same while we're away. You'll meet a bunch of chicks in college, and you'll forget about her. Second, she doesn't do serious. At least not yet. The moment we get to L.A., she's gonna move on from this little hero crush and find someone else who's closer. You're just gonna break each other's hearts and make the gang pick sides."

"Bullshit," I pushed him back and sighed, "look, I know it's your sister but… I love her. I really love her. *I'm in love with her*, Angel. And it feels like it could go somewhere… Just let me talk to her and see if she feels the same way and I promise I'll do right by her. *Please*."

He examined me for a couple of seconds. For a moment I thought he was going to let the guard down and give me a chance, but he shook his head and pushed me again against the wall.

"You're warned," he finally said, "kiss her again. Make another move and we're done."

I couldn't sleep for the next few days. Every time I was about to call Carmen, Angel's words haunted me. I wanted to believe he was wrong, but what if he was right? What if all Carmen felt for me was just hero worship? What if it was just a crush and wasn't willing to wait for me while I was away?

In the following week, neither of us brought up the subject. I wanted to pull her away and talk to her in private, but Angel wouldn't stop shadowing our every step. I couldn't find one single second alone with her.

I was frustrated. I needed to talk to her, kiss her again. Promise her to fight for her, even if it was against her brother. So, I made up a plan. I was going to confess my feelings and prove Angel wrong until he let go of his stupid tantrum.

I learned a song on Papa's guitar to serenade her and wrote a little speech.

Chip,

I know we haven't really talked in the past couple of days and I'm really sorry.

Angel found out about our kiss that night and he wasn't happy about it.

But I don't care what anyone thinks. Not even him.

I love you, Chip. I think I've always been in love with you.

I've always loved your smile, your laugh, the way you always make me feel alive and how you manage to make everything better when I'm sad.

You make me happy.

I know I don't deserve you, but I want to ask you for a chance to fight to be the man who could deserve you someday. I want to be the one who makes you smile and sigh. I want to be the only one who gets to kiss you and the one who tells you how beautiful you are inside and out. Because you are so beautiful it hurts not being allowed to tell you every day.

I know we're young and that I'm also about to leave for college. I don't have my hopes up. Still, I want to beg you to please wait for me and follow me to L.A. next year after your graduation. Next time I leave, I want to take you with me. We can work together so you can get into a good school and improve your photography so you can get a job at a sports magazine or the brand that sponsors me.

We make a good team and I know we could be perfect together. If you want to.

I will love you forever.

Please be my girlfriend.

I found the perfect chance to put my plan into action just a couple of days after. The gang was invited to a party at the house of this girl who had a huge crush on Angel. Ethan, Vince, Antonio and Alex were going to take the car Papá bought Angel and I to drive to L.A. and I was going to drive with Angel and Jacob in Araceli's car.

But I bailed at the last minute. I told the guys Papá wanted me to help him with a late installation and was going to get there later to bring them back. I wanted to go to Carmen's house while they were gone and come back with her as my girlfriend.

I rehearsed the speech and the song a couple of times and

headed to Carmen's house. I was almost there when I got a call from Papá.

"Mijo, donde estas?" *Mijo, where are you?* His trembling voice sparked my anxiety.

"On my way to Carmen's. Why?"

"I need you to come back now."

"Why? What happened?" I swallowed hard.

"It's Jacob. He and Angel… they were in an accident, and we need to get to the hospital." I could tell he was crying, "We'll be waiting for you."

He didn't say anything else and hung up.

My entire world froze for a second and I couldn't do anything else but to run as fast as I could, my adrenaline up to the roof.

I didn't know it at the time, but Angel had decided to leave the party way earlier than planned… shitfaced drunk. Antonio and Alex had tried to take the keys from him but he refused, stubbornly hopping on the car with Jacob next to him.

The guilt I felt the moment I crossed the sliding doors of the hospital emergency room hit my entire body like a ton of bricks.

I should've been there. It was me who was supposed to be driving that car. They're here because of me.

Antonio, Rocío and Carmen were hugging each other in the waiting room when I walked by. Carmen locked eyes with me for a couple of seconds, but I just dropped my head and walked away. What was I supposed to say knowing they were in this condition because of me?

Ethan jumped into Papa's arms when he saw us coming. He was sitting with Alex, Vince and Tío Vicente.

"He didn't stop, Papá." Ethan cried, "we were following behind them. We got to a red light and Angel didn't stop… that fucking truck trashed the car."

"It's okay, mijo." Papá said, scratching his hair, "they'll be okay."

I wanted to run towards Carmen, hug her and reassure her that everything was going to be fine. Tell her what I was telling myself, that people have accidents all the time and they don't always die. But the more details I heard from the guys, the guiltier I felt. I couldn't even look in her direction without feeling like the worst piece of shit.

Araceli and Carmela were yelling at the front desk nurse asking for answers when finally, a doctor showed up. I stood up immediately, praying for good news. He told us Jacob was in the ICU in critical condition, and then, the words I was afraid to hear left his mouth.

"As for Angel," he looked around, "I'm very sorry. We did everything we could but… we lost him."

The world stopped.

I could hear my heart ripping apart as I fainted and my head crashed against something I couldn't recognize. I still heard the sounds around me. Chattering, screams, cries for help. They all decreased little by little as the voices in my head kept telling me it wasn't true. That my stubbornness and betrayal didn't kill my best friend and sent my baby brother to the ICU.

No, he's not dead.

He's just mad because I kissed his little sister.

Where the fuck are you, man? Why don't you come out already and tell us it was just a prank?

Please. You're my brother. Mi compadre. Mi socio.

I'm sorry, Angel. I swear I'll stay away from your sister if you come back.

Just please. Come back.

"NO!" I screamed, kicking my blankets away. And for a moment I thought it had all been a dream. I was in my room, not in the hospital anymore. I looked quickly for my phone and dialed Angel's number but he didn't pick up.

"Come on! Come the fuck on!" I cried, "you can't be dead, motherfucker. Please… please pick up. Please."

Papá rushed inside the room and hugged me tightly. Turns out I'd passed out in the hospital and had no recollection of how or when we'd gone back to the house. I cried in my father's arms for what it felt like days, hoping I would wake up from this nightmare.

A slow hell burning me and all people around me from inside out.

And it was all my fault.

I didn't leave my room for days. I couldn't eat or sleep. Not even when my mother told me Jacob was out of the ICU. I couldn't gather the courage to face anyone, knowing I could've prevented the whole thing and didn't.

I just wanted to go to sleep and wake up years later.

The day of the funeral came, and I couldn't muster the courage to get up and say goodbye to my best friend. To my brother. Ethan gave me shit for not going, but I simply couldn't. I couldn't find the strength to even imagine seeing his face without his playful smirk, knowing I was never going to hear his voice again.

And I couldn't face Carmen, Antonio or Rocío.

Any of my friends.

Because I was the only one to blame.

So, I did the only thing I thought could save me.

I left without saying goodbye to anyone.

My parents weren't happy about my decision but still let me go.

Every mile I drove on my way to L.A. was heavy inside my chest knowing Angel should've been driving with me. Knowing my friends were going to feel betrayed. Knowing Carmen was going to ask about me and learning I left was going to break her heart.

I settled in L.A. and tried to shove away the avalanche of feelings that were haunting me but couldn't. Weeks passed but the pain never faded. Neither my love for Carmen.

It was the only thing I held onto. The only thing that kept me going.

I felt like shit knowing I'd left her when she most needed me. I wanted to call so many times but the guilt and shame for having left stopped me every time. I needed to go back home and beg for forgiveness. Find a way to repair the trust I'd broken and convince her to give me another chance.

So, I came back for Thanksgiving break.

I arrived on a Wednesday morning. I was going to surprise her after school and grovel until she forgave me. But when I got there, she was coming out with Adam Barret's arm around her shoulder. Angel and I had always hated the guy and in that moment, I wanted nothing else than to throw myself at him and rip his arm off my girl. That was until *she* cupped his face and pulled him down for a kiss.

What was left of my world crumbled to dust.

She was laughing. Looking at him with the same devotion she once looked at me with. Kissing him in the same way she'd kissed me just a few months back.

My heart didn't break. It fucking shattered.

The only thing that was bumping around my head was Angel's words.

See? Told you. She moved on from her crush. She found someone else.

That was the day I decided to ban her from my life and swore I was never going to put my heart on the line for her or anyone else again. I managed to ignore her for years, trying to focus on school and later on my business.

But once you taste a little of María del Carmen Morales, you can never go back.

11

oliver

Present

The familiar scent of spices and fried goodies invades my nose as we cross the doors of *"Las tres morenas,"* where my friends and I spent a good time of our childhood. Call me nostalgic, but I've had Central American food all over the country and nothing beats this restaurant.

Carmela says hi with a long hug to each and entertains herself with Juanito. We leave him with her while we walk to greet Araceli in the kitchen.

"Hola mami," Carmen says as we enter.

"Hi," Araceli says in Spanish, dropping whatever she's cutting on the table, "you can leave the bread on—" she stops to look at me with curiosity, "look at how you grew up so handsome. Long time, no see Santiaguito."

"Araceli," I greet her, "que bueno verla otra vez." *It's nice to see you again.*

"What are you doing here with us, the poor?" she laughs.

"Oh, don't say that," I scratch the back of my neck, "I'm here for a couple of months. I want to spend more time with my dad."

"I'm sorry he went through that horrible thing, mijo," she pats my arm, "Alberto is a good man. He's always been so good to us. He was like a father to my Angelito."

He's been like a father to your daughters too.

The thought stays inside my mouth and I can only smile. I always got the strangest vibe from Araceli. I never really liked her but after hearing what she said to Carmen after what happened with her asshole ex, my dislike has gone to another level. We always knew she was awful to her daughters but never witnessed it.

"So, what now?" Araceli chuckles, looking between Carmen and I, "are you dating her?"

Carmen and I laugh nervously, but Carmen interrupts. "Oh, no mom. We're just… we're friends like always."

"Of course," Araceli scoffs at Carmen, "look at him. That'd be aiming for too much."

What. The. Fuck?

I must've misinterpreted. There's no way she just implied her daughter isn't enough for me. *ME.* The guy who would *sacrifice a limb* without thinking twice, just to be worthy of her.

"Excuse me?" I ask, letting out an unamused chuckle, "you're kidding, right? The entire male population of the world is under-serving of a woman like your daughter."

Carmen lets out a loud gasp as Araceli laughs.

"Ay mijo, always so silly." She says, "you see her, right? Poor thing has always been so plain. Just like her dad. Thank God my twins got the good genes," she puts a hand on my arm and I fight my urge to shove it away. "Besides, she barely fries an egg and can't swipe the floor for the life of her. Careless. Helpless. It's a miracle she hasn't burned that house down. It's good she doesn't have time for anything with all of those jobs she has. She would only disappoint you."

I'm about to snap at her but Carmen takes my hand and shakes her head. Her eyes pleading with me not to say anything.

"Mami, please?" Carmen says, letting go of me and taking Araceli's arm, "can I talk to you for a minute?"

"Why? You don't like me telling the truth, do you?" Araceli lets go of her, "you can't even wipe your butt and you're already playing house by yourself." She turns to me, "you've been away for so long you don't even know, Santiaguito. It's like this. She doesn't like to be told what to do. She's a rebel. The moment you put your foot down and tell her who the boss is, she'll pack her things and leave you. She'll break your heart like she does with all men."

"MAMA!" Carmen snaps.

"See what I'm saying?" Araceli laughs without a flinch, "she's always disrespecting me like this."

I feel my eye twitching.

My urge to flip the table and force this woman to retract every single word she's vomited is almost impossible to contain. I want to roar in her face the never-ending list of reasons why she should be proud of her daughter. Carmen notices how I'm getting ready to snap because her teary eyes catch mine once again, this time she grabs my hand and pulls me out of the kitchen.

"We've gotta go," she says while we rush out. I pull a little bit. I want to go back and put Araceli in her place, but she pulls back again.

"Please, Ol. Let's just go, *please*."

Her broken tone brings my guard down and I follow her in autopilot, completely speechless and feeling so angry I could break something. Carmen rushes us outside without saying goodbye to Carmela. I pick Juan quickly and Carmela waves goodbye with tears in her eyes. When I go out, Carmen is already far ahead, and I have to run to catch up with her.

"Chip!" I shout, but she doesn't stop, "Carmen, wait."

I finally reach her and when she looks up, her beautiful face is red and covered in tears.

She needs a friend. Be her friend.

I don't think twice and take her in my arms. She doesn't resist and hugs me tight. Juanito sniffing and whining against her legs.

We stay like this for a couple of minutes while I rub her back and scratch her hair, her quiet sobs squeezing my heart.

I'm here now. You don't have to endure this shit alone. I'm fucking here. I promise.

She pulls away and smiles.

"I'm sorry," she wipes her face with her forearm.

"*You* are apologizing?" my voice shakes, "Chip, what the hell?"

"She's just… she hasn't been in a good place lately," she whispers, "she's just going through a rough time right now."

She starts walking and I go after her.

"A bad place?" I ask, "that seems like a very malicious place, Chip. Don't try to sugarcoat it. A rough time? Spitting venom to her own daughter?"

We keep walking in silence. I want to ask her so many questions but I know she'll try to justify Araceli. Just as she does with everyone who makes her feel less. She's always believed everyone has good intentions at heart, she's simply that good.

We go back to my parents' house and even Juanito looks tired. I can't shake the discomfort in my gut so, before we go in, I ask.

"Does she always treat you like this?"

"She's always been mean," she replies, head down. "But she's been this hurtful ever since Angel died."

Another fucking thing that's my fault.

I shake the thought out of my head and lift her chin up, "what does Rocío think about this?"

"She keeps telling me to stop seeing her," she sighs, "so I just don't say anything to her anymore."

"Well, maybe she's right," I shrug, "it's not fair to you. You don't deserve this you—"

"It is what it is, Ol," she takes my hand, "she might be cruel but I'm the only child she has close. Believe it or not, I love her." Tears start rolling down her face as she talks fast, "when I visit her, it lights my day. Seeing her healthy, being able to take care of her. Even when she doesn't notice a damn thing I do. It's still a blessing for me to serve her."

I stare in awe for a couple of seconds, wishing I had the same power to see the best in everything. To trust everyone just because that's what we should be able to do. To see the bright side, even when your own mother clearly thinks you're not good enough.

I love you. You've always been wonderful. Don't believe anything she says.

"How the hell do you do that?" I sigh, tucking a strand of hair behind her ear.

"How do I do what?"

"Find a good thing in a pile of shit… Find good things in people who just hurt you."

She laughs, "what other choice do I have? Get buried in sadness?" She cocks an eyebrow and purses her lips, "that ain't my style, bro."

I let out a soft chuckle and shake my head. She's the only person I know who could bring up the sass in a moment like this and actually make it work.

"God, I've missed you," I say, grabbing her face in my hands without thinking.

"Oliver," she whispers.

I swallow hard, "Chip, I—"

The front door of the house snaps open and we both pull away like two teenagers who were caught making out. My entire family comes out in a loud chatter. Mamá laughing at something Alex said, Papá in the middle of Antonio and Vince with their arms around him. My brothers arguing about something right behind them.

"Hey, there you are," Antonio says to Carmen as they all make their way to different cars and Papá goes back inside. I don't miss everyone's looks as they walk next to us, saying hi, giving gentle punches on my arm and patting my back.

"I was about to go find you," Jacob says to her, "where the hell were you?"

I kneel down to take Juanito's leash and push him inside to hide my wicked smile of relief. I almost kissed Carmen. *Thank God I didn't.*

"We umm…" Carmen clears her throat, looking around. I see Ethan and Antonio looking from afar as she talks fast, "we went to get pan dulce for Alberto but ummm… we talked and talked and talked. Time flew by. You know how it is. Right, Ol?" she giggles, "I know, right? Okay, I'll shut up now."

I chuckle and shake my head. Jacob raises an eyebrow and switches looks between both of us.

"We were just patching up our friendship," I shrug, "we're all good. She's ready to leave."

"Okay, good," he says, his expression still unsure, "you can drive with Ethan and Vince," he says to Carmen and turns to me, "you still have plans?"

"Yep," I lie and mock a salute, "we can keep talking later. Have fun."

Carmen smiles and waves, "see you, Ol… and thank you."

"Anytime, Chip."

That was close. Too close.

I put the bread on the kitchen island and throw myself on the couch. I'm in desperate need of a reality check and there's only one person who can bring me down from this cloud.

"Hey," Susan answers after the second tone.

"Hey, you," I say, my eyes closed, "how's Lake Tahoe?"

"Refreshing," she sighs, "how's Alberto?"

"He's great. His usual, witty self. Still a little weak but recovering just fine. You were right, that shit was traumatic."

"Definitely," she says. She laughs at something someone says in the background and clears her throat, "sorry about that. So, tell me. How are *you* doing?"

Confused. Scared.

"Can I book you a flight?" I blurt.

"What?"

"Just hear me out," I sit up and scratch my cheek, "I know you told me to get closer and make amends, *blah blah blah*. But it's doing the complete opposite of getting me closure, Sue. It's opening the wound even more."

"Have you talked to her about her brother? How you felt when you left?"

"Barely," I let out a long breath, "I just apologized for ghosting her and that's about it. She didn't ask anything else. She just plain and simple picked up where we left off... Like no offense was ever made," I wince, "dammit, Sue! She's still the same girl I fell in love with but... *more*... like the essence still there but more... matured?" I throw my head back, "God, *I'm fucked.*"

"My God. Breathe, Oliver," she laughs, "it makes sense and I'm glad that she was willing to give you another chance. That's a step towards finding your peace."

"I can't. I'm feeling too much already," I shake my head, "can you just *please* come and stay for a couple of days? I just need moral support."

She sighs, "Okay but you won't get out of this. We'll figure out a plan for the next few months and you'll close this chapter in your life, okay? I want to finally see you happy. You deserve it."

"Deal," I say.

"Let me check my schedule."

We check out flights and buy a ticket before hanging up. I have no idea what I'm doing, I just know I'm drowning inside a pond I thought I was never going to fall into again. Susan is the only ally I have, having her here for a couple of days will ground me.

At least I hope so.

12

carmen

Fifteen more minutes and I'm out.

Isn't it sad to feel like you're trapped when you go to work?

It wasn't always like this. I used to love my job back at the Agency with Fred. I was my bubbly and fun self all the time. But dreams are made of sacrifices and this dream of mine of being an extreme sports photographer has been there for far too long. Ever since Oliver handed me my first camera; I knew I was born to be a photographer. And not just any photographer. My second love was always Extreme Sports, of all sorts. BMX was obviously the first in line, but I learned to photograph it all.

However, budget and responsibilities got in the middle once I got to college. Graphic Design wasn't my first choice, but it was the most profitable at the time. It wasn't foreign to photography, so I took the chance and decided to climb the ladder from that point. And I've been doing it for the last six years. Not that I don't like what I do, it's just not my passion.

I don't care if I have to work for the male version of Cruella de Vil for a while.

I'm debating logging off early when I get a text from Alex. He left for Miami this morning and promised to let me know when he got home. After a couple of exchanges, I jolt at the sound of a throat clearing behind me.

"Carmen," Simon glares at me, "I hope I have those pages ready for tomorrow."

"I'm actually wrapping up, Simon," I fake a smile, "you know I'm *always* done in time."

"Look, I know you'd rather be behind a camera," he eyes me from head to toe, "but you need to find motivation in the part of the job you don't like first. You asked for a chance to prove yourself and I'm giving it to you," he smiles, "so, I suggest you take it seriously and stop wasting your time."

I swallow the ten thousand ways I can tell him to fuck himself and smile.

"Yes, sir."

Asshole.

Don't get me wrong, the guy is brilliant. But this *"I'm giving you a chance"* speech is just an act. He decided I'm his enemy and is up in my ass day and night, waiting for me to fuck it up somehow so he can get rid of me. He still has the power to take me off the X Games, so I need to behave as well as possible and that means to swallow my pride and do as he says.

Ten more minutes of this torture…

When he turns around, I put my head to my hands and massage my temples. I feel like I'm going to self-combust if I don't get out of here soon. I need to eat something sweet and vent. So, I take my phone and text the only person with enough patience to listen to my drama.

Carmen: Are you busy?

Rocío: Just coming out of a meeting, what's up?

Carmen: I'm calling you in twenty.

The moment I clock out I run towards the parking lot and dial once I'm inside my car. She answers at the second tone. I haven't talked to her in a week, so I take the time to update her with my entire drama, starting from the moment I saw Oliver at Hope Center just a few days ago.

"That *motherfucker*. Pedazo de mierda." *Piece of shit*, she mutters once I'm finished, "I'm so sorry, babe. How are you feeling?"

"I don't know." I close my eyes and rest my head back, "I think I'm just resigned. I've always known we're just meant to be friends and that's it. But I have a huge imagination and last night was playing with me big time."

"You were not destined to be friends only," she scoffs, "you were made to be together, but *he* fucked it all up. *He* was the one who abandoned us all and then ghosted you like you were nothing."

"He never loved me, Rosy."

"He did," she insists, "we all saw it. Even Angel saw it. He sure wasn't too happy about it but he knew it all along he just was a coward and never said it. Fuck him."

The same conversation as always. My sister always wanted us to be together, I guess that's why she also saw things that weren't there.

"He never made any promises, Ross. It's not his fault that he didn't feel the same wa—"

"Qué necia!" she interrupts. "You always do the same shit. You always make excuses for people who hurt you. Stop making excuses for that *cabrón*. He didn't stop to think he was going to hurt you, never did anything about his feelings and on top of that he left you without saying goodbye." She groans, "And now this? Jesus. I *can't believe* he almost kissed you; he's *engaged*. I should call him right now and give him a piece of mind."

My heart races at the thought of my sister cussing Oliver out over the phone.

"What? No!" I snap, "I said I think he wanted to… It could be my imagination."

"Well, I sure hope so. God, I'm so pissed… and his fiancée looks like she's a good woman."

"I know," I shake my head, "Oliver said they've been dating just for six months. Can you believe it?"

"Yeah, Tony told me about that. What an *idiot*."

"Him or her?"

"Both," Rocío huffs, "whoever falls in love with that idiot must be an idiot too."

She lets out a chuckle and I just groan.

"Ha-ha," I mock and let out a sigh, "but seriously, after all we went through, he gave me just one kiss after years of flirting and being inseparable. And *she* got him to propose in a matter of months."

My heart breaks a little as I say it. This is the one detail that hurts me the most. I don't like to compare myself to others, it's a useless habit. Everyone has their own story and unique happy ending that will come just in time. But some comparisons create themselves. When it's that one person comparing you to someone else without even knowing they're doing it.

"No, we're not doing this shit again, Maria del Carmen." My sister says with annoyance, "we're not diminishing ourselves or putting ourselves below the motherfucking pedestal. Stop it *now*. You are an amazing, talented, sweet, kind and beautiful woman. *Any guy* would be lucky to have you."

"Tell that to the parade of shitheads I've dated," I snap and put a hand on my steering wheel, "I'm a magnet for unreachable, emotionally unavailable guys, cheaters or abusive assholes."

"God, can you just stop?"

"I can't, Rosy," I sigh, "Oliver is the origin of every insecurity I've ever had, and I can't stop overthinking…" I put a hand on my forehead. "I just don't understand. I know I'm no super-model but I'm a good person. I think I have enough love for someone to want me for who I am, without trying to change me or leave me at some point because they found something different or got bored… I don't understand why the good guys never want me and the bad guys always manage to take advantage of me."

Rocío stays silent for a moment, and I feel a tear rolling down my left cheek. When I sniff, my sister talks again. Her voice soft and easy.

"What's up with that negativity, huh? Where the hell is my obnoxiously optimistic little sister and what did you do to her?"

I smile at the comment. From both of us I've always been the positive, happy-go-lucky sister with rose-colored glasses. But I'm a human being who has ups and downs too. And this one is very low: I never stopped loving Oliver and he's about to get married to the love of his life. And my dating record is way too depressing to feel encouraged to even think about dating again.

I take a deep breath and answer my sister's question.

"She got lost in a clean-cut beard and a flat cap."

She scoffs, "beards and caps are just makeup for guys so she shouldn't be that lost."

I let out a loud chuckle, "what are you talking about? Beards and caps are fucking sexy."

"Yeah, because they hide imperfections and men's egos." She says derisively, "did I ever tell you about this guy who asked me out on a date at a fucking pool?"

"No? Why would he want a first date at a pool?"

"That's exactly what I asked. He even had the nerve to tell me he saw this one tik tok saying he should because then he wouldn't be surprised later by my real looks. I laughed like a maniac, and I told him to shave his beard and take off the cap."

I let out a loud chuckle. "What did he say?"

"Nothing. He hung up and never called again. I used that Snapchat filter that shaves you and takes off all facial hair on one of his Facebook pictures. He looked like a fucking sperm, ew."

We both explode in laughter. If there's one thing I can count on every time I call Rocío, is that she's going to do anything in her power to make me feel better. Even if it's just for a little bit.

"At least I made you laugh," she says when the laughter dries down.

"That you did."

After a couple of seconds, she keeps going, "look, I'm sorry this whole shitshow with Oliver is making you feel so insecure again. But if there's something *you* have taught *me* is that whatever ball life throws at you, is for you to hit right back," I smile and she keeps going, "so hit right back, Chip. If you think you could still be his friend, then do that and get that closure once and for all. God knows you fucking deserve it."

"I really hope so. If friends are all we'll ever be, I'm fine with it. I just want the entire gang together again…" I say quietly, "I'm taking pictures of the family on Friday, by the way."

"Really?"

"Yes." I smile, "Alberto is excited about having his three boys back home and asked me for a photoshoot."

"Damn. That's going to be emotional. Do you really want to do it, or did you say yes just to make Alberto happy?"

"No, I really want to do it. I'm actually looking forward to it."

"Well, if that's the case… then have fun and make it a good time for you," she says and sighs. I can hear her moving stuff around. "Okay, I need to let you go. Tell Alberto and Martita I love them and to put a leash on his oldest son or I will."

I laugh again.

"Thanks for listening to me, Rosy, I love you."

"And I love you too. I'll text you later, okay?"

"Okay."

It's during times like this when I wish my sister lived closer. Although if she did, she probably would've broken Oliver's nose already. Still, I could use some sister hugs right now.

She's right, I need closure once and for all. I can't live my entire life longing for a guy to return my feelings. Ten years have been more than enough of this uncertainty.

Friendship has to be enough.

13

oliver

Positivity has never been my strength but I try.

Believe me, I try hard.

Looking at things with hopeful lens all the time is really hard for me, and my family knows it. Which is why I hate it when life tries to kill the little optimism I still have in my heart.

I spent all day yesterday with my parents. Ran errands with my mom, cooked for her and Papá. When Ethan and Jacob came home from work we all watched a Mexican movie my parents love and had coffee in the afternoon playing Monopoly cards. A game Papá nails every single time. It started off good, but the second time around Papá was having a little trouble making his moves. We teased him a little bit about it but he got too anxious, throwing the cards on the table and walking away.

I tried to go after him, but he locked himself inside the room and didn't come out until today. But that wasn't the worst part. When I came down, my mom was in tears saying that he probably was struggling to play the game. That he snapped because he didn't know what to do and we made it worse.

"He did not forget how to play the game, Ma!" Ethan insisted, "he was alright just a few moments ago."

"That's what I'm saying," she cried, "that's what he does. He's alright for a second and then he's not. Yo no estoy loca," *I'm not crazy.* "Did you see the look on his face? He was *confused.*"

"We probably went on about it too hard and he's still sensible, mami," Jacob interrupted, "he's still recovering. Still weak. Try not to read much into it, we don't want you to get sick too."

I stood there and listened, looking at the three of them going over the same thing for hours. I've been trying hard to believe we'll have a good outcome, but my mom let it all out. She recounted one by one the times my dad has forgotten what he just said, the name of the secretary at the shop, putting on his shoes the wrong way.

Doubt creeped in even deeper.

We finally agreed we weren't going to do or mention anything else that can potentially overwhelm him and won't make assumptions until he has an official diagnosis. It was two in the morning when that happened. Even with such tiredness, I didn't sleep shit. My heart is feeling heavy.

Now I'm at the airport, sitting near baggage claim, Juan next to me. The sliding doors open and I see a familiar, messy blonde bun coming out of the gate. Juanito immediately runs to greet her.

"Hey, baby boy," Susan says, kneeling down to kiss him.

"Hey," I say, pulling her into a hug, "I'm so fucking happy you're here. How was your flight?"

"It was okay," he smiles, "but I want to know how you are. You look tired."

I put my arm around her shoulders and walk towards the parking lot. I tell her about the events of last night and everything that went down with my dad. We have a little time, so I give her a little tour around the Twin Cities. She's never been to Minnesota before, and if there's something I like to talk about, is how underrated these cities are. They might not be big or famous, but they have the same action, culture, history and beautiful architecture as New York or L.A.

She takes pictures at the Prince and Bob Dylan murals; we have ice cream at the Stone Arch bridge and have lunch at my favorite taco truck Downtown. By the time we get back to my parents' house it's already coffee time for them, so we sit at the table, and I let them catch up with her. I try to pay attention to my dad, his body language, his expressions and although he's not engaging as much as he normally does, I can't find anything alarming.

Is it me? Am I in such denial that I can't really see something wrong with my own father? Or have I been away for so long that I no longer know him?
Shit.

Susan's laughter brings me back to reality, "I still feel so weird when you call him *Santiago*."

"No kidding," I roll my eyes, "I still don't understand why you would name us two names and call us by the second. Still, everyone calls us by our firsts."

"I wanted to name you after my abuelito, Ivan Santiago," Papá adds with a soft smile, "but your mom was obsessed with Oliver Reed."

"I was not, viejo mentiroso," *lying old man*. My mom gives him a playful punch on the shoulder.

See? His normal playful self.

"But what about Jacob and Ethan then?" I ask, still chuckling, "you named them *Andrés* and *Moisés* as middle names. They don't even rhyme."

"Where are they, by the way?" Susan asks, "I haven't seen them in a long time, I'd like to say hi."

"They have class at Hope Center today," Mamá stands up to take our plates, "they just started this new car mechanics class for kids who can't afford tech school and they're doing amazingly." She turns to me, "have you taken there already?"

I shake my head, "I was going to but figured she'd be tired by now," I turn to Susan, "we could go if you want. Jake and his friend Juliana have done great with the place."

"Ah, yes," she stands up, "I've heard so much about it I feel like I know everyone already."

We leave Juanito with my parents and walk five blocks to Hope Lutheran Church, where Hope Center's building is. When we get there, we find a wonderful chaos of chatter, music and people walking around. I introduce Susan to some of the people and give her the grand tour. We stop by the dining room and Susan stares with curiosity at the kids making a fun mess while eating.

"So, they come here every night to have dinner?" she asks, leaning against the doorway.

"Not all of them come every night, but most," I cross my arms against my chest, "they're kids from surrounding neighborhoods whose parents work overnight and can't cook dinner for them. There's also an overnight daycare and an after-school tutoring program so they can come and study or do homework if their parents can't help them."

"That's super thoughtful. I wish there were more places like this everywhere."

"That's Jake's vision for the next ten years. They want to partner with more churches and school districts to open more Centers like this."

"Let's find Jake," she takes my hand, "this is wonderful, and I *need* to get involved."

I grip her hand, guiding her towards the back where the garages are. When we turn around in one of the halls, we hear chattering inside a classroom that turns into an explosion of laughter.

That's when I hear that *unmistakable* chuckle.

Her chuckle.

I try my best to disguise my nerves and walk faster, but as we're about to pass by the door, it snaps open and all the students come out, still laughing.

"Bye, Carmen."

"Don't forget your homework," she screams, "and tell your friends about the exhibit next week."

Her face lights up the second she turns around and sees me standing there.

"Ol, I didn't know you were coming," she grins, but it's gone the second she sees I have company, "oh, hi there."

"Hi, I'm Susan," she says, eyeing Carmen and offering her a handshake.

Well, I guess this is happening.

I clear my throat, "Sue, this is —"

"Carmen," Susan interrupts me, shaking her hand frantically, "I mean to say *the* famous Carmen Morales. My goodness I'm so glad to finally meet you. Oliver talks wonders about you."

"Does he, really?" Carmen blushes.

Carmen looks as shocked as I am while still shaking Susan's hand and I silently pray the floor swallows me.

"For being Jake's best friend, of course," I say, giving Susan a look.

She lifts up an eyebrow at me like the smug she is, silently telling me *"You're screwed dude"* and turns to Carmen again.

"Right," she smiles, taking her hand away.

I put my hands inside my pockets and smile. I thought subtly was my thing, but this moment is proving me wrong. I forgot Carmen told me she teaches a photography class on Wednesdays and wasn't expecting to see her and having an awkward encounter with Susan.

"Heard so much about you too," Carmen says, "for how long are you visiting?"

In a perfect world, Carmen and Susan would be perfect best friends. They're both queens of small talk, they have sincere smiles and whenever they ask something, it's because they genuinely want to know. They're both caring souls.

But Carmen is slightly uncomfortable, I can see it by the way she grips her camera bag handle and how she's biting her upper lip.

"A couple of days," Susan looks at me briefly and tugs my arm, "just wanted to check on this guy and see how Alberto was doing. So, you teach here?"

"Photography on Wednesdays and English on Mondays," she smiles.

"You teach English to immigrants?"

"Yes, most of the parents we work with know too little or nothing at all," Carmen replies, "it's a basic conversational English class to help them communicate better but it's done wonders so far. We also offer free immigration advice and translation services for legal documents and tax filing."

"You told me about the art and sports stuff but nothing about this," Susan gives me a playful punch and I shrug. She looks at Carmen again, "this is so necessary for the community. Whose idea was it?"

"Mine actually," Carmen smiles shyly.

That catches *me* by surprise and I smile, "I didn't know that."

She looks at me and I see a tiny rose hue coloring her light brown cheeks, sending a thousand volts right to my heart that are impossible to ignore.

"Just thought about what my mom would've needed when we were growing up," she puts her hands behind her back, "we didn't know English until we started school, so she struggled for years whenever we went out and had to talk to people, pay bills or fill out forms. When we finally learned English, my siblings and I would argue all the time trying to decide how to translate all those legal words fast. Believe me, we *did not* want to get hit by that chancla."

Susan laughs and I find myself chuckling too, imagining the three Morales siblings around the big table, fighting for a piece of paper.

I never thought about it before but looking back, it amazes me how different we all experienced childhood even though we all grew up in Latino families and have similar backgrounds. There are so many differences and similarities, but language has always been the most interesting aspect to me.

Susan is so immersed in the conversation she even lets my arm go, crossing her arms against her chest as Carmen keeps going.

"After the sports and arts departments started booming, Juliana asked everyone for more ideas to help the community. This was the first thing that popped in my mind," Carmen shrugs, "we started two years ago with ten students and now we have almost fifty."

"That's amazing, Chip," I say, feeling proud of my people.

Susan lets out a soft giggle and looks up at me, "Chip?"

Oh yeah, I forgot I never told you about the cute nickname we have for her. I want to say, but Carmen talks first.

"Oh," she waves her hand, "that's just a foolish nickname my brother gave me when I was little and they never let it die. He used to say I looked like a chipmunk."

"Lovely," I whisper without thinking. Carmen looks at me with eyes wide open and I clear my throat, "yeah, ummm… you were always a lovely kid. Cute."

I look at the ceiling, trying to hide my embarrassment. I see Susan in the corner of my eye, shaking her head as she laughs. She's never going to let this one go.

"Anyway," Carmen clears her throat, "I'm heading out. It was nice meeting you. Let me know if you want to contribute with something, we're always looking for more volunteers and donors."

"I'd love that," Susan shakes her hand, "nice meeting you, Carmen."

"Bye, Susan," she smiles and looks at me briefly, "see you around, Ol."

"See ya, Chip."

When Carmen is out of sight, Susan pushes my shoulder. "Way to make her uncomfortable."

"Sorry," I mutter before we keep going.

We walk towards the back of the building and find the garages where Jacob, Ethan and Antonio have the car mechanic's school set up. Jacob is out on a date so it's only Ethan and Antonio. Susan chats with them for a little and say our goodbyes when we see the summer sun starting to set on the horizon.

Susan smiles as we walk back to the house but doesn't say anything. I know she has a lot to say about our encounter with Carmen and her silence is making me nervous.

"I loved Hope Center," she says as we approach a baseball

field. We take a seat on a bench and she keeps going, "Carmen is really sweet."

"She is," I whisper.

"And beautiful. The pictures you showed me don't do justice," she looks up at me, "and she has such a vibe with people."

"She… does," I take off my cap and run my hand through my hair, "can you just cut the suspense? I know you love to torture me but you're making me really nervous."

She laughs and kisses my cheek, "I sure love to torture you."

"No kidding."

"I thought you said she didn't have feelings for you."

Now is my turn to laugh, "it's true. She doesn't."

"Oliver, have you always been this blind?" she frowns, "because if you have, we might need to recap and find an explanation for what I just saw."

"There's no recap, Sue," I put my cap back and adjust it, "I was a crush for her while I loved her for years. She got over me and now she's fine without me. That's what really happened and that's the story I told you. What you saw over there was her being herself. The same she's always been with everyone else. I'm no special."

"Dude," she wipes her face with a hand, "you know, I always had the feeling I was missing something about this story. I knew I didn't have the whole picture and now I just confirmed it," I let out a frustrated sigh while she keeps going, "I need answers. But before we do that… I need to be honest about something else too. After seeing what I just saw, I think it's the right time." I snap my head towards her and she continues, "I want out."

"What? You want to call off the wedding? Because of this? Sue, I'm telling you the truth, she doesn't want anything to do with me, she—"

"Shhh… Easy," she puts her index finger against my lips, "Ol… I… I've met someone."

"What?" I chuckle.

"I met a guy," she smiles, her eyes glossy, "he looks at me the way you were looking at Carmen. And I look at him the same way she was looking at you."

I laugh in confusion again and she keeps going before I can say anything.

"I'm sorry I didn't tell you sooner, but I wasn't sure," she gives me an apologetic smile, "I guess I was trying to figure things out. You know how difficult it's been for me to trust after Caleb… His name is Will. He's one of the attorneys handling the contracts with the agency. It started with friendly coffee dates, some texts and calls… He's different. *My* type of different," she wipes a tear, "he knows about you, and nothing has happened between us. At least not yet. He went to find me at Lake Tahoe and asked me for a chance and I said yes. I came here thinking about how to tell you and after what I just saw… I know this was meant to be."

"Are you in love, Susie?"

"I think I am."

I hear the words and nod. I want to ask a million questions. Not because I'm frustrated or jealous, but because I'm thrilled for her. She deserves that kind of story. She deserves someone who worships the ground she walks on after everything she's been through. I can't hold her captive with this arrangement if she found her one.

"I'm happy for you," I kiss her forehead, "I have no objections and I really wish you the best kind of love."

"Thanks, Ollie," she pats my leg and sits on the floor, in front of me, "I'm happy and I want you to be happy too. So, let's talk about Carmen."

I take a deep breath and tell the story again. But this time, Susan pauses and asks more questions, interrupting when she thinks I'm missing an important detail. She winces, rolls her eyes and frowns in certain parts and when I'm done, she keeps nodding with her lips pursed.

"Makes sense," she says when I'm done, "so she never told you she didn't love you. She never said it to your face and you still moved to the other side of the country without looking back?"

"No," I narrow my eyes, "I *saw her*, Sue. With another guy and I just didn't want to know anymore."

"You just assumed, then?" she asks, her brows lifted all the way up.

"I didn't assume," I grumble, my heart twisting with a hint of annoyance, "did we talk about it? No. But it was crystal clear, and I didn't want to ask and endure the humiliation and rejection."

"So, you just left? Jesus, Oliver," she puts her hands on her face. "Why am I not surprised and how on earth did I miss this one little detail?" She looks at me again, "I don't know her at all, Oliver… but I know when a woman is in love. I know that look, dude… Maybe it's not the same as they were, maybe it's changed with time but… *Carmen has feelings for you.* It's obvious."

Don't play with my heart, Sue. Don't give me false hopes.

"I don't know," I sigh, rubbing my hands against my legs, "she's always looked at me with some sort of gratitude. I know the way she looks at me, but it's never been love. It's hero worship. I mean, I gave her my bike so she could learn how to ride and gave her first camera too."

"I know," she says, "now she's an amazing Sports Photographer. You really think that's all? You don't think this just added to what she already felt for you?"

"I guess it did at the moment," I shrug, "but it wasn't enough. I took her kindness and thought was flirting like an idiot. You should see her around others, she's that sweet to everyone. I'm no special. She just wants to be friends."

"Did she tell you that?"

"No, but—"

"You're the most frustrating man, you know?" she leans forward, putting her hands on my knees, "you assume a hell of a lot and communicate so little. I guess we just found your problem with women overall."

Ouch.

"Wow," I let out a surprised chuckle, "you came loaded and ready to shoot, didn't you?"

"I told you I want you to pursue happiness," she takes a seat next to me again, "and seems like Carmen is *that* and more."

I lean my head back a sigh, my eyes directed at her.

"So, you really think I have a chance with her?"

"One hundred percent," she gives my shoulder a squeeze.

I close my eyes, trying again to give into hope. To believe Susan is right and life is giving me another chance to have the girl that has always had my heart.

I laugh and run my tongue inside my lower lip, "I guess we failed in our quest to run away from love after all."

"I don't think we failed in anything," she smiles, leaning her head on my shoulder, "I think we were brought together to make each other ready for real love. I don't think I would've been ready without you."

I smile. Feeling grateful for her friendship and remembering how badly I wanted to fall in love with her but couldn't.

"Why did you say yes to me?" I ask.

"For the same reason you proposed," she stands up and takes my hand, "I don't want to be alone either, Oliver. You were offering me what I thought I needed without risking my heart. You're amazing and I'm a great catch," she shrugs and I laugh, "but we deserve to be with someone who thinks we're everything, not just a settlement or an agreement." She takes my hand and pulls me up, "and I get the feeling we're both about to have the happy ending we've always wanted."

"Will's a lucky guy," I say, pulling her into a hug "I love you, Sue. I hope he treats you the way you deserve."

"I love you too, Ol," she kisses my cheek, "and don't risk yourself only when it seems to be a safe landing. The biggest joys of our hearts come when we let ourselves fall and crash. Your heart is worth it." She laughs and gives me a hip bump, "and please learn how to communicate, you can't expect anyone to read your damn mind."

I laugh as we walk back to the house, underneath the street-lights. The next morning, I drop her off at the airport and say goodbye with a hug and the promise of my friendship forever.

I'm still not sure about Sue's intuition about Carmen, but I've loved her for so long that I can't miss another chance if that's what this is.

14

carmen

I spent the rest of the week looking for excuses to cancel the photoshoot with the Rodriguez Family but decided not to. I made a promise and I intend to keep it, even if seeing Oliver and Susan together today will kill me.

I know, I'm such a terrible person.

I almost passed out when I bumped into them on Wednesday. Susan was stunning in the pictures I found online, but face to face? Damn. No wonder she's a supermodel. It was the weirdest encounter I've ever had though. I never expected her to be that sweet and *never in a million years* I thought Oliver had been talking about me with such high praise. She's wonderful. And I hate that I hate that I don't hate her… I know, it doesn't make any sense, like everything that's going on in my world so far.

So here I am, at the Minnehaha Falls Park in Minneapolis where we agreed to meet. One of my favorite places for family photoshoots. I pep talk myself a little as I walk out of the car.

You can do this. It won't be that bad.

I see everyone from afar and wave. Alberto and Marta are sitting on a bench and the guys are standing next to them.

Sweet Mother Mary! Are they hot or what?

They're all dressed in button down shirts with rolled sleeves, letting all of those tattoos pop out deliciously. Formal jeans and Vans shoes. Ethan is even wearing a dark blue cap backwards. The BMX rider look has never been classier and hotter than this. And Oliver wearing all black? *Lord have mercy on me.*

Even Juanito looks elegant with a little red bowtie.

"Zzup, pretty boy?" I smile at Jacob, waggling my eyebrows as I fake a flirtatious tone, "are you a parking ticket? 'cause you've got *'fine'* written all over."

Jacob snorts and everyone else laugh.

"That was *lame* as fuck," he says, giving me a hug, "you look good too."

"Pfff… yeah, right," I scoff, "seriously, y'all look smokin' hot today."

I hug everyone, scratch Juanito's head and when I get to Oliver, I force myself to just smile. I'm about to turn around when he catches me off guard, pulling me into a hug. I freeze for a second, but I lose myself at his touch and give into his embrace. I use until the last drop of my willpower to stop myself from noticing how his big arms feel around my body and how warm his hands feel against my skin.

He's engaged.

I pull away at the reminder.

His smile looks different today for some reason, as if he wasn't planning to let go but had to. I shake the feeling away and quickly notice Susan isn't around.

"Where's your girl?" I ask.

He clears his throat and swallows, "she uh… had to go back to L.A."

"Oh, okay," I blink fast, "that's a bummer. Is she coming back soon?"

"I don't think so," his voice sounding unsure.

Yep, I'm a terrible person for feeling so relieved.

I truly liked Susan and I'm glad she makes Oliver happy, but not having to take pictures of them together takes a huge load off my chest.

"Alright, let's get this party started," I motion with my head so they can follow me.

We walk to an open area with freshly cut grass and I line them up for a few practice shots.

Here's my secret for a great family photoshoot: *The best pictures are the ones they don't know you're taking.* The trick is to let them pose for a few shots to get them comfortable with the camera and then encourage them to be themselves for the rest.

"Alberto, hug your wife for me," I shout," Ethan, stand next to Alberto, Jake and Oliver next to Marta. Let Juanito stand in front of you."

They take their places and I'm amazed with how obedient Juanito is to Oliver's instructions, standing so still. He even looks like he's smiling.

"Smile."

Snap, snap, snap, snap.

Game on!

"What the heck is that smile, Jake?" I scream, "you look like you're about to brush your teeth, bro."

The entire family explodes in laughter and Juanito barks a couple of times.

Snap, snap, snap, snap.

I made a couple of jokes to keep the energy and snap a couple of more shots before moving near the falls. I take advantage of them looking around and interacting with each other to get more natural photos while they're not looking.

When *Oliver* is not looking.

Snap.

This one I'll probably keep to myself like a stolen jewel.

His torso is posturing to his left, where the water is falling. His right hand holding Juanito's leash, his left arm is down, showing his sexy tattoos highlighted by the reflection of the water. His hand is gripping his phone in a way that makes his veins pop out. He looks pensive, determined, handsome and beautiful.

Forbidden.

I sigh and wave the thought away. This is more difficult than I thought it was going to be, even without Susan. I blink fast and try to concentrate on my job. I called them over to line them up again with the falls in the background. I let them talk and tease each other while I snap a few shots. We do all types of poses. The guys with Alberto, then with Marta. A few beautiful couple shots and a huge round with the guys hugging, goofing around, wrestling and jumping. Juanito got a lot of pictures taken too, he's by far the most photogenic dog I've ever seen.

We wrap up with a final photo where they're all smiling dreamily at each other.

"Thanks, Chip," Ethan says, putting an arm around my neck, "we haven't had this fun in a long time."

"It was Alberto's idea," I say, leaning my head on his shoulder.

"Maybe, but you made it happened," he kisses my temple, "thank you."

"Well, I'm glad I did, then."

"I was thinking," he scratches the back of his neck, "ummm… have you talked to Rocío? I haven't talked to her since her birthday."

"She's doing great," I say, "she just went full on Freelance on Entertainment and is meeting so many celebrities now. She just moved to a new apartment and it's massive."

"Huh… cool… uhh… still no boyfriend?"

I laugh, "with how busy she is right now? I don't think she has time for that even if she wanted to."

"Yeah… right." He laughs and lets out a long breath. "Well, tell her I say hi."

"I will… I talked to Nahomi the other day too," I say, waggling my brows and giving him a hip bump.

Nahomi was my best friend growing up. Ethan had a major crush on her since she moved into our neighborhood. We always thought she liked Ethan too, but when he tried to make things official, she locked him into the friend zone and lost the key. We still like to tease him, although he dates on and off, but I think he's already made peace with it.

The friend zone sucks, doesn't it?

Ethan shakes his head, "yeah, me too. She's hitting it big time on Broadway."

"Have you thought about visiting her?" I ask, "I bet she'd like to have you there."

He lets out a frustrated sigh and shakes his head again. "Jesus Christ, you're gonna start with that too? She's my *friend*, Chip. Always has been, always will."

"You never know what could happen, though."

He's about to argue again but the chatter behind us interrupts us. The family gathers around me, and Marta gives me a hug.

"Ay, mija linda. Muchas gracias," she kisses my cheek, "I can't wait to see the pictures. Now, how much do we owe you?"

"What?" I pull away, "are you kidding me, Martita? I could *never* charge you."

"Chip," Jacob warns, "ni te atrevas." *Don't you dare.*

"Seriously," I look at everyone, "I didn't do this for the money. It was a pleasure. I wanted to spoil Alberto and that's what I did."

"*How much*, María del Carmen?" Oliver's deep voice booms, sending a shiver down my spine. "If not, I'm writing you a check. Want it or not."

I swallow hard as I stare at his brows forming a straight line. Alberto's voice kicks me out of the trance.

"Beautiful day, don't you think?" he says, "I'm starving, Santiago. Why don't we all go have some dinner, huh?"

"Yeah, let's go get food," Ethan says, "you can stand a meal with all of us, right?"

Everyone looks at me with expectation. There's nothing I'd like more than having dinner with my favorite family.

"Absolutely," I smile.

As long as they stop trying to pay me, we're good. The only payment I need is for them to keep loving me as they do now.

15

oliver

If keeping my hands to myself was a struggle before, the challenge is almost impossible now. I couldn't help myself when I hugged her hello. I just couldn't. I had to feel her body near me and immerse myself in her arms for just a second.

Then, she had to go above and beyond, making this photoshoot one of the most fun days of our lives. The only way it would've been more perfect is if she would've been part of the pictures. Next to me, *where she belongs.*

I haven't told anyone Susan and I broke up. I'm not ready to answer any questions or give explanations yet. As my mother always says, "si no estás seguro de algo, mejor no lo hagas," *if you're not sure about something, you better not do it.*

So, I won't for now.

I want to test the waters first and make sure they can handle the news first, especially if I'm trying to win Carmen.

If I have a chance at all.

We drive to a pet friendly Italian restaurant in Downtown Minneapolis. I drive with my parents while Ethan and Jacob follow in Carmen's car. I wish I wouldn't feel so left out, but that's part of what I'm trying to fix.

All in good time, Oliver.

We take our seats on the patio and the waiter brings us water, breadsticks and sauce and a plate of dog snacks for Juanito. They all start talking about plans, work and Hope Center and as always, the beautiful woman in front of me takes over the conversation. My eyes don't leave her for a second and I can't help but getting lost in the sweetness of her eyes, her joyful demeanor… those full, luscious lips, the tanned swell of her breasts on that tight shirt she's wearing, the perfume I can smell all the way from this side of the table. It makes me wonder the way she tastes, how she would—

"What are you, a creep?" Ethan whispers to my ear, interrupting my thoughts. "Dammit, Oliver. You're eating her with your eyes."

"Sorry," I silently chuckle, looking away.

"Seriously, knock it off."

I clear my throat as the waiter comes to take our order. Mamá looks at me with worry in her eyes and I give her a reassuring nod, telling her they can order whatever they want. One of the things I'm most grateful for when I think of the kind of money I have, is that I have enough to spoil my family as they deserve. After a lifetime of seeing them working their asses off, what kind of son would I be if I wouldn't want to spend money on my parents? Especially after the scares we've had with Papá, money is the least I can give them.

"Jacob said you finally painted your living room," Mamá asks Carmen once our food arrives.

"I did," she smiles with excitement, "I finally got some time and did it in one afternoon."

"When did you moved in again?" Jacob asks with his mouth full, "One? Two years ago?"

"Almost three, can you believe it?"

"For real?" Ethan says, taking a sip of water, "it doesn't feel like it was that long ago."

"I'm so proud of you, mija," Mamá smiles, "you've done so much work on that house."

"If you still need a hand with stuff, just say the word." Ethan adds.

"Thanks, bro," she says, "I've done most of the little fix ups already. There are just some details left but probably too expensive for my current budget."

"What are you missing?" I ask, taking everyone by surprise, since I haven't been saying much.

"Well," she smiles shyly, "I need to replace some of the siding on the back and the painting on my kitchen cabinets. They're a little old and most of it is peeling off."

"Those are easy fixes, my niña," Papá says, taking a bite of a bread stick, "let me check the schedule with my brother Vicente and we can plan the job."

She smiles and gets ready to reply but I interrupt, relaxing against the chair, "I can do your kitchen. No charge."

I wish I could take a picture of everyone's looks. Jacob raises an eyebrow, Ethan narrows his eyes, Mamá couldn't raise her eyebrows any higher and Papá smirks like the cat who ate the canary.

Carmen looks at me with worry, "I couldn't let you do that, Ol."

I shake my head, "we let you do an entire professional photoshoot for free," I shrug, "let me do your kitchen and we'll call it even."

"You're here to be with your family," she laughs nervously, "I couldn't let you waste all that time fixing something that's going to take God knows how long."

I let out a frustrated sigh, "is it important to you?"

"Well, yeah, but—"

"Then it's important to us," I lean on the table, "it isn't a big deal. It'll take a day to tape your kitchen and take off the doors, two days to sand, two days to paint the doors, one or two to paint the cabinets and one to reinstall… it's one week out of the two months I'm here for."

We wait for her answer for a couple of seconds. I don't dare to look at my brothers, who I know will give me a lecture later.

"You're serious?" she asks.

"Bet," I shrug, bringing my glass of coke to my mouth, "let me do that for you."

"Ese es mi hijo," *that's my boy*. Papá says with a grin. "You can take a truck and the tools you need from the shop whenever you want to start."

"Thanks, Papá." I smile.

"Thanks for doing that for me," she says quietly.

I'd do anything for you.

"Anytime," I reply.

Whatever makes you smile, I'll do for you. Whatever makes you happy, I'll give you.

16

oliver

I can still hear my brothers' voices in my head as I drive to Carmen's house in Papa's truck. As I predicted, they were not happy at all.

"Ay güey, you sure love to play with fire," Jacob said before leaving last night, "I honestly hope you know what you're doing."

Ethan was less graceful. He glared at me the entire time since we left the restaurant till he left with Jacob.

"You better be doing this for the sake of friendship, Oliver," he warned me, poking my chest, "if you hurt her in *any fucking way*… you're gonna have a problem with *me*."

And this is one of the many reasons why I love my brothers the way I do. They've always had my back and *hers*.

I park in Carmen's driveway with a ball of nerves in the pit of my stomach. I told her I could start the project tomorrow and I was dropping off the tools I use today, but that was just an excuse to see her and start testing the waters to see if I have a chance with her or not.

"Hey, you," she says, coming out of the garage while I'm opening the trunk.

"Hey," I say, pulling her into a hug. This time, I force myself to let her go at a socially acceptable timing. Instinctively, I notice a few things in the five seconds I hold her:

1. She smells *fucking amazing*. A mix of clean clothes, warm skin and coconut shampoo.
2. She's wearing the shortest and tightest shorts I've ever seen, giving me a fine look of her beautiful, tanned legs and her gorgeous, spankable ass.
3. She's not wearing a fucking bra.

You're trying to kill me, María del Carmen.
"Need a hand?" she asks with a smile as I let her go.
Baby, you have no idea.

I shove that and every other dirty reply to that loaded question out of my head and nod, adjusting my pants as discreetly as possible as she distracts herself helping me.

I knew beforehand this wasn't going to be enough time with her, so I quickly figure out the perfect excuse to stay a little bit more.

"So," I say, leaning against the truck, "I was thinking, if you're not busy right now... we could go to Home Depot together and pick up paint and other supplies I'm still missing?"

"Oh," she tilts her head, "I thought you were going to decide on all that, I know nothing about painting."

"Well, it's *your* kitchen," I put my hands inside my pockets, "you need to decide what you want. I can give you advice, but *you* have the last word."

She considers for a moment, "Okay, give me a minute and we can go."

I stay in the same spots as she goes back inside, trying not to stare at the sway of her hips as she walks away.
Too late.
God, I'm fucked.

I feel my heart rate going up as I wait for her. I have no idea why my stomach keeps turning so much, I haven't felt this nervous since I was a teenager. She comes back in less than ten minutes, and I open the passenger door for her.

"Oh, we're going in your truck?" she asks with a quizzical look.

"What?" I chuckle, "not fancy enough?"

"No," she inhales, looking around, "just… trust issues, okay?"

"Get in the car, Chip," I roll my eyes, "what? You think I'll kidnap you?"

"I just don't trust other people driving, that's all," she says, letting out a frustrated sigh. She tilts her head and lifts up an eyebrow, "but just in case, just know I have six months of self-defense training and I can get *very* dangerous."

I want to laugh at her comment as she gets in, because I know she meant it as a joke, but I can't help but get half-furious and half-heartbroken. One, I knew she had issues with other people driving since the accident and completely forgot. And two, she should be free to walk on the streets at any time without fear of being attacked.

Women should be free, period.

I start the engine, deep in these thoughts and start driving in silence. I'd put some music on but it's an old truck and only has stereo FM and a cassette player.

"Hey, where's Juanito?" Carmen says, jerking her head towards me.

"Keeping Papá company," I say with my eyes on the road, "sometimes it feels like he they love each other more than they love me."

"I wouldn't blame them," she laughs, "you're not as cute or fun."

"You wound me, woman," I put a hand on my chest, and she laughs. The sound is like music to my ears.

"But seriously," she says, resting her head against the window, "how did you get Juanito? He looks purebred."

"He is," I give her a quick glance, "I ran one of those DNA tests for dogs on him."

"Deveras?" *For real?* "You're *that* rich?" She lets out a surprised scoff, "and there I was feeling bad you're doing the kitchen for free."

"Shut up," I chuckle, "wanna hear the story or not?"

"Yes, please."

I love to tell the story to anyone who asks. It was love at first sight, the moment that little devil and I found each other, I knew it was going to be *us* for a long time.

"I was on a hiking trip in Colorado with some friends about four years ago. We were walking through Rocky Mountain Park, and we started hearing these tiny hauls and growls coming from the woods," I smile at the memory, "I thought it was a baby wolf, but when I followed the sounds, I found him shaking and crying behind a rock. He must've been two or three months old. I still have pictures, remind me to show them to you when we get back."

"Oh my god," she gasps, "who would abandon a little puppy in the woods?"

"I thought the same thing. He wasn't even chipped," I rest one shoulder on the door, "I took him home with me and thought about giving him up with adoption but," I laugh, "he's always had this damn look and couldn't let him go. He's been my *compadre* ever since."

I stop at a red light and look at her for a second. She's looking at me with what I can describe as *admiration*. As if I was a hero. It takes everything within me to stop myself from leaning down and kiss her.

"That's so sweet,," she says after a sigh, "why did you name him Juan?"

"He looks like a *Juan* to me, don't you think?" I say as we enter the Home Depot parking lot, "besides, once I started calling him Juan, he responded almost immediately."

"It was destiny, then," she says, gathering her things.

"Yeah, I guess," I give her a weak smile, "the best type of love always is."

I wink and she swallows hard, but before either of us can say anything, I get out of the car. We get a cart and start walking around the aisles. We get some tape, wood filler and some foam rollers I knew I was missing. We keep talking about a little bit of everything. I tell her about my little shop, the things I do for fun, the welding team at the factory and the new bike we have in the making.

Her eyes, her laugh, her smiles, the way she listens to everything I say as if it was the most important thing in the world. Everything about her is giving my heart hope about what just a few weeks ago seemed more like a delusion.

"Primer?" she asks as I take two cans from a shelf.

"It's just to stabilize the surface after being sanded," I explain with a shrug.

It'll also give me two or three more days on this project to be close to you.

I take two steps forward and smirk at her, "do you trust the expert or not, *María del Carmen*?"

"Of course I do, *Oliver Santiago*," she bites her lip and walks past me.

We keep going through the aisles, discussing colors and types of painting. After a long time deciding, she finally chooses a Bone White that'll go with the Charcoal Gray of her appliances.

I let my mind wander for a little bit and imagine doing all this for our own house.

I'd fix the whole house just for her.

Scratch that. I'd build the whole damn thing from the ground with my bare hands just for her.

I. Am. So. Fucked.

A hint of dread freezes my belly for a second as I consider my worst-case scenarios. What if she rejects me? Am I really ten years too late? Is it really just a coincidence that all these mistakes and stupid distance are leading me back to her?

I try my best to shove those thoughts out of my head as we check out. I let her pay after an entire rant she throws at me in fucking Spanish when I took out my credit card. The woman is breathtaking, even when she's pissed.

We put the stuff in the trunk and head back. This time, she puts her playlists on the phone. We're rocking *"Uncanny"* by Anberlin when she turns her head in my direction.

"So," she says, "is your lovely lady joining us at the X Games?"

I knew I had to talk about this sooner rather than later, but I didn't think she was going to bring it up so fast. I need to be careful on how to respond to that question. I don't want her to think I'm like the lying, cheating assholes she's dated.

"I uh… need to tell you something," I say after a couple of breaths, "but you need to swear not to say anything to anyone, got it?"

"Sure," she turns her entire body now.

"And I mean *anyone*, Chip." I take a glimpse of her, and she eyes me with curiosity, "no one has to know, at least for now."

"Is everything alright?"

I take a deep breath, "Susan and I broke up."

"You… you what?"

"We broke up the night before she went back to L.A. We talked about it, and we decided it was for the best."

"What the hell?" She grabs my hand and squeezes, "are you okay, Ol? How are you feeling? Do you need anything?"

God, I love this woman.

"I'm fine," I smile, squeezing back, "it wasn't surprising to be honest. An interesting conversation, actually. But it's okay."

"No," she exclaims, "it's not okay to break someone's heart just before you're supposed to marry them. God, Oliver. I'm so sorry."

"She didn't break my heart, Chip. Stop worrying about me," I say, my eyes on the road, "I never gave her my heart in the first place."

"What do you mean?"

"We've always loved each other, but we were never *in* love." I sigh, "we're great friends who decided to get married for the wrong reasons. I didn't love her the way she deserves to be loved."

"Oh," she says, letting go of my hand a little, "did you… did you cheat on her?"

"God, no! I didn't cheat," I laugh and whisper the next words, "but… there's someone else. There's *always* been someone else."

My heart is hammering against my chest as I confess this. Her silence is terrifying. She doesn't say a word and lets go of my hand completely. I want to say something to break the awkwardness around us, but her phone stops the music and starts ringing. She looks hesitant but still answers. The volume is all the way up and I can hear *every. Single. Fucking. Word.*

"What's up, Papa Bear?" she says.

"Hey, how's my favorite girl?" the male voice on the other side says.

"I don't know about her, but I'm fine," she giggles, making me roll my eyes.

"Ha-ha," *Mr. Fuck-my-life* replies, "what are you doing tomorrow night?"

"I don't know, you tell me."

A punch of poisonous jealousy hits my gut as I keep listening. *He's asking her out on a fucking date…* and she's accepting without even knowing what's it about. She does have other options.

Why wouldn't she?

Five minutes with her and any bastard with half a brain will fall in love with her.

I grip the steering wheel as hard as I can, trying to canalize my anger and not snap like a jealous asshole like last time. I quickly glance at her, and she has a big grin on her face.

"Cool," he says, "I was supposed to go with Jason to this wine tasting at a vineyard we're about to sign with," he sighs, "but he's been so scared about leaving his wife by herself now that she's pregnant and on bed rest. I don't want to go alone… so don't make me go alone."

El güerito. Fred. It's got to be him.

I thought she said they were just friends and that sounds an awful lot like he's asking her out.

I don't like it.

At. All.

She lets out a soft chuckle, "am I sensing a crazy admirer I need to get rid of?"

"Could you please?"

She laughs, "who is it?"

"Umm… the director?"

"Damn, okay. I see you, Papa Bear," she teases, "what time?"

They both laugh and my stomach clenches. I pray. Beg. Plead that this doesn't screw it all up before I even have a chance.

"Pick you up at three?"

"Bet."

That's it. I'm making a move.

We approach our exit, and I can't wait for her to hang up.

I need to do something *today*.

17

carmen

"Papa Bear?" Oliver asks the second I hang up.

I have to give this man credit. He really tried to keep it cool while I was talking to Fred. Still, I don't know what the problem is. Is he really jealous? Or is it just brotherly protection? He just broke his *engagement*. He thinks he can fool me with that *"we agreed to break it up"* story but I know something else happened and he doesn't want to tell me.

As much as I want to know, I don't have a claim on him, and he doesn't have any claim on me.

We did a great job getting rid of that initial awkwardness but now it's all here again. Still, deep inside? I wish it was real jealousy. Because of me. Because he doesn't want to see me with anyone else that isn't him, especially now that he's single again. It's making my heart feel things I shouldn't. Wish for things I know I'm never going to have.

I don't want to act like the same girl who used to write *Mrs. Carmen Rodriguez* all over her History notebook. It's not going to end well.

"That's how we all nicknamed Fred back in the agency," I say, playing with a strand of my hair, "he was my supervisor and was super protective of us. Like a papa bear."

"That sounds too close for a business relationship," he replies, his face rock hard.

I raise an eyebrow at him. Is he really jealous?

He glances quickly when he notices my silence and softens his expression. I can see a tiny blush on his cheeks.

"I mean, that's how it sounds," he clears his throat and scratches his forehead.

I don't understand my urge to shake every doubt out of his mind, so I say, "well, we became very close with time. Especially since he started volunteering at Hope. I've told you this before."

"And?" he swallows hard and waits a couple of seconds, "you've never wanted to… date him?"

"Fred?" I laugh, putting my phone back in my purse as we approach our neighborhood, "not really. He's not my type and I could never see him that way. Even if I did, he's the type of guy who only wants to be my friend," *like most guys*, "he's so… I don't know."

"So what?"

Out of my league.

"What?" Oliver says, a little too loud, "are you kidding me, *Carmen?*"

Shit.

I don't say anything as he parks in my driveway. I want to get out and run, but he stops and doesn't move. I look at my lap and play with my fingers, feeling his eyes on me. I feel like I'm being scolded after playing a prank at school.

I look up and he runs his tongue inside his lower lip, his eye slightly twitching.

Damn, I think he's really mad.

"I uh… I wasn't supposed to say that out loud," I give him a weak smile.

"But you did," he takes off his cap and runs his hand through his hair, "Chip, why in the ever-loving fuck would you think you're out of that guy's league?" he puts the cap back on and turns all the way to face me, "if he suggested something like that, it's gonna get ugly for him."

"What? *No*," I take his hand, "he's never suggested anything about me other than I'm a good friend, because that's all we are. *Good. Friends*."

Not that's any of Oliver's business, but I would hate it if he'd think Fred's been an asshole to me.

"Then why did that even cross your mind?" he squeezes my hand, "I would say *you* are way out of *his* damn league."

Now it's *my* turn to roll my eyes. I hate it when people give me the *"honey, you're the prettiest"* lecture. I'm a confident bitch who knows who she is and gets what she wants but I'm also realistic. I'm well aware of who I am and who I'm not. Even if I was interested in Fred, he's not the type of guy who would date a plain-ass photographer who trips over her own feet and laughs at her own jokes.

"Oh, come on, Rodriguez. Cut the bullshit," I scoff, shoving his hand away, "you know exactly the type of girl I am and the type of woman I'm not."

"What the hell is that supposed to mean?"

"Nevermind," I open the door and walk away towards my house.

He follows me to the kitchen. I want to lock myself in my room, but his big, calloused hand grips my arm to stop me.

"Talk," he orders, pulling me closer.

My heart twists with humiliation and a sudden sadness and rejection I haven't felt in a long time. I try hard to ignore it but the frustration and disappointment of a lifetime of poor choices in the love department brings up the list of flaws I've been trying to get over. I can't help but open my mouth and let it all out.

"I'm not either a supermodel or a successful everything kind of woman that guys like Fred usually take on dates. I'm *average*, Oliver. And that's okay. I know I'm not ugly but I'm not extravagantly beautiful or refined. I've never been the kind of woman who stands out from the crowd or that has an entire line of guys that are waiting to date her," I sniff, "I'm almost twenty-eight years old and I'm still figuring out what makes me feminine. I've always been a tomboy who's never really cared for what other women do. I'm still super childish and immature sometimes. I'm disorganized and clumsy as hell… I know I have a lot of love to offer even though I know I feel too much and say it without filter but… for some reason I still can't figure out, it has only attracted guys who end up seeing me as just a friend after a couple of months or plain assholes. So, yeah… I don't know what type of guy would really be interested in me but I'm very sure of what type of guy isn't."

My breaths come in pants and Oliver cups my face with both hands, wiping my tears with his thumbs. His touch is gentle, sweet. He locks eyes with me with unbelief and concern. He lifts his eyebrows and licks his bottom lip.

"Do you really believe that bullshit?"

"It's not like I'm the only one who sees it."

"Just because your mother doesn't appreciate you and you've never dated a real man who knows how to love his woman doesn't mean you're not wonderful." He says softly, caressing my cheeks, "the guys told me about Alan."

I look away. I always knew Oliver end up learning about it sometime. I just never thought I was going to ever talk about it with him.

"I still can't believe someone would do that to you," he lifts up my chin, "I wish I could've been there to protect you, Chip. I'm so sorry."

"No one could've protected me but myself, Oliver." I whisper, "and well, I finally opened my eyes and that's what's important. It took a couple of broken bones and a broken heart. A lot of women never get to tell the story. I was *lucky*."

"I don't understand," he gives me a weak smile.

"I thought I was in love, Oliver," I hold a sob, "that shit messes up with your head."

"I'm not talking about you, I'm talking about that piece of shit," he shakes his head, "I don't understand what makes a guy put his dirty hands on a woman to hurt her. Especially if he has the god given privilege of being with a woman so beautiful, wonderful, selfless… so sweet, caring and loving as you," he caresses my cheek again, "bullshit. Everything you said about yourself is a huge pile of bullshit. You're the most amazing woman I've ever met and I'm ashamed of myself for not being here to tell you every day since I met you."

He leans down just about an inch. My heart racing and my body about to give out. His warm hand on mine consumes the last drop of logic in my brain.

"Oliver, what are you doing?"

"You deserved to be cherished, adored, treasured," he says, pulling me closer, "you deserve someone who would whisper to your ear how perfect you are, how much he needs you. How much he misses you when you're not around, how beautiful everything is when you're there. How much you lit up his entire body with just one look."

Madre mía, is this a fucking dream?

"Ol," I whisper, my eyes closed.

My body shivers as his hand travels from my cheek to my neck, still trying to wake up from this dream and commanding my mind to stop playing games. Our mouths are millimeters apart, my eyes wanting to open but I refuse, too fearful Oliver might disappear.

"The only cries he should hear from you," he continues, "is you crying out his damn name while he's worshiping your body."

He presses his forehead against mine, "I just wish I could—"

That's it, my brain just short circuited!

I don't even let him finish the sentence when I put my hand on the back of his neck and pull, bringing his lips to mine. He gasps for a millisecond of unbelief before giving into the kiss, gently pressing me against the island.

My heart is at the edge of every emotion I could feel. He kisses me back like a starving man who only has five minutes to live, and this is the last thing he'll do. With desperation. With his right hand on my cheek and his left hand resting on my hip. He kisses my mouth, my cheeks, my noses, my chin and softly goes back to my mouth, opening up to entangle his tongue with mine.

Gentle but determined.

Sweet but frenzied.

As if I'm all he's ever wanted.

As if he wants this moment to last forever just as I do.

My brain wakes up suddenly, stabbing my heart with reality: *He's just broken up with his fiancée.*

Angel's words come to my memory. The night when I stupidly confessed my crush to him, the night Oliver kissed me.

"You're gonna get your heart broken, Chip." He'd said, *"we're leaving soon and when we get sponsored, He'll be too busy for a high school type of relationship. He knows you've always had a crush and he just wants to have fun. I don't want you to get hurt when he finds a mature woman in L.A. and breaks things off with you."*

And now, I'm just a rebound. A consolation prize after his broken relationship.

He's leaving again.

Last time he broke my heart, next time he'll destroy it.

What the hell did I just do?

"No," I pull away.

"No what?" he says with a sigh, opening his eyes slowly as if he's coming back from a trance. A beautiful lazy smile playing on his swollen lips.

"I'm sorry for kissing you," I pull away, "but I can't do this."

"What?" he snaps his eyes open, "why not? And don't you dare apologize."

"I won't let you do that to me again."

He blinks fast, "Chip, I swear this time is different, this time I—"

"I'm going out," I ignore him, biting my lip, "help yourself with everything in the fridge. There's beer, Coke, Jarritos or the snacks in the pantry. Bathroom is the second door to the left in the hallway," I signal with my hand, "you can leave your stuff in the garage and park in the driveway when you come. Feel free to come with Juanito whenever you like. I love it when he's around and I'm not picky with animals around my house."

"Chip," he tries to grab my arm, but I shove it.

"There's a spare key in the upper left drawer of my desk, you can use it to come in. No need to let me know." I finally look at him, his eyes widened and unsure, "I trust you."

With that, I turn around and walk out towards my car.

"Chip, wait."

"Please," I cry, "if I ever meant anything to you. Don't say things like that again… and please don't try to kiss me again."

I literally jump inside my car and pull away as fast as I can. I still don't know where I'm going so I just drive, crying my lungs out and wishing his words were true.

Because they're everything I've always wanted to hear from him.

Because I've always loved him and I'm not sure if I'll ever stop.

But you need to love yourself more. Choose yourself first, Carmen. This man is going to break your heart and leave without looking back. When he does, you'll only have yourself to hold onto.

18

oliver

Holy fucking shit, she kissed me.

She caught me off guard and for a moment, I thought I was dreaming again. Once I realized what was happening, what a kiss it was. She pulled me towards her and kissed me like no woman has ever done before. Even if she pulled away, leaving me hotter and more confused than ever… that was a kiss for the books.

"If I ever meant anything to you. Don't say things like that again… and please don't try to kiss me again."

Everything, Chip. You've always meant everything *to me.*

You can't fake kisses like that, you can't fake that type of reaction. Carmen is an open book when it comes to her feelings and I'm sure I wasn't reading them wrong.

She felt so right. *We* feel right.

She feels like everything I never had with any other woman I've been with. Not that I've been with many, but enough to know no one is going to feel like her. Her rejection stings, but my hopes are all the way up now. This was the sign I needed.

She wants me. I have fucking chance.

Leaving the stuff we bought in the garage, I get the keys from her desk and drive to my parents' house in a fog of thoughts. Replaying the best and most life changing kiss of my life over and over.

"Don't try to kiss me again."

Maybe not now, María del Carmen. But you make me a patient man.

19

oliver

I know I'm in deep shit when not even BMX is enough to put my mind at ease.

I took Antonio and my brothers and joined some riders at a skatepark where Mickey, Carlos and Sean are filming some promo videos for Elite's new bike and other sponsors. I wanted to watch the session and use it as a distraction from the one thing that stole my sleep last night: Carmen and her friend tasting some wine.

So, it's the four of us on the floor against the park's fence and Juanito.

I slept a total of two hours last night replaying that kiss like a lovesick teenager, and couldn't stop making up scenarios in my head where Fred was the one kissing Carmen instead of me.

I'm helpless.

Bikes have always given me some solace in my worst days in one way or another, but today it isn't any consolation. Whatever riding has meant to me, doesn't even come close to Carmen's place in my life. BMX is a piece of my heart, but Carmen has my entire heart in her hands.

Hello, Misery, my old friend.

Sean jumps on a quarter pipe, landing on a perfect Tailwhip Barspin and the entire park erupts in cheers. I clap, trying my best to look enthusiastic because that kid makes that trick look like he's jumping on a rope, but my mind is a thousand miles away.

Well, more like seventy. *Yes, I googled the damn vineyard.*

It's 6:30 in the evening, which means Carmen is still with *Mr. Güero Perfect Smile.* Probably giving him all of her sweet smiles, laughing at his damn jokes, touching his arm, leaning in to whisper some made up crap to his fucking ear, all while trying to shove away that admirer from him.

"Dammit." I mutter under my breath, making the guys turn.

"Pst, *cálmate*, bro." Ethan cocks an eyebrow, "give Mickey some grace, 'mano. I know he's a Pro now but that doesn't mean he'll get it all perfect all the time."

"What?" I ask. I didn't even notice when Mickey entered the bowl. "Oh…no…I uhh…I wasn't thinking about him."

"Is it Susan?" Antonio asks, smiling *as-matter-of-factly*. "Let me guess, you didn't get laid, did you?"

Jacob and Ethan chuckle and I just glare.

"You know you can tell us if something's really bothering you, right?" Jacob says, allowing Juanito to lie down on his crossed legs, "it's not like we don't talk other than bullshit."

"Look, we all get it, alright?" Antonio continues, looking at the park for a second, "Sue went back hella' fast and not getting laid in a long time can put you in a mood," he winks at me, "we've all been there, Ollie."

They laugh and I get out a soft chuckle, shaking my head and giving him a finger. I want to kick him in the balls because… hell yeah, *I'm fucking horny.* That kiss only made me jerk off like a thirteen-year-old… twice last night and once today. But I'm not going to say that to the guys.

"Why don't we talk about that girl who's driving you nuts, eh Tony?" I say, motioning with my hand.

"For fuck's sake," he sighs, "I'm on my day off, relaxing with a good BMX session like the old days. Why on earth would I want to talk about the Spawn of Satan?"

We all explode in laughter. I've been so curious about this girl. Antonio used to be very laid back, playful and one of the most peaceful guys I've ever known. Ever since Angel died, all of that changed. He's uptight, super strict and meticulous about everything. Even though he doesn't always show it, he gets annoyed by the smallest things. We've always teased him about being a grump, but I don't think I've ever really seen him truly enraged. And I've known this guy my entire life. According to my brothers, this girl makes him fume and doesn't give two shits about his reactions. I need to know more about her.

"Just tell me what it is about her that pisses you off so much?" I stretch my back and face him.

"She smiles too much," Ethan jokes, making Antonio roll his eyes. He's about to say something but Jacob cuts him off.

"And she makes everyone laugh," he smirks, "you know how Tony is allergic to laughter. She's loud and funny, the complete opposite of his boring ass."

"Would you two shut up? This has nothing to do with Ramona being loud." Antonio says to them.

He turns to me, "You want to know what pisses me off about her, huh?" He scoffs and runs his tongue inside his cheek. "Slow Wi-Fi pisses me off, Oliver. *That woman?* She's a pain in *my fucking ass.*"

He counts with his fingers as he continues, "She has a smartass mouth and never shuts up, she tells the lamest jokes at the most inappropriate times. She's disorganized as hell and uses the garage as a pigsty. She's smug, conceited and thinks that she and her pink car covered in glitter are God's gift to the good old Midwest just because she was a big deal in California."

"Tony, Mona knows her shit," Jacob laughs, "you don't give her enough credit and you know it."

"It's never been about that, Jake," he scratches his beard, "she knows what she's talking about and knows her job but that's not enough when you put it into practice. She needs order, a plan. She just gets *excited*," he fakes a high-pitched voice, "and does the first thing she comes up with without thinking and planning first."

"There's a thing called teamwork?" I chuckle, "if she knows so much, I don't know… you could join forces, don't you think?"

"That's exactly the problem, Ollie boy," he scoffs sarcastically, "she does what she fucking wants. I already told her we should consult with each other before making decisions. The type of repairs we do and the type of cars we get are not the same as the rest of the shop. We're talking about car collectors, track races and rich car enthusiasts. But she gets defensive, jumpy and takes absolutely everything as a challenge. She loves seeing me annoyed." He cracks his neck, "but that's enough. We can stop talking about her now. Jake, at what time do you need to be at Hope?"

"We should go soon," Jacob says, still laughing and glancing at his watch, "why don't we call Chip? We could get Pho and watch something? Now that she and Ol are back to being friends, we could all hang out."

I sigh and look at the track again. "She's out at a wine tasting with *Mr. Perfect Smile.*"

I throw my head back to the fence and breathe in deeply.

"Oh, so that's why you've been such a cranky ogre today?" Ethan laughs, "Chip's on a date? She hasn't mentioned any guy lately. Who's she with?"

"*Fred,*" I say, faking a high-pitched voice.

"The audacity of that bastard," Antonio gasps, mocking offenses, "what a travesty that is."

"He should be ashamed," Jacob adds.

"We need to *save her,*" Antonio continues.

Ethan and Jacob laugh again, and I just roll my eyes. I know they love to tease me about this topic, and I usually let them, but the comment unsettles my stomach.

"Well, she was quite excited about it." I stand up and take Juanito's leash. "I don't think she really wants saving."

Juanito and I walk towards the parking lot but before we get to the car, I feel Ethan's arm slide around my shoulder while Jacob and Antonio follow behind us.

"Don't do this to yourself, Ol." Ethan says, making me stop. "You promised you were just going to be friends with her. Don't screw it up by torturing yourself when things like this happen or you're gonna be miserable."

No one says anything for a moment. I know I told them I would, but I was lying to myself then because it's impossible for me to feel any other way. Especially after what just happened between us. I consider coming clean about everything, but it would only end up in chaos.

I sigh and wipe my face with a hand.

"Look, we just want you to be happy." Antonio says, giving me an apologetic smile. "And if you think this is too much, maybe you should probably back off a little. There's a reason why you stayed away for years, no?"

"It's not that easy." I shake my head. "Especially *now*. No, I couldn't."

"It should be," Ethan shrugs, "considering you're getting married soon. You're here licking your wounds over something that is clearly not a date, but you haven't even stopped to think about how she could be feeling since you got engaged."

Antonio punches him on the shoulder and I blink fast, looking at them quizzically.

What the hell was that?

"Should we go now?" Jacob says after clearing his throat and taking Juanito with him. They try to switch topics as they start walking away but now I'm confused. *"What she's been feeling like"*. What does that even mean? She's had a whole life without me for ten years, she's dated, she's moved on. Yes, I'm sure she wants me now but not like I've wanted her, that's for sure.

Ethan and Jacob walk ahead with Juanito and Antonio stops me.

"Look, if you still love her that much, why don't you come clean with Susan?" Antonio mutters. "I'm not saying you should jump to look for a possibility with Chip like the desperate, impatient psycho you usually are, but at the very least, you should be fair to Sue."

I take a deep breath and hold back a chuckle. Not being reckless has always been Antonio's number one rule. I guess it's time for me to let this one thing out of my chest.

"Would you think less of me if I told you I already did?"

"What?"

"Bro, Sue and I have never loved each other or have anything more than a good friendship." I say quietly.

"We were never in love, everything was just…an arrangement. We'd get married, scare off potential heartbreaks and we wouldn't be alone for the rest of our lives."

I sigh before continuing. "But then she came here, had a ten-minute conversation with Chip which gave her some crazy ideas of me pursuing her and then dropped the bomb that she's met someone.he said it would be better if we broke it off."

"Holy shit." he pinches the bridge of his nose. "You're fucking crazy, you know? Who the hell does something like that?"

"You coming or what?" Ethan shouts from the car.

"You can't say anything yet, Tony," I warn as we rush towards them, "I don't want anyone to know yet."

"Oliver, you take masochism to a whole new level," he says before reaching the door.

We drop off Juanito with my parents and head to Hope. We start walking towards the door and just as if I had seen a fountain in the desert, I spot a dark red Forester across the street.

Carmen.

Not listening to my brain, I make my way over there.

Am I torturing myself? Maybe. But anything worth keeping takes a little bit of hurt and patience.

This woman? She's worth every single painful second of this wait.

20

Carmen

Oliver: I'll give you space because I know you need it, so this is the only text you'll get from me about this: We ARE talking about this sooner or later. That was one mind blowing kiss, Maria del Carmen. I can still feel it everywhere.

One text to send me over the edge. Just one.

He sent it last night after I got home from driving around Downtown Minneapolis for hours.

I hate myself for kissing him.

At the same time, I'm craving to kiss him again and again... and again.

Rebound. You. Are. A. Fucking. Rebound.

What was I even thinking?

Oh yeah, *I wasn't.* I knew it was a bad idea in the back of my mind but I still did it, knowing perfectly it would only mess everything up and fill my head with illusions of something that's never going to happen.

I've always been what I like to call: The crossover girl.

The good time before real love.

And the only real, long-term relationship I've ever had sent me to the hospital with a dislocated shoulder and a broken arm.

The difference is abysmal though, Oliver is the one guy I've loved the most in my entire life. I've never loved anyone as much for that long even though I've always known he's never felt anything else but temporary attraction for me. I'm being blessed with a second chance to have him in my life and hooking up with him so he can have a rebound would result in my heart being completely destroyed. Nothing against hookups, I just realized I'm not able to have casual sex. Especially with a friend, it would mess me up.

I've been back in my house for a couple of hours after a fun and interesting afternoon with Fred. That vineyard director quickly figured out we weren't together and was all over him the entire time. I could only do so much.

Back to my braless, loose t-shirt mood in the company of a nice cup of tea. I turned my computer on and have been editing the pictures I took of the Rodriguez family.

For a second I imagine my mom and Rocío in a photoshoot like this and the sadness takes over again. The last picture we have together is from ten years ago, for Angel and Rocio's high school graduation. Just a few weeks before Angel passed away. I stole it from my mom's drawer before moving away and I have it on my desk. One of the only happy memories I have of us as a family. The reason why it took me so long to be at peace with my brother's passing. The day he died, what was left of my family died with *him*.

I lose myself into the edits for a while, feeling a sense of calmness. After an hour of working on them, my eyes land on the picture I took of Oliver by the falls. I bite my upper lip and groan, smashing my face on the keyboard.

"You deserve someone who would whisper to your ear how perfect you are, how much he needs you. How much he misses you when you're not around, how beautiful everything is when you're there."

"Sweet talking *asshole*," I mutter to myself as I sit up and switch to another picture. I want to get rid of it, but it might be one of the best pictures I've ever taken. Not only because he looks like a model, but because *I'm a goddamned amazing photographer.* There's a glow in his eyes that allows me to really see him, the guy I've always known.

The one I fell in love with.

Rebound.

I take a few deep breaths before continuing when my phone pings with a text.

Mama: The car is not starting.

Primero que nada, buenas tardes (first of all, good afternoon). What happened to the woman who would pinch my arm if I didn't say hello first?

I roll my eyes and face upward before typing.

Carmen: OK, let me finish these edits and see what I can do.

Mama: I need to be at Hope in fifteen minutes.

Carmen: I'm a little busy right now.

Mama: It's your fault this car is always breaking down and you always have something more important to do.

I borrowed her car for an emergency about *a year ago.* Four months later, her engine overheated for the first time because she wasn't checking on the coolant, but she decided it was *my fault.* We've changed the head gasket several times and Antonio told us plain and simple it would be cheaper to get her a newer model instead. This is the fifth time it happens and as always, she's taking it all on me.

I sigh and wipe my face with both hands.

Carmen: Be there in 5.

The sooner I get this over with, the better.

When I arrive, I get out to help her with some of her bags, but she shoves me away and gets in the car without even looking at me. I lean down to kiss her hello, but she shakes her head away too, so I swallow my hurt and get the car going.

We drive in painful silence and the moment I stop in front of Hope, she hops out of the car without looking back or saying goodbye. I rest my head on the steering wheel and try to hold my tears for a couple of seconds.

I don't usually get this emotional about my mom anymore, but with everything happening now I wish I had her love to rely on. Marta is always there for me whenever I need that type of love. But I could never sit down and tell her everything that's happened between her son and me.

I take a few breaths with my eyes closed.

You're a badass bitch who kicks ass, Carmen. You've seen worse than this, you can do anything.

I scratch my eyes, blink fast and take my phone out. First, I'll take care of the problem.

Carmen: Hey babe, can you talk?

I wait a couple of minutes with my head resting against the window.

Rocío: *sad emoji* I'm interviewing Marie-Sabrina Andere in ten minutes.

Rocío: Unless you're dying.

Rocío: Please tell me you're not dying. *Upside down smiling emoji*

I smile.

Carmen: I'm not lol. But something came up with Mamá. She needs a new car. It broke down again today and Tony says it's better if we buy a new one. I was thinking about splitting with her so she doesn't have to pay for it all herself?

The text bubble appears and disappears a couple of times.

Rocío: Text me the amount and I'll Venmo you.

Carmen: Cool. Do you want me to send you pictures of the cars so we can decide together maybe?

She makes me wait five minutes for a reply this time and I know she's going to deflect.

Rocío: You are not going to believe this. I'm interviewing Christian Nodal next month before his concert here in Chicago!! He's giving me free tickets too, you want to come? Maybe the guys want to come to. It would be epic if we could all go.

Well, at least I tried.

Carmen: Sure. Let's talk about it and maybe we can plan it.

Rocío: Awesome. Talk to you later, love you.

I don't blame her for setting boundaries. God knows I need them too. But somehow I still wish we could be the tight-knitted family I always wanted. Seeing my efforts not getting any results I want still hurts a bit.

Our entire lives, Rocío was always inside her own world. She's always been a *romantic bookworm* like she calls herself. She was always supportive of us. Whenever she visited the skatepark it was always with a book in her hand, away from everyone else. Angel and I would always sit down and listen to everything she had to say about her books and TV shows. But when Angel died and she left for college, she changed so much it was so hard for me to recognize her anymore. She closed off completely and kicked Araceli completely out of her life. Not that they had a good relationship. It was always strained, but I could still see some love from Rocío towards Araceli. So, the way Rocío simply banned her makes me think that something else might've happened between them that I don't know.

I'm about to start my car when I see a shadow in the corner of my eye, quickly opening the passenger door making me scream and jump. I knock my head on the roof as the door slams closed.

"Oh, shit!" I close my eyes shut, holding my head. I open my eyes abruptly to see Oliver sitting next to me with a grin on his face. The asshole is laughing.

"Jesus Oliver," I punch his shoulder, "you scared the shit out of me."

"Shit, I'm sorry, Chip," he says, changing his expression, "we need to talk."

I glare at him and for a moment I look at his soft expression and pleading eyes.

Rebound.

"No, we don't." I say, turning the engine on.

He grabs my chin and makes me look at him. "Yes, we do."

"Oliver, please," I whisper, ignoring the cedary scent all over the car and the electricity of his touch, "if you want to apologize about yesterday you can do that tomorrow because I'm still pissed at you."

The idiot has the balls to smile and get closer.

"I don't think you really are," he shamelessly looks at my mouth.

God, why are you testing me like this? It takes herculean effort, but I pull away.

"What?" I scoff, "I am. Very pissed, Santiago."

"You know, I really don't think so," he smirks, "considering the fact that it was *you* who kissed *me*."

"I… well…" I stutter, "I'm sorry about that, I shouldn't have done it. I got carried away and I didn't know what I was doing."

"Bullshit," he says quietly, letting out a long sigh. "Anyways, apology not accepted. I actually —"

"What?" I interrupt. I close my eyes and press the bridge of my nose. My emotions revolting inside of me. "Ol, that kiss was a mistake. Neither of us meant it and we need to move on. I don't want to go back to what things were and that's how it'll be if we don't forget about it."

He stays silent for a couple of seconds and for a moment I think he's gone. But when I open my eyes, I see him looking at me. I know this look very well. It's the look they give you when they want to take you to bed but won't stay with you because the time isn't right, because the ex is back, because their career demands too much time, because they're "not ready" … Because you're not what they're looking for.

Because they think of you only when it's convenient.

Or because they never really loved you and just wanted to have a good time before settling down with someone else.

I've heard it all.

I've moved on from all.

But this is the guy I've never been able to move on from. Oliver is the guy with the most deceiving look of them all.

"Maybe *you* didn't mean it," he says after a long pause, "but *I* did. I don't regret any of my words or actions. I wanted that kiss more than you could ever know and I would kiss you again if you'd let me. So, I—"

"Oliver, you and I know this is a huge mistake," I interrupt again, "I am not going to ruin our friendship again just to be your rebound."

"What?" He panics, "Chip, that's not what this is, I—"

"Let's just go back to being friends, please," I turn to look at him, "we don't have to tell anyone."

"Are you gonna let me explain?"

"Not until you come to your senses," I close my eyes and then shout, "*Get out!*"

"I'll drop it for now," he says before opening the door to leave.

The only reason I don't cancel the entire kitchen project right now is because it would crush Alberto's heart. He's been so excited about Oliver helping me.

Besides, whenever it's done, I'll have something that'll remind me of him when he's gone.

21

carmen

I've successfully ignored Oliver for three days and I'm proud of it.

I'm tired as fuck. But proud.

I've taken as much workload as my physical and mental capabilities have allowed me. I also started logging into work one hour earlier than usual and logging off two hours later and volunteering at Hope Center for the rest of my free time.

Yes, tired as fuck.

It'd be easier if I could block him but he's still working at my house, and we need to have a certain amount of communication. He's been doing an amazing job, and I can't deny how impressed I am.

Still, I hope this is over soon or I'm going to have a serious breakdown. It's not even noon and I feel like I'm going to fall asleep in my seat.

I'm about to stand out to get some coffee when I'm called to Simon's office. I walk crossing fingers, hoping he'll send me to the car racing finals in Elko next weekend. One of our main photographers is sick and can't attend, only leaving me as an option.

"You called me?" I say, after knocking on Simon's door.

"Take a seat," he motions with his hand, looking at his computer. The tone he's using is more serious than usual and it unsettles my stomach. I sit and after typing some more and a couple of clicks, he finally looks at me.

"Carmen, I have good and bad news." he says with an apologetic look. "The good news is that we need you to cover up for Sierra in Elko this weekend." My heart jumps but sinks at the same time. "Now the bad news is… we decided to hire five freelance photographers for the X Games coverage. We won't need you there anymore."

I remain calmed, but internally? I'm screaming and wrecking his entire office. I have to thank Araceli for that, living with her has taught me to keep my cool in the worst situations.

"Um… can you tell me why?" I swallow hard, gripping the chair arms.

"It's the busiest weekend of the year for us and we can't afford to take anyone from the building," he takes his glasses off and leans forward, "I would make an exception for you, believe me, I would but… we need everyone in their own field. You've proven yourself an excellent designer and we need you here, your experience as a photographer isn't—"

"How can I get more experience if you won't let me?" I interrupt. This time I can't hold my tears.

"You will have your chance, I promise," he continues, "I know you're talented and I swear I'll get you another event if you—"

"You've been saying this ever since you were hired," I get up and snap my hands on his desk, "two years ago, Simon! I haven't touched a camera for this magazine for two years." I point my index finger to him, "I might now have experience in editorial photography but I sure as hell can photograph any sports event, especially during the X Games," I take a deep breath, "I've ridden BMX myself since I was thirteen years old. I know every sport in that event like the palm of my hand and have an extensive portfolio to prove it. I'm more than qualified, more than capable. Now tell me once and for all what your problem is with me because I'm starting to believe this is personal."

There. I said it.

I know I'm a good Graphic Designer. I am one of the best in the building. But that was only a means to an end. Graphic Design is *what I do*, not *who I am. I am an Extreme Sports Photographer*. A damn good one. No matter if one person believes me or not.

He considers me for a moment, playing with his pen. He gives me a look that says, *'are you done with your tantrum already?'* and smiles at me.

"Why don't you take the rest of the day and come back on Monday?" he says, "take a few days for yourself to breathe and come back fresh next week? All paid."

Hijo de su re-puta madre.

I want to give him a finger but if I do, I might end up fired. I'm not going to give him that satisfaction. So, I walk out of his office, turn off my computer and leave. I know Oliver will be home, but that awkwardness is the least of my problems. I just want to curl up in bed with my giant stuffed Totoro, drink an entire bottle of tequila and fall asleep.

After that, I can come up with a plan, because I will slap the asshole in the face and prove him wrong.

You think you can make me quit? Remain seated and wait, Simon baby.

22

oliver

Three days.

Carmen has been avoiding my ass for *three. Torturous. Days*.

I've tried to look for excuses to text her. Needing more sandpaper, asking where she keeps the cleaning supplies, telling her where I'm leaving her stuff so she doesn't have to look for them.

Is it pathetic to feel happy about getting short responses and emojis?

Her comment about this being a rebound gutted me. Still, I refuse to think my chances are ruined. It only encourages me to wait for the perfect opportunity to talk to her, that's why I've been delaying the kitchen project as much as I can. I taped all the kitchen and made a plastic wall around it before taking the doors out to sand them… slowly. I'll start applying primer tomorrow and will hopefully take three more days than what we originally planned.

I'm tired.

Hopeful though.

Juanito and I are coming out of the bathroom when Carmen

storms in through the garage door, sobbing her lungs out. Juanito immediately jumps to follow her to the bedroom. I feel my heart beating faster and panic rises from my chest.

Beware of the tension between us, I decide to approach slowly. When I open the door, my heart breaks at the sight of her hugging Juanito, kneeling down in front of the bed.

"Chip?" I ask, knocking the door, "hey," I kneel down to reach for her, "hey, what's wrong?"

She turns around and looks at me with reddened eyes and the sight shakes me to my core. I've never seen her this sad in my life. For a second, I think she'll tell me to fuck myself, but without a warning, she throws herself to my arms and starts sobbing again. I put my arms around her and hold her tight, letting her cry while I rub her back and Juanito whines right behind her.

I hug her for a couple of minutes. When she's done crying, I scoop her in my arms and take her to the living room. I wait for her to argue, but she puts her arms around my neck and lets me carry her.

After I lower her down on the couch, Juanito jumps next to her. I toss a blanket at her and she scoots to hug my dog again. Without saying a word, I walk to the temporary kitchen we set up in the dining room and make her a cup of tea. When I come back, she's rolled in the blanket as a cute burrito.

I sit next to them and look at her swollen eyes and red nose. Her makeup all faded, and her braided hair messed up.

She looks devastated.

Still, she's the most beautiful woman I've ever seen in my life.

"Want to talk about it?" I ask as she takes the first sip of her tea.

She nods and after a shaky breath, she starts talking.

Simon Motherfucking Miller.

I want to find the guy, kick his ass and use all my resources and contacts to bury him alive, and make sure he never works at a sports magazine in his entire life.

"That's fucked up, Chip," I say when she concludes, "he can't do this to you."

"Technically he can," she shrugs, playing her fingers around the cup, "my contract specifies he can change tasks at any given time. I checked a couple of months ago."

"Then quit," I suggest.

"What?"

"Quit," I scoot forward, restraining myself from touching her, "I can get you a better job. I have friends and contacts. You could work for Elite too, whatever you want. I'll make it happen. A better magazine, brands, stores, you name it. You don't need to prove anything to that shithead."

"No," she puts her cup on the table, "I couldn't let you do that, Ol."

"Jesus," I mutter, throwing my head back, wiping my face with one hand, "no seas necia, Maria del Carmen," *don't be stubborn*. I sit straight, "you can't move forward if pride is blinding your view."

"It's not pride, Ol. I made a commitment with *myself*," she sniffs and wipes her tears with her sleeve, "I've never listened to haters. Their words only feed the fuel. I don't back down from challenges, especially if the prize is something I truly want. I said I was going to make a name for myself at that magazine and I will. I never give up. *Never*."

Then why did you give up on me?

I shake the thought out of my head.

"I understand that," I say, "but part of knowing your worth is knowing how to leave a place that's not only holding your wings but also cutting them," I softly grab her chin, "and sometimes you need a little help to do it. Not because you can't do it by yourself but because the people helping you are the ones who believe in you and want to see you shine." I caress her cheek and she blinks slowly, "and listen carefully, the person who doesn't let you shine to your fullest, doesn't deserve your light."

She deserves the largest stage, all the lights pointing at her like the star of the most amazing show. She deserves a standing ovation, not to be hidden backstage.

Carmen doesn't say anything for a moment and just looks at

me. Tired, sad. I'm not sure if my words are making any difference but I don't want to give up on trying to make her smile. An idea pops into my head and before I chicken out, I talk.

"Let's go out," I stand up, extending my hand.

"What?"

"Let's go out," I repeat, putting my hands inside my pockets, "you have the day off and I'm already done for the day, we could do stuff."

She bites her lower lip, "as friends, right? It wouldn't be a date."

I let out a soft chuckle and shake my head. "Not a date, I promise."

After a couple of seconds, she takes my hand and smiles, "Okay."

She stands up and walks to her bedroom to change. When the door closes, I allow myself to bite my fist and make an exaggerated happy dance, careful not to make any noise so she won't hear my excitement. I'm dying to talk to her about the kiss, about the possibilities… but right now, she needs a friend. That's exactly what I'll give her.

I'll do or be anything that she needs to be happy.

Even pretending we're not on a date.

We drive separately to leave Juanito with my parents and she waits for me while I change. Then, we drive together to the Mall of America, rocking her 2000s punk-rock playlist. We talk about anything and everything. Sharing *memories*. Memories that in another time, with another person would've made me sad. But not with her.

Everything with Carmen Morales makes me *hopeful and grateful*.

When we get to the mall, we go directly to the ticket kiosk of the Nickelodeon Universe, the amusement park right in the middle of the mall. We go on a couple of rides, eat cotton candy and grab a burger at her favorite place at the food court. I know she doesn't want to leave yet, so we decide to walk around the mall.

"Remember Angel and Rocio's sixteenth birthday party?" I ask, taking a straw of my drink, leaning on the handrail in front of the park.

"Dios mío," she laughs, "only you would think it was a good idea to have *one last ride* after we devoured all of those pizzas."

"Hold up," I turn to face her, "Angel and Ethan were the idiots who got on the line first, we just followed, so don't blame me."

"As always," she chuckles.

I shake my head, turning to the park again, "I still remember running to the bathroom and taking turns to throw up in the stalls. I couldn't even smell pizza for a long time without gagging."

"Damn, me too. Your mom was so pissed at Alberto for letting us do that," she pauses for a couple of beats, "Rosy was so happy."

There's a hint of sadness in her tone. I know she misses her sister dearly. But Rocío took the longest to recover from Angel's loss. It only fed her already reserved personality, in contrast with Carmen and Angel who were always loud and outgoing. We've talked over the years; she always texts me for my birthday or Christmas and I do the same even though I know she still resents me for going away.

"I know," I say, tucking a strand of hair behind her ear, "how is she doing, by the way?"

"She's alright. Or at least that's what she always says," she gives me a tight lip smile, "although I feel like I share more with her than what she shares with me. I know she opens up to Tony, though."

"Do you have any idea why?"

"She has this wall around herself sometimes." Her voice breaks, "I think I pushed her a little way too hard when we were younger when she made herself clear that she didn't want to be around Mamá… I just wanted us to be a family, I didn't want to push her away."

"I know," I whisper, "maybe she's just trying to protect herself and doesn't know how to let you in. Boundaries are important."

"I just wish she would be closer to me… I wish she wouldn't live so far away."

"It'll happen. She'll be back, I know it," I smile, "it's impossible not to come back to you, no matter how much time it's been."

Because you're home.

BMX always meant familia to me, but Carmen has always been my home. The home I belong to, where I want to live and die. The place where I'm whole. The home I finally came back to, and I get the feeling that whenever the time comes I won't want to leave. I want to say all of this but don't dare. She gives me a teary smile, as if I just said exactly what she needed to unlock something important inside of her.

I swallow the thoughts and look at her again.

"You deserve all the love," I sigh, "you really are the most amazing person I've ever met and I'm sorry we didn't talk for a long time. It was such a knee-jerk reaction to what happened, and I truly regret it." I take her hand, "I missed how you always made me feel seen, warmed and understood you."

"And I missed how much you've always believed in me." She whispers.

I imagine myself leaning down to kiss her, but I don't want to scare her away and ruin the moment. She's in a vulnerable place and I'm lucky it's me who she's opening up to. So, I just smile.

I love you. I still believe in you.

I'm about to suggest the candy shop as our next stop, when I feel someone tapping my shoulder. I turn around to find a tiny brunette smiling at me.

"Excuse me," she says, shrinking her shoulders, "are you Oliver 'the quokka' Rodriguez by any chance?"

Carmen softly grips my arm and my cheeks feel hot. It's been a while since someone has called me by that nickname.

"I uh—yeah. Hi."

"Oh my god, I can't believe it!" She squeals excitedly. "Would you sign this for my husband?"

She hands me a napkin and a black pen. "You're like, his *idol!* He used to follow you and Angel Morales around when you guys started doing all of those contests at Freedom Union park ages ago. He won an amateur competition once and has a picture with both of you framed in our living room." Her smile drops. "My husband doesn't ride as often anymore, but he has your Premium Angel bike and all of his wardrobe is Elite. He just got a tricycle for our three-year-old."

I chuckle and scratch my chin, trying to hide my blush. It's not that I don't ever bump into riders. I don't have a lot of public presence and I don't have any social media. The people who follow the sport closely know my face, but I've never had this kind of attention.

This interaction hits differently, though. This is the very first time I bump into someone who's been with me every step of the way. It's people like this who make me miss riding even more.

And I'm glad his wife is in this with him too. A lot of people I know have stopped riding because their spouses or partners haven't been supportive at all.

I quickly glance at Carmen, who is covering her mouth with her hands. I smile and go back to the conversation.

"I'd be honored," I take the napkin and the pen from her. I sign it and return it with a smile, "you know what? If you're comfortable with it, why don't you give me your information? I'd like to send him a box with brand new stuff. I can have some of the L.A. riders to autograph it all."

Both women gasp, Carmen looking at me as if I just saved a kitty from drowning.

"Are you serious?" the brunette says, making me focus on her again.

"Of course," I say, "it's really not a problem."

"He's going to be so happy," she says, "thank you so much,

Oliver. And sorry I interrupted your date," she smiles at Carmen, "you have a beautiful girlfriend."

I look at my girl as she blushes and shakes her head.

"Isn't she gorgeous?" I ask, not taking my eyes off her.

"She definitely is."

I take out my phone and she gives me their names and address. I type a quick text to my assistant in L.A. asking him to send a poster, a couple of t-shirts, hoodies, caps, two pairs of handle grips for his bike and a signed helmet for their kid.

We say goodbye and are left alone again, grinning as if we can't believe what just happened. My heart is fuller than it's been in a long time, as if everything is coming full circle and I was meant to have this exact moment next to Carmen. We walk for a little with her tucked inside my arm, neither of us mention how I referred to her as my girlfriend.

"That was so nice of you, Ol," Carmen says, "and she called you 'Quokka', I haven't heard that nickname in a while."

"I still can't believe there's been people following us around since then."

"What are you talking about?" She stops and faces me. "You guys were legends around here. You all still are."

"Angel was, he deserved all the recognition, not me." I say with a smile.

She grabs my hand this time. "Don't say that. You were both working hard to really make it. Maybe if you would've followed the original plan, you would've been better than he could have been. And I say this with all the love I have for him."

Through the years, my friends have implied that I was a better rider than Angel but have never said it so bluntly before. I've always refused to even consider it. From both of us, Angel was the most determined. The bravest one. He was the one with the ideas, the vision and who taught and pushed us all to our limits and achieve what we never thought we would. He deserved every opportunity I was ever handed on a silver platter and he was robbed the day he died.

I don't say anything for a while, we're now walking hand in

hand as if we're a couple. I have no idea at what point everything shifted but it did and I'm grateful. Still, there's a pinch of sadness in my chest. The knowledge that everything I have and everything I am now, is a reminder of what we lost.

Angel isn't here to enjoy any of these moments, and he never will.

"I miss him," I whisper.

"Me too," she says, giving my hand a squeeze, "he was my hero. My best friend. I know he was proud of me."

"He was," I kiss the top of her head, "he loved you more than anything in the world."

"He loved you too, you know?" she leans her head on my shoulder, "he must be so proud of you and what you've done."

We walk to the ice cream shop and buy two waffle cones. This time I let her pay. We sit on a bench and start eating in comfortable silence.

Not a date, my ass. I suppress a chuckle.

When she's done with her ice cream, she turns around and narrows her eyes at me. I get ready for a bomb.

"Why did you never go Pro, Ol?"

Boom!

I sigh. How do I tell her it was because I'm a coward? That I felt unworthy? Guilty?

"I didn't feel like it was my place anymore," I say instead, "it was a dream for me and Angel. It felt wrong without him."

She tilts her head, "that doesn't sound like you at all.."

"I don't think I really was myself back then so… I did a lot of things that weren't my nature."

Like running away from you.

"Well, I understand everyone mourns in different ways, but honestly?" she leans forward, crossing her legs on the bench, "not seeing you on a bike ever again hurt like hell. It was like losing you too. You were the best, no one ever came close to you. I understand how grief made you stop but seriously… I can't figure out what made you quit."

I shake my head, "I felt like somehow I wasted my time all of those years, losing myself in something that was going to die anyways," I confess, "even though I miss it like crazy… all the memories feel… empty. Like they're there for nothing and I wasted years of my life."

I turn to look at her.

"Are you kidding me, Santiago?" She grimaces and puts a hand on my knee, "you didn't waste time on BMX. Even if you don't do it anymore, it gives you so much. A greater purpose. The means to do something bigger with the sport than just riding… it taught you a lot of disciplines you're still applying today, a business that sells *more* than bikes. A brand that gives kids a passion. A hope our generation didn't have when we had to choose between following our dream or having a job," her voice cracks, "and most importantly, it made you happy. That alone makes it all worth it. Every second invested in the best way."

I feel my heart twisting inside of me. She flipped my self-pity coin and slapped my head in the most loving way. My girl is the epitome of true joy and positivity. Not the one that denies bad things happening, but the one that shines through them and finds the way out with determination. Not wondering but *knowing* there's something good at the end of it.

"And here you are doing it again," I whisper, shaking my head with unbelief, "finding the light at the end of a tunnel with no ending."

"There's always a way out, Ol," she takes my chin and shakes it tenderly, "and if there isn't you make one yourself."

I smile at her words as her warm hand caresses my face. She smiles back and the last iceberg inside my heart melts and evaporates. She looks at me like she's about to say something and stops, narrowing her eyes and smiling mischievously.

"You know what you need?" she stands up, "you need a ride, bro."

I froze at her words and open my mouth. "I haven't ridden in ten years. I must be so stiff I won't be able to even jump on a Bunny Hop."

"There's something called *muscle memory*, Santiago." She extends her hand, making me stand up, "come on."

"What?" I grip her hand and pull her closer to me, "you gonna teach me some new tricks?"

I regret my words the moment they come out. I promised myself I was going to behave. But instead of getting mad, she licks her lips and lifts an eyebrow.

"I can teach you a whole new set of tricks, alright," she says with a flirtatious tone, "let's go."

I clear my throat, feeling myself blush from my face all the way to my dick. Never in a million years would I have expected a reply like that. As much as I love it, I know she's seducing me into a bike ride I know I'm going to embarrass myself with.

"I don't own a bike." I say, leaning a little closer to her face until our foreheads almost touch "But even if I did, I don't have one handy."

"You're the co-owner of one of the biggest BMX brands in the country and you don't have a bike of your own?"

"I told you I haven't ridden in a while."

"Well, lucky for you," she touches my nose, "I own two. Let's go."

That alone should be the ultimate warning. If those are the two bikes I think she might be referring to, I won't come out of this alive. However, those demons have been there for far too long. I've been waiting for the right moment to let them out and be done with them.

Once again, María del Carmen Morales anticipates what I need and gives me a chance to not do it alone.

The time is now.

23

oliver

The drive back to her house is a blur.

I'm nauseous, my hands are sweating, and my heart rate is going up with each passing second. To anyone else I would've said no, but Carmen isn't just anyone. She's *the* person, *my* person. Everything she does, she does with love and faith, that's why I trust her blindly.

We park in her driveway and I wait for her to change into jeans and tennis shoes, her hair braided and her camera hanging around her neck. Without a word, I follow her to the storeroom in her backyard. I hold my breath as she opens the door, my eyes catching on the two bikes that have been preserved neatly.

"Are those…?" I don't finish the question, swallowing the lump in my throat.

"Yes," she gives me a teary smile, "good as new."

I lean on the doorframe, feeling my legs giving out as I stare at the 2008 Haro 5X I gave Carmen and next to it, the Subrosa my dad got for Angel's seventeenth birthday.

The last bike he rode.

"Why did you never buy a new one?" I ask after a long pause, "there are so many lighter bikes that would work even better now."

She bites her lips and considers before answering, "let's just say I'm more sentimental than practical," she shrugs, "I've just been changing the tires, pedals and grips," she signals with her hands, "recognize these?"

I let out a silent chuckle when I notice the Elite logo on one of the pedals, my heart pounding a thousand beats per minute.

"You should've told Jake or Ethan about it; you didn't have to buy them. I could've just sent some to you."

"I guess I won't have to now," she winks, "which one do you want to use?"

I chuckle softly and look at her eyes full of hope. I smile back in silence and take the Haro after a deep breath. I can see her face lighting up as she takes Angel's bike to follow me.

"Same spot?" She asks as we reach the sidewalk.

I nod, "let's do it."

With a grin, she hops on the bike and starts pedaling.

Now or never, bro.

I grip my hands on the handle, take a deep breath and push my right foot forward on the pedal. My heart starts beating faster and the adrenaline starts rushing through my veins as a powerful energizer. The familiar sound of the chain rolling on the sprocket feels like a hammer inside my heart, the warm summer breeze crashing my face with flashbacks.

For a second I think I might not be able to handle all the emotions popping up, but once I start gaining speed to catch up with my girl ahead of me, I start feeling less weary.

Carmen quickly glances at me and the smile she gives me makes me feel like that teenager I used to be. The one who wanted to show off for her. So, I lift up my body into the air in a Bunny Hop. I don't realize I've jumped until she lets out a squeal.

"I knew you still had it in you."

"Don't get too excited," I pant, "I'm already tired."

My legs are starting to feel heavy. But I don't want to stop, I haven't even tried anything complicated but that enthusiastic and brave teenager inside of me wants to make his way out.

She's bringing him back. She's bringing you back.

We ride about six blocks and get to Freedom Union Park. Our spot. Our home. The park we fought for. We spent months gathering signatures and getting the entire community together so the city would approve the admission of skateboards and BMX bikes.

The park where I kissed Carmen for the first and last time.

The second we ride across it, the familiarity is almost overwhelming. It seems like time never flew by. My entire being is entering a warzone. My brain fighting against my conscience, who is reminding me of all of my mistakes. Making me see how different things are and how the only thing that's left are memories.

We stop in front of a quarter pipe. Carmen leaves her camera on the floor and pedals around. She starts by dropping into one of the bowls and flying out with a playful smirk.

"Don't look at me like that," she laughs and approaches, "I just wanted to try, it's been a while for me too."

"I wouldn't dare judge you, Chip. I don't even know if I could do *that*."

"Well, the only way to know is trying, so try." She smiles.

Fear sweeps over me and I shake my head, gripping the handlebar again. I'll probably end up with a broken arm if I try to do the same. Instead, I pedal on a flat section of the track and start with a couple of Bunny Hops and a lame Manual around the bowl. My legs are feeling heavier by the second, my muscles haven't been active in anything other than my home gym. Somehow along a manual that I manage to hold for more than five seconds, as if my body has suddenly remembered something, I find myself strong enough to turn all my body and spin it into a 180.

Carmen claps and cheers, pedaling towards me.

"Okay. Enough playing amateur, Big Guy," she says and my heart freezes for a moment.

Big Guy.

That was her nickname for me. She gave it to me when we were still very young. She said it was because she always felt so tiny next to me. She's been calling me by my name ever since we saw each other again. I didn't pay much attention; I knew I deserved her coldness after all. But the way she said it just now moved something different inside of me, as if she's also able to see that old Oliver somewhere inside of me. I ignore the feeling and shake my head.

"Maybe tomorrow," I scratch the back of my neck, "I think I just spent my quota for the day."

"Muscle memory, remember?" she softly punches my shoulder, "If you could do a 180 like that, a Feeble Grind shouldn't be that hard. Come on, I want to take real pictures."

I chuckle at her enthusiasm. I love that she believes in me so blindly, but I don't think my body can give more. These few tricks I tried, even though they're some of the easiest in my record, have already drained me physically and emotionally.

But Carmen isn't the giving up type, remember?

I stand still, trying to catch my breath.

"Come on," she tugs my arm, her eyes widening, "don't you want to make me smile?"

Always.

I swallow hard, "of course."

"Then do it for me, come on," she shakes my arm, "I want to see that fucking Quokka smile back when I edit." She takes the camera and starts pedaling towards her backpack. "Water break and you'll give me a Feeble Grind on that small ledge."

I make my way there and drink the whole bottle in two swigs. My mind is pleading with me to stop but my heart and my body are itching to get back on the bike. As if my spirit has been sleeping and it's slowly waking up. I pedal towards the ledge and hop, getting my front tire close to the edge but once I pull my back peg, the front tire slips and I fall to my right side.

"Shit," I groan, rolling onto my back.

"Do it again," Carmen yells, "get up."

I try it four times and fail each one. The fourth time I yell, kicking the bike. I hear Carmen pedaling behind me.

"Come on, Rodriguez," she says as I turn around, "don't slop on me. You used to do this every day. Wait a second," she says and takes a piece of wax from her backpack. I have to laugh at her sweetness. She really was prepared for everything. She rubs the wax on the ledge and gives me a thumbs up, signaling me to try again.

I sigh, throwing my head back in frustration. I will never hear the end of it if I quit now, so I take the bike and pedal around the park to get air and mentally prepare to try once more.

Just once so she knows you're not a quitter.

Without thinking about it too much, I pedal towards the ledge and jump once again. This time I can feel the peg aligning with the front tire as they perfectly slide in a straight line along the ledge. My entire body snaps with the realization and I automatically lift the bike again as I reach the end, landing on the ground as if it's the most natural thing in the world.

"Hell yeah!" I throw my fist to the air as I pedal around.

"Woohoo!" Carmen cheers, standing up from where she's sitting, "see? Now go to that quarter pipe and give me a Tuck no Hander."

Pumped with excitement, I pedal towards the ramp and take off. But as I do, I lean back way too much and fall backwards, hitting my ass in the concrete.

"Fucking hell!" I hit the ground hard, the bike flying to my right.

"Good," she encourages me, "get up and do it again."

I'm tired, my muscles are sore and tomorrow morning I'm going to have back aches because of this fall. I think I've had enough, but I understand why she's pushing it, though. This was my signature trick. The first one she photographed of me. What first give me my "Quokka" nickname. So, I stand up and try again. This time I go up, I have a major freak out in the air and let go of the bike. I land on my feet, but the bike bounces on the floor and hits me in the face, making me fall backwards again.

This time, I don't get up right away, choosing instead to close my eyes shut and listen to my surroundings. I can hear the crickets, the air blowing warm and nice as a car drives by. A surprisingly quiet park for a Tuesday afternoon until the silence is interrupted by the approaching footsteps of the woman I love.

I open my eyes to find her staring at me from above.

"Get up, you big baby."

I do as she says with a groan.

"I think we can stop now," I say, lifting up the bike. "Thanks for the fun ride. Wanna watch a movie when we get back to your house?"

"Okay, what the hell is wrong with you, Quokka?" she asks, stepping in front of me. Her mouth twitching a bit as her brows pull down in a frown. "Where's that BMX legend who made me cry until I learned to land on a fucking Barspin?"

"I can't, I told you," I sigh, "I'm stiff and can barely lift up the bike. This might've been the lightest bike back in the day but it's not anymore," I shake my head, "nothing is the same. I am not the same guy I used to be. Everything changed when he left," my voice cracks, *"I* changed."

"Of course everything changed, Oliver," she says, cupping my sweaty face, "it was going to change anyways. We're not supposed to stay the same for the rest of our lives. And just because it hurt like hell to lose him it didn't mean we weren't worthy of a beautiful beginning right after." Her hands fall, "you can't quit when things change and you don't like it. You can't quit when things get too hard, and you most certainly do not *quit* just because you fell."

She laughs humorlessly. "Do you remember what you told me the first time I grabbed this bike to learn?" she signals to my bike, *"If you fall, you still have something to learn in the air before you land."*

"I don't remember saying that."

"I remember everything you said that day. See? That *was you.* The *you* that's still here but it's hiding and scared. I get it, change is scary, Ol, but it can bring amazing things if you let it. Changing means *growing.* It means you're ready to move from where you are," she smiles, "you don't cut the caterpillar from the tree when it starts to change. You let it adapt so it can fly later. It's the same bug, but bigger, stronger and more beautiful… You've been running away from a change we all moved forward from a long time ago, Ol. It was as if you would've died to yourself when Angel did… but you aren't dead. You're still here," she places a hand on my chest, "he would've been so mad at you for letting yourself die like this."

I feel tears rolling down my eyes, her words lighting up every single dark spot in my heart and crumbling down every wall I've been putting up through the years.

"Let's go," she pushes me towards the bike, "Tabletop, now."

"What?" I laugh with disbelief.

"It's a simple Tabletop, Ol," she rolls her eyes and jumps on her bike, "here, let me show you."

Without too much bullshit, she pedals around the quarter pipe to gain momentum, jumps bending her left knee and gracefully crosses it over the front tube, pulling up through the other arm like a fucking Pro. When she lands, I erupt in cheers.

"Your turn," she calls out, grabbing her camera again.

She seems to have the video mode turned on, because the moment I start pedaling, she follows me with camera in hand. The moment I bend my knee in the air and land nice and neatly, my hope goes up, taking me back in time again.

I don't know what it is about seeing her riding next to me with a camera in her hands that gives me all the energy I thought I drained in the last hour. Once I touch the ground, I want to do it again.

When I make another round along the park, I can feel Angel himself pedaling next to me, teasing me and encouraging me with bets and challenges.

"Don't make me laugh, loco. It was just a scratch." I can hear him saying. *"Just jump on that shit and do it again, cabrón. I've seen you fly higher."*

This is for you, compadre.

I fly higher this time and land stronger than ever. Now… now it feels like I'm unable to stop.

Tabletop
Can-Can
Toboggan
Wallride
Walltop
No foot
Tuck no fucking hander.
One after the other.

Suddenly, I'm riding around my park as if I'm dancing on a cloud. I can barely believe it. Just when I thought I'd made peace with not doing this ever again, with not feeling this way ever again.

But this wasn't my doing. It was all Carmen. Her love, her patience, her faith in me is what slapped my idiotic head and forced me out of my shell.

She keeps following my every move, capturing every angle like a master.

It's the same adrenaline, the same excitement. The same love for this bike coming out of the grave, taking shape and filling my lungs with life again.

I'm flying out of a bowl when I hear her laugh right behind me. The melody that makes my soul surrender to hope, that makes me fearless. In the heat of the moment, I instinctively jump on a ramp, pulling my entire body to bend my knees as I kick the back tire hard. Before I realize what I'm doing, the frame spins and I land on the pedals.

A perfect *fucking Tailwhip.*

What the hell was that?

"HOLY SHIT, OLIVER!" Carmen squeals, leaving the bike and the camera aside, running towards me. "That was amazing."

I jump off the bike and lift her in my arms to hug her. When I put her down, I finally look at her eyes tearing up. I hesitate for no longer than two seconds and close my eyes, bringing my lips to hers. My heart races when I feel her arms around my neck as she kisses me back. I cup her face, rub her cheeks. My tongue sweeping hers, my teeth caressing the softness of her lips, my heart drinking her kiss like the fountain of life.

"Thanks, Chip," I say against her lips, pressing my forehead to hers. My eyes closed. "I don't know how to pay you back for pushing me to do this. Remind me who I am. The passion that's still inside me."

"What are you talking about?" she says, pulling away a little bit, "I never even knew what my passions really were until I met you. You believed I was going to be good at them before I even tried."

"And I never knew what passion really was until I met *you*," I wave my hand toward her, "I never felt more than when you were around. You always made my life better. You made me stronger." I kiss her forehead, "you always were the engine that pulled me through."

I feel my heart coming out of my throat as I confess this but the moment her smile fades and steps back, I feel how it starts breaking again. I replay my words to pinpoint exactly what I said to make her this angry and right when I'm about to ask her she grabs her bike and shoves it away again. She turns to face me one more time, biting her upper lip.

"Then why did you leave me like that?" she raises her chin, her eyes filling up with tears, "if you felt that way about me, then why did you *use me* and then left me?"

Used her?

"What?" I ask, feeling the stab of her words, "I did what?"

"We were such great friends and then… then you had to ruin it all when you kissed me and acted like it never happened. Never talked to me again. You never had real feelings for me, Oliver and that's fine. It was just a kiss for you, but you *broke my heart*… I thought it had meant something to you. I at least deserved to know you weren't coming back instead of waiting for you like a lost puppy." A single tear falls from her eye, "you didn't even show up to Angel's funeral. When… when I needed you the most."

"Chip, I know I screwed up, just… just let me explain," I

interrupt, trying to get closer, "you have to understand, when he died I… I lost it, I lost myself and—"

"*You* lost it? *You* lost yourself?" she pushes me, "what do you think it happened to all of us, huh? You think it was difficult for you? Guess what? I had to go back to that house without him. I had to hide the bikes from Araceli so she wouldn't throw them away. It was me who cried herself to sleep alone every night. Everyone left, Oliver. *Everyone*… not even my sister stayed for too long. The guys retreated to their own thing, and you just vanished… It was only *me* asking God why I had to lose him… what I did to push *you* away." She shakes her head, "meanwhile you were a thousand miles away… when I most needed you. Not as a boyfriend… just as a friend."

"Chip, I—"

"You did exactly what he said you would and like an idiot I didn't listen."

"What the hell did he say?" My words come out deep as a growl.

"Oh, don't act so surprised," she gets closer again and pokes my chest, "I always knew that's what you thought. I was just a naïve groupie with a crush for you, right? Did you have a good time in college after all? Did you find a woman to replace what this *little girl* couldn't do?"

Tears are coming out of my unbelieving eyes as I listen. I acted like a coward, and I own that. I feel like a worthless piece of shit seeing the pain in her eyes, the betrayal in her tears. What I've caused. But as I process her words, another reality sinks in: She also did what Angel said she would. Not because I didn't mean anything to her but because he made her think I was going to leave her heartbroken.

And I did just that. Fuck my life.

That's why she doesn't trust me, what she meant when she stopped our kiss. This is what Antonio was talking about.

Oliver you're a fucking idiot.

"I can't believe he said that to you," I wipe my face with a hand.

"I was his baby sister, of course he was going to warn me about his player best friend."

"No, that's not why I can't believe it," my voice breaks, "it's bullshit. I *never* said that."

"He's not here to back it up, so don't call him a liar."

"He *did* lie to you, Carmen," I lower my voice, getting closer to her, "I didn't disappear because I didn't want you. I left because I was stupid and broken and couldn't handle the guilt," I breathe hard, "it was a dick move, I know it and I regret it with my life. But I couldn't see you in the eye knowing I could've prevented that crash. And it felt disloyal to make a move on you when we were both mourning and knowing he didn't want me with you."

"He didn't want us together because he wanted to protect me from *you*."

"That's fucking bullshit," I raise my voice, making her jolt, "he knew I was in love with you, and I never implied I just wanted to have fun. *Ever*."

Her eyes widen little by little but doesn't say anything. My deepest secret is out, and I can't stop myself from letting it all out.

"I was out of my fucking mind in love with you, Carmen," I grab her face, "you always knew how to make me laugh, how to make every single thing amazing, as simple and minimal. I wanted to be where you were all the time. You were my light. You made me feel like the king of the world." I let her face go and shrug, "I learned to love and enjoy the world through your eyes, through your heart… in ways I wasn't capable of doing by myself. You changed me. The only change in my life that never hurt me."

She covers her mouth with her hands, and I keep going, "Angel saw us the night we kissed, and he was livid. He threatened me… and believe me, I didn't give a shit at that moment. I just wanted to be with you. But the night he died… you know how things went down… I was supposed to go with them to that damn party but didn't… I bailed last minute because I wanted to go to you."

"Wh—why did you want to go to me?"

"I was going to your house and ask you to be my girlfriend for real... I wrote you a note, I was going to sing *1, 2, 3, 4 by Plain White T's*... your favorite song?" I feel my cheeks getting hot, "I was going to ask you to wait for me and follow me to L.A. when you graduated. But when everything happened... I freaked out and bailed. When I came back for thanksgiving you were with that douche—"

"Adam..." she adds, "I was already dating Adam."

"I saw you with him and it fucking *gutted me*," I find her gaze, "it crushed my heart. I saw you two kissing and it destroyed me... I never wanted to give up, but you moved on so fast, and I thought... I thought you didn't want me anymore, I thought..." I shake my head, not wanting to justify my stupidity anymore and grab her hands, "I'm so fucking sorry, Chip. I'm sorry I disappeared instead of talking to you and work things out. I'm sorry I didn't come back. I'm sorry I didn't call. I'm sorry... You have no idea how much I regret it."

"And I thought you just felt bad for playing with me and just went away," she cries, "I just... accepted it. But you... you loved me?"

"Like crazy," I sigh.

Right when I'm about to kiss her, I feel two drops on my face and the sky starts darkening.

"Shit," she mutters.

Without even glancing at me, she grabs her backpack, camera and jumps on the bike to make her way out of the park. I follow her like I'm committed to do for the rest of my life.

Antonio was right, there's too much we need to say to each other, and this conversation is far from over.

24

carmen

"I was out of my fucking mind in love with you."

I'm still trying to convince myself those words weren't a dream. That this moment isn't a dream. The look in his eyes, the pain in his voice. Trying hard to accept that my brother lied to me and made both Oliver and I believe we weren't meant for each other.

It makes sense, Angel was the most possessive person in the world, I can only imagine the rage Oliver had to endure from him when he told him he loved me.

When we arrive at my house, we rush to leave the bikes in the storeroom and get inside as the rain starts pouring. I walk across the living room in a trance, thinking how to restart the conversation without making it weird. Because we need to talk about this. This new information changes everything.

I turn around at the sound of his steps. He's looking directly at me, his heavy breaths mingling with the sound of the rain. None of us has said a word but my eyes are communicating in silence.

Yes, I forgive you.

Yes, I want you.
Yes, I loved you.
Yes. I still do.
Yes, I will always love you.

I let him kiss me at the park in the heat of the excitement. After his confession, there's nothing I want more than his lips on mine and his hands on my body. I've been craving them for ten years and one little glimpse of his touch will never be enough.

"Oliver," I whisper, putting my arms around his neck, "*kiss me. Please.*"

A smile slowly forms on his lips as he leans down, cupping my face with his left hand and resting his right on my hip. He brushes his nose with me and kisses the path between my cheek and my mouth. When he touches my lips, I open up for him and slightly pulls his neck to bring him closer. My heart debating how much it should let him in.

Hopeless, naïve, sixteen-year-old Carmen is telling me to let him all the way in.

But *scattered, born from the ashes, badass Carmen* is reminding me he was getting married until a week ago. That there's still a returning ticket to L.A. with his name on it and he is going to leave,

Have him for today, my heart whispers. *Next time he leaves, he will take a piece of you with him.*

Oliver slows down the pace of our kiss, gripping my hip as he lets out soft moans against my mouth. The heat between my thighs is getting too strong to ignore as he tries hard not to press me against the wall, even though I want him to.

I want all of him, feel every part of him. I pull him even more, deepening the kiss and asking his body to give in. Suddenly, I feel his erection against my belly.

I let out a long sigh and throw my head back, but he pulls away a little.

"Sorry," he whispers, "can't help it when you kiss me like that."

I smile at the sight of his swollen lips. His eyes deep in thought as they scan my face, looking for the shadow of the doubts that made me reject him the first time. But now, I can only give him what we both want. What's always been his.

Even if it's just for today.

"It's okay," I glide my lips along his neck and take his right hand in mine, moving it under my shirt. I use his hand to move the cup of my bra to the side and squeeze the top of my breast. I pull back to catch his gaze as it widens with each movement.

"Fuck," he cries, closing his eyes shut and pressing his forehead against mine, "baby, please don't torture me. Not with this. Please."

"Big guy," I moan and cup his face with my free hand, "look at me," I whisper. He opens his eyes a little as I go on, "I want you. Please, tell me you want me."

He looks at me as if he's in pain, his eyes roam between my eyes and my mouth.

"I've wanted you for half of my life," he says within a sigh, his hands frozen where they are, "ever since I understood what wanting a woman was I've wanted you."

"Then please," I say as I gently bite his bottom lip, "take me to bed."

"You sure?" he says. When I nod, he swallows hard and takes my face in his hands, "Okay, but if you want me to stop, just tell me. No matter what the reason or how far we're into it. It's your call. Your decision."

Who said consent isn't the biggest turn on in the world?

"Okay," I whisper, letting out my most seductive smile.

The embarrassment I was getting ready for dissipates when he hungrily takes over my mouth. His insecure demeanor changed into something primal, urgent. Biting hard, sweeping his tongue deep into my mouth as if there wasn't enough time.

Breaking the kiss for a moment, Oliver helps me to get rid of my shirt and jeans leaving me in my underwear. He looks at me from head to toe with wonder before devouring my neck, pulling me closer as he caresses my back, down to my ass.

"This huge, *gorgeous ass*, mami!" he groans against my neck, giving me a hard spank that makes me moan and press my body onto his. He squeezes hard. "This ass has been killing me for days."

I throw my head back and let out a loud chuckle, but it dies down when he suddenly grabs me by the waist, tossing me over his shoulder like a caveman and walks down the hall towards the bedroom.

He puts me down once he closes the door and turns the light on the nightstand. He's about to take his cap off but I stop him.

"Don't," I roam my hands under his shirt, "leave it on, please."

He smiles mischievously, "you like how I look with the cap on?"

I've imagined you on top of me, under me and many other ways with your cap on.

"I do, very much," I say, lifting his shirt so he can take it off, "you've always looked so hot with your cap backwards."

"Your wish is my command," he groans as he tosses his shirt away and pulls me for another kiss.

My hands are against his strong chest, his travel from my legs to my back again, and with one light click, I feel my breasts set free. He breaks the kiss and looks at my chest with a smile and brings his hands to my shoulders to slowly slide the straps down my arms. When he finally tosses the bra away, I think for a moment he stopped breathing. He finally looks up and kisses me again, bringing both hands to cup my breasts, playing his thumbs against my nipples. I moan against his mouth, electrified by the contact, feeling my knees weaker with each passing second.

"Perfect," he whispers against my mouth, "*fucking* perfect."

I let out a long sigh, painfully putting a little space between us, taking his hands and pulling him back towards the bed. Oliver gently pushes me until I'm completely laid down and covers my mouth with his again. He puts my arms above my head and starts kissing my forehead, my eyes, my nose, my mouth and down the rest of my body. When he gets to my chest, he brings my right breast to his mouth, making me gasp at the touch of his tongue on my nipple. He spends a long time there, switching between my breasts.

I can't explain how it makes me feel as if my body doesn't belong to me anymore.

"Fucking. Hell." I moan as he releases my nipple with a pop. I close my eyes shut as the heat of his breath travels down my belly. His teeth find my thong, which he slowly slides down until he shoves it away.

"This ain't hell, mami," he chuckles as he starts going down, "I'm about to taste fucking *heaven*," he slides his hands up mi thighs, "now spread these amazing legs for me, please. Me muero de hambre." *I'm so hungry.*

It was a request, but my body obeys the command in his tone. When I do, he lifts my leg over his shoulder as he kneels down and starts kissing my inner thigh, pushing two fingers inside of me, murmuring things I'm not able to recognize. My brain is completely shut off, my heart is racing, and my entire body is crushing down with pleasure.

He slowly slides his hands up to grab me by my ass before burying his face between my legs. The first sweep of his tongue makes me let out a loud whimper, but as he keeps circling against my clit, my moans become cries. I slide my hands and cup his head over his cap, feeling all my nerve endings lighting up like a line of gunpowder until my entire body explodes with the most intense orgasm I've ever experienced in my life.

"Holy shit," I pant.

"Heaven," he whispers against my thigh, "*sweet heaven…* but I'm not done with you yet," he whispers as I try to come out of this post-orgasmic trance.

Oliver stands up, dragging me to the edge of the bed so I can sit up, where he stops and takes off his pants and boxers. When he's completely free, my brain stops working.

Unable to connect with lungs. Oxygen just left the chat.

"Sweet mother Mary, you're fucking huge." I gasp, biting my lower lip.

He turns completely red and lets out a long chuckle. He's

about to kiss me again, but I stop him. I need to admire this fucking delicious view because… *Dios mío.* I thought women who bragged about their man having huge dicks were full of shit.

This thing is real. Fuck.

I stand up and start scanning this glorious piece of manliness with my hands, tracing his quadriceps, his abs and muscular chest and arms. He's covered in tattoos for the most part and I start kissing one by one, as he buries his face in my neck, caressing with his hands. I take a step back to get another look, when I spot a familiar tattoo on his left pec… right above his heart.

Our tattoo.

Angel's tattoo. The same one I have on my back.

"I didn't know you also had it." I say, planting a soft kiss against the ink. The emotion I've been holding inside is bursting as I wrap my arms around his neck and pull him down for another kiss.

"How could I not?" he says against my lips, moving to kiss my cheek with so much sweetness that my eyes automatically close at the sensation.

I'm sure you've heard about the famous butterflies in the stomach. Well, I have three fucking parrots fighting to get outside my body right now. This is too intense, too much for this little heart of mine. These are ten years of believing this moment was just going to be a fantasy forever, a forbidden dream. And here he is, kissing me like I'm his everything, pleasuring my body as if I was the most precious thing he's ever touched.

He breaks the kiss and smiles, walking backwards to sit at the edge of the bed. He pulls my hand this time and I take control, straddling his lap. We're touching, kissing and exploring with our hands and lips. The sensations in my body intensify the feeling in my chest as he brings his hand to one of my breasts. His palm rubs my nipple as he traces a path from my neck to my earlobe with his tongue. His other hand caressing my back all the way to my ass.

This is when it hits me.

I will *never* get enough of this.

This is the hottest, most beautiful man I've ever seen. How will I be able to say goodbye after this?

"I can't wait any longer," he whispers to my ear, "I need to be inside you *now*. Make you mine *now*."

I've always been yours. I want nothing else than for you to be mine. Only mine.

The thought dies in my head as he rolls us over. He's on top of me, both completely bare and vulnerable. Skin against skin. I force myself to hold my tears as he lifts himself up a little bit to scan my body. His mouth slightly open and his eyes glossy.

"Don't ever think you're average, okay?" He leans down to kiss me. "You're stunning, baby. You're fucking beautiful."

I throw my head back and sigh, pulling him with me. I lean up to lick his neck and that hot ear piercing and whisper.

"Nightstand, second drawer."

Oliver gives me a quick smooch and makes his way to the nightstand. I move up in the bed and lay down again, putting my head on the pillows while he puts on the condom, stroking a few times before crawling to meet me.

He kisses my nose and caresses my face.

"Hey," he smiles down on me.

"Hey Big guy," I say, roaming my hands around his chest.

"I've been dreaming about this for so long."

"Deveras?" *Really?*

"La mera verdad." *The honest truth.*

He nods and kisses me deeply, grabbing my face. "No matter what happens, this isn't just a hookup for me, Chip. You *are not* a rebound—you could never be that. You're special to me. More than you'll ever know."

I'm speechless, scared to ask what he means and what he expects. Right now, I just want him to fill me. Imprint this moment in my body and my heart forever.

"Get over here." I lift one eyebrow and open my legs for him, bringing his mouth to mine.

Oliver gets closer without breaking the kiss, he positions himself and thrusts inside. His right hand is on the pillow above my head while his left is gripping my hip. I feel my heart about to burst at the friction and I let out a long moan as he starts moving slow but incredibly firm.

"Open your eyes, mi amor." He whispers, our foreheads against each other. My right hand is entangled with his and my left hand gripping his ass. I keep my eyes closed, ignoring his request and the tone of his voice.

I can't look at him, he will see right through me, and my heart wouldn't be able to handle it.

He takes me hard, not too fast but not so slow. His whole body pressing against me, as if we would never get close enough.

It has never felt this way before.

Heaven. Definitely heaven.

A dream I don't want to wake up from.

Oliver's hand slides from my leg, all the way to my breasts where he starts playing with my nipples, prolonging the sensations.

"Please, look at me Mami," he insists.

This time, I lazily open my eyes. When I see him, I find him smiling with his face flushed. I can't help but return the smile and cup his face, pulling him into a kiss.

"There you are," he whispers, "I need to look at you while you take me all in, baby." He lets out a soft moan that makes me shiver, "I love it when you look at me like that. Never stop looking at me like I'm the only one you see."

Because you are.

The thought dies in my head as I feel my orgasm in the horizon, so I hold onto him tightly, lifting my hips to find his thrusts and crying out his name to his ear. I've never been a screamer in bed. But this intense, fervent sensation in my body tangled up with the fluttery feeling in my chest is too much to bear.

"Come for me, mami," he groans as my pleasure starts building up, "let go, mi amor. *Damn,* I knew you'd look this damn beautiful coming for me."

Oliver speeds up the pace and when it hits, I dig my nails into his shoulders and kiss him again to keep me from stupidly confessing what I've been feeling for so long. He speeds up even more and a little after that, he comes letting out a strong groan that sends shivers down my spine.

"*Holy. Fucking. Shit.*" He pants as que drops himself on top of me, "that was amazing."

"I know," I laugh, pushing his heavy body as I catch my breath, "and there's more where that came from."

He laughs again and gives me a long, deep kiss before we take turns to go pee. When it's my turn, I sigh and let reality sink in…

I just had the best sex of my life… with Oliver!

He comes back and finally takes his cap off, throwing himself on the bed for a tight, long snuggle. I look over his shoulder to see my phone and it's already nine at night.

"Hungry?" he asks, as he looks at his phone too.

"Could eat an entire cow," I place a kiss on his chest.

"Wanna order something?" he looks down, "I burned a thousand calories on that bike ride and another thousand with you."

I drum my fingers on his abs, "how about pizza and chicken wings?"

"Bet," he places a kiss on my forehead.

We put his clothes in the washing machine before taking a long hot shower together. We order the food and devour it in the living room while watching a movie. But just as I supposed, Netflix and chill becomes another make out session that ends up with me riding Oliver on the couch.

After we resume the movie in my bedroom, we end up between the sheets again and again and *again.*

"I don't want to go," he says against my hair after a little break. His arms around my waist, my face resting against the curve of his neck.

I can hear the insecurity in his voice and my heart doubts for a second. I could ask him to leave, thank him for this amazing night and settle for that. But is that what my heart really wants?

What does *he* really want?

He's going away anyways, isn't he?

I'm too scared to ask him. My heart gets heavier just by thinking about it… and I really don't want to let him go.

"Then don't," I whisper against his neck.

"You sure?"

"I want you here with me."

He snuggles closer and kisses my temple before covering us with a blanket.

I'll ask him tomorrow.

I love you, is my last thought before falling asleep.

25

oliver

Bliss. Complete. Absolute. Pure fucking bliss.

I'd never had this much sex in one night before last night.

Scratch that. I'd never made love to anyone —*with* anyone before last night.

I can't even begin to describe this state of mind. I'm bewildered. In awe.

I never knew nothing in this life could be this wholesome, this happy. I was shocked and moved to my bones when she threw herself at me, asking me to take her to bed. I knew the moment I was helpless before her, her heart, her body.

Waking up next to her has surpassed any fantasy I've ever had about us. Because she's always been the ultimate dream. Utopia and Shangri-la bundled and incarnated melting in my arms, taking her pleasure from *me* and only *me*. Feeling my love inside her body.

Damn, I love her.

More now than I ever did. I will love her for the rest of my life. Carmen Morales is *everything*. I'm not giving up until she's fully convinced I'm worthy of her love, that *we* are worth a shot. That I'm not the same guy who once left her.

But I need to take it slow, I can mess it up.

I lift myself up and feel the soreness of my body. Too much physical activity in one day but worth every single second. We spent all night making love and slept about two hours. My phone says it's 8 in the morning, but she doesn't have to go to work today, so I'll let her sleep in.

My girl deserves it. I don't want to get up either yet, so I just cross my arms behind my head and enjoy the bliss.

"I can hear you smiling Big Guy," she says with a lazy tone. She's laying on her stomach, face buried in the pillow. The sheets are covering only her lower body. I carefully lean to caress her bare back and kiss her hair.

"Good morning," I whisper, moving her long hair to one side to kiss along her neck.

"Not gonna happen, buddy. Sorry to disappoint your *big ass* morning wood," she says, turning her face to me, "I can barely move, and I can't feel my lower body. Otherwise, I would've been on top of you ten minutes ago."

I let out a painful chuckle and pull her into my arms. I can't believe this tiny person can make me this full and joyful. She snuggles and kisses my cheek. I turn to look at her and she has her eyes closed. The way she's breathing and how tense the rest of her body is sends a wave of worry down my belly.

"Hey," I caress her cheek, "what's going on, *hermosa*? What are you worrying about?"

She slowly opens her eyes and looks at me with a hint of sadness. My heart starts sinking as she bites her lip.

"I–I just–I just want to know what we're doing here," she places a soft kiss on my chest, "I know you said this wasn't a rebound—"

"It's not." I interrupt, sitting up straight and bringing her with me. "I swear it is not—I've been wanting this my *entire life*, Chip."

I brush her lips with my fingertips, "The truth is, Susan and I never loved each other, and we never should have gotten engaged to begin with. Hell, we should've never even *dated*. We were just lonely, sad and done with dead end relationships. We decided to get married so we wouldn't be alone for the rest of our lives. So no, she wasn't heartbroken over it—neither of us are. I don't need a rebound nor do I ever want one. Especially not with you. I swear it."

"Alright, I believe you." She still looks unsure. "But I still don't know what you want."

I want you to be my everything. My wife, the mother of my children. The one who slaps my head when I'm being a coward and an idiot. The person who believes in me when I can't, the one I tell everything to. The one I trust the most. The woman I can come home and make love to till I forget my worries.

The words die in my throat. I can't scare her away with too many expectations. Not yet. She doesn't owe me anything, it's *me* who has to earn her love and a place in her life without pushing her to give more than she can.

"Look, I know what you're thinking," I give her a little peck on the lips, "we don't have to label anything or decide what to do now. I know this isn't exactly taking things slow, but we can take it one step at a time. Have fun for now?" she looks at me with uncertainty but after a couple of seconds, she nods. I kiss her forehead as she gives me a lazy smile. "And can I ask you a favor?"

"Sure."

"Can we not tell anyone about us for now?" I swallow hard, "I just don't want anyone to assume things… put pressure?"

The guys would be livid if they knew. The last thing I want is anyone thinking I'm playing with her or pushing her to accept me. I want to make sure she trusts me completely before putting us out there. I need to take my time and not let anyone interfere.

I'm dying to tell her I love her and that I want her forever, but coming out too intensely has the potential of freaking her out and breaking my heart again. This time forever.

I almost have her.

Messing this up isn't an option.

carmen

"Whatever you need, Ol," I say, swallowing my tears and closing my eyes again.

Fun is fine. You're used to this, remember?

You saw him leaving once, you can do it again.

Just enjoy this while it lasts.

26

oliver

I take back what I said. Utopia and Shangri-la have nothing on María del Carmen Morales.

It's Saturday morning, which marks the second night I've spent in her bed. Since I don't own a place in Minneapolis, hiding this from my family hasn't been easy. I'm not one hundred percent sure they've bought the stories I've made up to justify why my rental car has been parked in her driveway this entire time, but since I'm not planning to stay the night often, I think I can cover up.

Hopefully.

We'll have to tell them sooner or later, but I want to enjoy her without everyone sticking their noses for a little. And most importantly, I need to make sure she feels as strongly about me as I feel about her.

It's 9 in the morning and while Carmen is taking a shower *—which she strictly forbade me from interrupting lest I make her late—*I decide to wash the dishes after cooking breakfast for both of us.

She's getting ready to pick up her Araceli and buy a new car for her. I'm not really excited about her spending so much time with her mother while not having anyone to defend her if necessary, but I understand that she needs to do this by herself.

I hear her speakers playing an old reggaeton song in the bedroom and I make my way there. I find her braiding her hair in front of the mirror, already dressed in a high waist mini skirt and a sleeveless crop top I want to peel off already.

"Hey, *hermosa*," I say, grabbing her waist from behind, kissing her neck, "damn, you smell good."

I feel my body getting hot within seconds as I see goosebumps spreading along her arms and neck. She turns around and kisses me.

And what a fucking kiss this is.

These three days, she's been the Queen of PDAs. She's always been physically affectionate, but I'd never experienced it at this level. We went to Lake Harriet Park to walk Juanito yesterday after I was done for the day and she wouldn't stop hugging, kissing, caressing my face and tugging my arm or holding my hand while we walked. We came back a little late after dropping off my dog with my parents and took her for dinner Downtown. All like a normal couple.

"Hey, you," she smiles as we pull away, "you'll be okay without me for a couple of hours?"

"I hope," I kiss her nose, "I need to finish some stuff with the kitchen and might take my parents for a drive somewhere."

"I'm glad you're going," she pulls away to put her phone and makeup bag in her purse, "you've spending too much time here."

"Worth every second," I sit at the edge of the bed, pulling her to my lap, "but you're right, I haven't spent that much time with them, might tell the guys if they want to come."

"Aw," she puts her arms around my neck, "you know I'd love to go with you, but I want to be done with this damn car sooner rather than later."

"I know, baby," I say, caressing her cheek, "we should do something with them tomorrow. Maybe take them for brunch or something?"

"I love that idea."

With a smile, I cup her face and bring her beautiful lips to mine. I meant it as a soft kiss, but once I have her melting against me, it deepens so much I start rubbing her back with my free hand.

She pulls away and we both start laughing.

"You're so mean," she gives me a playful punch on my shoulder, "you want to make me late but don't worry," she softens her tone, "I'll make it up to you. Promise."

Her promise hits me right down my sweatpants and I need to adjust myself before walking her to the car. She goes away with another long kiss goodbye.

The car disappears and I close my eyes, feeling her scent in my nose and her kiss beating on my lips.

Dear God, I don't deserve this woman and you still gave me this chance. Please, please *don't let me screw this up.*

I sigh hard and walk back to my chores in the garage. I click on my Spotify playlist and start a private concert in the garage. The same song I've been playing on repeat, thinking about my girl.

"*Candlelight*" by Relient K. I use a roller sponge as a microphone and sing the lyrics from the bottom of my lungs.

What would she think if I learn this song on my guitar and play it for her? Would she think it's lame? Not to brag, but I'm not that bad. We all inherited music talents from Papá. From the three of us, I'm the one who hasn't used them often until now.

Because of her.

Don't want to put my hopes all the way up but it's impossible.

I keep singing out loud, closing my eyes from time to time like a lovesick kid. Suddenly, the music stops completely, and I jolt in surprise as I feel a hand on my shoulder.

"*FUCKING HELL!*" I shout.

Antonio's high-pitched howl fills the entire garage as I catch my breath. Well, that's a surprise. I haven't heard this guy laughing like this in years.

"The fuck, Oliver?" he says, still laughing.

"Hell, Tony." I punch him on the shoulder, "What the fuck?"

"My mom made some Pepián last night. I'm just here to drop it off." He lifts the pot in his hands, still laughing.

"Well, I'm glad almost shitting my pants is the cause of the laughing dry spell being broken. I'm honored."

"Shut up."

I shake my head and laugh too, signaling with my head and walk towards the door.

"I was about to ask you how you're doing," Antonio says as he puts the pot inside the fridge, "but I can tell you're pretty good."

"Good? Hell no, I'm happy," I cross my arms against my chest and lean on the wall. "No, that's too light. Umm… cheerful?" I put my hand on my chin, "No. Elated? Overjoyed? Out of my mind-ecstatic?" I sigh, wiping my face with both hands, "is there other fucking word for how fucking euphoric I am?"

Antonio studies me for a couple of seconds and a frown starts forming on his brow as he slowly clenches his jaw.

"Holy shit, you slept with her, didn't you?" he mutters between his teeth and closes his eyes shut, pressing the bridge of his nose with his fingers, "Oliver I swear to God I'll *fucking. Kill you.*"

I laugh and walk towards him, taking his head in my hands and giving him a hard kiss to his cheek.

"Yeah, I did," I open my arms wide while he wipes his cheek, "go ahead. Kill me. Now." I hit my chest twice with my fist, "I can die right now as the happiest man *in the world*, loco. I'm so. Fucking. Happy and in love, cabrón. *I'm so in love with that woman.*" I shout the last part.

"Gross. For the love of God shut the fuck up," he covers his ears and shuts his eyes, "I don't need to know."

"You don't get it, right?" I take his hands off his ears, "Tony, I have a chance. It's a miracle. I think this time we're *really* going to be together. It's unreal."

He sighs and glares at me before going back to the fridge for a beer. I know it's a little weird for him. After all, they were raised together as siblings. But the dude needs to suck it up, he's the only one I can trust right now. From all of us, he's always been the most analytical and down to earth.

"Okay, so you actually talked to her?" he drops himself to the couch, "you opened up, clarified what you needed and asked for forgiveness?"

"Yes and yes."

"Okay, great," he smiles, "that's good. How about the future? What are you guys going to do? Is she moving to California with you? Are you coming back? What's the plan?"

"Whoa, hold up," I laugh, "the plan? What are you talking about? It's only been two days."

"Yes, *the plan*, Oliver. After you told her you love her." He runs his tongue inside his lower lip, "you didn't just jump into bed asking for a good time, right?"

"I ummm…" I scratch the back of my neck, "we didn't really… I mean, we did but…"

"No puede ser. You did just that, didn't you?" He leans forward. His brows in a straight line. "You told her you wanted to have a good time without setting expectations? Is that what you did?"

"No," I sigh, "I told her I wanted to take things slow, have some fun and see where things go. I know she's scared and I want to—"

"*Qué la chingada*, Oliver!" he wipes his face with both hands, "what are you? Eighteen?"

"I just don't want to pressure her," I take a long swig of my beer and sigh, "I don't understand you, you know? You're always preaching about not being impulsive and how being reckless leads to disaster and now you want me to push things with her?" I close my eyes for a moment, "we have too much baggage to rush into things, Tony. I don't want to scare her away. She seems open to giving me a chance after the biggest fuckup of my life and going on too hard, too fast can kill it. I–I can't lose her again."

"This isn't about not being reckless, Ol," he sighs, "this is about being assertive before it's too late. You're only going to lose her again if you're not clear with your intentions."

This. This is exactly what I wanted to avoid. I have no idea why Antonio is pushing this, he knows exactly what's at risk, everything I could lose if I don't make things right.

"I. don't. want. To *pressure her*," I snap, "we agreed to leave the past behind, but the fact is, it still happened. There's still a lot to unpack and figure out. I don't want to rush her. I don't want to put so many expectations she might not be ready for."

"Oliver," he lowers his voice and shakes his head, "this isn't some chick you just met and hooked up with. This is the woman you've been in love with *forever*. You can't give me that bullshit, you've had ten years already."

"What aren't you telling me, Tony?" I stand up and pace around the living room, "why are you pushing this? I'm telling you I'm not ready."

"You're never ready, Ol," he laughs sarcastically and stands up to face me, "you're never ready to talk, never ready to *stay*… you weren't ready before and if you keep going like this, you never will. And this time?" He shakes his head fast, "there won't be any do-overs. You will really lose her and won't *ever* get over her."

There's something not sitting right with me. This is the same tone all of them have used whenever they'd mention Carmen in the past. Hushing each other, exchanging glances with one another like they have a secret.

"Tony, we've been friends our *entire lives*, cabrón," I put a hand on his shoulder, "we know each other better than other people can say they know their *siblings*… So, I'll ask you one more time and I hope you can be honest. What the hell are you not telling me?"

"Mierda," he swallows hard and shakes his head. After a small pause, he talks. "The day you asked us never to mention her again we knew things. Things we wanted to tell you that we knew could solve it all, but you shut us off and Chip didn't want to talk about it either. So, we made a pact of never talking about it so we wouldn't mess things up even more," he clenches his jaw and scratches his beard, "so if you ever wanted to solve things, you'd have to figure it out yourselves.

I need to honor that vow I made to the guys but just because you're about to fuck up the only chance you'll ever get, I'll tell you one thing only," he pokes my chest, "be honest and open about your intentions. Be clear about your feelings. Tell her you fucking love her and prove it to her with your actions. Tell her you're in for the long run. Don't be afraid to ask her exactly how she feels and what she wants. Stop *assuming* you know… Do you trust me?"

"With my life." I say quietly.

"Then do it before it's too late," he pats my shoulder, "you're braver than you think you are. I'm proud of you for talking to her about the past, that must've been tough," he smiles and pats my cheek, "but you deserve it, and she does too. You're my brother and she's my sister, I don't want you to get hurt. And contrary to what Angel ever said and thought… I've always known you're meant to be together."

I just nod and he smiles. We finish our beers and walk through the kitchen and garage, showing him the progress. We grab more beers and he helps me finish the rest of the doors. When we're done, we call my siblings and agree to go to my parents' house to play videogames and watch movies with Papá.

Antonio's words don't leave my head for the rest of the afternoon. I'm not entirely convinced this is the right way to go but I do trust him. And I'm willing to do anything to keep her with me, even doing what scares me the most.

I just need to find the right time.

27

carmen

Fuck my life.

How difficult can it be to choose a car, test it and buy it? How long should that take? One? Three hours at the most?

Four seems like a lot but it still seems like it's too little time for Araceli Morales who made me go to four different car dealerships in Minneapolis and she didn't like any of them. She managed to find the most ridiculous things to complain about in every single car we tried out. She cussed out the clerks for not being able to please her and proceeded to cuss *me* out for not knowing what the hell she wanted.

And how many did we buy? None.

Nada.

And who did she blame? Yes, of course me and my sister, her ungrateful and cheap daughters who obviously grow their money on trees and don't want to buy her the extravagant car she says she deserves that would cost more than what we do in a year.

I'm so pissed I don't even know what to do with myself. As much as I try and give everything in me, I can't seem to please my mother at all. Nothing is ever good for her. Nothing is ever enough.

And as much as I want to believe I can change it, I am never going to be good enough for her.

I had to listen to her whining and complaining about it the whole way back to her house. She wanted me to go in and help her find another dealership online but I made an excuse, told her to let me know when she was ready to go to another dealership and left.

I felt so frustrated and sad that I had to pull over in front of a park and calm myself down. I texted Oliver to let him know and then my sister Rocío, who told me to text her when we chose a car.

Oliver replies first.

Oliver: Mujer hermosa *three kiss emojis* I'm sorry it didn't go well with your mom. I'm over my parents with the guys. When you're done we can take Juanito and get something to eat, whatever you want. You deserve it.

Carmen: Need *teary eye emoji*. We could do that or we could go home and cook together if you want? We can pick up groceries on the way. What would you like?

Oliver: As long as I can eat all of you first, I don't care what we eat later. *six drooling emojis*.

Who the fuck needs panties anyways?

And this is why my heart is so *confused*.

I take a deep, shaky breath and reply.

Carmen: I like that idea *kiss emoji* see you in a little bit, guapo.

I see the three dots on the screen, meaning that he's replying to the text when a Facetime call from Rocío comes in. I hit the green button at the first tone and I can see her also inside her car, her hair pulled up in a ponytail and no makeup on. Her skin is radiant as always.

God, my sister is gorgeous.

"Hey babe," I say with a lazy tone, "where are you?"

"I just came out of the nail salon. I was getting a mani when you texted me," she says with her eyebrow lifted, "but all the excitement flew away when I read it, what the fuck does that woman want?"

I let out a long breath, "I have no idea. You should've seen her how she treated those people. That poor guy at Honda had a Latino last name and she kept speaking to him in Spanish even though he kept saying he didn't speak it... She shushed me so many times when I tried to translate, she didn't give a shit. I felt so bad, he was so embarrassed."

She groans, "no, please don't tell me. I don't want to know."

"I don't know what to do, Rosy." I cry, "no matter what I do, no matter what I say or how much I show up, she is still not happy with me."

"So don't," she shrugs and shakes her head, "I already told you but you don't listen, Maria del Carmen. You need to stop trying to make her love you like a devoted mother would. She is not and *never* will be. If you keep trying to make her act like the loving mother she isn't... that broken arm is going to be sweet tea compared to what she could be."

Araceli's involvement in the incident that got me a broken arm is something I rarely mention, so hearing my sister reminding me of it makes me feel like she sucker punched me in the gut. I want to fight it, tell her that she isn't that evil. That she's just sick. That I still believe she can change if we just help her but first, that would open a wound that's already forgotten. Also, deep inside I know she's probably right. Maybe we just didn't have any luck when it came to our parents. I know how bad intentioned and mean mom can be. I know what she's capable of. Still, I can't seem to have it in me to pull away completely.

"I'm sorry for being too harsh," she keeps going, "I just want you to be happy. And being around Araceli will do the opposite."

"I just want this car thing to be over already." I let out a long breath and rest my head on the window, "I have a lot going on right now to deal with her on top of everything."

She lifts up an eyebrow. "Is Oliver still giving you shit?"

I feel my cheeks going hot at the mention of Oliver. Rocío

seems to notice because she stares at me with a quizzical look in her eyes and when I don't say anything, she asks.

"Chip?" she gets closer to her phone, "is there anything you need to tell me?"

I groan and wipe my face with both hands.

"I've been sleeping with him." I say, still covering my face.

"Excuse me," my sister says with an unamused chuckle, "I think you said you slept with Oliver? I'm sure it's another Oliver because it cannot be possible that you slept with the same Oliver Santiago Rodriguez we know?"

"I'm not saying it again if you don't want me to." I uncover my face.

"What?"

In a couple of minutes, I tell her everything. How Oliver ended up fixing my kitchen, my debacle at work. And how a little comfort from Oliver ended up in the best night of my entire life.

"Okay, first of all," Rocío says after I'm done, "your boss is a fucking jerk. I already told you, you should quit and start your own fucking business. God knows you're capable of it. And second, at least tell me the sex is good."

I ignore the comment of me quitting my job and take a deep breath before answering.

"Good?" I scoff, "that's an understatement. I can barely walk and my heart is going to explode."

"Okay, so he pulled his head out of his ass, I don't see what the problem is then?"

"The problem is that he doesn't want anything serious," I purse my lips, "he wants to *see what happens* and you know that's a code for disappearing later."

"Cerote, hijo de puta," *son of a bitch*. "He really said that? Those exact words came out of his mouth?"

"Right after an entire night of banging my headboard against the wall." I drop my head back, "He said it wasn't just a hookup and I mean…I do believe what he said about Susan and his engagement but… I just have a bad feeling, you know?" my voice breaks, "that whole *take it slow* doesn't sit right with me. We already had ten years and it feels like it's just an excuse to pack his things and leave me when the time is up. It's happened before."

Rocio looks at me with concern, "look, you know I love him and hate him at the same time… but maybe he really is trying to take things slow. He's an idiot but I don't know, I don't want to think he's a player… what do the guys say?"

I let out an unamused chuckle, "well, he asked me not to tell the guys, how about that? I don't even know if he told them he broke up with Susan."

Her expression drops immediately and a frown forms on her brows. She knows how big that is, we tell each other everything.

"Oh baby," Rocío says, "I wish I could hug you right now."

My tears start falling. Rocío doesn't say anything and lets me cry for a little bit.

Why is it always like this? I don't need a guy to make me happy, I've been happy by myself for a long time. It's just that sometimes I crave that closeness with another person. I crave being with someone who wants to share that happiness with me, someone who thinks I'm the most amazing person. Oliver keeps making me feel like that but wants to hide it from the world when I have been waiting for years to say it out loud.

"Why do I always have to be the one they want to hook up for a while and then toss away? I don't get it. I know I deserve better but goddamn, why does it have to be this difficult?"

"Babe, I'm sorry to tell you this but I'm glad none of those assholes have stayed. None of them deserve you."

"Well, I guess we'll never know."

"What if you talk to the guys? Maybe Tony or Jake can talk some sense into him."

I shake my head, "I don't want to cause any trouble between them."

"Well, you are worth the trouble," Rocío raises her voice, "you're worth standing up to them if there's any trouble to begin with. You only hide something you're not proud of and you are *the motherfucking prize*. You need to either talk to the guys or talk to him... Be honest with him... if he cares for you as a friend he needs to respect your feelings over a fling."

"I... I don't know," I whisper, "I think I'd only humiliate myself if I do that. Besides... Even with all my doubts I can't stop hearing a little voice that says that maybe this time will be different."

"Carmencita, look at me mamita," Rocío says and I look directly at the phone, "love is meant to be proven, not just performed. Love is a decision. Love is a fucking *choice*... That's it, that's the bar... you need to either make the bar clear for him and be clear with what you need or... you have to analyze if this is all worth the hurt you'll go through when the time's up," I nod and she keeps going, "if this was another guy you just met I'd say you have fun because you deserve all the orgasms," I laugh through tears, "but this is the guy you've loved since you're seven... and you deserve to be loved back. It's a two way street... we're not made to give all of ourselves without receiving all of the other person in return."

God, I love my big sister. She always knows what I need to hear, even if it breaks my heart for a good reason.

I know I don't need validation, I know I don't need to prove I'm worth loving. I did it for years with my mother and later with all the assholes I dated. But on the other hand, I can't lie to myself, I don't want to break things off. I do want to see where this goes. My mind is telling me I should run but my heart is asking completely different questions. *What if he stays this time? What if this is the one time it all works out?*

"I can handle it," I say after a couple of seconds of silence, "I really want to give him the chance to prove me wrong."

Rocío blinks a couple of times before she talks, "Okay, I'll trust you... but just keep in mind: Just because you're used to pain, it doesn't mean you have to endure it."

Wow.

I let out a shaky breath and let that sink in. Am I so used to this type of pain that I just welcome it in my life? Maybe, but the truth is, I've spent ten years of my life thinking there wasn't any chance for Oliver to come back into my life. Not even as a friend. I can't waste this chance. I *have* to try. I *have* to know.

"I'm here for you, mi reina," Rocío says, "even if we can't see each other in person all the time. I'm here and I love you. You have no idea how much."

"I love you too, hon." I smile.

We say our goodbyes as I dry my tears and start my car. I try to calm myself down as I drive to Marta and Alberto's house.

If all turns out the way I'm afraid of and a fling is all I get, I just hope he wants to stay friends next time he leaves.

Even if he takes my heart with him again.

28

carmen

It's been a month since Oliver and I started this secret adventure. Three weeks of falling more in love with him and having the best boyfriend I've ever had. Not even being my boyfriend.

We see each other almost every day. The nights we don't spend together, he sends me texts like *"Good night, mi amor"* and *"Good morning, belleza."* He calls me when I get off from work to ask about my day.

When he does spend the night, he wakes me up with a kiss and makes me breakfast while I'm showering. When I get home, he has hot food for me, rubs my feet and my back… and makes love to me all night long.

He finished the kitchen just a few days after the first night and the results are beautiful. He even offered to remodel the living room to match it but he already did too much, I don't want to take advantage.

Everything he says and does scream *forever* to me but he hasn't actually said he wants it. He hasn't asked me to go back to California with him or hinted he wants to stay in Minneapolis. I'm too scared to ask, to burst the little bubble we're living in where everything is perfect and we love each other, even though none of us have said the words.

Work has been a warzone. Simon has been more annoying than usual since he kicked me out of the X Games. He got me a photoshoot with a retired Pro Jet Ski racer a week ago and since then he thinks he's a fucking hero. It was a simple interview inside a studio, no action, no movement. *So much for an Extreme Sports Photographer.* Simon said it was better than nothing, but that fucker doesn't know who I am.

I'm no *'better than nothing'* kind of *girl.* I'm a go big or get the fuck out of here kind of *woman.*

I'm driving with Araceli once again to pick up a car for her. This is the sixth dealership we visit and I just hope it can be the last.

When we get to the dealership, the host directs us to a waiting room. My mom goes to the bathroom while we're assigned to a clerk. I'm sitting down with some coffee I got from one of the desks and my phone chimes with a text.

Oliver: Crossing fingers for you, mi amor. *heart emoji* I just got to the hospital, we're just waiting for them to call Papá in. I'll miss you tonight but will stop by tomorrow with coffee and donuts.

Be still my little heart.

Alberto has a checkup with his cardiologist today and Oliver wanted to be present. They will go to the mall afterwards to buy a stationary bike and a treadmill so he can exercise at home. I wanted to go with them but I need to get this done already or it'll drive me crazy.

I haven't said anything to Oliver but I've secretly been researching Alzheimer's. Oliver refuses to talk about it but I've started seeing certain things in Alberto that worry me. I stopped by the other day to pick up Juanito from their house and caught him with his shirt wrongly buttoned up and having some trouble using the microwave. When I tried to help him out, he shoved my hand off and glared at me. Something that's never happened before. He blinked fast, apologized before leaving the plate on the counter and going up to his room.

I don't want to assume, I don't want to say anything to them that might upset them or worry them before they get a diagnosis. It really could be nothing. Alberto's appointment at the Mayo Clinic is in a week and even if Oliver doesn't say anything I know he's worried.

I have faith, though. I will stay hopeful but still prepared if they need me to help with anything.

Carmen: Can you be more perfect? *drool emoji*

Oliver: Only when it comes to you, mi vida. *wink emoji*

Carmen: Jeez, are my charms that seductive?

Oliver: Want me to show you?

I feel myself blushing and suppress a chuckle.

Carmen: OMG *open mouth emoji* You're offering nudes, Big Guy? I'm in a public place with my mother, remember?

Oliver: Holy shit, Maria del Carmen. You have a hella dirty mind and I fucking love it.

Oliver: I was going to offer to get tacos after you drop off Araceli.

Oliver: You thought I was sending nudes? I'm in the waiting room of a hospital with both my parents. Orale. *devil emoji*

I start chuckling. These funny moments, the flirty banter, the way I can be myself with him without any barriers. Without having to walk around eggshells every time I talk to him. I've never had this with anyone. This connection isn't casual. This is something more.

Then why do I feel like he's going to leave anyways?

I shove the thought away and reply.

Carmen: OK, my bad. *eye roll emoji* See? You corrupted my innocent mind. Anyways, I have class at Hope after this. Couldn't do tacos until much later.

Oliver: You made me laugh so hard people are staring. Yeah, I forgot it's Wednesday. I promised my parents to cook dinner for them later.

Oliver: Anyways, I'm really going to miss you tonight. I promise I'll make it up to you, hermosa.

Carmen: I'll miss you too. I'll let you know how it goes.

Oliver: *fingers crossed emoji*

My mother is still in the bathroom when the host comes to get me and direct me to a clerk. When I see the guy standing, my heart completely stops and I feel a cold wave of air freezing me completely.

My nightmare, the worst mistake I've ever made in my life smirks at me as I approach. A mix of anger and complete terror takes over my stomach and for a moment I feel like vomiting.

"What the fuck are you doing here, Alan?" I hiss as I get closer.

From all the places I feared I was going to bump into him, this was the last one.

Alan Danfrie, my ex-boyfriend.

The *last* boyfriend.

29

carmen

The past

I've dated my fair amount of assholes.

And I thought I had a very good bullshit meter when it came to them. I thought I knew how to spot them and dodge the bullet as it came. That's why meeting Alan was like meeting Lucifer himself.

A demon dressed up as an angel.

I ended up falling in love with the devil thinking he was God.

The scariest part? You don't even notice the flames until you're already calcined.

People always criticize women for falling for these pieces of shit but reality is, none of them knows how difficult it is to recognize the signs when you're being treated like a queen. When they give you everything you thought you ever wanted. When you feel like they're asking you about your life and your past pain because they really want to know, not because they're actually saving ammunition against you later.

I met Alan my second year of college in a Marketing class we took together and flirted for months. He's quite a looker. Tall, dark hair, green eyes and the type of body that belongs in romance books. I had never considered myself prettier than average, all of my exes had ended up with the opposite of me, so I always doubted myself more than I'm proud to admit. So when he started smiling and winking, when he made any excuse to talk to me after class or sit next to me… I let my head and heart go all the way up.

We were paired up for a big project at the end of the semester and the excitement in his face made me melt.

"My lucky day," he said.

"Is that so?" I smiled.

"Very much so," he winked, "I've been waiting to talk to you for so long. You have no idea what you do to me, Carmen."

He asked me out just a week after we started working on that project and didn't leave each other's side for months. He would pick me up every morning and walk me to class. We would spend every single second of the day together and when we were apart, we would text nonstop or talk over the phone for hours.

He bought me clothes.

He took me to fancy dinners.

And something I haven't told anyone… he was the one who took away my virginity.

Yep. I was a late bloomer. Not that I didn't touch myself and took care of my needs on my own, it's just that I was so scared of being intimate with a man and getting hurt. But Alan was so sweet, so convincing and even though he never made me come once… I couldn't take the risk of losing him.

I was so codependent I couldn't see straight.

I thought that finally, *finally* I was going to be able to move on from Oliver because this was exactly what I wanted: Undivided attention and protection. Someone finally needed me so much that he wouldn't let anyone near me because he was scared of losing me.

I should've seen it for what it was when the little things started happening. Like when he started ordering my food in restaurants because he said I was getting chunky. Or choosing my clothes because he said the "skater style" wasn't "too feminine". Maybe if I would've seen it right then, it wouldn't have gotten as far as him refusing to touch me because "I gained weight and it was starting to feel gross to him" or the never ending fights every time I wanted to go out with the guys and he wouldn't let me.

"How many times have I told you Jake and Ethan are like my brothers?" I would say.

"That's the issue, Carmen. They're *not*. Men and women can't be friends."

"That's so stupid… and I already told you Antonio is going to be there. You can't tell me you don't even trust him."

"Did you just call me stupid?"

"I didn't call you stupid, I said the idea is stupid."

"Don't you ever call me stupid again!" He yelled, "I don't know if I could be with someone like this, Carmen. I don't know if I feel safe in a relationship where all of your friends are guys and you don't respect me. If things keep going like this…"

"No, please don't." I would say, feeling a rush of dread around my body, throwing myself in his arms, "I promise I won't ever call you like that. I will watch my words. I'm sorry. I'm sorry."

"You know I love you, right?" He kissed my temple.

"I know, I know and I'm sorry. I'll call them and say I can't go. But please don't leave me."

Every fight we ever had ended up like that. When I didn't want to get up early on a Saturday morning, when I didn't want to go to the gym, when I refused to change majors. When I refused to sale my bikes. Between school, job hunting and trying to make him feel important and secure in the relationship I became a prisoner without even noticing. I thought that was my contribution to the relationship. That he was the one settling for less.

Still, I didn't see the downfall. The jokes he laughed about were no longer funny. The pictures I'd take weren't good enough anymore. My efforts to make things better didn't work. I didn't know what to do to keep him happy, to bring back the Alan I fell in love with at the beginning.

I was so blinded that I thought it was me who was fucking it all up. He had been the only one that had wanted to stay and I needed to fix it. Even if I had to throw away everything else that made me happy.

"I don't like him," Antonio said to me, "I don't like the way he talks to you and I don't like he's isolating you from everyone in your life. We barely see you anymore, Chip… Ethan says you've left him on read and Jake is sure you blocked him, what the hell?"

"School is crazy, Tony," I lied, "It's my last year and I need to focus. That's all."

"Just know we're here. Always."

Now that I reflect on it, I can acknowledge that deep inside I knew he was right.

But after Angel died, everyone started building a life on their own. Even when the guys started working at the same shop, they were in their own little car world. My sister was far away and I never really had any friends besides them. I didn't have anyone. I was scared of being alone. I was scared of being rejected by the only person who didn't grow up with me that thought I was worth his time.

So I did the unthinkable.

I didn't tell anyone about my graduation so they wouldn't show up.

I thought it was going to give me some peace of mind but I was fucking miserable. Devastated. I sent them all an email apologizing after a couple of days and instead of resentment I got emails back telling me how concerned they were.

Still, I kept trying to make Alan happy.

Just a couple of months after that, Alan and Araceli finally convinced me not to work. I spent a long year secluded in my mother's house doing chores, helping my mother in the restaurant and going to church with both of them on Sundays. At this point, the guys were panicking. Antonio kept sending me emails with articles about how to recognize abusers and signs of emotional and mental violence. I read a few but once they became more and more relatable I stopped.

It was during that time that Hope Center started to flourish after Jacob and Juliana spent years working on this project. When I told Alan I wanted to get involved, he laughed at my face. Even though Araceli started helping out because her friends from church were.

"You know that creating a non-profit requires money, right?" Alan said, "that little project isn't going to save the world. It's not worth your time, baby. You should invest your time in something you can profit from."

I was gutted. But the more Jacob and Antonio emailed me about it, the more I wanted to know.

One day, I secretly slipped out of the house while Alan was having drinks with his cousin and met Antonio at Hope Lutheran Church. They were using the Sunday School classrooms at the time and had already bought the piece of land next to the church. He showed me the plans for the building, the written project and the list of donors.

I fell in love with it. It was a dream come true for the community. My heart ached for it and I couldn't say no to getting involved.

"Chip, I want you to meet Bernie Garza," Antonio said as we entered Juliana's office, "she's the director of Sullivan Creatives, the advertising agency that donated the money for the land. They will also make a fundraising event to get more donors."

"Oh my goodness, I'm so thrilled to meet you," I said as I shook Bernie's hand, "I've never met a Creative Director before."

"Nice to meet you, Carmen," she said, "Antonio showed me some of your work, you're very talented. Sullivan is actually looking for a couple of Graphic Designer interns if you're interested."

"But... but... I don't have any experience," I laughed nervously, "and you don't even know me."

"I know enough," she smiled, "and well, that's what internships are for, aren't they?"

We talked for about fifteen minutes and exchanged emails. She guaranteed me a spot in the agency with the promise of a full time job after six months if I did well.

And I noticed that for the first time in almost four years, I didn't care if Alan was going to be happy with this or not.

I said yes.

For me.

And for no one else.

But just as I expected, Alan gave me hell for it.

"You think an agency like that is going to be flowers and rainbows?" He said, "they're going to take advantage of you. It's either that or making copies and pass on coffee. Besides, you don't have a car, you don't even know how to use the bus. I can't take you, I have to work too. What are you going to do without me?"

I'm not going to lie, I was scared about every single thing he mentioned. But the moment I crossed the doors of that office, I didn't care anymore. I was in full learning-mode and wanted to take on the world. More than I ever was in college.

Fred and Bernie moved me around every department for three months so I could learn from everyone and try my potential in every area so they could see what was the best fit for me. They put me to work, just like everyone else. And when Fred discovered I was a photographer, Bernie handed me the most expensive camera I've ever held in my life right away.

I loved my job.

I didn't care if I didn't have a car. I learned how to use the bus and walked everywhere no matter the rain, blizzard or if God was baking cookies outside. No matter if my mother or my so-called boyfriend didn't approve.

And I still stay with him.

Because he was there.

Because from all the girls in the world he could choose, he was choosing me.

Simply because of that.

My first solo photoshoot with Sullivan was a Motocross event for one of their biggest clients. I wasn't feeling confident but Fred and Bernie thought otherwise.

The night went on so fast and I was having so much fun I didn't realize it was getting late. I was supposed to ride with a co-worker and neither of us could move until the event was over. So I texted Alan I was going back later than expected.

Right when the night ended, Fred and Bernie pulled me away to offer me a full time position with a *Senior* salary. I was ecstatic. For the first time in my life, the hard work had finally paid off.

When I called Alan, I didn't notice the 96 texts and 63 missed calls.

"Hey baby," I said, putting the camera on the bag, "you'll never guess what just happened. I just got hired! I have a full time job!"

"So that's what you've been doing?" he said, his voice hard. Almost macabre, "fucking some executive all night so they'll give you a job before six months. Nice. My lying girlfriend is also a cheater."

"The fuck, Alan?" I scream-whispered, "I've been working. Working. You can call Fred or Bernie. They've been here all the time."

"You're a fucking whore, that's what you are. You're not going to take that job or we're done. You hear me?"

Tears rolled down my eyes with each word. I was angry, hurt and I felt like the veil had finally dropped. How did I put up with this for such a long time? When did I start believing I deserve this? I gave up my energy, my love, my passions, dreams and family… for this?

"Wait a goddamn minute." I muttered between my teeth. "You have no right. No. Fucking. Right to talk to me like I'm a worthless piece of shit," my voice broke, "I've been faithful and loyal to your bullshit for the past four years. Even when you've told me how low you think of me. You're not my fucking dad to give me orders. I'm tired of you. I'm done. I'm not letting you do this anymore."

"You ungrateful bitch," he laughed, "I've been putting up with you all these years and this is what you do? You really think I'm an idiot, don't you? You think I don't know you've been cheating on me this entire time and I still stayed with you. There's no fucking way you'll get a job like that without giving them a cheap fuck. You're lazy, mediocre and plain. Now you better be at home in thirty minutes or we're through. I'm calling your mom."

My heart ached. This is what he always thought of me and never had the balls to tell me plain and simple. It hurt. Too much. But I realized it wasn't because I loved him. It was because for the first time in four years I realized I didn't deserve this.

God, is this as good as it's going to get for me?

I felt a breath of fresh air the second the question crossed my mind.

"That's it," I said, "we're done. You and I are over. You can call my mother to whine about it because, guess what? I'm not coming home. Ever. Don't call me. I don't want to see you ever again."

I felt as if someone had just lifted a huge weight off my shoulders. As my tears fell free, I dialed the only person I could think of.

"Hey," Antonio said. His voice was groggy but I could hear the concern in his tone, "everything alright?"

"No," I cried, "I uhhh–I was wondering if I can–if I can come stay with you for tonight?"

I heard him moving the second I finished the sentence.

"Where are you?"

"Watertown, I can get a ride to—"

"Send me your location, I'll pick you up."

He showed up half an hour later with Jacob, Ethan and Vince. None of them asked me questions, they just held me, scratched my hair while I cried and spent the rest of the night watching movies and eating junk with me. I cried, ask for forgiveness a million times and they kept telling me it was Okay. That they had my back and they'd never hold it against me.

The next morning, Antonio helped me pick up my things from my mother's house. The neighbors probably thought she was being killed by the way she was screaming and crying. We even had to call Tia Carmela so she wouldn't try to slap me.

The next part of the story has two versions. The one everyone knows is that Alan convinced me to talk a few weeks later. Then I met him at a mall where he tried to kiss me and when I pulled away, he broke my arm.

It wasn't quite like that. But I kept it that way for the sake of peace.

It wasn't Alan who called me, it was Araceli. He convinced her to set up a meeting with me at the restaurant. He kneeled down and cried like a baby, apologizing. Asking for another chance and telling me how much he loved me and wanted to make things right. I was fed up already and didn't want to listen to him, so I turned around to leave but the moment I did it, he grabbed me by my left arm.

"Alan, you're hurting me," I cried, trying to get him off me.

"You're hurting me more," he said, twisting harder, "I love you. I fucking love you. How can you do this to me? How can you not forgive me if I'm telling you I'm sorry."

"You're fucking crazy."

"You are making me crazy, Carmen."

I screamed for help but no one heard me. Araceli and tía Carmela were already gone and we were so far back in the building no one would ever hear.

He pulled my hair and twisted my arm so hard I felt I was going to faint. When I heard the crack, I finally passed out. I woke up with my entire body in pain and couldn't move for what felt like an eternity. I didn't know where my phone was, so with the little strength I had left, I walked myself to the next door tienda and passed out in front of the owners.

I woke up in the ER with a cast and an IV connected to my vein.

I'd love to say it was my feminist spirit and high dignity what encouraged me to press charges, but it was the hospital staff after questioning me about the incident who figured out I was attacked.

I was embarrassed.

Angry.

Scared.

I felt guilty for letting things go this far, but after a long talk with the Sheriff and the station's counselor, I was convinced it was my responsibility.

I wish I could've hidden this from the guys, but it was after midnight when I got back to the house. I'll never forget the panic in their eyes when they saw me coming out of the cab. They'd been calling me nonstop. The four of them were worrying sick, Antonio and Jacob had their eyes swollen when they held me tight.

They were about to report me as a missing person.

I couldn't lie to them about Alan, but my heart still wanted to protect Araceli. Even then they went crazy. I had to assure them over and over that he was already in jail because otherwise they would've killed him with their bare hands.

I just wanted everything to be over and finally be at peace.

It took me a while to talk to Araceli again, especially because she insisted for a while that Alan wouldn't have done that without a good reason. That he was a good man in love and he didn't know how to prove it to me.

That was the catalyst I needed to put a down payment for my own house and never go back to my mother's house again. I had to call my sister and ask her to forgive me for pushing her to talk to Araceli. We cried so hard that night I told her what really happened and got even closer afterwards.

I told Oliver once I'm grateful for my mother and that's true. Although I still have many unresolved issues, I can't find it in me to dismiss her from my life completely. Maybe I'm just hopeful that she really isn't a villain.

I hope one day I get to know for sure.

30

carmen

Present day

"Well, hello there," Alan extends his hand.

Don't fucking touch me, asshole," I shove my hand, "what the hell are you doing here?"

"Delicate and soft as always," he laughs, "well, I work here. Good to see you too."

Alan is charming as fuck, his smile and tone look so genuine you'd think he's a saint. That's why he's always been great at sales. But I know this smirk. I know this tone.

"How?" I whisper, "you're supposed to be miles away from Minneapolis."

"Is that so?" he straightens his back, "I'm supposed to be miles away from you. Which I have for a while. This isn't me doing anything wrong… I know it's a little disappointing to know you didn't ruin my life after all."

The restraining order was supposed to be only 300 ft away but

I know his attorney suggested he moved away. Last I knew, he was living in Wisconsin. It'd given me a little peace for a while but knowing he's here will add another layer of anxiety to my already stressed out heart.

"Me? *I* didn't ruin your life, *you* ruined mine."

I see my mother in the corner of my eye and I rush to her, "we need to go."

"Why?" she frowns, "I like it here," she looks over my shoulder, "Alan?"

Shit.

She walks right by me and even pushes me a bit, throwing herself to his arms.

"So good to see you, Araceli," he says in Spanish. He pulls away and looks at me from head to toe. "I can ask someone else to take care of you."

"No," she says, patting his hand, "I want you. You know us so well, you'll take care of us."

"Mamá!" I scream-whisper.

He puts his arm around her and looks at me, "If you let me, I think I'll be able to help you."

That evil smile. It looks so familiar that I feel nauseated and want to smash it into the concrete at the same time.

"Mami, please?" I say, pulling her away from him, "do you remember what he did to me?"

"Yes. And you sent him to jail after he said he was sorry. I'm sure he's a changed man now," she whispers, "besides, this is his job. We're already here." She pats my cheek, "you're acting like a child."

Of course from all the places she will want the one where the asshole who ruined my life is working. Just my fucking luck.

She smiles and turns around to tug his arm. He walks towards his desk and starts asking her about the type of car she's looking for and what kind of model she would like to see first.

I follow them and limit my words to yes and no answers and very minimal information about our budget and her basic needs. I let her do all the rest. While we go to the lot to see the models, I try to think about happy thoughts but it's almost impossible with my mother complaining with him like a longtime friend, playing victim the way she does with everyone she crosses paths with.

"I am so lonely. Carmen doesn't even visit anymore."

"I think the Lord will be taking me home soon."

"I'm sick, you know? But none of my daughters want to take me to the doctor."

"I ran out of medicine last week… I think I might have to ask for financial aid."

Major *fucking* eyeroll.

I don't understand why she needs the attention of this asshole when the only thing I've ever done is give her mine. Why does it have to be him? Is she really that oblivious?

It's in moments like this that I envy my sister and all the distance she's put between her and Araceli.

My mother finally decides to try a Honda Pilot 2015. We test it around the neighborhood in silence and return to the dealership when she finally makes her decision. Even though I feel relieved that she finally picked a fucking car and this is almost over, I still need to endure the never-ending paperwork and payment arrangement talk that takes forever. By the time we get to it, it turns out there's a problem with my mom's insurance that will take until tomorrow to solve.

"There's no way I'm coming back here," I say to Araceli.

"Of course she can't," she laughs nervously and looks at Alan, "she works in the morning and comes back pretty late."

"Still working at the agency?" Alan asks.

"None of your fucking business," I say between gritted teeth, "when can we pick up the car?"

"I can give you a call, why don't you leave your pho—"

"In your fucking dreams, Alan Danfrie," I interrupt, "cut the bullshit. What time?"

"Patoja abusiva." *Disrespectful child*, Araceli scolds me. Slapping my arm before she turns to him. "I can get a ride from my sister. Can I give you my number?"

He hasn't taken his eyes off me and I try to glare to disguise my panic. I'm sweating cold because of the way he's looking at me. He does it for a long time then curves his lips into a malicious smile. He blinks fast and looks at my mother.

"Absolutely," he says, handing her a piece of paper, "I'll give you a call as soon as everything's ready. Shouldn't be later than noon."

She returns the piece of paper and gives him another hug before we get out of there. I could give her a long lecture about how abusive and toxic her behavior was today, but it'll be like talking to a dead wall. I can't believe I'm saying this but… I think I'll limit my visits again.

I drop her off without saying goodbye and make my way to Hope. I'm glad to have this safe space to get my mind full of positive vibes.

31

carmen

I teach my class and let myself relax. These kids crack me up and give me the best time. They're talented, quirky and know how to turn every class into a party. Still, I'm not feeling like myself, even some of the kids noticed.

When I'm done, I make my way to the front door. I can hear a music class in the background and the chattering of the kids lining up in the dining room to get their food. I stop at the door and I laugh as I notice Fred serving today and a couple of teenage girls trying to flirt with him.

I'm about to turn around when I hear Jacob singing my name from behind me.

"Chip, Chip, Chiiiiip," he sings before exaggerating a kiss on my cheek, "*muaaahh!*"

"Hey, what's up?" I pull him into a hug.

Damn, I needed this hug and I didn't even know until this moment.

I don't notice I'm holding onto him for too long until he pulls away and looks at me.

"Hey," Jacob frowns, "you doing Okay?"

"Yeah, I'm fine," I laugh nervously and start walking away. I only take two steps and trip over my feet, bumping into a desk, making all the pamphlets and pens on it fly away.

"Shit." I mutter as I kneel down to pick them up.

Jacob chuckles silently and kneels down to help me. When we're done, he lifts up an eyebrow and gives me a knowing smile. I swear this guy has supernatural vision, he looks through me as if it was his job.

"Want tacos?" he asks.

"Same place?"

He motions with his head and I follow.

We drive separately to my house to leave my car and then walk a few blocks to our favorite taqueria. We order our usual: *tacos de birria* for him and *al pastor* for me. We start talking about him and he smoothly changes the subject until he plain and simply asks me what's bothering me.

Horrified.

That's the only way I can describe the shake of his head and heavy breathing as I talk.

"You need to call the police," he says, leaning forward on the table.

"He didn't do anything wrong, Jake," I say before I take a bite of my taco, speaking around my food. "He was just doing his job."

"Then why the hell didn't you turn around and leave?"

"It was the only way that Araceli was going to finally buy a fucking car," I look down in defeat, "I tried to talk to her and go somewhere else but then—"

I stop myself and look away. After the Alan fiasco, I got used to hiding the details of what Araceli did or didn't do to me. I already know what they think and I don't want to keep having the same pointless conversation.

"Then what?" he tries to catch my gaze, "what, Chip?" I look back at him and I can see him getting annoyed. "For the love of God, María del Carmen. What. Did. She. Say?"

I let out a frustrated sigh, "that he asked for forgiveness, he must've changed."

"What the fuck?" he exhales.

"It's just the way she was raised." I shrug. "She believes you should forgive a man as many times as possible when he says sorry. She's that old fashioned."

"Bullshit, that's not being *old fashioned*," he wipes his mouth with a napkin, "knocking your head with a chancla being twenty eight is old fashioned. Refusing to learn how to use a dishwasher is old fashioned… dammit! Persuading you not to leave home until you get married is old fashioned. Taking sides with your daughter's abuser is not. I'm sorry, I know it's your mom and all but this is so unhealthy for you, Chip." He shakes his head, "she's been hurting you for a long time and it needs to fucking stop." He starts shaking his leg and breathes hard for a couple of seconds. "Let me ask you a question here. Have you ever thought that maybe, *just maybe*, you think you love your mom just because you feel obligated to?"

The question feels like a bucket of cold water over my head.

"What?"

"Think about it for a sec," he leans forward and motions with his hands, "we're raised to love and respect our elders even if they don't do shit to earn that respect. Don't get me wrong. I love my parents and I love Tía Carmela too… they're great… but there are some shitty relatives I'm better off without. *'es familia y hay que quererla'?" They're family and you have to love them*, "That's some insanely toxic bullshit. You don't have to love someone who's being abusive. No matter who that is and how old they are."

"No, I…" I stutter, "I love my mother, Jacob."

"Do you really?" he shrugs, "why? Give me one reason. One thing about her that makes you love her."

"I… because," *think Carmen. You know you love her, don't you?* I bite my lower lip and swallow hard. I think about it for a couple of seconds and the only reason I have is the same and the realization brings a wave of panic down my throat.

"Because she's my mom, that's why," I slap my hand on the table, "I can't help but love my mom."

"I rest my case your honor," he says, crossing his arms. After a couple of seconds, his face softens and takes off the cap he's using to scratch his head. "You need to tell Oliver."

"What?" I scream-whisper, "why would I do that?"

"I'm worrying sick about your safety and he's the only one who's not busy all day."

"What are you talking about? He's leaving anyways, what will you do when he's gone?"

"He could stay alert while he's around," he throws his hand in the air, "we can't let you be alone with that motherfucker being so close. Maybe Ol can—"

"No."

"He cares about you," he says, softening his tone, "just as much as we do and he knows about what happened with that asshole."

"Yeah, I realized that." I take another bite.

"Sorry, Chip. He figured it out."

"*Sh'* alright," I say with my mouth full, "he *wash* going to find out anyway."

He chuckles, "how are you doing by the way?"

"What do you mean?" I say, knowing exactly what he's referring to.

My love for Oliver has never been a secret. Jacob knows more than anyone else. He held me many times while I cried hearing news about him. I know he's been worried about me and I was already wondering when he was going to bring it up. I'm thankful for the change of subject but half panicked at the same time. I knew it was a bad idea for Oliver to stay so many nights at my house as much as I love it. The guys aren't idiots, they were going to suspect sooner or later.

"Come on, Chip. Don't give me that bullshit," he laughs as he takes a sip of his horchata, "look, the guy hasn't been exactly subtle. He practically forced himself into your house to do the kitchen and now he uses any excuse to ask you to come over or to go to you." He purses his lips, "I tried to tell him to take it easy. I'm sorry."

"It's Okay," I give him a tight lip smile, "we're on good terms if that's what you're worrying about."

"You know why I'm worried. In fact, we all are." He sighs, "look, I know we've had this silent agreement not to talk about what happened but I'm not an idiot… I know you still love him and you're hurting because he's getting married. I don't know if you should keep spending so much time with him."

"Jake I…"

Don't say it. He asked you not to say it.

I wish I could tell Jacob about us, tell him my fears, my doubts. Ask him for advice on how to figure things out with Oliver without scaring him away but I can't. If they knew about us, they will try to force things he might not be ready to talk about. There would be arguments and fights. Everything would be ruined. I'd rather die than seeing my family break.

"I'm fine," I sigh, "We're friends again, much better than ever and that's what counts. Even if he's not mine to keep."

"Girl, it's okay to stay away from someone if you're hurting." He takes my hand and kisses it. "I love Oliver and I know he won't intentionally cause you any pain. But he's hurting you anyways, I can see it."

God, I love this dude.

"I swear I'm fine. He did an amazing job in the kitchen and he's really been making up for all these years. Like the other day, I came home crying from work and—"

"What?" He interrupts, "what happened?"

"Shit, I haven't told you." I sigh, "I'm out of the X Games."

"Are you kidding me? Why?"

"*Ese hijo de puta* hired five freelance photographers and left me and Chucky out," I inhale deeply, "same bullshit about *experience*. Don't look at me like that, I'm not quitting."

"I'm not saying anything."

"But you're thinking about it."

He lets out a silent chuckle. "So, Ol was there when you got home?"

"He was," I suppress a sigh. "He made me tea, let me cuddle Juanito while I was crying. Then he took me to Mall of America for a much needed distraction. He was sweet."

He rode a bike for the first time in ten years because I asked him to and took me home to bang me until I forgot my name.

"I see," he eyes me suspiciously, "and you're one hundred percent sure you're Okay with him being back in your life just as a friend?"

"What else can I do, Jake?" I say, playing with a lock of my hair, "I'm resigned. I think I'm finally ready to move on."

"Okay, I believe you," he gives me a look that tells me the opposite. "Still, if you need me to kick his ass just let me know."

"I'll even throw the first punch."

He laughs, "as if you need me to kick ass for you anyways." He shakes his head, "and please, try to stay away from that car dealership. I'll try to find where he lives so we can stay alert."

"I swear I just bought a car and that's it. I'm not even picking it up tomorrow. Araceli is."

"Alright," he stands up, leaving a tip on the table, "we're still good for Friday night, right? Vince is back in town by the way, he's bringing his boyfriend Daniel with him."

"I know, I can't wait," I follow him towards the door, "seven sharp."

"What are we having?"

"I don't know, Ol is cooking. I'll help him." I shrug as we walk and I catch him looking at me and swallowing his laugh. "What? I told you we were friends."

"Orale, ya te dije que te creo." *I already told you I believe you.*

Yeah, I know buddy, I don't even believe it myself. But that's the thing about lies, when you tell it to yourself enough times, you might end up believing it.

32

oliver

Slow Bachata is playing on the speakers while my girl and I cook my signature spicy chicken enchiladas. Juanito is peacefully sleeping on our couch while we wait for everyone. *Her* couch.

Vince couldn't believe it when I told him Carmen and I were close again and I almost spilled the tea then but like Papá always says, *"todo a su tiempo"*. All in good time. Which I think might be closer than I thought. I'm getting to a point where I can no longer contain myself when we're around other people. Scary or not, Antonio is right. The future is getting closer and we need to put our cards on the table to move forward.

I'm not ignoring the fact that I need to go back to L.A., but the opportunity to leave it behind without throwing away everything I've built might be closer than it seemed before. Damian and I have been talking in the last few days. Sales are exploding all over the country and Elite Bike's popularity is starting to go worldwide. The board is asking us to open two more factories and an extension of headquarters in the Midwest. Damian suggested I take charge in a Minneapolis location. I wanted to give him a solid yes, but I haven't talked to Carmen.

My family is tighter than ever, I'm finally getting the girl and I'm sure dad will be just fine. All of that gives me a good feeling but my fears and doubts are making their way inside my head. What if I say yes and she gets cold feet? What if she realizes I'm not what she wants in the middle of the process? What if she ends up saying no?

I simply could not survive it.

Live in the moment. Enjoy today.

I'm stirring the chicken in the pan when Carmen lets a knife fall to the floor.

"Shit." she mutters when Juanito jumps from the couch to whine against her.

"You alright baby?" I say, taking her hand.

"Fine," she gives me a sad smile, "just cut my finger."

"Here, let me see."

It's not a deep cut, so we wash it and put a band-aid on it. Still, I feel like there's something else in her eyes. Her usual joy is gone and I'm afraid of whatever she has to say. She's been acting weird since she bought the car for her mom. She's told me several times she's fine but I know my girl and I know Araceli. She's an expert at sucking the joy out of her daughters.

"Hey," I kiss her cheek, "it's alright."

Her eyebrows are high and her eyes teary so I take her in my arms, letting her put hers around my waist. Her weariness sends a wave of panic down my spine.

I clear my throat, "It's gonna be okay, mami. Did something else happen?"

"No," she says. After a long pause, she starts talking very fast. "I'm just so nervous, Ol. It's the first time we have everyone in the same room at the same time for an entire meal. I get so clumsy when I'm nervous. Everyone's gonna know, I'm gonna give us away and everything will be ruined and —"

I cut her off by taking her beautiful face in my hands to kiss her.

"Maybe it won't," I whisper against her lips.

I've restrained myself from telling her I love her because I want to find the right moment. But every breath I take, every kiss and every fragment of my attention has been full of my love for her. I think it's time for me to actually say the words.

"What do you mean it won't?"

I'm about to tell her when Juanito rushes to the door and starts scratching it. Not three seconds after, it slams open letting Antonio, Jacob, Ethan, Vince and who I assume is Daniel. Carmen and I push each other away and walk over to welcome them. The guys take turns to pet Juanito while we hug and Vince formally introduces us to his boyfriend. Carmen takes some beers out and we all take a can.

"The kitchen looks amazing, Chip," Vince says to Carmen while he and Daniel sit on the high stools by the kitchen island.

"It was all this guy," she points at me with a wooden spoon.

"I thought you said he was a businessman," Daniel tells Vince.

"I am just as surprised," Vince says, looking at me, "what else did I miss?"

We tell him about the photoshoot and how I ended up fixing her kitchen. I take my phone out to show him some of the before and after pictures of the renovation. It really looks amazing.

"Hey, are Mamá and Papá walking or driving?" Jacob asks from the living room.

"Alberto wasn't feeling good," Carmen says, "his blood pressure was a little high when we got back from Vicente's house and was having a headache."

"Besides, we're heading to Rochester tomorrow for his appointment," I add, "he wanted to be well rested for the drive."

I can see the disappointment in everyone. They canceled last-minute and I was really bummed out too. We'll head to the Mayo Clinic tomorrow morning. He still has a couple of scans they need to make and some other tests they will run before we get to talk to the specialist and he's been a little nervous. To be honest, I am too but I want to hold onto hope. Everything's starting to make sense in my life again and I know brighter times are coming our way.

It's the Carmen effect.

The air starts to feel thicker but Ethan decides to break the silence.

"Are those spicy enchiladas?" He asks as I take the pan out of the oven.

"You whining about this again?" Carmen laughs, "they're not even that hot. But if your delicate mouth can't handle it, you can have a glass of milk later."

"Look," Ethan says after taking a swig of his beer, "I don't have a delicate mouth, alright? I have a delicate ass… I don't want to spend all night sitting on the throne."

Jacob and Antonio instantly look at each other with a smirk and start singing at the same time, "*Ay ay ay ay! Ethan no llores!*"

We all erupt in laughter. Ethan has the most fragile stomach and we all love to tease him about it.

"You all laugh now," he winces while the laughter dies down, "but you well know you won't be able to use the bathroom ever again if I get there first."

"Well, I guess you're right about that," Antonio replies, "we definitely do not need to tear the whole house down and build it again, do we?"

"I still don't understand that stereotype, you know?" Ethan talks with his mouth full of chips, "why do people think that just because you're Mexican, your stomach is made out of steel when it comes to spicy food?"

"Then just say no when you're offered," Vince shrugs.

"You and your gringo half," Daniel laughs, "Vinny, even I know rejecting food in a Latino household is a cardinal sin. And I'm the whitest dude on earth."

"Aw, I knew I liked you Daniel," Carmen says, making him smile. Everyone else nods and say their yeses as Carmen brings the enchiladas to the table while everyone else take a seat on the table.

"If someone took the time to cook for you, the least you can do is eat," Antonio adds.

"Food is a religion for Latinos and *this* is the church, que no?" Jacob says as he sits, "can I get an Amen?"

"Amen," we all say, raising our beers.

Not to brag, but I do make a mean meal when I want to spoil my family. I used to cook a lot when I was younger but became a culinary genius in college. When you're used to your Mama's cooking and suddenly have to live with a bunch of guys who survive on protein bars and cereal, you take your cooking skills to another level.

"Damn, Ol," Antonio says, taking another round of everything, "you killed it."

"Thanks, Tony," I smile, "I'm glad you like it."

"I fucking missed your food, dude," Jacob adds.

"Hey, I almost forgot," Vince says, rubbing his hands, "just a few more weeks and we're down to the X Games, bro."

"He's been talking about it forever," Daniel says.

"VIP, baby. Tell me, how is that *not* exciting?" Vince tells him and turns to Carmen, "Chip, you need to send me some of those pictures later."

"If you're okay with a phone picture of my T.V., I can." Carmen says, pursing her lips and looking at her plate.

"I already told you I'll get you tickets," I take her hand under the table.

"Wait," Antonio interrupts, "what are you talking about?"

She lets out a disappointed sigh and tells the story. By Jacob's expression I can tell he already knew but the others start making frustrated noises. Antonio clenches his jaw and shakes his head, Vince narrows his eyes and Ethan looks like he wants to hit a wall.

"Fucking asshole," Ethan says as she concludes, "tell him to fuck himself. Oliver can get you a better job." He turns to me, "Ol, get her a job. You know she's the best."

Everyone starts talking at the same time, saying the same thing with different words.

"I've told her already," I say while the chattering slows, "*I could hire her as a freelancer or get her hired somewhere else, but she's a hard headed woman.*" I say, looking at her glaring at me,

"I told her we could even use those pictures she took of me the other day as a hook with another magazine."

Carmen's eyes go round as she squeezes my hand under the table.

I hadn't even realized what I said until Jacob asks us, "What pictures?"

When she showed me the pictures she took the day we went for a ride, I asked her not to show them to anyone. Not because I was ashamed, but because I didn't want them to assume I was going to pick it up again.

Everyone looks at me waiting for an answer and I can't help but to be honest.

"I um–we–" I stutter, "Chip took me for a ride the other day."

Their jaws drop almost at the same time, looking at us as if they've just seen a ghost.

"A ride?" Vince asks, blinking fast, "a *bike* ride?"

I can see Carmen smiling and nodding in response.

"You guys went for a *BMX* ride?" Antonio asks again, signaling with his finger between Carmen and I.

"Yeah, we went to Freedom Union," I bring my beer to my mouth, trying to sound casual, "she still has my old Haro and Angel's Subrosa intact."

"You've got to be shitting me," Jacob whispers with tears in his eyes, "there's no possible way you've gotten this guy on a bike."

"Is it really true, Chip?" Ethan looks at Carmen.

She rolls her eyes and laughs as she stands to get her iPad. When she sits again, they all stand behind her chair to look through the pictures and videos. The *"ooh"*s and *"wow"*s and tons of unbelieving cuss words don't stop as they study all of them. The smile on their faces as they see me going back to my first love, what made us family… has no price in this world.

"I can't believe this," Ethan leans towards Carmen and kisses her cheek, "thank you. Only you could've brought Oliver's ass to life."

"Now don't get your hopes up," I chuckle as I stand up to get another beer, "I'm not planning on pick it up again, I don't even know if I want to keep doing it for fun, I was just… venting."

"We don't care if you do it again or not, Ol," Jacob stands in front of me, "you still don't get it, do you? We didn't just lose Angel in that car accident. We lost *you* too. And we're so fucking happy you're back."

The gates of guilt open up just a little as Jacob's words take me back to reality. *I'm back but Angel is not. He should be here. He could've been here.* I shove the thought away and try to smile. Despite the guilt and pain, I can't deny the fact that this is the first time in ten years I've felt this happy, this whole, this strong. I feel like myself again with the people I'm supposed to be with.

It gives me hope that I might be ready to leave the past behind for good and finally come back to them.

To *her*.

As she keeps going through the pictures and exchanging anecdotes from our ride and our younger years, the idea of that new headquarters office sounds less scary.

33

oliver

The night flies away. We say our goodbyes almost at 1 in the morning. I drive with Antonio to disguise in front of my brothers and come back to my girl at the speed of light.

It's time to stop the trial and start paying a premium. Time to really go back where I belong.

I find Carmen cleaning the kitchen and I join her in silence. We steal glances, I kiss her cheek when she walks by me. I still don't know what's going to happen once I go back to L.A. or what the future holds in my professional life, but whether I stay here or I move back… I want her with me.

I'm tired of pretending my life without her isn't void. She's the light I haven't been able to see in ten years, no matter how many widows I've opened.

"Thanks for everything," I say as I take her in my arms and kiss her forehead.

"Thank *you* for cooking, Ol," she kisses my chest, "Martita taught you well."

"I'm not talking about tonight," I caress her cheek, "the guys are right, you know? Only you could make something like this happen. You make everything wonderful, María del Carmen. You make me a better man."

An unbelieving smile forms in her lips. After a couple of seconds of silence, she shakes her head. "Ol, you're an amazing man. With or without me."

"That's where you're wrong," I take her face in my hands, "this man you're talking to? This whole, happy man? He only exists with you," I press my forehead to hers and close my eyes, "this is the only version of me you know because it's the version you pull out of me. The *me* I like the most, the *me* they've missed." I smile, "the happiest version of myself is back. All because of you."

A single tear falls from her eye and I kiss it away. She lets out a soft, almost inaudible chuckle and I drink it as I claim her mouth with mine. My lips devoured hers. My desire for her body blending with my need to have her completely.

"Make love to me, papi," she hisses against my touch, bringing all my will power to her feet.

"Damn," I groan, "I love it when you call me papi."

I feel my defenses vanishing as I kiss down her throat, her left shoulder and the swell of her breasts. She brings her hands under my t-shirt and pulls it up before doing the same with her sundress. I lift her in my arms and carry her to the bedroom. Juanito jumps to follow us, he's been sleeping with us in bed but he knows he needs to go when mom and dad need some alone time.

I close the door with my foot and put her down. I unclasp her bra and slide her thong down her glorious ass, leaving her beautiful body bare to me. She pulls my neck down with one hand to kiss me before sliding it down to quickly unbuckle my pants. I laugh at her rush and help her kick my pants away along with my boxers.

I grip her waist and pull her towards me.

Without breaking the kiss, I lead her as I walk backwards till I sit on the bed. I scoot up and she crawls until she's on her knees, straddling my lap. My hands travel her skin as I trail the path between her sternum to her breasts with my tongue. She cups my head with her hands as I take one in my mouth. Just when I thought my cock couldn't get any harder, she lets out a moan as I suck her nipple. I feel my entire body on fire, wanting to get inside her. But I want her as desperate as I am right now, so I bring my right hand down her beautiful pussy and rub two fingers against it.

"You're so fucking wet, baby," I pull away just a little to see her flushed face. Her back arched and her entire skin glowing with pleasure. I lean forward to kiss her chest, the side of her breasts and her belly as my fingers still rub her clit as she moans and thrusts her hips against it.

I take her mouth again and kiss it.

"I can't get enough of you," I whisper, "no matter how many times we do this. I can't get enough. It'll never be enough."

My body feels light, my chest growing a few sizes as I see her come undone. Once she comes in my hand, I take her lips once more.

"Please," she hisses, taking my cock in her hands. "Please, Oliver."

"You want to ride me, baby?" I whisper against her chest, "is that what you want?"

"Yes," she whimpers once again as she opens her legs, positioning herself on top of me and sliding down.

"Do it," I say, putting my hands on her hips and help her down, "take all of me."

With a gentle thrust, she starts sliding up hard as if her life depends on it. The pleasure comes the second we make contact, we both shiver as we feel each other in pure bliss.

I breathe her scent before pressing my lips to hers once more as she puts her arms around my neck. She moves with intent, moaning my name in my ear and I can't help but caressing her sweaty face as she slows down the pace. But I can't stop. I feel like my heart will stop if she does.

We've been going without condoms for a couple of days after having the clean/pill talk. Although it felt different in many ways, there's something about today that beats all other times. The intimacy, the depth of each sensation. The emotion behind every touch. The intensity.

It's different.

Something that I've never felt before with anyone else.

Her thrusts are slow but frantic. I can't keep my hands still, massaging her legs all the way to her ass with my right hand and bringing one of her nipples to my mouth while she keeps moving.

I feel my heart filling up with gratitude. For finding her again, for making ten years of pain worth it.

"Oliver," she moans, her hands sliding up and down my chest, "Oliver please don't leave me."

Fuck.

I feel each word of her pleading twisting my heart and I give her ass a squeeze.

"Never," I whisper, flipping her over so she's under me, "I'm here," I say, looking into her shiny eyes as I start moving inside of her, "I'm yours baby. Always been yours."

I always tell her to open her eyes while we make love, but this time it's me who needs to close them. I can't look her in the eye without feeling disarmed and vulnerable. Without her knowing that I need her more than I ever did.

I take her left hand over her head and interlace our fingers while I kiss her, feeling my orgasm close. Not too long after, she comes with the most beautiful, breathy moan I've ever heard in my life. I feel my heart coming out of my ribs and I follow. When I'm completely spent, I can't keep my feelings to myself anymore.

"You're everything to me," I say, pulling away just a little to see her face, "I love you, María del Carmen Morales. I never stopped loving you for one second. I'm so in love with you I don't think I can live without you anymore." I swallow hard, stroking her smiling face, "you don't have to say it back if you're not ready, but I need you to know. I need you to hear my words saying that you own me entirely. Heart, body, soul… everything is yours."

She lets out a teary giggle and pulls me down for a kiss. I'm getting hard again but my phone starts ringing for the third time and I groan against her neck.

"Go get it," she smiles, "it's been ringing, it could be your parents."

"I'm not done here," I mutter against her mouth.

"Who said I was going anywhere?" she smiles mischievously.

"Hold whatever you're thinking then," I say making my way out of the room and I roll my eyes when I see Damian calling me from L.A.

"*Way* to kill the mood, dude," I say, opening the door and letting Juanito in the room.

"Ol, my man," he chuckles, "I know it's not the perfect time, but hey, you know you missed me."

"I can't sleep, can't eat," I tease and we both chuckle. "Tell me what is it that can't wait until a more respectable hour?"

"Alright, don't hate me," he laughs again, "I just wanted to let you know we have a meeting first thing tomorrow and we'll be needing your decision yesterday," I sigh and he cuts me off before I can say anything, "now, before you freak out on me, let me tell you as your friend and not as your business partner. I think you should do it and do it soon."

"Why does it have to be now?" I ask as I sit on the couch. "I already told you, I need to talk to my girl first."

"You and I know she'll say yes. There's no better time than today."

I laugh, "bro, your mama never taught you not to make decisions for a woman?"

"She also taught me how to smell a pile of bullshit from Minnesota to California."

I want to keep up with the mood and change the subject, but he's one of the most persistent people I've ever met. I don't know what Carmen will decide, and even if she says yes, I don't want to start on that never-ending rollercoaster ride of meetings, budget planning, trips back and forth and the stressing part of this business before enjoying every single second I have left of my time here.

When I don't say anything, Damian breaks the silence.

"What are you really scared of, Oliver?"

The question almost makes me choke. I clear my throat. "What?"

I can hear a door slamming and Damian's engine starting.

"I'm telling you this with all the love in the world, bro: *Move on, motherfucker!* It's time to look back and wave goodbye."

"I… I don't know what you mean."

"Oh you do," he laughs, "look, your dad's situation isn't ideal, you still need to figure things out but he's happy having you all there. You've got your bros all in one same place for the first time in ages and you finally got your girl. But, are you really at peace with what happened?"

Insightful son of a bitch, he can always look through my soul. Fuck him.

"I am," I stutter, "I wouldn't be here if I wasn't."

"Then why do you want to delay shit? It's like you want to live inside the dream but not make it a reality because you know reality looks a little different than it used to be. Isn't this what you wanted? Having all your family together again?"

We're not all together again. He's still not here. He'll never be here again because of me.

I shove the thought away and sit up straight.

"I just don't want to stress out during my vacation," I argue, "I would have to put things on hold and I want to enjoy it for a little longer before the pressure starts."

"Bullshit, if that's true you would've talked to Carmen already. Stop making excuses, Oliver." I hear a honk before he keeps going, "make peace with the past, dude. With yourself. The sooner you get your ass to work and start the entire transition, the sooner you can get your life back. It's time to go home. Your family needs you there, your girl needs you there and now, Elite does. Are you seriously telling me you don't want to make this permanent?"

I want to ignore the unease his words give me and focus on what I want.

I want to see my parents smile every day as we do the simplest things together.

I want my mother's food and be able to hug my dad whenever I want.

I want to punch my brothers and my friends on the shoulder every time we say hello instead of a simple wave through Face-Time. Show up at their places as if they were mine and spend real time with them.

I want Carmen in my arms every day. Kiss her whenever I feel like instead of just my dreams.

They're worth the work and effort.

"Do you remember what you told me when we started Elite?" he continues, "you said some events in life are just a platform to set the ladder on and climb where you're destined to be. L.A. was your platform, Ol. You need to get over your fear of heights and start climbing that shit."

I let out a trembling breath and drop my head back. I'm not taking this decision for Carmen, I want to lay down the choices so she can make one. But he's right, this is where I want to be. This is where I belong.

"You're right," I sit up again, "it's time to climb the ladder."

"Yeah," he screams, "that's my boy."

"I still need to talk to Carmen, though," I warn, "I'm not making decisions without her. I'm ninety-nine percent sure she'll say yes, but you never know."

"Wise man," he teases, "speaking of, let's talk later. Kat's cravings are driving me insane and I need to go back with these tacos before she threatens to chop my balls. Sorry for the cock-block."

"Meh, I forgive you for tonight. Let's not make our ladies wait then. Tell Kat I say hello."

"Will do. I'm happy for you, bro. I've never seen you this happy before."

"Thanks, man. See you in a few weeks."

I make my way back to the bedroom and find Carmen already in deep sleep. Her face buried in the pillow, Juanito snoring at her feet on the bed. I don't want to wake her up, she's been tired and today was a lot of work. I scoot between the sheets and cover her back, placing a kiss on her temple.

"I love you baby," I whisper, before spooning her.

She lets out a soft groan and turns around, putting her arms around my waist, squeezing a little before kissing my chest.

"I love you too, Big Guy. So much." She whispers back. My heart is so full and my body so weak I'd fall if I'd be standing. I cover her with my arms and bury my face in her hair.

She loves me.

I could die a happy man right now.

Damian is wrong. I'm not scared. What could I possibly be afraid of when I have all I ever needed inside this bed?

Nothing, right?

34

carmen

Cinderella singing "So this is love?" has nothing on me right now.

Not that I'm actually singing. Oliver would probably question his sanity and would run away the second I let out the first howl.

It's my heart who's singing. It's loud, clear, directly to my ear and letting me know last night was real. A perfect song, uncanny and familiar at the same time.

A song out of a dream I'm afraid I'll wake up from.

But I don't. The moment I open my eyes, he's still here. I'm facing his back, the sheets covering just a little down his naked waist. His breathing is soft and smooth but I can still hear him. I sigh and cover my face with a pillow.

Last night was magical. He made love to me in a way I've never experienced before.

"I love you, Maria del Carmen Morales. I never stopped loving you for one second."

I've heard similar things in the past and believed them all. I've even loved some of them, but none of them were this true. None of them felt like this or sounded like this. None of them even tried to show me with each day's actions what those words meant. They were just feathers in the wind.

None of them were Oliver.

I feel him turning around before I see him. He sighs, putting his arms around my torso and gives me a soft kiss on the lips. "Good morning, mi amor."

"Good morning, baby," I whisper, taking his face in my hands, giving him another kiss. When I pull away, he's looking at me with his eyes wide open.

"What?" I ask.

He studies my face, "you called me *baby*."

"I did."

"You haven't called me any pet names outside of sex time."

"You don't like it?" I ask quietly.

"Oh, I love it," he says, rubbing his right hand on my ass, "it's just… exciting to hear it for the first time."

"Huh," I move my lips along his jaw and down his neck, speaking between kisses, "for a second I thought I had to change it to, I don't know, let's say," *kiss,* "*mi amor,*" *kiss,* "*handsome,*" *kiss,* "*papi?*"

I moan the last word.

"You're really thinking this through." He groans, giving little bites along my jaw, "I already told you I love it when you call me that."

"It's my favorite too," I smile, bringing his lips to mine.

Our kiss starts getting heated. I quickly look at my phone and we still have a couple of hours to spare, so I let myself go and we end up making each other come one more time before we get up.

"You need to get ready, Ethan and your parents will be waiting for you," I say, trying to catch my breath.

He groans and shakes his head, mocking a tantrum and making me laugh.

"You're such a baby," I laugh. He closes his eyes for a moment and hugs me tight. Today's an important day for Alberto and even if Oliver doesn't say it, I know it's weighing on him.

"Hey." I murmur against his chest. "You doing alright?"

He lets out a long breath and turns to look at me.

"I think so," he says, "I gotta be honest, I'm a little scared but… I feel confident. I mean, you've seen him. I don't think it's as serious as Mama thinks it is. Besides, I've been doing some research and there's a high chance Papá might be just stressed out. With his rushed lifestyle it wouldn't be surprising. Alzheimer's doesn't run in our family and only five percent of the people diagnosed with it are in the early onset. The probabilities are very low."

"Well, that's comforting," I say, trying with all my heart to believe this will be the case.

"It really is," he smiles, "it gave me high hopes."

"Well," I say, running my fingers against his chest, "no matter what happens, we will face it together."

"Without a doubt," he says as he leans down to kiss me. We kiss with abandon, with all the love we confessed just last night. It takes a lot of effort, but we finally pull away.

"Okay, coffee time," he says, pulling away the sheets.

We get up and Oliver goes straight to the bathroom. I dress lightly and tie my hair in a messy bun. Juanito stands up and follows me to the kitchen, where I put food in his bowl. While Oliver showers and gets his bag ready, I make some eggs, refried beans and warm up a stack of tortillas. I'm putting the grinded coffee in the coffee maker when he approaches to kiss my cheek.

"We need to talk, babe."

For some reason, I don't like the tone he's using. I inhale deeply as I press the brew button and turn around, faking my best smile.

"Okay," I tuck a strand of my hair behind my ear.

He takes two cups from the holders and puts them on the counter.

"Last night we said a lot of things."

"We did."

"I ummm… did you mean it?" he lowers his tone and talks to the cups, "about… loving me?"

"I did," I don't notice I'm panting until I keep talking, "oh

God…. Are you… having second thoughts? Are you breaking this up? Is this because I didn't say it back right away? Am I being too clingy already?"

The word vomit is humiliating, but my entire load of insecurities are making their way out without permission. Oliver visibly panics and turns around, putting his strong arms around my waist and silences me with a kiss.

"Hey, no," he pulls back, "no, baby. I'm so sorry, that's not what I meant at all. Dammit, there's no way I'd think you could ever be clingy," he laughs, "cling onto me all you want. I've been dreaming about it my whole life." He pulls away, "I'm asking because I also meant it. I've never been more serious about anything in my life. *I love you* feels like an understatement. And if you feel the same way, we need to figure out what's going to happen after this. I've thought about it for a long time and I… well… I want to know your thoughts about how we're moving forward."

I let myself breathe a little, taking the pot to pour in our cups.

"To be honest with you, I didn't think that far ahead but I'm listening."

"What? Why?" he laughs, taking our plates to the island. "What exactly did you think was going to happen?"

I was getting ready for you to leave me.

"I thought you said you wanted to have fun and live the moment?"

"Well, yeah," he says, "but I meant to live the moment and figure out if this could really work between us. We don't exactly have a memorable past in that department," he sits and kisses my hand, "but that's not important now. What matters is that we love each other and we want to be together. Which brings me to the next topic."

I feel a wave of nerves tangling inside my belly but I decide it's hunger. I'm not myself when I'm hungry, so I take a tortilla and make a little taco with eggs and beans as he continues.

"The call I got last night was from Damian." He takes a sip of coffee, "Elite is in high demand. Sales are exploding after Mickey's bike came out and the board is asking for expansion. They want two more factories and move me to a new headquarters office. Damian thinks Minneapolis is a good location and he suggested I move back here to manage operations." He shoves a forkful of eggs to his mouth and a tortilla bite, "we discussed it a couple of days ago and I still need to give him a final decision but... I wanted to ask you what you think."

Talk about making things official.

Is it me or is he asking me if I want him to move back or not? *Of course I do.* But this isn't him looking for a job here, he's talking about moving his multimillion-dollar business to the other side of the country. I can't help but feel a wave of panic up and down my spine. I can't make this decision for him, it's a huge responsibility that isn't mine.

"What do I know about business, Ol?" I laugh.

"Har, har," he teases, "I'm not asking for business advice, Chip," he leans forward to kiss my cheek, "I'm asking you if you want me to move back. If not, we'll find another way but I need to know what you want."

"You moving back and you moving your multimillion dollar business because I say so are two different things." I say, "What I want shouldn't be your deciding factor."

"This conversation isn't going the way I was hoping," he scratches the back of his neck. "Can you just tell me plain and simple what you want to do?"

I feel like that scene from *The Notebook*. Allie definitely had a point.

"No es así de fácil," *is not that simple.* "Why are you loading all this on me? It's too much. It's your business, your life and it should be your decision."

"*Tú* eres mi vida," *you are my life.* He gets off the chair and moves to stand between my legs, taking my face in his hands. "You are the one who matters the most. I don't care if we live here, or L.A. or Mexico or in fucking Mars as long as we're together."

What if I say yes, he moves back and he realizes I'm not what he wants? He will regret his decision and our lives will be a living hell. What if he fails and business doesn't go as he wanted? He would resent me. I can't make this decision for him, he has to be the one who takes action.

Because action is what really matters.

"Of course I want to be with you, of course I love you as much as you love me… but that doesn't make things automatically perfect," I whisper, looking him in the eye. "There's a lot to consider, we haven't been dating for that long. God, we're barely figuring out what this is. You can't take that kind of risk just because I say so, it's *you* who needs to decide."

"You're worth it," he presses his forehead to mine, "you're worth every risk. Nothing could ever make me happier than giving you what you want and making any move you want me to make."

"Then do it because you want to. Not because of me."

"But why?"

The look in his eyes breaks my heart but I can't deny to myself that deep inside I'm scared shitless. He thinks so highly of me already but… what if I can't meet his expectations and he regrets it later after making this huge of a move just because of me?

I hold onto his arms. "You have to make decisions with your head, Oliver. Not with your emotions… You're just dazzled with how great things are. I am too… but you need to think if this is what you really want for your future."

I pull away from him completely and walk towards the sink. He follows me, his brow frowned, his jaw clenched.

He turns me around and covers me with his arms.

"Hey," he says and we spend a couple of seconds holding each other before he finally talks, "baby, you really need to check on that beautiful heart of yours, rewind and record on top of all that bullshit you've believed about yourself," he pulls away and looks at me, "I understand it's scary and difficult to move past the line of assholes that made you believe you don't deserve to be treated like the ultimate queen that's walked the earth," he adjusts his shoulders, "and I know I also have my part in that. But I'll be patient and will prove you wrong. I'm not giving up on us."

He cups my cheek and kisses me softly on the lips, "can you at least think about it? I don't want to make decisions without you being fully happy."

"Can you please understand I can't make that decision for you? Whatever it is that you need to do, you have to decide yourself. I'll be happy with whatever."

He groans and shakes his head. He looks like he wants to argue but his phone chimes with a text. He types something quickly and wipes his face with a hand before facing me again.

"I have to go, my parents are waiting for me," he gives me a soft smooch, "but this isn't over. I'll come home Monday night, have a nice dinner and will talk this over." He kisses my forehead, "I love you. I've never loved any woman that hasn't been you. *Ever.* I've loved you and dreamed about this for so long and I'm not giving up on us again," he kisses me again, "I'll call you tonight."

We hold each other for a couple of seconds before he takes his bag and leashes Juanito. He turns around and goes away, closing the door of my house and I instantly feel cold and lonelier than ever.

I turn to our unfinished breakfast and can't help but let my tears out. At what moment did everything turn into this swamp of doubts and fears?

Why can't he decide to stay on his own? Why can't he choose to stay without me telling him to do it?

I can't lose myself in another person again knowing he could change his mind at any time. If he wants to take that risk, it must be his own decision.

"Why do I feel like you're going to leave anyways?" I sob with my face buried in the cedary scent of his pillow.

Next time you leave, please don't go without me.

35

oliver

Can the world please stop for a second?

One second is all I need.

When is life going to stop fucking with me? The moment I start seeing a light at the end of the tunnel, everything grows dark again. The moment I want to see things differently and believe things can get better, life punches me in the gut *again*.

I've been sitting on a bench outside Hope Center for I don't know how long. We came home early this afternoon and the same sentence keeps bouncing around my ears since we officially got a diagnosis for Papa.

"Your father is in the early stages of the early onset Alzheimer's disease."

One second, that's all it took the doctor to deliver the news. After three days of physical exams, neurological evaluations, lab work and brain imaging. They checked every part of his body to rule out other memory loss related diseases, mental health disorders, thyroid imbalance, brain tumors and so many other things. We talked to four different doctors, all of them asking me and my family every single detail about Papa's lifestyle and symptoms. I felt hopeful for a moment, almost relieved. But when they started showing us the scans, talking about abnormal protein accumulation, plaque tissue around something called hippocampus and memory and reasoning tests not coming the way they expected for a person his age… my heart began to disintegrate.

There's no doubt now.

The suspicions were true.

"The good news is that you're getting the diagnosis on time." The doctor said when he started to explain the options we had to start treatment.

On time for what? Sure, we're going to do whatever it's needed to prolong his life, but his mind will fade away anyways. We will be nothing to him, even if he still has distant memories about having a family. There's no way to go back from this, no way to save his brain. No way to stop the damage and bring his life back as it used to be.

One second.

I dissociated from that point forward. I could hear Ethan and Mamá asking questions and the doctor talking about medication, how it's going to work and how to take it, lifestyle changes, mental stimulation and memory training programs for Alzheimer's patients but I couldn't concentrate. I couldn't take my eyes off Papá. His eyes looking at a wall in deep thought, a sterned frown in his brows, probably trying to make sense of what was happening.

We left in a somber silence, as if we were heading to a funeral. My mom made all the calls from the car and the moment she talked to Carmen, my phone was bombarded with texts and calls from her but I just didn't have the energy. I even asked Ethan to drive because my body felt like it was drained from everything that allowed it to move. I know he's as devastated as I am, but he's always been able to balance his emotions better than anyone else.

Papá has Alzheimer's disease and there's nothing we can do about it.

When we got home, Papá said he was tired, excused himself and went for a nap while Ethan and Jacob began to make the arrangements to get his medication and Mamá cried nonstop over the phone, talking to her sister in Texas. So I decided to go for a walk to clear my head. I just wanted to find a safe place and break down freely, so I found a bench in Hope Center's property and cried until my lungs hurt. I cried for what felt for hours and now I'm here drained, feeling my entire body in pain.

I wish I could just go away, disappear and forget about everything.

My phone hasn't stopped ringing, Jacob and Ethan asking me where I am and Carmen saying she'll be home soon.

Carmen.

My anchor. My only love. My everything. The only person who could bring a little light to my broken soul. I need to break down in her arms and even if she can't make this any better or make it go away, we can share the burden. We can hurt together and maybe help each other find healing, because I know she's hurting as much as I am.

I glance at my phone again and realize she must be home by now so I collect myself and walk out of the building. I'm about to cross the street when I see Carmen's Forester parked on the other side.

She's here?

I run inside the building like a desperate man in a desert, looking for a drink of water. When I don't find her in any of the classrooms, I go to Juliana's office and knock on her door.

"Hey, Oliver," she says, looking up from her laptop. "oh, are you alright?"

"Hey, Julie," I put my hands inside my pockets, "yeah, I'm just… wondering if you've seen Carmen? Her car is parked outside. I was looking for her."

"She was here just ten minutes ago letting me know she might suspend her classes next week. She got a call from her mom, it sounded a little urgent, so she left for the restaurant."

"Good, thank you," I say, feeling a cold wave of anxiety down my spine, "I'll see you later."

She waves goodbye and I make my way out as fast as I can. The thought of crossing words with Araceli in this state of mind and with this situation weighing on my soul makes me feel nauseous. But I need Carmen as much as I need to breathe right now and I don't care if anyone knows anymore.

I open the door of the restaurant and scan the entire room looking for her. There's only one person paying at the register, where Araceli is currently serving and no one else. She smiles at me when she sees me and waves.

"Hi, Araceli," I say as I approach, "I was looking for your daughter."

She doesn't even look at me. "She's here, but I don't know if it's a good time."

"Oh, okay. I can wait."

"You can wait if you want," she shrugs and leans on the counter, lowering her voice, "she's in the back with an old boyfriend. I think they're coming to an understanding."

No. Not possible.

"Ummm…" I swallow hard. "Are you sure?"

"Yes," she says, excitedly, "didn't she tell you? They used to date a long time ago and she broke it off because of a misunderstanding. We bumped into him the other day when I bought my new car, he works there and we didn't know. Seems like the flame is still there. They're reconnecting, so it might take a while."

My legs feel weaker with each word coming out of her mouth. My head is literally spinning and I feel like I'm going to pass out at any moment.

She lied. She fucking lied to me.

I knew something was wrong from the moment she came back home from that damn car dealership. I couldn't point a finger to it but she was acting weird, more anxious, completely off. Was it really because of this?

No. She isn't like this. She loves you and you know it. Araceli *is the one lying to you.*

"I need to use your bathroom." I say, my voice trembling and my legs shaking.

I walk towards the office door and look through the little window. I can see her back and a tall guy approaching her. He takes her hip and leans down to kiss her. I feel my eyes close shut and I can almost hear my chest being ripped open and my heart getting stabbed.

I can't bear to see what comes next and I step away from the door, making my way out of the restaurant. I don't even bother to say goodbye to Araceli. I need a place to sit down and breathe deeply or I'm going to throw up.

I make a quick stop to shake my head, as if doing it would erase what's happening. What am I going to do now? I refuse to believe she would do that to me again. Today of all days, the day she knew my heart was broken already. After all we've been through. After telling me she loved me.

Did she ever love me? Was it a game my mind played because I wanted so hard for her to love me that I dismissed the red flags as I did back then?

You know that thin sound you hear in your ear when everything is silent? That's all I hear as I force myself to keep walking. The cars are passing, the sun is shining in the horizon but I can't hear anything, feel anything. The earth just emptied and so did my heart.

My legs are moving out of instinct, no direction, not even acknowledging the motion. My body is here but *I am not*. Not anymore.

The scene replays thousands of times in my head. The lips I kissed hundreds of times for the last few weeks. All of those nights with my arms around her, her body against mine, all thrown to the trash as if they were nothing, as if it never meant anything. As if *we* didn't mean anything.

She fucking lied to me about everything. About what I meant to her, about her love for me. About that day in the car dealership. She was planning on going back to him while I was getting the most devastating news. Everything she said to me about me not being able to make decisions was just an excuse, she's doing the same thing she did to me back then.

Has she been seeing him this entire time? Was this some sort of revenge?
Is there any way to stop thinking? Stop feeling?
It hurts. It fucking hurts too much.

Please. Make it stop. Please, God. Please. I love her. Don't take my life away. Please, make her love me. Don't take Carmen away from me. Don't take my dad away from me. Please. They're my engine, they're my everything.

I find a bench in the park a couple of blocks away from Hope and drop myself on it. I'm panting with a stinging pain in my chest. I don't know how on earth I'm going to be able to get up from here.

The disbelief in the past few hours makes me stand up in a jolt. Angel was right after all… He knew it all along. She was going to get up and leave when the crush became a serious relationship. She blamed me for having gone away but she turned her back on us first. She never wanted to give me a real chance.

I'm tempted to go back and tell her no one is ever going to love her as much as I love her but seeing her with another man twice in this lifetime it's too much for me. I don't have the mental, emotional or even the physical strength to do it.

What did I do? What did I miss? Why, Chip? Why did you play with me again? Why couldn't you love me?

I didn't even know I was crying until I let out a painful sob.

If I close my eyes I see her face, her lips calling my name… but if I open them, I see what she's left of my heart… nothing.

I scream to the air and fall to my knees.

After minutes or maybe hours, I stand up and throw myself on the bench again and take my phone out.

I change my return flight to L.A. for tomorrow.

I turn off my phone.

I'm done.

36

carmen

"GET YOUR FUCKING HANDS OFF ME!" I shout as I slap Alan's hideous face.

"I… I'm sorry, Carmen," he says, holding his cheek. Smiling like an asshole, "I had it coming, I know. I was out of the line and I'm sorry. This wasn't why I wanted to see you. I just wanted to apologize for everything I did in the past but… I still can't resist you."

Araceli did it again.

She wouldn't stop calling while I was talking to Juliana about taking off next week. I didn't take the news about Alberto too well and I need time off to process and be with Oliver and the rest of the family. I hadn't been there for too long when Araceli texted saying there was an issue with the car payments. I've been ignoring most of her calls and texts since the day we bought her car and even though she loves to play dumb. She *knew* this was going to get me here. She asked me to wait for her in the back office while she finished with a customer, only to realize this creep was waiting for me here.

I was pissed more than I was scared. This time, I backed off and tried to run but he did the same thing as before. He stopped me and kissed me. I didn't even notice what was happening until his hand grabbed a hold of my waist and felt his disgusting mouth pressed against mine, trying to force his tongue in.

So I pushed him and slapped him.

"You can take your apology right up your ass," I give him a finger, "now leave before I call the police, you're violating a restraining order."

"Come on, Carmen, don't be so dramatic." He backs up a little, "It all turned out so wrong. I was wrong about you… all this time… I… I've hated myself for what I did. I swear I've changed… I love you."

I know I should be angry, but I'm amused. So I start laughing.

Is this motherfucker for real?

"Fuck you, Alan," I say within a chuckle. I shake my head. "I feel sorry for you. You have no idea what love is. Not one. I know how it looks, how it feels. So please, leave now." I step back and signal to the door.

Alan considers me for a couple of seconds, I can see a hint of red in his bearded cheeks.

"Is there someone else?"

There isn't someone else. *There has* only *been Oliver.* He's the only one who has ever shown me true love… and the one I've doubted the most. My heart starts breaking at the thought. I can't wait to have him in my arms again and face whatever is about to come together. I know my doubts are reasonable, but there's no doubt my heart will only belong to him. No matter how many insecurities we have to fight.

"Who the fuck do you think you are to ask me a question like that?" I scoff, "you know what? You're free to stay. *I'm* leaving."

I start walking towards the door and he stops me.

"Please, listen to me," he says as he gently takes my hand.

I'm disgusted by the contact, so I grab him by the shoulders and knee his balls.

"You fucking bitch!" he groans before struggling to make his way out of the restaurant by the back exit.

That will show him not to mess with me ever again. I start walking to the front door when Araceli stops me.

"What are you doing, María del Carmen?" she grabs me by my arms. "Do you know how much it took me to convince him to see you?"

I fucking knew it. I feel nauseated with each word and my head feels like it is about to explode.

"What's wrong with you, mother?" I scream, shoving her arms away from me, "how could you do this to me?"

"No seas necia," *don't be stubborn*. "I'm thinking about you, about your future."

"How in the world do you think conspiring against me with a fucking abuser is thinking about my future, huh?" I feel tears rolling down my eyes, "estás igual de loca que él." *You're as crazy as he is.*

I haven't even finished the sentence when I feel her hand slapping my face. I put the hand on my cheek and look at her, seeing for the first time in my life what I've refused to see for so long: *pure, diabolical and evil.* Jacob's words come to my memory, now understanding fully what he meant.

"No me hablés así muchachita idiota." *Don't talk to me like that, you idiot girl.* She mutters between her teeth. "I'm your mother and you're going to respect me."

Dear Lord, did I ever love her?

Have I just felt sorry for her? Felt like she needed me because no one else seemed to do so? Because I didn't want her to be lonely? I also lost myself and my worth in her just because she's my mother and I'm supposed to love her even though she's done nothing but manipulated, humiliated and degraded me? How many times did Angel stop her from beating us and threatened her to take us with him to never return? *This* is what Rocío has been warning me ever since she took her car and drove to Chicago to never come back.

"I don't want you to end up alone, Carmen," she grabs my hand and squeezes it, "I don't want you to end up like me."

"So you'd rather see me dead than alone?" I say within a sob, "I mean that little to you?"

"En lugar de andar de puta cogiendo con un hombre que te va a dejar," she says, "hacele caso a este que al menos por lástima te va a mantener. Te pidió perdón ¿qué más querés? Te está ofreciendo buena vida aun así como sos de simplona. Mujeres como vos y yo no nos podemos enamorar, después nos dejan por otra y quedamos hechas mierda." *Instead of fucking like a whore with a man who's going to leave, take this guy who at least will take pity and will take care of your bills. He asked for your forgiveness, what else do you want? He's offering you a good life even being so plain. Women like you and I can't fall in love. Men will always leave us and make us feel like shit.*

"No necesito a un hombre que me mantenga, madre," I say, shaking her hand off me, "Yo no valgo la lástima de nadie, puedo sobrevivir sola. Vos y yo no somos iguales, yo sí sé lo que valgo y eso lo aprendí solita." *I don't need a guy to pay my bills, mother. I'm not worth anyone's pity, I can survive by myself. You and I are not the same, I know my worth and I learned that by myself.»*

"I'm gonna ask you to please stay away from me too." I say, reaching for the door, "You crossed a line you can't easily return from today, and I don't know if I'll ever forgive you."

I make my way out of the restaurant to Hope Center where I parked my car and slam the door shut, letting bitter tears out. This is it, the last straw. From all her slaps, this has been the one that hurt the most. My idiot head thought that maybe she'd learned the lesson by now, that she felt at least a little remorse after the first time, but as always, I was dead wrong.

I sob all the way to my house. I call Oliver twice while I'm on the road and he doesn't pick up. I need him so much right now. Jacob was right, I need to tell him what's been going on. I didn't think Alan was going to be a big deal, but now that Araceli brought him back I can't deny how much is scaring me. I try to call Oliver one more time but it seems like he turned off his phone.

But maybe it's better like this. I know he's still processing Alberto's news and needs time and space to clear his head and figure things out. If he finds me like this he might go homicidal and will try to find Alan to kill him with his hands. I can't call any of the guys either, none of us are in the right headspace to put more weight on their shoulders. I better wait for Oliver to come home tonight and talk to him when I'm calmer.

I throw myself on the couch, feeling the most abandoned I've ever felt in my life, sobbing, letting out an entire lifetime of rejection, humiliations…and fear that I'm not one hundred percent safe with Alan around. Thinking how I will never be enough for my mother but still how blessed I am for having the opportunity to choose who I want my family to be.

We will figure everything out in the morning…*together*.

37

carmen

I walk into my office feeling even worse than my worst hangover. I slept, but I don't think I rested. The worst and weirdest part of all this is that Oliver didn't come home last night. I woke up today to an empty bed with no missed calls or texts. I'm scared of what that means. Jacob texted me earlier last night to tell me they all made it well back to Minneapolis and that Oliver had spent the night at their parents' house.

I've been calling nonstop but the calls go directly to voicemail. I know he needs time to process but I thought he'd run to me for comfort, not away from me. If work wouldn't be so tense right now, I would ask for the day off. I need to know how he's doing. I need to be there for him… and I need to tell him what went down yesterday.

Araceli sent me a text almost at midnight but I deleted it and blocked her number without even reading it. All she's ever wanted is someone to manipulate and control and I'm not that person anymore.

I am my own person, the master of my own life. I know what I want and who I want… And I want everything with Oliver.

I'm starting my computer when I get a call from Simon's assistant, asking me to go directly to his office.

Great. Just great.

"Called me?" I say, letting myself in.

He doesn't even ask me to sit but gives me an apologetic smile.

"Good morning, Carmen," he says, "I got some bad news this morning from headquarters in Manhattan and… I'm afraid we have to let you go."

The fuck? I realized I slammed my hands on his desk the moment I felt the sting of its cheap oak rasping my palms.

"You're kidding." I mutter with tears in my eyes.

He sighs and looks at me with his eyebrows raised. "The magazine is downsizing the staff all over the thirty states we're in and the creative department is the first one on the line." He stands up and moves across his desk to take my hand, "I swear it had nothing to do with me. I actually tried to keep you. I think Chucky is next and I don't know how I'm going to tell him now that his daughter is in the hospital."

"I can't believe this." I feel tears rolling down my eyes. "The only thing you can reproach me about is me being so stubborn about taking pictures. That's all, Simon. Please. You can't do this to me."

"I know, Carmen." He wraps his arms around me and for some reason I lean my head on his shoulder. "I swear I'm terribly sorry about this."

This is the first time I've ever felt him so sincere. I sit on the chair and bring my hands to my face and cry before signing the layoff papers with dignity.

This hasn't been my season at all. I thought I was making the move of my life as a Sports Photographer when I found this job. In reality, I only found the worst obstacles I've ever faced in my career.

"Look, I'm not supposed to help you but… I could probably get you a job in a small sports publication that's starting out." He writes a phone number and an address on a piece of paper. "Let me know if you're interested."

"Thanks." I force a smile before heading out.

I don't think I'll miss this job, it was a total downgrade from Sullivan Creatives. My entire team even cried on my last day and Fred gave a tear-jerker speech. Still, this isn't fair and feels like shit.

I get to my car and cry a little before starting the engine. I call Oliver twice and it sends me to voicemail again.

Weird.

I dial again and this time, I leave a voicemail.

"Hey. I know you probably need space and this isn't the right time but... I need you." My voice breaks, "I need you so much, baby. I ummm... I need to tell you something that happened the day I bought my mom's car and also something that happened yesterday that really scared me. I don't feel safe right now and don't want to be alone. Also, I ummm... I got fired today. I know you're not in the best place emotionally and mentally with Alberto and all but... I just need you. I love you, Santiago. I'm sorry if my doubts made you feel like I don't want a future with you because I do. Reality is I...I want you to stay. I want to be wherever you are but I'm not going to lie, I would love to be near our family and be all together again. I'm sorry if I made it so difficult last time we talked about this, reality is... I am so scared because I've *always loved you.* From day one I've known you're the love of my life and I'm scared you'll leave me again... And sometimes my fears come out too strong. I love you, Oliver. Call me when you hear this."

Maybe I will accept his offer to photograph for Elite Bikes. Wouldn't that be epic? Both of us making our dreams come true together?

He's the only person I need now. I've been blaming myself for what others have done to me that I pushed him away and not only do I need to apologize for that, but also need to start forgiving myself for it.

I get off on my exit and drive directly to his parents' house, feeling a ball of nerves revolving inside my belly. I don't want him to get annoyed for not respecting his space but I don't know what else to do.

I knock on the door twice and suddenly realize my makeup must be all wiped off.

Relax, Carmen. He's seen you like this before.

The door slams open and I smile at Martita. Her eyes are red and swollen and I throw myself into her arms.

"Hola mija," she whispers before pulling away, giving me an apologetic look, "are you here to say goodbye to Santi?"

"I was here to see how everyone is doing, I haven't heard anything from him since yesterday and I—" I jolt, blinking fast, "wait, what do you mean to say goodbye to him?"

She frowns and brings her hand to her chest. "Oh, please don't tell me you didn't know."

"I didn't know what?" I can't help my tears from falling.

No. Not possible.

"*Hijo de su chingada madre! Me va a escuchar este pinche cabrón.*" She cusses to the air before turning to me. "Carmencita, he left for L.A. about an hour ago."

"He…he left?"

He fucking did it again. He left me after saying he wouldn't.

"Ay, mija! I'm so sorry." She says moving forward to hug me as I stand there sobbing uncontrollably. "He said he had an emergency but I'm not dumb… With everything happening with Alberto I thought he only needed to breathe and calm down but something else happened. I know it, Carmencita."

I feel myself fainting and fall to her arms again. I know I freaked out bad the other day but taking it this far? Didn't he say he wasn't giving up on us? He was so sure of himself when he said it.

Why did I have to be so dumb to believe him?

As I fall into Martita's comfort I try to remind myself of what I know: I'm a badass bitch who kicks ass. I am enough. I'm worth a person who loves me unconditionally and despite my frustrations, confusions and traumas.

I deserve a person who thinks all the things others have rejected are worth loving.

I deserve a guy who decides to stay.

I don't deserve this pain. I don't. I don't deserve this. I don't fucking deserve this.

"Tell me what he did, mija," she says as she's still hugging me, "did he promise you to leave Susan? Is that it? Did he say he was going to call off the wedding and he's marrying her anyway?"

I feel so stupid as she says this, as if the veil has finally come down and see beyond Oliver's empty promises and words of love: He hasn't even told his family he's not engaged anymore. He hasn't given them the indication that he wanted to be with me. He dropped the entire Elite decision speech on me because he didn't have the balls to face the fact that he wanted to find an excuse to leave anyways.

And he did.

Martita insists on taking me inside and telling her what Oliver did but I can't stay here another minute. He's grinded my heart to dust but I refuse to turn his own mother against him.

And I...I still have myself.

I have a dream and a life that can't stop just because a man decided not to be in it anymore.

"I'll be fine," I pull away, "I don't want you or Alberto to worry about me."

"Mija, this is your house," she cups my face, her eyes filled with tears, "I might not have carried you in my womb but I love you. You and your sister are my daughters."

"Oh, I love you so much, Martita," I try to smile.

"I love you too," she shakes her head, "If you need anything, please come right away. I don't want you to be torturing yourself for that *cabrón*."

"I'll come back, I promise."

She hesitates but lets me go. When I get inside my car, I dry my tears, take a deep breath and make a mental checklist of what I need to do.

Like Ethan always says: *You don't let yourself die for anyone.*

First, I need a job. I drive to my house and when I park in my driveway, I send a text to Simon.

Carmen: Sorry to bother you. I really need this job, can you connect me with that publication?

Simon: Of course. Meet me at the address I gave you in half an hour. I can give you a tour and introduce you to some people.

I drive about twenty minutes to the outskirts of Saint Paul. The GPS takes me to an industrial area, full of factories and warehouses. When I get to the place pinned as the destination, I realize it's an abandoned building.

There's got to be something wrong.

I take the piece of paper out and it's the same address. I sigh and scratch my head before getting out of the car, dialing Simon. It's hot as hell and the guy keeps sending me to voicemail. I dial once more and decide to leave a message.

|"Hey Simon," I begin. "I'm here at the address but there's got to be a mistake I—"

A huge hand slams against my mouth pressing hard and another one taking my hand, making me drop the phone. For a moment I feel a wave of panic taking over and try to scream and pull away but the person grabbing me is stronger.

"You're exactly in the right place, baby." I hear Simon's fucking voice in my ear.

Using my free hand I grab his arm and try to use the self-defense technique I know, but the moment I lift my knee up, I feel another pair of hands taking me by my legs.

"My balls are still hurting from that kick." Another voice says and my tears start to fall the moment I recognize him.

Fucking Alan.

"But you're about to make it up to me. Told you she was going to fall for that," he looks at Simon, then back at me, "when Simon mentioned this pain in the ass photographer who insisted on photographing the X Games, it wasn't so difficult to make the connection." He laughs, "what are the odds? My cousin being the boss of the long-lost love of my life?"

Cousin? I am a fucking idiot!

I start screaming and trying to bite Simon's hand, still pressing against my mouth but both of them are grabbing me with so much strength that I'm unable to keep moving. They take me inside the building to a little room in the far back and push me against a wall where my head slams back. I start screaming the word *fire* when I feel my mouth fee, as I was taught to do, but it's useless. There's no one who could hear me. I can hear my voice slamming the walls with an echo and there's not even the sounds of the cars on the road.

These guys are going to rape me and probably kill me.

I keep screaming my lungs out as they take me but stop dead as Alan approaches and punches me in the face, making me lose all my balance and fall to the floor hitting my head.

I don't have the strength to stand up again.

I lay down on the floor and just feel the movement as they move me across the floor. I don't know how, but I have to fight back.

I close my eyes and start sobbing, and for the first time in my life I can't see any light at the end of the tunnel.

38

oliver

About two hours earlier

I think I was disowned by my entire family today.

After pulling myself together, I gathered my entire family to drop the news that I was going back to L.A. Even reassuring them over and over that I was coming back soon, they still all yelled at me and let me know how much of an idiot I am. I know they suspect Carmen is the main reason. After everything that happened with Papá, there's no other motivation for me to pack my things and go this way.

My mom went mad, threatening to take out the wooden spoon and whoop my ass like a ten year old if I didn't tell her what's going on. She gave up after Ethan talked to her. She didn't come down when I said I was leaving. Papá didn't say a word. When I said goodbye, he gave me a pat on my shoulder and asked me to call him when I get home.

Antonio and Vince also gave me a piece of their minds. Antonio being the hardest.

They will all get over it. They always do.

Ethan and Jacob took the day off from work to drop me off at the airport. Ethan glared at me since he jumped to the driver's seat and Jacob can't even look me in the eyes, so he decided for the back seat with Juanito as his company. I know they're pissed but if I tell them one word, they'll want to dig deeper into the issue and that won't end well. I have enough heartache to add their lectures on top of it.

We fall into an uncomfortable silence as we slowly make our way to traffic and the tension becomes unbearable.

"You're really doing this," Jacob says as we merge into the freeway, breaking the silence. "You're really going away after everything that's happening… I can't believe this."

"I already told you I'll come back." I sigh, "I just need some time to think."

"Where have I heard that before?" Ethan says with a sarcastic tone, "oh yeah. Maybe ten years ago when you said the same shit after Angel died?" He nods slowly, "yeah, I remember you took *just a little* time to think."

"I am. Coming. Back." I hiss.

"When?"

I decide not to reply because I don't know the answer to that question. The silence thickens the air again and I drop my head back.

"Talk to us, Ol." Jacob pleads, meeting my eyes through the rear mirror, "we can't help you if you don't talk. Bailing on Mamá y Papá in a moment like this? Not showing up at the X Games anymore… Not saying goodbye to Chip? *It's us*, dude. We're more than brothers, we're best friends."

"There's so much you won't understand." I say lazily.

"Yeah, because we never do, right?" Ethan scoffs sarcastically, "this is the biggest of all your asshole moves, Santiago. I don't even know why Sue's still marrying your ass."

Just what I needed. I feel how the guilt starts creeping over my entire body, I haven't been honest *at all* with them and maybe that's why I deserve everything that's been happening. Maybe if I would've told them from the start, everything would've turned out the way I wanted. Maybe not… but I know I can't really go back home without coming clean and lifting that weight off my conscience.

I bite inside my cheek, "I broke up with Sue."

"You what?" Jacob says, almost in a whisper. Ethan looking dumbfounded at the road, clenching his teeth.

I stretch my back before I talk. My arrangement with Sue, her visit and how we decided to part our own ways. I open the window to get some air, I feel like they're both sucking the oxygen with their glares. When I finish, Jacob talks first.

"I'm going to overlook the fact that you hid this from us and tell you straight away you're the biggest asshole who's ever walked on earth, Oliver Santiago." He snaps, "if you've been single this entire time, then why in the hell not have some balls and talk to Carmen once and for all? Why not take a chance on her already?"

I look at him with surprise. This is the first time he's talked so clearly about the subject. I never thought he would think of me and her as a good idea after all this time. The thought encourages me to open up even more.

"It would never work," I close my eyes, "she's not that into me. She…" *don't say you saw her with someone else. Don't turn them against her.* "I guess… Angel was right after all."

"Angel is dead, Oliver!" Ethan yells, making me snap my eyes open, "you can't keep living as if he's still here. *He's gone*, dude." He glances at me, "what he said and did to both of you was a pile of bullshit. But I'm sure if he would've been alive he would've been over it already."

"It doesn't matter. He was right anyways… and then he died because I didn't listen…" I look between them, "he died the night I was supposed to be there for him and decided to stab him in the back."

"That was shitty luck and irresponsibility," Jacob interrupts, "we were drunk driving like morons, you think that had nothing to do with it?"

Juanito barks once and I turn around, "Oh, you're taking their side? Nice job, best friend." I turn to Jacob, "I was supposed to be driving that car, Jake. I was supposed to be there instead of hitting on Carmen."

"Why the hell do you always talk about this as if you had the entire responsibility, huh?" Ethan signals with his hand, "you think it's been easy for us all these years knowing that we were the idiots who let him grab the keys knowing he was wasted? No, *pendejo!*" He punches me on the shoulder, "we were *all* responsible. And none of us should've been there to begin with. You were exactly where you were supposed to: finally asking Chip to be your girlfriend."

I feel tears clogging up in my throat. I'm not trying to avoid their responsibility or trying to diminish their pain and guilt. I'm just owning my part. I went after the forbidden girl and ended up with my best friend six feet underground and my heart broken. I did it again and now it's the 2.0 remix, *fucking reloaded.*

It wasn't meant to be and I still pushed it till it broke.

"Would've ended up in tears anyway," I mutter, "she did to me now what I knew she would. The minute shit got real, she freaked out and bailed."

Shut up, Santiago. Shut. The fuck. Up. They don't need to know.

"What is that supposed to mean?" Jacob asks, his eyebrow raised.

My heart freezes and I'm on the spot again. I wanted to take this to the grave, but when have I ever been able to keep secrets from them?

"I… uhh…" *whatever the hell.* "I hooked up with Chip."

I hear a tiny gasp and they both stay silent for a second.

"When? The night of the crash?" Jacob asks.

I sigh, taking my cap off to scratch my head.

"No… since I started the kitchen."

"What?" Jacob says at the same time Ethan yells, "are you damn serious?"

Ethan makes a sudden turn in a random exit, breathing hard and muttering something I can't understand. He parks in an empty street and lets out a few deep breaths, calming himself down.

"I *fucking knew it*," Ethan slams his hand on the steering wheel after I'm done and looks at Jacob through the rear mirror. "I told you Jake! You didn't believe it when I said they were sleeping together. I was seeing things, huh? Of course I was fucking seeing it."

"Yeah, I figured it out myself when we all had dinner on Friday… but I couldn't believe Chip would sleep with this asshole while being engaged."

"*I DID NOT. CHEAT. ON SUSAN!*" I snap, turning my face to him.

"I didn't know then! But that's not the point. You fucking slept with her, Oliver! And now you're going back to L.A?" He says, leaning forward. "You're a fucking asshole."

"Tell me something I don't know," I put my cap back on.

"Gladly," Jacob says, sarcastically, "she's too good for you, you know that? You pushed her away for ten years without giving her a goddamn reason, showed up out of nowhere to hook up with her just to leave her again? Are you really this piece of shit?"

"I would've avoided her if I could have." I feel stupid as the words come out.

"You really think we're that stupid, cabrón?" Ethan laughs, "you were all over her from the moment you saw her. You didn't even *try, mano*."

"She's going to die when she finds out you're gone," Jacob continues, plastered on the back seat, his hands on his face, "you're going to fucking *kill her* and when you'll come back with your tail between your damn legs she won't ever forgive you." He takes a deep breath and leans forward, "you know she's always been in love with you, right?"

"Jake, don't," Ethan warns, turning to him.

"I…" I stutter, blinking fast, "we did say *I love you*."

"I'm not talking about now, I'm talking about *always*."

What?

"Güey, ya párale." *dude, stop it.* Ethan insists. "We already said too much."

Jacob is livid, his cheeks are red and his hands balled in fists. This dude listens to no one when he's mad.

"No. It's time for us to talk about this." He points with a finger, "I've had enough of this mess already. I've had enough of her thinking she doesn't deserve better and tired of this *pendejo* running away because he's a fucking coward." He turns to me, "she's been in love with you since we're *seven years old*, Oliver." He clenches his jaw, "the only reason why she's jumped from asshole to asshole it's because she wants to get over you by lowering her standards. Angel said those fucked up things to both because he knew you were going to leave him out the second you got together. But it backfired, and now she's convinced herself you were always just a crush because she thinks she'll never be enough for a good guy like you. She thinks you'll end up leaving her like you did before."

It's when Jacob catches his breath that I lose mine. All the missing pieces in this painful puzzle are now taking place. Is this why she was so freaked out when we first kissed and why she wanted to settle for friendship?

I'm not just an idiot, I'm *the High King of all idiots.*

I swallow hard. "Did she tell you that?"

"About her being in love with you?" Jacob laughs, "I think you're the only one who never knew."

"If the little hearts with O+C all over her notebooks weren't an indication." Ethan snorts.

I suddenly imagine little Carmen's handwriting and try to keep the sweetness of it in my head, but I can't let that other thought go.

"I meant… about her being with other guys."

"She doesn't need to. I know her like the palm of my hand, Ol. She was devastated when you left. That shit broke her. She cried for days when she found out you were gone, we were all there seeing her trying to get comfort by dating guys who never deserved her." Jacob says, his tone getting harsher with each word, "but we swore we'd never meddle because it was *you* who had to fix it. Everything could've been solved years ago with a simple conversation and a little groveling, but you're both stubborn as hell. We made a pact and stayed out of it because we love you both and could've messed up more, even though it hurt. But *this* is insane. You crossed the fucking line."

"You're an idiot." Ethan exhales. "She's been denying how much she loves you but it's been common knowledge."

I try to process every single word and they click perfectly in all the empty spaces. There I was, thinking I was courting her and winning her love when I already had it. Then why didn't she tell me plain and simple when I asked her what she wanted? I quickly tell them about my possible move to Minneapolis and my last conversation with her.

"She didn't *say* she wanted me to stay, she didn't say a thing," I conclude, "she just had to snap her fingers and I would've made the move without thinking twice. I would've given her anything."

"She wanted *you* to make the decision for yourself. She needs you to *want* to make those decisions because you're *choosing* her on your own. She never asks what she wants because she's afraid of others thinking she's manipulating the situation." Ethan says before running his tongue inside his cheek, "besides, you left her once and she's still waiting for you to find a reason to leave. Why ask you to stay if you're going away anyways? Come on, Ol. She's not the type of girl who would throw herself at your feet and beg you not to leave her. That woman will *open the door* and wave good-bye, even with a broken heart."

She was giving me the opportunity to show her I was here to stay because I wanted to and I blew it. Is that why she looked for that in another guy? If she loves me like they claim she does, if she's loved me as long as I've loved her… then why was she kissing someone else? Why did she lie to me about him? It doesn't make sense.

"You still believe what Angel said about her, don't you?" Jacob asks *as-matter-of-factly.* "You still believe you're just a crush to her and will dump you when she finds someone better like he said. And you don't *want* to fight to deserve her because that's what you think he would've wanted." He shakes his head. "Ten fucking years and he's still manipulating you from the underground?" He laughs sarcastically. "I always knew he was some persuasive guy, but this is another level. *Unbelievable.*"

"*That's not true!*" I feel my blood boil, "I was about to confess my feelings the night he died."

"But you still left, carnal!" Ethan signaling towards me with his hand. "You ran instead of talking to her."

"You left to stay loyal to him, because you refused to accept he wasn't here anymore." Jacob adds, waving a hand in the air, "congratulations Oliver, you managed to stay second to him like always. There! I said it."

"What the fuck is that supposed to mean?" I clench my jaw.

"Come on, Ol." Ethan says calmly, "We all knew you were the better rider from all of us. Better than *him*, even if you refused to accept it. He was great and we all loved him."

He points to me quickly, "But you were the most charismatic, the most dedicated and fearless; everyone followed *you—Carmen being the first one in the line*—but he always wanted to be first. He wanted to be *you*."

No, that's not it.

"But," Jacob continues. "You loved and respected him so much that you kept him on a pedestal your entire life. And you still do it. That's why you never became a Pro and why you refused to know anything about Chip for ten years. That's why you keep going for slightly less than what you deserve and why you unconsciously believe everything he said to you about her."

"You still see her through that lens." Ethan agrees, "You still believe you're his second. That's why you're so reluctant to make the move Damian and the board are asking. Because it will be the summit of all the things he didn't have and you know he would've wanted."

I'm speechless. It's like that scene in *The Truman Show* when he finally realized he'd been living in a lie that everyone knew except for him. The pain in my chest intensifies as I realized it too: *I've been loyal to a ghost and everyone noticed but me.*

"Are you two making this shit up right now?" I ask, "Or does everyone feel the same?"

"We've talked." Jacob says scratching Juanito's neck. "We all came to the same conclusion years ago. He fucked you guys up without even knowing the consequences it would cause and both of you are stubborn as hell to listen to reason."

"I told her I loved her." I breathe, my eyes closed as I suppress my tears, "I literally took my heart out and placed it in her bare hands."

"And yet, here you are, on your way to the airport," Ethan laughs, "doing *exactly* what she was afraid of."

"She needs someone who's willing to *fight* for her." Jacob says leaning forward again, this time smiling. "She needs you to be clear, and back up your words with *actions*. She's had enough empty promises and shit partners…God, that asshole broke her fucking arm, Oliver. She's already had too much bullshit, even from her family." He leans back again. "Araceli has always made her feel like shit and Rocío cuts her off and doesn't even visit her because she doesn't want to bump into Araceli."

"She—" Ethan clears his throat, "she has her own load of issues, okay? Don't put her at the same level as Araceli."

We look at him quizzically, but he ignores us looking away to the window.

"Whatever." Jacob says, shaking his head. "The point is, why would she think your words mean a thing if you haven't taken the time to prove them."

"You *told* her you loved her," Ethan says, starting the engine again, "but you left her once and you're doing it again. She got what she was expecting, even if you *did* tell her."

It makes sense, even though it doesn't explain why she lied to me about the car dealership and why she was seeing this guy behind my back. Still, I believe everything they're saying, which makes me realize there's something that doesn't add up with what I saw yesterday. This behavior is not like her at all.

Can I still fix this? Can I go back to her and find an explanation after what I just saw and work through our insecurities to finally be together?

Not if she finds out you're gone.

"Fuck," I say, burying my face in my hands.

"What are you going to do now?" Jacob asks.

It takes me two seconds to conclude. *She is the one true love of my life, she deserves that I fight for her with everything I have. My parents need me here more than ever, my brothers too.*

"I can't leave," I sit up straight again and fix my cap. I can see them both smiling as Ethan starts making his way out to the freeway.

"But I need to do something first." I say, "get off on the next exit."

Ethan makes his way between the lanes and I suddenly find the silver lining. I resisted the idea of coming back for so long because I knew the moment I faced her, I wouldn't stand a chance to make my life what it's always supposed to be.

Thank God I did.

I need to kneel down to beg for her forgiveness.

But first, I need to talk to someone.

It's time to let go.

39

oliver

Seems like the air was taken away from the earth the moment we open the doors of the car and start walking along the cemetery. My siblings lead the way through the garden and the fear that's been creeping my soul since he left intensifies as I realize that until now, I didn't know the way to his grave.

I see it before they signal, my legs feeling heavier with every step as we get closer. The air feels cooler. Summer is still far away from ending, but I feel winter coming at me when the golden letters engraved in that green stone freeze my heart one by one.

Angel Ramiro Morales

June 17th, 1990 – June 30th, 2008

*We will never forget you, son, brother and friend. Our beloved **ride or die.***

I feel my heart slamming against my chest, my stomach twisting and my breathing intensifying when we finally stop. The three of us lined in front of the gravestone. When I told my brothers I wanted to come here, I said it without even thinking how hard it was going to be. I just knew I had to, no matter how out of my comfort zone this is.

I can feel him here, though. As if Angel wanted me to come here to finally face the one thing I refused to ten years ago.

"Angel is dead, Ol."

Angel has been dead for a long time, and I kept him so alive that I still lived my life as if he'd been a thousand miles away from me all this time. As if the plans we once made were still on hold.

"Qué onda, güey?" *What's up dude*, Ethan says quietly as he touches the gravestone, "long time. So much that we need to tell you."

"What's up, loco?" Jacob steps forward, putting a packet of Angel's favorite bubble gum on top, "it's been quite a month. But we'll have time to catch up, we brought you a surprise. Look who's here."

I let out a silent chuckle as I hear them talking to him with such familiarity after so many years he's been gone. I can't help but feel a little guilty again. They were right earlier, this wasn't easier for anyone. Jacob was in a coma for two weeks after the crash and has no recollection of that night. Ethan and the rest of the gang saw the entire thing happen with their own eyes. The physical, mental and emotional consequences have been a heavy cross to bear for all of us. Still, they *stayed*. They dealt with the guilt and loss instead of running away from them.

You're not running away anymore.

Ethan takes Juanito's leash out of my hand as I kneel down. I freeze for a moment, still unable to grasp the idea of being here so close to him after ten years. Suddenly, I feel a familiar vibe in my heart and I picture him right in front of me. I close my eyes and take a deep breath.

"Hey, bro," I say, my voice breaking a little, "I'm sorry it took me so long to come visit. I just… I never really got used to the idea of being here without you."

I stay silent for a couple of seconds, trying to keep my face and voice straight but the tears start rolling down anyways.

"I miss you, man. Now more than ever. I ummm… A lot has

happened since you've been gone." I shake my head and sigh, "I didn't make Pro. I'm sorry." I smile, running my hand against the stone.

"I figured out that was your calling not mine. But I didn't give up on BMX—on us. We have an entire line of welders in these cool factories making some of the best bikes in the world. I even named a bike after you. I hope that made you proud."

A sob comes out of nowhere and I put my hands on my face. I can hear Ethan pulling the leash as Juanito starts whining.

"I… I need to talk to you… about Chip." I breathe, "I honestly don't think you knew how bad things were going to get and I don't think you meant to hurt us the way you did… but you still did. But you know what? *I forgive you*." I wipe my face with a hand, "I love you and miss you and that's more important than anything else. I know you loved her and you loved me. Possessive as hell but you loved us all. " I sob, "I did what you wanted though. I tried to ignore her, forget about her, I tried to stay away but I can't… not anymore. I *love* her. *Like crazy*. That never changed, it only got deeper and stronger." I point a finger to him, "I've messed up every relationship I've had because my heart has always belonged to that woman." I feel a hand on my shoulder, "I've been far away from her for too long and I can't keep lying to myself. I need her. She makes me feel alive bro. You know how she always makes everything brighter, better. She sees things I can't. Things that make life beautiful even when everything sucks and right now… everything sucks. She makes me a better man, she makes me *brave*. She made me get on a bike again, can you believe it? After I swore to you I was never going to if you weren't here."

I laugh through tears. "And I'm not asking you for approval anymore. I'm here to let you know I'm marrying your sister." I hear Jacob letting out a soft chuckle as I go on, "well, she hasn't said yes yet… but I have a ring already. I bought it a few weeks ago. She's it for me. My everything." I sit down and cross my legs, "and I swear to you here, in front of some of the most important people in our lives, that I will work *every day* for her and our family. That none of your sisters or your mom will ever lack anything. I swear I will love that woman till the day I give you the next fist bump.

"One more thing," I choke on my tears and sniff. "I know I have no right to ask you, but would you watch over Papá? He… he's going through some rough shit now. He's going to need you. We're all going to need your strength… this… this is so fucking hard." I pause for a moment before sobbing again, taking my cap off and running my hand through my hair, "dammit, Angel. I miss you, *socio*. I love you. Always have, always will. You've been in my mind every single second since you left. And I'm sorry. I should've been there, should've kept my promise. I should've been brave and *beat the hell out of you* until you were okay with me dating her instead of bailing on you like I did. I'm sorry I didn't show up at the funeral. I just… I couldn't see you in a fucking casket knowing you couldn't hear me or talk to me. I couldn't say good-bye, we were not supposed to say goodbye. I refused to bury you and I chickened out and ran the opposite way. I'm sorry I never came back for her, for the gang. *I'm so sorry.* But I'm here now. I promise. I won't leave again. I won't."

I finally break and can't talk anymore. I let out the tears I've been holding for years of being a coward. My two brothers kneel down to hug me tight as I sob like a little kid. I can hear them both sniffing too.

Papá always says, "llorar hace a un hombre más fuerte y más blando." *Crying makes a man stronger and softer.*

I never understood what he meant until now. I see it. I feel it. These tears hurt, but it's a pain of relief. Like when you have a splinter deep in your hand and you finally take it out. It still hurts, but you're set free. That's exactly how I feel… *free.*

Let go.

"It wasn't your fault, Oliver!" Jacob takes my face in his hands, "whatever had to happen did. It hurt, it still does but it was life. Not you… this time we'll get through it together. That's what we've been doing all of these years… we've just been waiting for you."

"We never blamed you, man. Damn, we didn't even blame each other." Ethan says, kissing my cheek, "not us, not Chip, not

Rocío or Tony… Alex, Vince. No one has ever blamed anyone for what happened. We only just wanted you to come back home. And you're here now."

"No more letting guilt ruin your happiness, *please*," Jacob adds, "stay here with us? We're familia. *Your* familia."

I nod and smile through my tears. We stay there in front of the grave for a couple minutes, feeling more at peace than I've ever felt in a long time. Healing is not an overnight event, but the first step is the most crucial. And it's never too late to take it. The road seems rocky ahead, but I won't walk alone.

I'll have my familia. I'll have my girl.

"I think it's time to get your girl back," Ethan says as we stand up.

The statement pulls me back to reality. I need a plan, grovel hard and make decisions, but first, I need to know how bad things are.

"Yeah, but," I put my cap back on, "there's one thing I haven't told you."

In less than five minutes, I fill them in with the painful details of the last couple of days and the last drop that made me change that ticket. I can see Ethan visibly cringing and Jacob bringing a hand to his mouth.

"Oh shit," Jacob mutters the second I finish while Ethan talks over him.

"No, there's no way," he shakes his head, "she wouldn't do that to you. It must be a mistake. She's not a cheater, Oliver. You weren't in the right headspace and you didn't stay that long, there's gotta be an explanation, she would never—"

"This isn't good," Jacob interrupts him, bringing his hands to his head, "God, this is not good. *I'm such an idiot.*" He turns to me, "what did he look like?"

"Ummm… white, bulky, way taller than her," I shake my head in confusion, "why?"

"Did he have black hair? Thick beard and seemed older than her?"

"Uh, yeah. Why?"

"Fucking Alan," Ethan blurts when he realizes.

"What?" I yell, feeling my heart coming out of my throat.

"Shit, we gotta go to her, now!" Jacob shouts as he runs towards the car.

We follow him and as we make our way out of the parking lot, he starts telling us about the day she bumped into him at the car dealership and how scared she was about telling me. I quickly turn my phone on after almost two days and my heart almost stops seeing tons of texts and missed calls.

One single voicemail left just a couple of hours ago.

"Hey. I know you probably need space and this isn't the right time but… I need you."

My heart breaks with each word I listen from the woman I've hurt more times than I can count when the only thing she's ever done is love me and wait for me. I can hear the fear in her voice, the sadness and abandonment in her tone as she tells me over and over how much she loves me and needs me.

"I want you to stay."

"I've always loved you."

"I'm scared you'll leave me again."

My body tenses up and my head is about to explode. She didn't lie to me because she was having an affair. She hid what happened because she was scared. She didn't kiss him, he probably forced himself onto her and I turned around and fucking left her when she needed me to protect her. She *was* going to tell me what happened…

I made her worst fear come true.

A wave of panic mixed with anger slams my body as my head starts making up worst-case scenarios and I try to fight my mind as I've never done before.

All my hope was drained out after this weekend of hell and I just pray that little drop I still have left is enough for what's coming.

40

oliver

Jacob dials RideXtreme after we listen to Carmen's voicemail for the fifth time. She left the building not too long ago. We try calling her from all three different phones while we're on the road and when none of us get an answer, we come to the conclusion that something else is going on.

"Is it giving you a tone?" I ask Jacob, trying to keep my voice straight.

"It is, but it keeps ringing until it gets to voicemail," he says with the phone against his ear, "I'm so stupid, I should've said something to you."

"You just trusted, Jake. She asked you not to say it and you didn't." Ethan says as he merges between lanes, "any of us would've. She'll be okay. We'll get to her and keep her safe."

We dial the rest of the guys on our way. Antonio asks us to pick him up at the shop, Vince tells us he'll go to her house and Alex asks us to keep him updated. We stop quickly at my parents' to leave Juanito and my luggage. When Mamá tells us she was here just half an hour ago, my heart splits between hope and hurt, knowing she might be fine but also learning she now believes I'm gone.

You just need to kneel down and beg, but she's fine.

We don't give Mamá much detail but promise to fill her in as soon as we find her and hit the road again. We pick up Antonio and head to her house. I feel my stomach tangling up with my intestines as we drive through these blocks slightly over the speed limit, praying she'll be safe and sound. When we turn around her block, I feel my body giving out as I see Vince standing in the driveway.

"She's not here," he says in pants as we pull over, "do you know anything?"

"Not yet," Jacob says, "should we go to the restaurant? If she's with that son of a bitch. Araceli might know where she is."

"I don't know," Antonio says, "knowing her, she'll say whatever crap just so we don't get in the middle."

"Have you talked to Juliana?" Vince asks, leaning on the window, "maybe she's at Hope."

"I did," Ethan says, "she hasn't seen her since yesterday." He closes his eyes shut, "we still don't know if she's with him. We might be freaking out for nothing."

"She was laid off just a few hours ago, if she's fine, why hasn't she said anything to any of you?" I say, my hands in my face, "What.. what if she did go back to him?"

"Not a chance, cabrón," Ethan says, cupping the back of my neck, "I can assure that with my life. She's waited ten years for you, she would never do that."

If she leaves me because she can't forgive me, I will have to go on with my life and accept it as my punishment. But if something happens to her because of some psychotic motherfucker? I could never forgive myself. I could never live with that pain.

"Wait." Antonio snaps, taking his phone out. "We added each other on Find my Friends when she knew he was out of jail."

Antonio pulls up the app with his trembling hands. It takes a couple of seconds to get her location and I feel time slowing down. The blue dot finally stops and it pins her in an industrial area Downtown Saint Paul fifteen minutes ago.

"I know where that is," Vince says, opening the door to get in. "There are only storehouses and factories there."

"It's not that far away." Ethan says, starting the car again.

If I don't shit myself as Ethan switches lanes like Toretto, it's because my mind is full of anxiety prayers. Asking God not only not to be pulled over but also pleading she's okay. We finally slow down as we approach the destination on the GPS and as soon as I recognize her car parked in front of one of the buildings, I open the door and run towards it.

"Oliver, wait!" Ethan screams after me.

The front door of her car is open, and my entire body paralyzes for a second when I see the keys still in the starter and her phone thrown on the floor.

She's here. She's in danger.

"Could you at least wait for us?" Jacob says as I pick it up and show him.

"Call the cops," I mutter, "now."

I see Vince taking out his phone and dial in the corner of my eye when we hear a loud and sharp scream inside the building.

"Over here!" Antonio says when he finds an open door in a far corner.

We get inside and the screams are deafening, my heart hammering and adrenaline pumping hard as we run. The building is completely empty, making her voice clear, directing us to a room located in the back. Vince is still talking to the cops, giving them our location when we run towards the small office and I'm *livid* with what we find the moment we step inside.

Two motherfuckers, pinning her against the floor.

One of them taking her arms and the other one by the legs. My heart shatters as I see my strong, beautiful woman trying to fight back. We throw ourselves against the guys, knocking them down to the floor.

Ethan and Vince slam one against a wall while Jacob and Antonio get to the other.

"I've got you," I pant as I throw myself to my knees to take her, "you're safe baby. We're here, we've got you."

Her hair is covering her eyes. I carefully take her head and brush a strand away to let her look at me. When I do, a burning wave takes over me from head to toe as I see her nose bleeding and her left eye red and swollen.

Every one of the times I ever thought it was the angriest I've ever been turn to nothing compared to what I'm feeling now. The current stage of my entire body and mind has crossed the line of boiling fury. It intensifies as she opens her eyes, blinking slowly as if she's trying to figure out where she is. She gasps when she notices it's me who's holding her. Her chest comes up and down very fast as she starts crying in my arms.

I look at her and shake my head, still unable to believe someone was capable of doing such a thing. I look to my right and I recognize the guy Vince and Ethan are trying to hold.

I can't control what my body does from here.

I gently lower her down and kiss her cheek and without giving a damn, I walk two steps until I'm in front of him. His disdainful look and challenging posture of his head is the last thing I notice when my fist starts punching his face over and over without control.

The guys move away. I throw my entire body weight on top of him with my knees against his chest without stopping.

"Ol, stop." Ethan says, trying to pull me away. "That's enough. You got him."

Ethan tries his best, but I'm a heavy dude on a mission. Disfiguring this monster's face is the least he deserves.

I'm still punching him when I hear the sirens approaching. I don't notice how tired I am until Vince and Ethan finally pull me away from him. He groans and tries to stand up but falls to the side. I don't think he'll try to run.

When I hear my girl crying, I turn to look at her. She's being held by Antonio and Jacob while the others are holding the other guy, who also has his nose bleeding and a few red spots across his face.

The police finally make it through the door and take them away. Carmen gives out their names and I can't believe it when I learn the other guy was actually her ex-boss. I feel my brother's arms around me while we talk to another officer. When the ambulance gets here, I take her in my arms to the paramedics. She doesn't protest. As I walk she finally looks up and I resist the weakness in my knees when tears start falling from her eyes.

"You left." she whispers.

"I know. I'm sorry." I tell her before kissing her forehead, "I swear I'll explain later but I'm sorry I put you through that."

"You left *again*, Oliver."

"Fuck baby, I'm so sorry," I say, taking a seat inside an ambulance, holding onto her for dear life, "I'm an idiot. I'm so stupid. *I'm sorry.*"

"You said you wouldn't leave me and you did," she sobs, "still… thank you for coming to get me."

I look at her through my tears and tuck a strand of hair behind her ear. "It's the least I could do for the woman I love."

We both let out our tears as we hold onto each other for a little while before the EMTs examine her. We're all taken to the station afterwards and end up leaving around ten at night.

While we drive back, we finally set our stories straight. I can't even look her in the eye as she tells everything Araceli did, how she tricked her into seeing Alan again and… that the moment I turned around to leave the restaurant, was the moment she slapped his face.

I sure have a lot of groveling to do.

None of us think she should be alone in her house and Antonio offers his so she can stay there for a while and she accepts. She'll be safe with him and will give me some peace of mind.

We get to Antonio's house and we all step out of the car to shield her as she walks in. She has a broken nose, a concussion and a mild damage in her throat. Thankfully nothing that will permanently harm her other than scars across her face and her heart.

I offered to pay for a lawyer and therapy. She was reluctant for a moment but everyone else encouraged her to accept and she did.

Everyone says their goodbyes in Antonio's living room leaving us alone for a moment. She's sitting down on the couch and I kneel down to talk to her.

"I understand why you turned around and left," she says with tears in her eyes, "believe me I do. You were already broken about Alberto and Araceli made it worse. So, I get it that you thought you saw something that wasn't there… But that's exactly what scares me, Oliver. This is the second time you do this and it *terrifies me*," she cries, "it scares the hell out of me that you'll find it too hard or too scary at some point and will have this knee jerk reaction again instead of talking to me. I survived it ten years ago, but I don't know if I could do it next time. I love you *too much*. More than before." She whispers the last part, "I… I need time… a couple of days to clear my head… and you need time to think if this is really what you want, if you're not going to leave when things get scary or too tough."

I stop breathing as pain takes over my chest. I wipe my face with a hand and shake my head.

"I know I don't deserve your trust," I say, "but you're my everything. I love you. You're it for me, Chip. And I won't stop fighting till I earn your trust again."

"I–I don't know. Just think about it and—" She looks away, her eyes red. "If you want to leave again–just–would you please say goodbye this time? *Please*. Have the decency to say goodbye like I mean something to you."

The remaining pieces of my heart shatter with each word. But this time, I'll make it right.

"No need to say goodbye." I smile through tears, "next time I leave, you're coming with me," I whisper as I wipe the tears from her beautiful cheeks. "Otherwise, I'm not going anywhere *ever* again."

41

oliver

Why is it that when someone asks you to wait, time slows down? It's like it knows you're anxious to get some news and the universe intentionally decides to make it worse.

It's been a week since Carmen was abducted and everyone's been working as a team to ensure she has everything she needs. Alex took the first flight from Florida as soon as Ethan called to tell him what happened. He's staying with her and Antonio so she isn't alone when everyone's at work. I've been stopping by from time to time to check on her without pressing out for much more and spent most of my time with my parents. Papá might go back to work soon, now that his heart is a little stronger and he started with medication for Alzheimer. We're still debating whether or not it is safe for him to drive. The doctor said he only needs a little help to go on with his days and he doesn't need to change his routine just yet. We just need to adapt with him as time goes by. As Ethan said, we're not losing him yet. We're going to make sure he has the best life in any way we can.

Mamá is talking to me again, after what went down with

Carmen she was so pissed at me for going away, but once I asked for forgiveness and explained what happened, she broke down in tears and held me for a long time.

As soon as I could, I texted Damian with my definite answer. He was very clear saying that I might need to get to L.A. sooner than we thought. I have a stupid amount of meetings I need to attend for planning and budgeting, but the sooner I get through it, the sooner I can come back home.

It's Friday night, Ethan, Vince and I are at my parents' house, playing Call of Duty. Mamá is cooking dinner at Hope Center and Papá is watching in silence. I've been distracted all day and have been killed three times already.

"Cheer up, man," Vince says, shoving the control to the coffee table, "I know it's easier said than done but, patience is key."

"I don't know," I say, throwing myself to a bean bag, "I feel like I've screwed up too much."

"Not as bad as you think," Ethan stands up to get a beer from the kitchen, "she loves you. Take hope in that."

I let out an unamused laugh. "I wish it was that simple. I doubted her, reassured her insecurities and fears and on top of that, I left her alone when she most needed me… *again*. What if she decides she can't trust me?"

"Give her what she needs, mijo. I know waiting feels like you're burning inside, but that's love." Papá says, standing up to kiss my forehead. "Love is pure gold. The only way to test if gold is real… is through *fire*. Is she worth the burn?"

I swallow tears. "Yes."

"Then wait for her just as she waited for you," he pats my cheek and goes upstairs, leaving the three of us in shock.

"Wow," Vince whispers.

"I know," Ethan replies, "he's the wisest guy on earth. He knows everything."

Even going through his own pain, he's still managing to be the father I need at this very moment.

We're not even paying attention to the game, so Vince turns off the console and takes out his iPad, where he has all the pictures Carmen took of me the day we went for a ride. I hate bragging but I look amazing. She was born to do this.

When the head director of RideXtreme knew what happened, he contacted her to give her job back but she refused. She didn't want to go back to the same environment that was so draining for her and we all supported her. I just wish I could help her to achieve her goals.

"I can't stop looking at them," Ethan says with the iPad in his hands, "you should frame this one."

It's the Tailwhip I did at the end. The picture shows one frame with several shots in sequence with a clear view of the process, every motion and turn over the quarter pipe. It's so well edited that my body contrasts perfectly with the sunset behind me.

"I might," I smile lazily.

I let my mind wander for a little bit, imagining a studio in a big house where I'd keep the pictures of her and our family. A corner table with this picture framed and all the pictures she'd take when she becomes a BMX Photographer like she's dreamed about.

There's got to be a way to help her without me influencing directly.

"You should send it to a magazine," Vince continues, "I bet a lot of people would kill for an exclusive. You're still *The Quokka* of Minneapolis after all."

And there it is!

"Wait a minute," I jump from the bean bag, taking my phone out. The guys look at me quizzically as I make my way to the deck.

If this idea works, I will have to make my first trip out of state soon. Knowing I might not get the warmest and welcoming answer, I take a deep breath and dial the number of the only person who can help me right now.

She picks up at the second tone.

"You son of a bitch!"

I sigh. "Hey, Rocío. How are you?"

"What the fuck, Oliver?" she keeps going, "why would you do this to my sister, huh? Do you realize she's the motherfucking *prize?* A *damn queen?* How on earth can you be so stupid and do the same thing that got you both heartbroken twice? *Twice? Idiota, estúpido y pendejo.* When you have a woman like that next to you, you don't leave her to the wolves and run away. You man the fuck up and stay with her once and for all like you've always *fucking wanted.* How difficult is that? *Jesus.*"

My stomach drops with each word. I know I deserve her hate and then some but I still try to keep my shit together.

"I know," I say, leaning on the railing, "I know I'm an idiot. I'm sorry."

"Of course you are, you're a man." I can hear her heels on the floor as she talks, "men are always sorry but they never take real action to make up for your fucking mistakes. Inútiles de mierda." *Useless pieces of shit.*

"I *want* to make it up to her."

"Oh is that why you're calling?" she huffs, "you need help from big sister? *The fucking nerve, you asshole.* You don't deserve her, did you know that?"

"*No one* deserves her, I don t think anyone ever will," I say firmly, "that's a fact. I'm not going to say that I do… but I *fucking want to,* Ross," my voice breaks, "I swear to you I want to be the man she deserves, even if I never come close to it. I want to spend the rest of my life proving to her that giving me one last chance wasn't a waste. Because I might not be worthy of her but I'm sure as hell no one is ever going to love her the way I do."

Rocío doesn't say anything for a long time. My anxiety picks up and I feel my hopes slowly going down until she breaks the silence.

"Keep talking."

"She asked me for time but I know she wants to be with me. She told me that," I say hopefully. "I understand that and I can give her time, but I want to help her out with something else, that's where I need you."

She lets out a long breath. "What do you have in mind?"

I sigh and cross my fingers. "How would you feel about

writing an exclusive about the businessman and Minneapolis BMX legend who jumped on a bike again after ten long years."

Rocío remains silent for a couple of more seconds and I pray to every saint I know of in both English and Spanish.

"If you hurt her one more time, Oliver Santiago Rodriguez," she mutters, "if you get fucking cold feet once again and leave her again I swear to god I'm gonna get you in your sleep and cut your damn dick off."

The thought makes me cringe a little bit but the relief I feel in my chest makes me let out a chuckle.

"I'll sharpen the knife for you." I smile.

After checking our schedules and exchanging emails, we make a quick plan and discuss how to execute it.

"I'm not going to lie." Rocío starts. "I'm actually pretty excited about this idea, she's gonna love it."

"I really hope so." I sigh, "thank you, Ross. You have no idea how much I appreciate the help."

"Just don't fuck it up," I can hear the smile on her tone, "and Ol?"

"Yeah?"

"Give Alberto a hug from me," her voice breaks, "I promise I'll visit more often."

I smile and reassure her before I hang up and come back inside. Vince and Ethan shoot me a confused look.

"I'm going to Chicago for the weekend," I say with a smile, "you guys want to come?"

They look at each other, still confused and then look at me.

"Sure," they say at the same time.

I book a flight for tonight and I start explaining my plan to the guys as we go back to pack. They're both rooting for me, although I can see Ethan's a little bit more enthusiastic about the trip than I was expecting. Jacob and Antonio drops us off at the airport and in less than five hours, we're in our seats waiting to take off.

I know Carmen might freak out if she knows I'm gone suddenly, so I take my phone and send her a text.

Oliver: I won't be able to see you during the weekend. I'm sorry. I have an interview in Chicago and they need me to be there ASAP. I'm taking Vince and Ethan with me. I just wanted to let you know I'm coming back in a couple of days.

Carmen: Thank you for telling me. Good luck in your interview, you guys have fun. *Kiss emoji.*

Oliver: Thanks, baby. See you in a couple of days.

She doesn't reply, but she doesn't need to. I make myself comfortable as the plane starts to move and I fall asleep, knowing I will be hearing her sweet laugh again very soon.

42

carmen

| Fear is a bitch.

It eats you up and doesn't let you move. It keeps you away from people and away from your dreams.

Asking Oliver for space was scary and hard but so necessary. All I want is to run to his arms and tell him I'll love him forever but… *fear is a bitch*.

He's been more than understanding and has given me what I needed. Just not in the way I expected. He stops frequently to leave food, groceries or just to check up on me. He asks me if I need anything without trying to kiss me or hug me, kisses my hand and leaves.

He even let me borrow Juanito.

This cutie is the most effective therapy dog on earth and my heart has been full with his company.

It's been two weeks since the incident and although Alan and Simon are in jail and will spend a long time there, I still can't be alone. I'm having nightmares every night, I'm tired all the time but can't sleep and everything I try to eat makes me gag.

I already had my first therapy session, but healing takes time. I hate that I have to wait to actually feel better. For that same reason, I'm about to take the bull by the horns and do the one thing I haven't done to start letting go completely.

"Are you sure you want to do this?" Alex says as we walk through the doors of *'Las tres Morenas'*. This dude is six-feet, five inches, a tank of muscle who has fought two wars and kicks ass for living…still, he's the biggest and mushiest teddy bear ever.

"I am." I smile.

"I'll be here if you need me," he says, taking Juanito's leash and sitting down on one of the booths.

"She's in the back," Tía Carmela says as I kiss her cheek hello, "you don't have to do this, mi amor. She's already done too much damage."

"I have to, Tía," I smile, "I need to let it all out. For me."

She gives me a teary smile, kissing my cheek. She's been so worried, apologizing nonstop every time she sees me, as if it was all her fault. I've always wondered how on earth this loving woman could be sisters with Araceli.

I knock on the door of the kitchen and let myself in. She's cleaning and stops when she sees me.

She studies me for a second. Even though my black eye and scars are fading, it still looks bad. I know I just made an impression. I can see her swallowing tears. Pride. Always pride before showing any emotion or real care for her daughters.

"You came." She says. "I've been calling."

"I know," I take two steps, "I needed time before seeing you. I'm okay if you care to know."

She blinks fast and looks away, "Yes, good…thank you."

Thank you?

Is she fucking kidding me?

Two words I've never gotten from her and the one time she says them is today, the day I show up beaten up by the guy she schemed with to hurt me.

"Really, Araceli?" I blink slowly and breathe hard, "I don't know why I was expecting an apology. I'm always wrong about you…always." I stand in front of her, "Why mother? I want to know why you hate me so much?"

"I don't." She takes a deep breath. "Everything I've ever done in this life is for you and your siblings. I've worked all my life for you. I've given you everything your father didn't. If I hated you, you would've been in the streets a long time ago. That's not hate."

"But that isn't love either," I say quietly, "That's just being responsible. Meeting a need you know you have to meet." I shake my head, "Our entire childhood Rocio and I saw you treating Angel like a king while you treated us like trash. Even Angel couldn't understand why you manipulated us and humiliated us. How every single word from your mouth implied that we were not enough for you," I feel tears coming out of my eyes, "I've been here for you all this time doing my best to make you happy. Even after what you did with Alan last time…I still stayed. Now you not only lied to my boyfriend about Alan but you also tricked me again to see him when you knew what he'd done to me. Did Carmela tell you he tried to *rape me?*" She's still looking away and I feel my anger taking over. "LOOK AT ME!" I scream, making her turn her head towards me, "is it because we look like your ex-husband? Is that it? Do Rocío and I remind you of the man who left you?"

She shakes her head. A disdainful look in her eyes.

"You're so naïve." She lifts up her chin, "Do you think he was the only man who left me? Men always leave, María del Carmen. Women like us don't get to keep a man. We don't get to choose them. They choose us."

Her words hurt me, not only because she thinks I'm worth so little, but because she thinks the same about herself.

"This is the second time you say something like this and it makes me so mad." I gently grab her hand. "There are good men out there willing to fully love good women, mother. Men that stay present and when they show up, they don't give their love in crumbs. They believe in you, they protect you, comfort you… they'll go to an empty building to rescue you from a rapist."

I let out a sob. Oliver and the guys love me. They saved me.

They thought I was worth risking their lives to find me and get me. They are the good men she thinks don't exist.

"Good men don't humiliate, diminish or manipulate you." I continue, letting go of her hand. "Good men don't hit their partner and they sure as hell don't rape."

"I didn't believe he was capable of that." She shrugs, holding onto the broom in her hands. "He said he was sorry for what he did. Do you know how many times I forgave your father after he came in drunk smelling like cheap perfume? He pushed me for being clingy, slapped me... the last time he did he packed his things and left. He didn't care if I was begging him to stay, he—"

She stops herself and I see a tear falling from her eye.

"He what?" I whisper.

A sob falls from her lips. "I told him I was pregnant with you, and he kicked me...with you inside me. He left because I wouldn't let it go. I should've let it go and I made it worse. I pushed him away."

The moment she says that I feel those kicks inside my heart. I knew he never loved us. I knew he'd ran away with some woman but I never knew he physically abused her and how hurt my mother really was.

"I can't believe this." I shake my head angrily. "You're blaming yourself because he was a piece of shit? Are you serious?"

"He was *my life*." She wipes her face with her apron, "so sweet and romantic when he wasn't drunk. And I messed that up because when he left me I had nothing."

Outrage takes over my body.

"What do you mean you had *nothing*, Mamá?" I take her face in my hands. "You had three children who loved you. A sister and a nephew who moved from the other side of the country just to be with you. You didn't give up and didn't settle for cleaning bathrooms in an office building. You built a damn business from the ground, knowing how difficult it was for a woman of color... let alone an undocumented immigrant who didn't speak one word in English." I let out a long breath. "You've managed to keep that business standing to this day. How can you not see the value in that?"

Her worth, her entire identity depending on one person. How do you come back from that?

I continue before she can respond. "Not only you let yourself die for a worthless man but you decided that just because you endured the worst of him just to keep him, I should do the same too?" I close my eyes for a second, "you threw away your own effort and raised us to believe we weren't worthy of true love just because one guy didn't love you?"

"True love doesn't exist for us," she grabs my arm, "you're as naïve and dumb as I was at your age."

I shake my head. "You and I are not the same. You lost yourself when that piece of shit didn't appreciate you. I might still be working on my self-love but I know who I am. I know I deserve good things. I know I deserve love… my own love most of all."

She breaks down in tears and my heart breaks even more. I'm still incredibly pissed at her but I'm worried about her. It scares me that she'll never be happy because she doesn't think she deserves better.

"I'm sorry, but you're not well in here," I gently tap her chest, "I'm worried about your mental health. You've never been okay. Healthy people, no matter how wounded they are, want something better for their children," I feel tears rolling down again.

I sniff back my tears as I continue. "A healthy mother encourages her daughters and empowers them to be who they are. A healthy mother doesn't manipulate, and sure as hell doesn't put her daughter in danger. I'm not asking you to love me, I'm asking you to let me help you to love yourself…so maybe one day you can love us."

"And how is loving myself going to change anything?" She scoffs bitterly. "Angel is dead, your sister doesn't even call, and you…you're going to leave with that Rodriguez kid," she crosses her arms, "Loving myself won't matter when I'm all alone. And I'm telling you now, you'll live in Fantasyland for a while and when he leaves you for another woman, you'll come back saying I was right."

I don't know why but that makes me laugh. The way she describes Oliver only shows how little she knows him. How little she knows *me*.

"Yeah, Angel is dead and I'm sorry we can't bring him back." My voice breaks again, but I clear it and continue. "But believe me, if I could,I would've done it from the moment he died."

I wipe my tears with a napkin and take a deep breath.

"Rocío is just choosing herself over this hell. And yes, I will probably marry Oliver. But he's one of those good men I was telling you about and I know he'll never leave me."

I give her a calm smile. "But if he ever should, well, mamá, that's when loving myself will come in handy. I would piece my heart back together *myself* and go live my life without him."

Ignoring her curled lip, I lean on the table closer to her. My voice is strong as I speak the truth.

"I matter mom and you do too, but you're too hurt to believe it."

"I'm not crazy." She clenches her teeth.

"I didn't say that," I take her hand, "I'm saying you're sick. I can help you if you want. We can find someone to help you get through these problems, like a therapist, so you can heal and understand yourself better."

I kiss her hand. "Just think about it and call me if you decide to take a leap of faith in self-healing. In the meantime, for my own good, I'm saying goodbye."

With that, I kiss her cheek and walk out the door.

This was probably the toughest conversation of my life. Understanding the root of it all and finding out how close I was to repeating the same pattern by believing a lie she passed on to us. Now I see it; I've been so scared of everyone leaving because she made me believe that's what I was destined for. That I wasn't worth staying with. I believed that lie so much that I ended up abandoning myself.

I don't want to believe any more lies, not even my own.

The lie stops here. *The toxic cycle ends with me.*

Alex, Juanito and I make our way back to Antonio's house in comfortable silence. Alex is opening the door for us when my phone chimes with a text.

Fred: Just checking up on you.

I don't know if it's the entire situation but I feel more emotional than usual, every single thing my friends do for me makes me tear up. We get inside the house and I reply.

Carmen: Best Papa Bear of all. Holding up. I feel a lot better today.

Fred: I've heard holding babies is good therapy.

I gasp with excitement. Our friend Jason's wife had a healthy and strong baby girl last week. I frantically type a response.

Carmen: Are you going to Jason's? Are they ready for visits?

Fred: Yes and yes. I can pick you up if you want.

I turn to Alex, who's plastered on the living room floor with Juanito, scrolling through the Netflix menu. "Do you mind if I go away for a couple of hours?"

His body tenses and sits up straight. "Not by yourself."

"No," I laugh, "my friend had a baby last week and she needed a few days before getting any visitors. Fred will pick me up."

"Oh, the dude who looks like Alex Pettyfer?" He asks, softening his posture. I laugh and nod, "Just checking, don't blame the Security Guard." He turns to the T.V. again. "The guys should be out of work soon, I'll just hang out with them." He gives me a soft smile. "You sure you're alright?"

"Better than ever." I smile back, laying down for a little on the couch to wait for Fred.

I actually would be much better if I could see Oliver, but with everything he's been doing with Elite opening an office in Minneapolis, I'm sure he's busy. It hasn't been that long and he's already getting interviews, time must be so tight for him and I understand. My insecurities want to tell me he's annoyed and upset with me, but I know better.

Anxiety! Fuck you, bitch.

He's been doing everything he can to ensure he's there for me, that he's not going anywhere.

Then why are you making him wait for so long?

What is it that I have to think about so much when I perfectly know he's everything I've ever wanted and he feels exactly the same?

Am I still scared? Fuck yes. But isn't that what true love is about? Putting your heart at the risk of break, trusting that the other person will take care of it instead?

Do I trust Oliver?

I do.

I am ready.

Then what the fuck am I waiting for?

I'm about to call Fred to cancel when he texts me he's here.

Well, that was fast.

My stomach drops a little, knowing I'll have to delay my talk with Oliver, but I know meeting this precious baby will cheer me up too. I leave Juanito with Alex and jump in Fred's car.

"How's the job hunting going?" he asks after a couple of blocks.

"It's… going," I shrug.

Advertising yourself as a Freelance Sports Photographer isn't easy. I've been submitting my pictures *everywhere*. Antonio insists that I use my Graphic Design skills again but I feel like I'm ready for the next step in my career. The X Games are off the table, but there are still other national competitions and hundreds of riders from all Extremes Sports I could work with. There's got to be a place for me.

"You know you can come back to the agency at any time, Carmen."

Right when I'm about to tell him I want my old job, my phone starts ringing. The ID shows a Minneapolis number.

"Sorry, I'll take a second," I tell Fred before answering, "This is Carmen."

"Ms. Morales," says a female voice, "Eleanor Jones from Hard Sports Today here. We received information regarding your Freelance services as a Sports Photographer and would like to request a quote. I know you usually send emails for these requests, but since it's a big event in just a few days we're trying to cover, I wanted to call you to check your availability first."

I have nothing but availability.

"I would love to," I look at Fred excitedly. He's smiling at me and pulls over while I keep talking, "can you send me a text with your email? What kind of event do you need to cover?"

"We're talking about the X Games at the U.S. Bank Stadium next week," she says while I put a hand on my mouth, "I know it's very last minute, but we need experienced photographers on the field. We've seen the wonderful shots you've taken and have no doubt you're exactly who we need."

NO. WAY.

I think I just shit my pants. *Sorry, not sorry, Fred.* I grab Fred's arm with my free hand and squeeze it hard, making him chuckle silently.

"Are you kidding me?" I laugh, "Of course I can, email me with the details and I'll send you a quote right away."

She sighs, "you just literally saved my butt."

"And you saved mine," I beam, "may I ask who referred me? I don't remember sending my portfolio to this magazine."

But if by mistake I did, thank God.

"That wasn't necessary," she says, "That BMX Hall of Fame article this week was more than enough."

The what from where?

"Oh, yeah. Right. That." I laugh, "I almost forgot I did *that*."

"Well, I'll let you go right now," she says, "I'll text you in the next ten minutes."

The second I hang up, I let out a loud squeal and Fred hugs me as I freak out for a moment.

I'm going to be at the X Games.

AS. A. PHOTOGRAPHER.

How in the world did that happen?

Eleanor sends me a text and I reply through email right away. She says she'll email me with details and schedule for a meeting later this week. I tell Fred about the call and that I might not need my job at Sullivan after all. But there's still one thing I don't understand.

"Call me paranoid," I continue, "but I think she might have the wrong person, though."

Fred laughs, "you think there's another Extreme Sports Photographer in Minneapolis whose name is Maria del Carmen Morales?"

"You never know," I laugh nervously, "but… she mentioned a *BMX Hall of Fame* article and well—"

"Oh yeah," he interrupts, ""I almost forgot about that! Those pictures of Oliver are amazing, the guy still got it."

"Wait what?" I shake my head. "What pictures?"

He can't be talking about the pictures of our BMX session. He told me those were personal.

"You're telling me the most prestigious BMX magazine in the country used your pictures without your permission?"

"Do you have the article?"

He takes a stack from his backseat and hands me a copy of the magazine, dated two days ago. I can't believe my eyes when I see it.

The front cover is the picture of that amazing Tailwhip Oliver did when we went out for a ride. I start turning the pages and see almost every picture I took that day, and when I start reading, my heart begins to speed and my tears start to fall.

Behind the Smile of The Quokka
By Evelyn Rocío Morales
Photo Credits: María del Carmen Morales.

If you grew up in the streets of South Minneapolis during the decade of the 2000's like I did, the name Oliver Santiago Rodriguez will sound familiar to you. Flying on a bike like Superman, stealing dozens of glances, making BMX have good representation in the most needed communities as a sport for the brave and the dreamers, helping more kids to get involved with the movement and inspiring hundreds to reach for the stars no matter what obstacles were ahead.

June 10th, 2007, the date of the last Street Jam at Freedom Union Park. Attended by more than two hundred people with contestants from all over the country. Organized and run by Angel Morales and Oliver *"The Quokka"* Rodriguez, as he was known around the neighborhood for his signature smile. They both had embarked a long and sacrificial journey in search for a more ambitious use of their talents. They spent the entire next year afterwards winning high category contests and creating a solid presence in the Extreme Sports scene with the purpose of achieving professional sponsorship. They were both accepted in UCLA and the future looked brighter than ever.

However, the dream was shattered in the summer of 2008, when Angel Morales passed away in a tragic car accident.

We didn't see or hear anything about the smile of The Quokka for the next few years. What no one expected was the next time he'd show his face, wouldn't be as a professional rider but as a *sponsor for future* riders.

After years of studying Mechanical Engineering and experimenting with titanium and carbon fiber, Oliver and his good friend—*and fellow BMX rider*—Damian Williams designed the first Elite bike for a developmental project at UCLA. This was the moment other riders started asking them for parts and even entire bikes. They didn't know they were going to capture the attention of retired BMX Pro-rider Aaron Johnson, who discovered the potential of the bike and offered them a deal to manufacture and distribute their idea which would catapult them into being one of the most sold bike brands in the country.

Elite Bikes Co. not only sells BMX Freestyle bikes, but also a variety of BMX Racing Bikes, Mountain and Cyclocross bikes and will soon be launching a line of Electrical Bikes to the market that is already being expected. Not to mention the clothing line that includes t-shirts, caps, beanies and hoodies for people of all shapes and sizes.

We didn't see the Quokka on a bike for ten years until very

recently, as he went back to his roots on a nostalgic visit to his hometown in Minneapolis to support the newest additions to Elite's team. Three riders from his own neighborhood are competing at the X Games Championship this year for the first time. He went back to his very first bike which he still preserves as good as new, and had a photoshoot done at the park that saw him being born as the BMX legend he is now. In the pictures we see the Quokka flying in the air with the passion and very specific style that characterized him during his first years and the same smile plastered on his lips.

I was lucky to be one of those enthusiastic fans who grew up seeing The Quokka in action in his early beginnings and it was an amazingly pleasant surprise to receive the exclusive pictures in my hands, seeing him come back to his first love. I had the honor to talk to him about it and it's a great pleasure to share with you an excerpt of the interview.

It's nice to see you again, Oliver. Thank you for this interview.

It's so good to see you again, Rocío.

Riding a bike after ten years must've been a challenge for you. How did it feel to put your feet on the pedals again?

Surreal. There's no other way to describe it. It felt as if time had stopped the day I last rode and continued when I put my feet on the pedals again. That's what happens when you love something that much, it will always feel natural.

Couldn't have said it any better. Even though you never rode professionally, you did leave a mark on people's hearts with your bike and hard work for the sport. What do you think about all of those fans who still remember you from your early years?

It's because of them that I am who I am now, it's because of them that I was able to gain credibility when Damian and I made the first Elite Bike. They were the ones who believed in me, no questions asked and I'm honored to have their trust and loyalty even after all these years.

You left the bike ten years ago, but you never left BMX. It was really a surprise when I first heard you were not pursuing professional sponsorship anymore. What made you stick from the sidelines?

Love. When you love something or someone with all your heart it's difficult to let go completely. You try other things trying to feel the same way you did before, just to find out it won't ever be the same. I could've never let go of BMX for good. It's in my blood.

And here we are, looking at these amazing pictures of you not too long ago. What made you jump on a bike again? What's the reason behind the pictures?

The same reason I've always had a smile on my face in each picture: The photographer… Your sister, Carmen Morales. The love of my life. *Quokka* wasn't just a nickname for me, it was a reminder of what was making me smile. I smiled because BMX makes me happy and she was the only one who understood why. She taught me how to feel the sport, how to live it to the fullest. It was her love and support that made me jump on a bike after ten long years and remember why I started in the first place.

That's an epic kind of love.

A love for the ages.

What can we expect from The Quokka and Elite Bikes Co. for the future?

We are already expanding Elite Bikes, we are in the process of extending headquarters and opening a factory in Minnesota. There's also a project for a free roofed park in the Twin Cities area in the making, and a few trips for future sponsorships. We want a team of at least ten international riders and we will be traveling to Mexico, and Central America to catch talent.

My best of luck for you in everything that you do. I'm sure this is only the beginning of a wonderful new journey.

I'm sure it is.

"Oh my God!" I say without being able to read the rest of the article.

He did this, he put himself out there because of me, even when he didn't *want* to do it. And *my sister* helped him. I can't believe she would write a piece on him, on BMX!

All this for me.

I put my head in my hands and start sobbing. *This* is what he was doing in Chicago. They planned this to help me put my name out there as a photographer and my work known.

I need to see him now.

"You deserve this happy ending, Carmen," Fred says, hugging me again and realization sinks in.

"You knew about this?" I ask, pulling away. He smiles knowingly and I gasp, "we were never going to Jason's." "No," he laughs, "we needed to get you out of the house without expecting anything and Alex to be able to leave without you noticing."

"You damn actor!" I laugh and I give him a playful punch, "wait, where is Alex going?"

"The most important question here is, where do you want to go now?"

I don't even reply to his question and take out my phone.

Carmen: I can't believe you did that.

Oliver: I would do anything for you.

Carmen: Can I see you?

Oliver: Of course, are you still with Fred?

Carmen: Yes, I can be at your parents' in ten.

Oliver: Good, come to the backyard. There's something else I need to show you.

43

carmen

I love a driver respectful of the speed limits, but *come on, Fred!*

My heart has been on my throat, beating so hard it might come out. I haven't stopped crying and trying to guess what he's going to show me. I don't care about anything material, I just want him.

Fred encourages me with a hug before getting out of the car. The moment he takes off, I see a couple of cars parked in the driveway. As soon as I start walking, Juanito comes from the backyard to greet me.

"Hey, buddy," I kneel down to let him lick me. "Where's daddy?"

Muttering and a couple of voices shushing each other capture my attention and I make my way to the backyard of the house, calling Juanito to follow me. The fence and part of the siding of the house are decorated with tiny lights and as I turn, I see Jacob, Ethan and Oliver, sitting on three high stools, guitars in their hands, surrounded by little candles.

The moment Oliver sees me, he smiles and taps the base of his guitar, "1, 2... 1, 2, 3, 4."

I recognize the melody immediately. *"1, 2, 3, 4"* by Plain White T's.

My song.

The song Oliver was about to sing to me the night we lost Angel and our lives changed forever.

I put my hands on my mouth and try not to sob loudly.

Oliver takes over the main verses, never taking his eyes off me. A warm wave of joy spreads from my chest to the rest of my body as he smiles or winks whenever he sings an *"I love you"*. Jacob and Ethan join him to sing the chorus parts in perfect harmony. I knew they could sing, but never knew they were *this* good.

When they get to the solo part at the end, the three of them smile proudly at each other. I take the chance to walk towards him with shaky legs, Juanito following me. When they stop, Jacob takes Oliver's guitar and Ethan takes Juanito with him, smiling as they walk past me.

The most beautiful man that's ever existed is now in front of me and before I can find any words, he takes both my hands and kisses them. The contact automatically lights up every part of me that has been dark since the day I saw him last.

"What are you doing, you crazy man?" I ask through tears.

"I'm picking up where we left off," he smiles and kisses my forehead, "I'm pressing play where everything stopped and went to shit. This–this is my do-over." He takes a deep breath and continues, "you've heard about the fight or flight reaction, right? When fear shocks you and you have that natural response?" he asks, when I nod, he continues. "I've always chosen *flight*. It has been the easiest for me. I chose it when Angel died and couldn't live with the guilt and the reality that he wasn't here anymore and been choosing it every time things change or get hard." He presses my hands to his chest, "But from now on, I'm choosing to fight. But I choose to start fighting *for you*. For *us*."

He wipes a tear from my eye, "Baby you scare the shit out of me. You're too perfect and you don't even know it. My biggest fear is that someday you'll realize I fall short of what you deserve and will leave me for someone better."

I feel my body giving out with his words and I fall to his arms. He holds me for a moment before continuing against my ear, "I don't deal well with change and pain. It freezes me out, takes my mind from reality and my solution has always been to avoid it," he pulls away for a moment, "I've done that many times and I've hurt everyone, I've hurt myself and I've hurt *you*. And the realest thing of my reality is… that there hasn't been anyone else for me but you and it won't ever be." He kisses my forehead, "I love you and I'm asking you now to let me prove to you I'm in this with you forever. Please, baby, forgive me for everything I've done to you. I love you and I promise you today next time I run away it will be to you, not away from you. Please give me another chance."

I let out a teary chuckle and pull him into a kiss.

"Of course I forgive you," I whisper against his lips, "you're the love of my life, Oliver. I can't see my future without you in it. Of course I'll give you another chance."

He sighs in relief and brings his beautiful smile to mine again while putting his arms around my waist, mine cupping the back of his head. I kiss him with forgiveness, with a promise to not only love him but to always be there when he's scared or insecure.

Our entire family comes out of the house with cheers and claps, gathering around us to celebrate. His parents and siblings, Vince, Antonio, Alex and even Tía Carmela. They all take turns to hug us. The guys surround Oliver to give him a messy group hug that ends with a couple of playful punches and pushes.

It's loud.

Messy.

I love it.

Oliver puts an arm around my shoulder as we walk inside, where Martita and Tía Carmela have homemade tacos for every-one. Juanito hasn't stopped jumping, rolling over like a smug and sniffing around us. He must know mom and dad are finally together. No doubts, no reservations.

Alex connects the speakers and plays his favorite Salsa and

Merengue playlist. The chattering and joking hasn't died down. The laughter goes on for a long time.

Oliver sits on the couch after we're done eating and I sit on his lap. He takes his phone out and pulls me into a selfie, him kissing my cheek.

He sends it out in a text message but I don't get to see the number. Not two minutes later, his phone chimes and hands it to me.

Susan: Yassss!!!! Congratulations, Ollie! See? I TOLD YOU. Tell Carmen I can't wait to see her.

Right after that, another message comes in, this time with a picture of Susan in Yosemite National Park. She's wrapped up in the arms of a handsome Black man who's kissing her temple. My heart flutters. I might not know Susan but I can tell she's as happy as I am now.

I do have some questions, but right now, I want to enjoy his glances, his smiles, his kisses on my cheek, his lips on mine whenever he catches a breath from talking to everyone. And I don't overlook his restraint as he grips my waist or my leg without going further.

He must know what I'm thinking because he leans to whisper to my ear, "I've missed you so much," *oh, I know that tone,* "can't wait to get you home."

"I've missed you too," I say against his mouth before kissing him, "thank you so much for what you did with the pictures, for talking to Rosy."

"Anything to make you happy, baby." He softly kisses my cheek. "You've worked so hard. I'm so proud of you."

I'm about to say I love him when Ethan cuts me off, yelling from the other side of the living room.

"Yo, can we keep it PG-13 for just a bit there?" He grimaces at us. "We can't wait a little bit for the gross PDAs. Get a room."

I can feel myself blushing while everyone laughs. Oliver lets out a loud chuckle and gives him a finger, shaking his head. I'm happy Ethan is lighting up his mood. Jacob and Antonio told me he came back a little sad and gloomy from his trip to Chicago with Oliver. I might ask him later about it.

"What? You jealous?" Jacob says, pointing at him with his beer. "Why don't *you* get a woman and a room?"

He scoffs, "Just wait till I turn on the charm."

"Always the smug," Alberto says, patting Ethan's back. "You're here talking about being irresistible and making your lady wait."

Ethan's color drains from his face and stutters. "Wh—what are you talking about *viejo*? I don't have a lady."

"That's what *you* think." Alberto smiles mischievously. "If you don't open your eyes already, it might be too late when you finally do. Just look at these two." He points at us. "I knew it all along, they just needed a little push."

"Oh," Ethan replies, looking relieved. "Yeah, of course."

What was that?

"Te saliste con la tuya, viejo metiche." *You got your wish, nosey old man.* Martita says, interrupting my thoughts. "My hero, I don't know how you did it but you did."

I let out a surprise chuckle and Oliver sits straight, laughing hard as everyone talks at the same time, asking him to tell the story. When the laughter stops, Martita tells us how Alberto conspired for years to get Oliver and I together and then meddle here and there so we could reunite.

"Sly old man! I knew you were up to something." Oliver says standing up to hug his dad. "I love you. If there's one thing you never forget, let it be that. Eres mi héroe." *You're my hero.*

"I love you too mijo." Alberto says as he gives him a kiss on his cheek. "I will always love you."

Oliver tears up a little bit and I swallow my own tears while he says something else to his father's ear. I wish I could protect his heart from every harm, but the only thing I can do is walk with him through it and help him heal when pain is inevitable. Life will happen and sadly… Alberto *will* get worse. But he won't be alone. His familia will always be here with him.

"By the way," Alex interrupts with an emotional tone, "Ollie boy, thank you. I'll gladly be your best man."

"You asked Alex to be Best Man? Seriously?" Ethan punches Oliver on the shoulder as Alex starts laughing.

"That's low, *loco*." Antonio pushes him from behind. "How can you decide these things without all of us?"

"I thought I was going to be Best Man?" Jacob says from the table while Vince shakes his head.

"Jesus Christ," Oliver interrupts, wiping his face with a hand and turning to Alex, "I haven't even fucking proposed. What the hell?"

I laugh while they follow the argument like little kids. I suddenly remember I still need to thank someone, so I take my phone and send a quick text.

Carmen: Thanks, Rosy. I love you.

She doesn't wait to reply.

Rocío: I love you too, Chipmunk baby. I'll visit soon. I promise.

Oliver smiles at me from where he's standing and mouths *I love you* before winking at me. I make my way where he is and wrap my arms around his waist, while the guys keep talking to him. I look up against his chest and he's already looking at me as if I'm the only one in the room. He leans down to kiss my nose, I realize he probably thinks I am.

This isn't my happy ending. This is my hopeful beginning, a beautiful baby root born from my own ashes.

I can't wait to see how beautiful and amazing it gets.

44

oliver

Can your heart explode from happiness?

The plan was a success thanks to my family and some other strings I was able to pull last minute. It wasn't too hard to get Fred on board. Güero has a soft spot for my girl and didn't hesitate to help out. The idea was to put Carmen's name out there and hope for a call, but I didn't expect Eleanor's call that fast. When she called me to ask for information about the photographer who took the pictures for the article, the missing piece fell into place by itself. She's a sucker for romance stories and was more than happy to call Carmen at the right time.

We ended up going back to Carmen's house almost at one in the morning, where we made up for the lost time *all night long*.

The next day, we went to Angel's grave hand in hand, where we asked for his blessings and promised to always take care of each other. To always remember him and to tell our future kids who he was and how much we'll always love him.

The rest of the week flew by fast.

Carmen had a couple of meetings with Eleanor and got her badge for the X Games.

When the day finally came, she blew my mind with her talent. We didn't spend much time together during those four days but it was well worth it. I introduced her to Damian, who arrived here just the night before the X Games started and it was friendship at first sight.

She was a little tense and exhausted during and after the competition, but the energy she carried around and the satisfaction in her body language made her glow in a way I'd never witnessed before.

The best pictures she's ever taken after my solo session, according to her.

Nothing like witnessing the badass love of my life making her dreams come true.

Sean Williams won Gold in Dave Mirra's BMX Park best trick with a Front Flip Tailwhip and Mickey Acevedo won Bronze in the BMX street category with 88.3 points, just a little bit under the second place. Carlos was bummed he didn't win this time but he will still be remembered as the youngest Latino rider competing in the X Games. Even though they didn't compete directly representing Elite, I feel more than proud to see these guys making history. They're all already accepted in major universities with full scholarships and I will do my best to ensure they can make a living out of the sport they love.

It's Monday morning after the X Games, we were wiped out last night and came directly to bed after the closing concert. I temporarily moved in with Carmen. My parents had no problem with it even though I don't have much time left in Minneapolis. They know I'm coming back soon and they're thrilled to have Carmen and I finally together.

I wake up with her delicious scent caressing my nose and her legs tangled with mine, her arms around my waist.

"Am I squeezing you too tight?" she asks against my chest.

I smile, "not tight enough."

She starts squeezing tighter and tighter until the pressure starts tickling and I explode in laughter. I take her laughing face in my hands and kiss her deeply. When I pull away, she smiles lazily and closes her eyes.

And I'll get to do this every day for the rest of my life.

"I can't believe the games are over already," she says, still with her eyes closed.

"I know, it was too fast."

She kisses my jaw, "what's the plan now, Big Guy?"

"Well," I look over her shoulder to check the time on my phone, "right now, I want to spend the rest of the day with you doing whatever you want before we meet the guys and get Juanito back, then…" I caress her hip, "I do have to go back to L.A. eventually and start the entire transition back. Now, listen," I kiss her hair, "I want nothing more than to take you with me. You wouldn't have to worry about anything, I can take care of you and we can find freelance jobs as we move forward. You already have a bunch of followers in your new Instagram profile and after this weekend you'll have a rain of offers. But, if you want to find a job and stay here while we decide what the next step is, I'll hate it… but I'll support whatever you want to do. I'll be coming back to you as much as I can and you can fly there to see me."

"Are you kidding me," she snuggles closer, "I'm not leaving your side ever again. When do we leave?"

I sigh in relief and kiss her again. "As soon as you want to, baby. I can book a flight for tonight, tomorrow, whatever you want."

"I love the sound of that," she lifts up an eyebrow.

I snort, "I bet you do."

"For how long are we staying?"

"It depends. Could be one or two months the first time," I caress her back, "we'll be going back and forth for a while until we're settled and ready to start operations."

Now that she's coming with me, she'll have to make a lot of arrangements regarding her house and other belongings.

"Sounds like a plan to me," she sighs, "let's take a couple of days off and rest."

I nod and take a couple of seconds to watch her smile. For the first time in my life I feel like everything is in its right place. I have everything I want, every dream I ever dreamt.

There's only one thing missing.

"What?" she whispers, "why are you looking at me like that?"

"Marry me," I blurt.

Her expression changes and I can see tears already forming in her eyelids.

"Stop playing," she smiles.

I laugh and shake my head. Without saying anything I get up and go to the kitchen, taking a small velvet box I'd hidden in one of the cupboards a few weeks ago. When I come back, she's sitting at the edge of the bed and I get down in one knee in front of me.

She covers her mouth with her hand and gasps.

"I didn't have a plan when I bought this ring," I smile, taking her hand, "I just knew I wanted to see it on your finger sooner rather than later... Maria del Carmen Morales, I've been waiting my entire life to ask you to be my partner in crime, to be the first face I see in the morning and the last one at night. To be the mother of my children... to let me see you shine that beautiful light of yours from the front row. Be my wife? Please?"

She kneels down in front of me and kisses me like she's never done before. She pulls away with tears in her eyes and a smile on her face.

"Yes," she whispers, "yes, yes, yes, yes."

I laugh and kiss her again before sliding the ring on her finger.

My fiancée.

My future wife.

We go back to bed full of excitement and hope for the future. We laugh, talk, kiss and make plans like we have no other care in the world. I'm sure we both want to call the entire family to share the news but that can wait. I want to celebrate in private for a little longer.

"Do you think he's looking down on us?" I ask with my forehead pressed onto hers.

She knows I'm talking about Angel. In the past, the thought of him would've gotten me shivers, my stomach would've twisted with regret and pain, but I'm already working through those feelings so one day I'm completely at peace talking about him. That's why I already scheduled my first therapy session online. I want to be able to heal that wound and remember him with joy and not with guilt anymore.

"I think he is," she smiles, "I think he's happy to know we really do love each other."

"I still wish he was here," I swallow hard.

"I know baby, I wish he was too. We'll always feel like that."

"You know," I clear my throat, "I still can't help to feel responsible for his death but… more than that, I feel privileged that I had the chance to be his best friend, to learn from him, to love him like a brother. And grateful… because in that process, he brought you to me. No matter how many times I left, I was always going to come back to *you*."

I wipe a little tear from her eye as she beams at me.

"And now," she tilts her head with a huge smile, "we're leaving together."

"Only for a little while," I caress her cheek, "next time we're coming back to stay."

I lean down to kiss the most delicious lips that ever existed and let myself get lost in her embrace.

I can't believe I'm saying this but, I love how things are changing.

epilogue

oliver

Two years later

I walk across our new living room and put the last moving box on the floor, declaring us officially moved back to Minnesota.

Carmen flew back a week ago and has been staying with my parents. Ethan, Jacob, Vince and I drove with all our things from California and came back yesterday. Everyone is helping out today, and I'm waiting for Carmen to arrive with Antonio and his fiancée.

Yep, this dude is getting married next month. Quite a story there; I can't wait for him to tell it.

When Carmen and I got engaged, we spent a few months in California and got married on December 9th in the Leopold's Mississippi Gardens in Minneapolis during a beautiful snowfall. Rocío was Carmen's Maid of Honor and stood by Jacob and Fred as her Bridesmen. Papá walked her down the aisle where I waited for her next to all of the guys, as my Best Men team, because I couldn't pick just one.

I'm opening up some boxes in the kitchen when I hear the front door opening, my heart beginning to race when I hear the steps of two little shoes echoing the house. I step out of the kitchen and kneel down with my arms open.

His little eyes land where I am, his voice bouncing as he sprints toward me.

"*Dadaaaaaaaaaaaaaaaaaaaaaa!*"

"Hey, here's my little guy," I say, gathering him in my arms while I scratch Juanito's neck when he comes running behind him. "What's up, mijo? You had fun driving with Tío Tony?"

I say hello to Antonio and his fiancée before then carrying him around while I move some things out of the boxes.

I thought getting married to the love of my life was the peak of all happiness.

I was wrong.

Exactly one month before Carmen and I got married, we found out she was pregnant. And the day *Angel Santiago Rodriguez* was born, my eyes saw a different light.

I flew our entire family, including Araceli, to California so we could all welcome him to the world.

You hear things about the day your kids are born, but nothing prepares you for the real thing. It's the most terrifying yet most beautiful experience I've ever had and made me admire and praise the strength and power of my badass wife on a whole new level.

Felicidad pura, *pure happiness*.

We flew to Minnesota with him a couple times while I made the last arrangements for Elite's new home and we officially started operations last week, the day Angelito turned one.

He's the perfect mix of Carmen and me. He looks exactly like me —he even has my dimples— but his laugh, his goofiness and wittiness are the incarnation of his mom. The guys take turns to babysitting whenever it's needed and he's gotten Rocío to visit more. The guys were making bets of what was going to be his first word and I turned out to be the winner. He can't say anything else other than "*mama*" and "*dada*" but we all talk to him in English and Spanish so he can grow up bilingual from the jump.

Araceli was officially diagnosed with several mental illnesses just two months after we got engaged. I wish I could say she's getting better, but she rejected therapy from the moment they told her she needed medication and be hospitalized in a mental clinic to get better. She kept telling us she wasn't crazy and she refused to go through "*such an embarrassment*". She was so bitter after that and didn't even attend our wedding. So, we did what we needed to do and put some space between her and our family. For sake of our peace and especially for my wife's mental health. When Angelito was born, we took him to see her so she could meet him but when she asked us to let her spend time with him, Carmen was firm in the conditions: *She'll take the medication and go to therapy*. She said she was going to think about it, but never gave a response. That was a year ago. Carmen took it well, although I know it broke her heart, therefore, it broke mine. But I'm proud of her for putting those boundaries all the way up.

"Dada, dada, dada," Angelito keeps mumbling, tapping my shoulder and I laugh at his insistence. When I turn my head to give him my full attention, he starts mumbling nonstop. Juanito following us and wagging his tail at the sound of his voice. He's been his personal bodyguard since he was born and has never left his side since we got him home from the hospital.

"Little dude has been drooling like crazy," Antonio says as he takes a bib from one of the boxes. He's drooling on his Elite t-shirt and I know he just changed. Carmen has been trying to match my outfits on him.

"Understatement," I laugh, taking the bib and putting it around his neck, "Doctor says he must have another tooth coming."

Antonio laughs and looks around, "hey, where's everyone?"

"Ethan and Jacob are at IKEA picking up this little guy's closet," I say, kissing Angel's cheek, "Vince and Daniel are on their way."

"Are Alberto and Marta coming over?"

"I think so, Papá was feeling a little down this morning."

"Oh, okay" he nods with a sad smile, "I'll go see him if he decides to stay. Haven't seen him in a week."

Papa's been weaker and slower with time. He hasn't had another heart attack but we're constantly checking his blood pressure and heart rate. He exercises with frequency and takes medication daily. His memory is slowly fading, he loses his train of thought easily and has trouble reading. He doesn't engage in conversations as he used to and little by little he's been needing more help with certain tasks, but he still has more lucid moments than bad ones.

Alzheimer's doesn't affect everyone the same way and the doctor said the first stages can last for a long time and it was difficult to know how fast they may progress. He's still functional and goes to work frequently but drives with Tío Vicente. He loves and enjoys Angelito, just as my mom, even though he doesn't always remember his name. Not too long ago, he asked me where Angel was. It took a minute for me to realize he wasn't talking about my son and I almost fainted. My mom—as the queen she is, reassured him and didn't contradict him in anything. She's been going to a support group for Dementia and Alzheimer's caregivers, where she found a beautiful community with people who can understand her and support her through this process.

Carmen and I have also been going to therapy. I've been able to work through my emotions and learned so much about myself. I can see that being reflected in my relationship with my wife, my family and in how the guilt and pain for Angel's death have been easier to handle. I even joined everyone for the first time last year to the picnic in his gravesite to celebrate his and Rocio's birthday. It was hard and emotional, but good for my heart.

We're tighter and stronger than ever.

"Hey, where is my wife?" I say to Antonio," she was driving with you, right?"

"Miss me already?" she says, making my son and I turn automatically.

The moment I see her, the world spins again. The love of my life, the woman who drives me crazy in every sense of the word. Who rants at me when I leave a wet towel on the bed and can't stop taking pictures of my son and I when we're sleeping.

My *very pregnant* wife. Yep, we have another bun in the oven… and it's a girl. Amelia Valentina Rodriguez is due in three months.

"Mama!" Angelito starts squealing, shaking his chubby arms and legs when he spots her.

"*Mi corazón!*" she squeals back, walking towards us, "you were waiting for me, chiquito lindo?"

She kisses his cheek and murmurs something to him. My heart melts every time she does that. I put him down for a little and he runs after Juanito. I take advantage to lean and kiss my wife in the lips.

"Sorry I didn't come in right away," She says as I pull away and start walking towards the backyard. "The neighbor's daughter is having a birthday party and she was inviting us." She sighs. "Then Bernie called me saying she wants to bring Ellie to play with Angelito tomorrow." She stops and caresses my face. "What's up big guy, you missed me?"

"All day," I sigh.

"It's only been like four hours," she laughs against my mouth.

"Too damn long," I pull her for another long kiss, rubbing her swollen belly. I break the kiss at the sound of Angel muttering something to Juanito while he plays with his tail. I turn toward her. "Should we let him sleep with us? He always yells all night when he sleeps in new places."

"Nah, we just need to wear him out and he'll sleep just fine."

Parenting with Carmen has been an adventure and although we've had our highs and lows. It's because of her that our son is growing up so beautifully strong and independent. I love to see her spreading her joy and positivity on Angelito and at the same time, teaching him how to be respectful, fair, loving and empathetic from a very young age. It makes me fall more in love with her to see how safe he feels around her. We are so lucky to have her.

"You know everything, baby." I kiss her cheek.

"Oh." She gasps, taking my hand and putting it on the left side of her belly. "Did you feel that?"

"I did." I smile. "She's been kicking hard since last night."

"It's your voice," she says, "she doesn't kick like that with other people around, she must've missed you this week."

"I'm here, *princesita*." I say, kneeling down to kiss Carmen's belly. "Did you miss daddy? Daddy missed you so much, I can't wait to finally see your beautiful face."

I wait for a couple of seconds with my face pressing against her and she doesn't kick again. *Well then.* I stand up and chuckle at my daughter's sass, the one she's obviously inherited from the Queen wrapped around my arm.

Carmen built a solid name as an Extreme Sports Photographer since we moved to California. She's photographed riders from all over the country for many magazines and brands. Just starting this year, she got a picture of a sequenced Barspin 360 published in the Annual Book of Photography. She's always being solicited but she's taking a break now we're close to having Amelia.

I open the sliding door and let all my family out to see the nice layout Antonio, Vince, my brothers and I spent almost two weeks building. We left a portion with small pots so Carmen can plant her flowers. On the other side, we installed a platform with a quarter pipe, a rail and a small ledge across the deck and I'm building a little shack at the end of the yard that I'll use as a carpentry and welding shop. I got everyone a bike and have been going for rides from time to time just for the sake of fun. I already got Angelito his first BMX tricycle for his birthday and will surely teach him and Amelia to ride like their dad and his Tío Angel did once.

"Are you scared, Santiago?" She asks against my cheek.

She knows me so well.

"Shitting my pants." I confess as I laugh seeing my little boy tripping over my dog and squealing something at him. I turn to see her longing look in her eyes. "But you guys make me brave."

"And you make our family strong." She smiles.

The yellows, reds and oranges of the golden hour are already painting the sky. As I sit here enjoying my beautiful family before going back to the craziness inside, I make a silent prayer giving thanks to the Guy upstairs for giving me so much and to Angel, for making us all a family.

I sigh and shake my head, still unable to believe how blessed I am.

"God, I'm so glad we're finally back." I say before kissing my wife.

For the first time in my life, I don't want to be anywhere else.

THE END

Thank you so much for reading Carmen and Oliver's happy ever after. Don't worry, they will come back soon. Don't miss out on Antonio and Ramona's story, coming Spring 2024.

acknowledgments

Am I really writing my acknowledgments? Is this for real? Did I really get to this point. It feels surreal. This is going to be long, I have so many people I'm thankful to.

First of all, I want to thank God for this opportunity. Thank you for giving me everything I've wanted, exactly as I've wanted them.

My mom and sister Ale. I don't know what my life would've been without you. I owe you everything I am. I wouldn't be here without you, I wouldn't be who I am if it wasn't for you. It's always been the three of us against the world and I don't think I could've written this book without you. I love you with every part of my soul.

To my stepdad Marky, I love you so much and I hope you didn't get spooked by all the things you read in this book. Thank you for your love and all the cheers.

Mario Eduardo, thank you all the stories and the support I needed it from the very start. I will never forget it.

My family: Mama Alis, my aunts, uncles and cousins. Ya'll knew I was going to write a book someday and I'm happy you never gave up waiting for it.

Galo, you knew this was possible when I thought it was just a fantasy. You believed in me when I didn't know I could believe in myself. I love you to infinity and beyond.

Papá Juan: Escribí un libro papito. Me hubiera gustado tanto que lo vieras hecho realidad. Te amo por siempre. Te extraño por siempre.

Tía Carmen, por todos esos libros que me conseguiste de

pequeña y por influenciar mi amor por la lectura. Carmen, la protagonista, es una pequeña dedicación para ti. Te quiero mucho.

My stepsister Kolina, thank you so much for giving me the push I needed to start writing in English when I thought I had absolutely no future in it. You helped me build my confidence enough to even try it and here I am. I will never forget it.

My cousin Gabby (My very own Chipmunk), I love you so much. Thanks for your input on the very first draft of this manuscript. I hope you're proud of me. I love you and miss you.

Zack, you have no idea what your support has meant to me. We met during a time when I didn't really know this was going to be a reality and having you in my corner and feeling genuinely happy and proud of me while I make this dream come true has meant everything. I can't thank you enough.

To Lilian Sosa, my friend, number one fan and my very first reader. Thank you for the encouragement and support.

Anna Lindgren and Carly Wilson, thank you for getting excited about this idea and being there with me every step of the way as I wrote the first scenes. I love you. Carmen and Oliver wouldn't be who they are without you both.

My beautiful romance boos Anna P. and Lila Dawes. For the millions of Whatsapp messages, video calls, audio messages and memes shared along this journey, the banter, the laughs about everything and nothing, brainstorming and idea exchanges. I love you more than words can say and I couldn't do this without you in my life. I would walk through hot coals for you.

Michelle Helgerson, booksta-bestie and alpha reader extraordinaire! Your excitement and love for my books are an inspiration. Thank you for always being there for me to talk shit, books or anything in life. Your friendship has been a highlight of my life, I love you.

My BABWKAs Natasha Bishop and K. Rodriguez. This book, my writing and my life overall wouldn't be the same without you in it. I bless the second in time you came into my life and made it better. Your friendship is one of the most amazing gifts I've ever been given and I promise I won't ever, ever take it for granted. I fucking love you, bishes.

Tori Alvarez, it all started with me gushing and daydreaming about your books and here you are now, as my mentor and friend. I have no words to express how much you mean to me and how thankful I am for all the love, feedback, ideas and guidance you've given me through this entire process. I've got your back, woman! Always and forever.

Carla Peterson, mi vida. You've been there for me from the start. The way you hype me up is so fucking incredible and I have no words for how amazing it is to have you in my life. Thank you so much for your friendship and for believing in me before reading this book!

Marianne, my dear. You have no idea how much your friendship means to me. Thank you for taking the time to read and love this story and for helping me out pinpointing trigger warnings like a damn pro. I hope you know how much I love you!

My early beta readers, Author Felicia Bleadel, Author Vivian Mae, Diana and Pricilla. I couldn't have shaped this book into what it is now without you. Thank you so much!

Hannah Holt, for giving me all the feedback on all the scenes where all my guys were together. Thank you so much.

Staci Hart and her author support group. You were the start of everything. Thank you.

Sarah Smith and Skye McDonald. You introduced me to this beautiful reader/writer community when I had no idea where to start and I will always be grateful for your love, support and friendship.

Authors Andrea Hopkins, Eve Kasey, Kristen Granata, Melissa Grace, Rebecca Gannon, Kristin Turnage and S. J. Tilly. Your books inspire me every single time. Your constant encouragement and support means everything. I'll always look up to you. Thank you for being such an inspiration.

My sensitivity readers, Cathy and Melissa. Thank you so much for sharing your stories with me and helping me shape Alberto's story in the most authentic way possible.

To my editor, Colby. I couldn't have asked for someone better than you to edit this book. Thank you for the help, your friendship and all the time you put into this project. Working with you has been the best.

Paul and Stephanie. My beautiful cover models. Thank you for being part of this journey and letting me put your beautiful and extremely photogenic faces at the front of this whole project.

Mistre, my friend and photographer. Thank you so much for your friendship and letting me show my readers some of your amazing talent.

Last but not least, to all the Bookstagram community. I've never been so welcomed, loved and appreciated in my entire life as I've been by these amazing Authors and Readers. Ever since I started my Bookstagram account I've met some of the most amazing people around the world and I'll never be able to express my gratitude for all the love I've been given through this community.

ARC team, THANK YOU! I still can't get over the excitement you've shown since I started promoting this book has filled my heart with joy. Thank you for giving me a chance.

And to you, my dear reader... you're the ultimate dream come true!

about the author

Andrea is an author and photographer who breathes, eats and drinks music and romance stories but can fit in a Fantasy or Historical Fiction book anytime.

She's always been a hopeful romantic, a reader, coffee drinker. Born and raised in Guatemala City but has found her forever home in the suburbs of Minneapolis, Minnesota where she can be found either singing out loud, reading, writing, gushing about her favorite book boyfriend online, watching reruns of her favorite telenovelas or old seasons of Survivor.

You can find her on Instagram as @andreagonzalezromance and her reader account @chula.is.reading.romance.

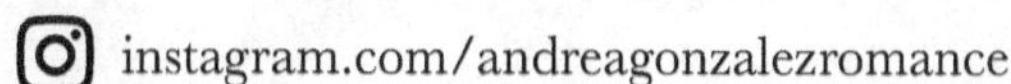 instagram.com/andreagonzalezromance